THE
GILDED
CAGE

THE
GILDED
CAGE

A Historical Novel

Book Two of the Emily Alden Trilogy

Sidney S. Stark

Momentum Ink Press

New York

AUTHOR'S NOTE

This book is inspired by actual events. While the main characters and plots are all fictitious, some of the secondary characters and subplots are not. It is, therefore, a true composition of historical fiction.

Published in the United States by Momentum Ink Press, New York.

PUBLISHER'S CATALOGING IN PUBLICATION DATA
provided by Five Rainbows Cataloging Services
Names: Stark, Sidney S., author.
Title: The gilded cage / Sidney S. Stark.
Description: New York : Momentum Ink Press, 2020.
Identifiers: ISBN 978-0-9975239-9-7 (paperback) | ISBN 978-1-7358893-0-6 (ebook)
Subjects: LCSH: Women musicians—Fiction. | Man-woman relationships—Fiction. | Families—Fiction. | Reconstruction (U.S. history, 1865-1877)—Fiction. | Great Fire, Chicago, Ill., 1871—Fiction. | Historical fiction. | BISAC: FICTION / Historical / General. | FICTION / Women. | FICTION / Family Life / Marriage & Divorce. | FICTION / Sagas. | GSAFD: Historical fiction.
Classification: LCC PS3619.T3739 G55 2020 (print) |
LCC PS3619.T3739 G55 2020 (ebook) | DDC 813/.6—dc23.

https://theunblockedwriter.com
https://momentuminkpress.com

For information about special discounts available for bulk purchases, sales promotions, fund-raising, and educational needs, contact the author at sidney.s.stark@gmail.com

Book design by Kathryn Holeman

For my grandmother and granddaughter.
So much to teach and so much to learn.

BOOKS BY SIDNEY S. STARK

THE EMILY ALDEN TRILOGY

Certain Liberties
The Gilded Cage
Tried as Silver

Twilight Perspectives:
Essays of Life and Death

For more details, join us at
https://TheUnblockedWriter.com
where you'll find inspirational essays,
writing news, and event information.

PRAISE

The Gilded Cage

"Stark follows the fortunes of a talented violinist and her family into the tumults of Reconstruction in this sequel to *Certain Liberties* (2019) . . . As in the previous novel, Stark weaves her characters' trajectories into the larger events of the time . . . Stark's detailed recreation of the time period—culturally, linguistically, and philosophically—should please those who like nothing better than escaping into previous eras . . . Stark's prose is elegant and ornate, evoking the Victorian novels that were popular during the time period . . . An unhurried and painterly novel of a musician finding her voice." — *Kirkus Reviews*

"As in her first historical novel, *Certain Liberties*, Sidney Stark excels at making the past relevant and enthralling in her latest novel, *The Gilded Cage*. Her meticulously researched, riveting story guarantees that her characters will remain vivid long after you've read the final page."
—**Paul Pitcoff**, author of *Cold War Secrets* and *Beyond the Foster Care System*

"What a glorious accomplishment to have researched and written such a stunning book. I find the parallel of the Reconstruction and the redirection of Emily's life's journey wonderful . . ."
—**Nancy French Achenbach**, President, Sag Harbor Historical Society

Certain Liberties

"The author masterfully sets the historical stage—the United States as it devolves into the Civil War—and she addresses the issue of slavery with nuance and rigor. . . a riveting storyline." — *Kirkus Reviews*

". . . a wealth of historical detail woven into an intriguing plot, Sidney Stark has written a wonderful novel with a roster of lively characters. It's a spell-binding read . . . not to be missed."
— **Jia Kim**, Cellist, Director of the Central Chamber Music Series
& Stowe Chamber Music Society

PRAISE

Tried as Silver

"Stark's 19th-century violinist proceeds to London for her final act in this, the third in a trilogy of historical novels. After two decades in Paris, famed British-born American violinist Emily de Koningh (nee Alden) and her family are relocating to London . . . There is a new energy in London's music scene . . . where the Royal College of Music was recently founded to compete with the storied conservatories of the Continent. Are Emily's prospects about to experience a similar renaissance, or is her fragile ensemble of friends, relatives, and lovers about to disband for good? Stark's novel displays a depth of research and command of history." —*Kirkus Reviews*

Emily Alden is a Nineteenth Century heroine battling the turbulence of society's demands. *Tried as Silver* roils with suspense as Emily, surrounded by actual and imagined characters from the Victorian age, redefines the meaning of family, parent, performer, and lover . . . a page turner causing readers to examine how their own lives are "tried" by the pressures of modern society. Don't miss this third book in the trilogy."
—**Paul Pitcoff**, author of *Cold War Secrets* and *Beyond the Foster Care System*

"In *Tried as Silver*, Sidney Stark propels her polished historical fiction with the pace of a thriller, and completes her trilogy (*Certain Liberties*, *The Gilded Cage*) about the highly acclaimed virtuoso violinist, Emily Alden. Spanning the Victorian era, Emily struggles with the timeless and universal themes of managing family and profession. Notably, the author invites a solution as elegant and crafted as her language, her historical figures, and her dealing with the restrictive sexual mores. Stark, like Emily, finds her forte in music and musicians of the times."
— **Denise B. Dailey**, author of *Listening to Pakistan: A Woman's Voice in a Veiled Land*, *Riko: Seductions of an Artist*, and *Leaving Guanabara*

CONTENTS

CHAPTER ONE

THE WINTER OF 1859 was by all accounts one of the most arbitrarily severe Americans had ever experienced. But in New York City, they finally hailed the opening of the enormous public works project later known as the Central Park. It was anything but haphazard. Twenty thousand workers from the United States and Europe reshaped the rocky landscape to create a romantic pastoral setting. It was said more gunpowder was used to blast out the Manhattan granite than was later fired at the Battle of Gettysburg, and laborers moved over three million cubic yards of soil and planted more than 270,000 trees and shrubs. That winter of the park's inaugural, thousands of New Yorkers skated on lakes built on the site of former swamps fed by underground streams. The park was designed to sustain the souls of people, mostly working people, starving for the balm only Nature could provide. But its commissioners initially restricted its use for the individuals, mostly wealthy, who could afford daily late-afternoon carriage parades worthy of such a beautiful setting.

Although the Central Park Zoo quickly became its most popular highlight, unlike the park itself, the zoo happened accidentally. Its spontaneous evolution started when New Yorkers dropped off unwanted animals at the arsenal, where they were confined in misery in its basement. Just before the Civil War, the legislature authorized some new buildings to house the growing collection of beasts, and the Central Park Menagerie was placed behind the arsenal just inside the park's Sixty-Fourth Street entrance. A path leading in from Fifth Avenue sported fashionably dressed couples, families of four, and clusters of children shepherded by stern, imperious governesses, all moving in a continuous flow of expectant humanity. They came to see the wild, caged animals donated to the park by rich and famous Americans who no longer wanted to care for them. Parents were also there to show themselves and their children off (and their elegant carriages), seeking a gentler and greener place than the city streets they were leaving behind, as well as to escape the din of traffic for a while.

The participants of the scene appeared a far cry from the deprived immigrants the park had ostensibly been designed for. Long skirts, colorful jackets, and large, tilted hats on the women were mimicked by their daughters, just as young sons were dressed in the formal jackets and trousers of their fathers. A dynamic tension seemed to hold most of the children captive, obviously expected to be polite, quiet versions of their well-dressed parents. At the same time, discomfort flowed around the families on their own, those mothers and fathers unused to being with their children without the help of a governess.

❦ ⚶ ❦

On this fall day in 1871, everything seemed in order around the zoo's new permanent quarters built just over a decade after the park's opening, except for the upset of one little boy whose moans were almost drowned out by coach traffic bustling along New York's Fifth Avenue. Horses attached to parked carriages and each other stamped with impatience. Tired of standing around waiting to serve, the elegant barouches swayed back and forth, moved by currents of irritation eddying around the animals. In a desperate attempt to disappear, the unhappy child pulled on the folds of his mother's three-quarter-length cream-colored skirt. This young woman with a boy on each side of her had a spring in her step and smile on her face engaging two notable dimples. They suggested her pleasure in anticipation of the outing and adventure ahead. Yet the fact that she was alone with her children, and the bonnet ties, meant to be fastened tight under her chin were left to swing loose, gave her a slightly daring and casual air.

The elegant cut of her small, waist-length jacket matching her skirt, and stylish maroon velvet-trimmed bonnet identified her comfortable affluence. Her two little boys, dressed alike in sailor suits, were nonetheless distinctly different. The older boy looked the epitome of order and cleanliness, while the younger seemed naturally disheveled, his shirt hanging outside his shorts. The pretty woman's attention moved from the animals in cages to her smaller son, whose distress she'd finally noticed.

"What's the matter, Connie? I thought you'd love the Menagerie." Emily de Koningh dropped her hands to her younger son's shoulders, rocking the child back and forth against her legs almost imperceptibly. The movement and gentle tone of her voice soothed him enough to encourage him to look up, or maybe he just needed some air. She smiled down at him with her dimples deepening. "That's better," she said. "I truly thought you'd both be thrilled by your first glimpse of a live bear."

"We are, Mother," her older son insisted. "He's just being a baby." William pulled himself up tall, enhancing the impression that he was much older than his actual five and a half years. The age gap between the boys in fact seemed greater than their real eleven months. With smooth dark hair, William was unusually tall for his age, making his naturally high, childish voice the only giveaway. Seemingly out of nowhere, he said, "Many men died in the War Between the States, right, Mother?" An odd comment for one so young. Overhearing the child's question posed at the often-grating level of a small boy demanding to be heard, passersby frowned and looked more closely at the woman with her two sons. William seemed to have a way of throwing people off balance, a trait his mother traced back directly to her own father, Sir William Alden. It was a characteristic she wasn't fond of, though she understood she might be overly sensitive to the challenging tone.

Like their appealing mother, both children had dark, dancing eyes and even features. The dimples deepening at the corners of her mouth as she talked were mirrored in their small cheeks. In truth they'd have seemed to be twins if their coloring and builds weren't so utterly opposite. "Good Lord, Willie, why do you ask?"

Emily leveled a look at her older son, trying to read the motivation behind his query about war deaths. She turned from the four-year-old at her skirts, though she continued to lovingly coax his wavy blond curls into place with her gloved fingers. "Now that we've put a little time between us and the Civil War," she said with some exasperation, "can't we just leave those poor, tired souls to rest in peace? It wasn't all men who died, anyway," she added, holding William's eyes with hers. "There were plenty of women, both African and white numbered with those who lost their lives."

"How many?" the boy asked, snatching her response like a torch in a relay. "My teacher in school said it was one half million. You wouldn't think there'd be anyone left in the country if that's so." He glanced around at the people roaming past the animal cages of the Central Park Menagerie, noting with pleasure that one or two were now obviously listening to him as they walked.

There always seemed to be a commotion at another cage rather than the one people were looking at, and the sense of missing something important spurred enthusiastic visitors to roam restlessly from one place to another without notice of whose view might be blocked by their moves. Emily knew there was time to get around to the panthers and swans, as well as the Swiss mountain sheep triplets, without rushing from one to the next. She had no idea how to find General Custer's rattlesnake and wasn't sure she wanted to; or General Sherman's African Cape buffalo, claimed as one of his prizes from his march through Georgia. But between them and all the animals the inventor Samuel Morse had donated, she knew there'd be plenty to spark and hold her young sons' interest for their morning adventure together.

"Actually, I'm sure one day we'll find out the death toll from the Civil War was even higher," Emily muttered. "Oh look, Connie!" She put her hand back on top of the younger child's head, as if in affectionate blessing. "The black bear is waking up!" Her abrupt change of topic distracted the older boy, too, as she'd intended, and they all pushed closer to the bear's pen to see better. A woman in a huge hat resembling a collapsed silk layer cake turned from her male companion to look more closely at Emily guiding the boys to the bear's cage, demonstrating the outrageous belief that children should have the best vantage point from which to observe the cages and their inhabitants if they were to learn about them firsthand.

"Does he actually attend school?" the layer cake lady asked, glancing warily at William as if he was another park specimen. "He looks distinctly too young." The casual surroundings seemed to make people more familiar and less polite, so Emily decided to err on the side of ease herself in the park's more relaxed atmosphere.

"He does indeed go to school," she answered the woman. "He's in his second year already. He started just as he turned three, as did his brother," she added, smiling down at Connie, still clinging to her skirts.

"I don't like this place," Connie whimpered. A few more stylish bonnets and tall beaver hats moved, as ladies on the arms of gentlemen standing around the animal pens turned to look down at the child. "I don't like it," he repeated, burying his face in his mother's skirts.

A tall, thin, elegant man, looking as if he had a bad smell under his nose, asked, "Really? Is that quite natural . . . to go to school so young, I mean?"

"It is in a Dutch household," Emily replied, working to keep a growing irritation out of her voice. "My father-in-law's relatives in the Netherlands were sending their children to school at a young age over two hundred years ago," she added, matter-of-factly.

"Discipline should always be taught in the home. Surely treating children thus is an invitation to anarchy," the man sniffed. Emily tightened her grip on her younger son's shoulder imperceptibly. She took a deep breath to calm herself, and William glanced up sideways at the tall interrogator before looking back at his mother. Her tone was a warning he knew to heed, even if it wasn't directed at him.

"Dutch parenting is characterized by warmth rather than punishment," she said. "It makes for happier children and happier parents, too—a better family situation all the way around," she finished, nodding her head slightly to the opinionated couple and turning away from them in a purposeful spin, gathering both children to her skirt and moving up closer to the bear's cage.

"No, Mama, I want to go home," Connie whimpered again as he held back.

"Oh, you're just a nimenog," she announced.

"What's a nimenog?" William asked. His brother still held on to his mother's skirt, but he twisted up to study her face more closely.

"Oh, just a very silly fellow," Emily answered. "It's really slang, but it's not so offensive it shouldn't be used, I don't think. It's onomatopoeia," she declared, grinning at both of them. "That means a word that sounds like its meaning. Don't you think *nimenog* sounds like a silly fellow?" They both stared at her for a second and then laughed together, pushing up against the bars of the bear's pen to look at him.

The huge creature watched them watching him. Emily struggled to resist the temptation to pull back. They were completely safe outside the cage, after all.

"How did they get him in there, Mama?" Connie asked, gripping the bars in two small, chubby fists as if to press through them to join the bear on the other side.

"Back up, Connie," Emily said, unable to stop herself from pulling on his shoulder gently. "He's been here since the Menagerie opened about ten years ago. I think he was given to the park as a cub, along with some black swans, by an extraordinarily rich man who got tired of caring for them on his estate."

"Why did he have wild animals on his estate?" William asked, eyeing a boy of his own age nearby who held a small dog on a leash. Turning in place to watch the pet, William leveled an unmistakable glower of jealousy as the child walked by, the pet virtually ignored by its owner. William slipped a small ball out of his pants pocket, bouncing it once or twice as if to engage the dog whose young master pulled the pet to his side with a violent jerk.

"It's always been something people of wealth want," Emily said, unaware of her older son's drifting attention. "Royalty down through the ages used the size of their personal menageries as a sign of power."

"But we don't have any royalty here in America, Mother, right?" William pulled himself back to their conversation, returning his ball to his pocket. Four-year-old Connie still clung to Emily's skirt with both hands, hobbling her as if to reassure himself of her closeness.

"That's right, Willie, but we have a lot of newly wealthy men and women here who forget that and would like to be royals. I'm sure that's why the idea of private menageries came into fashion."

"This one's not as good as the zoo in London, is it, Mother?" William looked around at the other pens, having clearly lost interest in the withdrawn bear.

"It's one of the first zoos in any American city, Willie. Only the Philadelphia Zoo came first, and I think ours has many more animals in it than the one in London—something like three hundred fifty, at last count. Anyway, it certainly pleases New Yorkers because I've read that seven thousand people come here every day!" William looked impressed and was blessedly silent for a few moments, but a strangled sob from the folds of Emily's skirts broke the peace and made her jump.

"What in God's name is wrong now, Connie?" She dropped to her knees to look at the little boy's tear-streaked face.

"I hate it here!" he cried. "That poor bear hates it, too. He's been in prison since he was a baby and he's never done anything wrong."

"Cornelius de Koningh, you've mistaken a zoo for a jail," she laughed, gently.

Connie pressed his chubby body up flat against the cage, pushing his forehead against the bars so he could make eye contact better with the bear. "He's so sad, Mama. Look how he sits so still. He doesn't even walk back and forth like the lions. Please, let's go. I can't look anymore." Emily stared at the child, amazed that her attempt to give him pleasure had gone so wrong.

"He has a point, Mother," William chimed in, always ready to join any argument. "Funny," he added with a slant glance at Emily, "we just finished the war and now we go lock up all the wild animals we can find as if they were our prisoners."

Emily rose slowly to her full height and looked from one child to the other. "Fine," she said, clearly exasperated. "Let's go." She turned away from the bear pen with a hand on each child's shoulder, but another wail from Connie stopped them, causing groups of park visitors to spin around and stare.

"My leg!" Connie cried. "It's stuck! My knee is stuck between the bars and I can't get it free!" The little blond boy's mouth formed a gaping, mute howl. He tried to squeeze his chubby leg through the narrow opening between the wrought-iron railings of the bear's pen.

The flesh around the kneecap was swelling up on both sides from his struggle to pull it out, which made him pull all the harder. Everyone froze, watching in stunned silence. Emily bent down and reached through the bars to push from the other side, which made the bear finally stand up to pay attention. He growled, protective of his small space. "Help!" Connie screamed, tears pouring down his cheeks in a tidal wave of panic. "I can't get loose!"

"Maybe they'll have to cut his leg off, Mother, just like the soldiers," William said, eyes wide. The rising buzz of park visitors calling questions about what was happening only upset Connie more.

Emily, too, was worried about the bear's disposition and pulled her hand away. "Hush, Willie. Don't be ridiculous," she hissed. "Maybe you could do something useful like getting one of the attendants we saw when we came over here. Back up, everyone," she commanded, pointing William toward the perimeter of the crowd and giving him a little shove. "You're frightening the child even more by pushing in to stare at him like that." She glowered furiously at the group of sightseers gathering around them. "Get help, please," she said between gritted teeth.

William knew his mother must be frightened, or she would never have lost her temper in public. He'd sometimes traveled with her when she and his father performed in concerts together. There were plenty of things that had frightened him then, like the performances themselves in front of hundreds of people, but his mother had never lost her calm. Yet this was different. William could see fear in her face as she shoved people away from his brother. He saw her drop to her knees to soothe and quiet him. He heard her reassuring Connie he wouldn't spend the rest of his life stuck in the cage, but she looked desperate, and that frightened William, too. He ran in search of the attendant they'd spotted feeding the sheep in the first pen at the edge of the crowd.

It seemed to William like an hour, but it took only a few minutes to find the helper and bring him back to the bear's pen. In a few more minutes a cake of lard soap the attendant had in his cleaning bucket had coated the iron railings wedged around Connie's swollen, chubby knee, and only a few more moments of sliding and pulling freed the little leg. Emily had both arms around Connie as she talked and whispered to him, her face pressed alongside his. It was over as suddenly as it began, and the little family clung together in an anticlimactic ending to the panic.

A tall gentleman got down from his carriage and started toward them, wading against the tide of people now leaving the scene. He was well dressed without pretention and clearly in robust physical condition for a middle-aged man probably in his forties. With broad shoulders and a powerful torso held perfectly erect, yet relaxed, he would have looked like a prize-fighter except for his obvious prosperity. Stopping next to Emily, he waited for her to look up after administering to Connie's needs.

"I'm glad to see the child's misadventure ended so well," the gentleman said. "Can I offer you three a ride home?" His voice was an odd mix of Irish brogue, Scottish burr, and something else unidentifiable, as he lifted his top hat with a small bow.

"Thank you, sir, but we need the walk to calm down. We don't have far to go." She nodded her now bare head of dark hair, piled up supposedly under the small bonnet that had slipped off somewhere during the excitement, and putting Connie's hand in hers, Emily started toward Fifth Avenue with her sons on each side. She suddenly felt exhausted and no longer relished the walk ahead.

"Madame," the muscular gentleman called after her. "Are you the High Art m-musician who performs and plays the violin in Europe with her husband? I think I could not m-mistake your face."

Emily stopped and turned slowly back to look at him. "I am undoubtedly the same, sir. I know no other women who play the instrument in public accompanied by their husbands." She assessed the handsome, athletic-looking man with a slight stutter more closely. His wave of auburn hair over his forehead, and matching brows and mustache, gave him a decidedly rakish look which combined daringly with his expensive, tasteful outfit to set him apart from most of the upper-class visitors to the park. She felt she might have seen him before but couldn't be sure.

"I'm sorry, I don't recall your name," he said, taking his hat off to hold in his gloved hand in obvious deference. "I really know nothing of High Art, but I know what I like, and no one could mistake the beauty of your playing."

"Thank you, sir," Emily said, with a small nod of her head, but no self-introduction. He had, after all, not introduced himself, either. "However, we must be on our way now. It's been a trying afternoon for us all. I bid you good day." And with that she steered the children forward as she left her admirer behind, watching the three of them disappear through the fall foliage just inside the park.

"Mother, we should have gone with him. We can't walk all the way home," William grumbled.

"Of course, we can, Willie. It's not much more than a mile from here. And besides, I'm sure Grandfather Klaas's carriage will be down for us any minute. We'll be able to spot it when we get past these houses in the next few blocks."

"Connie can't walk all that way, can he?" William eyed his brother who was moving quite quickly to leave the scene of his and the bear's entrapment.

"Certainly, he can," Emily said. "He needs to move the knee and get some circulation going." But she glanced behind her to see if the handsome gentleman was still there with his carriage. She was a little disappointed to find he was not.

They progressed slowly along a path inside the park paralleling the avenue, taking time to allow the offended knee to loosen up while keeping its owner's mind off his troubles. Emily was walking a tightrope between too much attention and too little sympathy for her four-year-old son. They strolled in silence for a few blocks, clearly enjoying the peace and beauty around them in the park as they finally started to let go of the tension from their ordeal. Obviously cheered with relief, Connie suddenly piped up. "I had so many people trying to help me get free, Mama, but nobody helps that bear. He'll never get out of the pen and go home, will he?"

"I don't know that he wants to, Connie," Emily answered, thoughtfully. "Remember when the animals broke out of their cages last year and then just stood around waiting to be put back in? They've never known any other life."

"I think he wants to go home," Connie said. He looked decidedly grim for a usually cheerful little boy.

"Why don't we try to help them?" William suggested, his eyes sparkling with the brilliance of his idea. "You know a lot of people, Mother, and you could do it."

"Willie, we're not getting involved with the workings of the Central Park Menagerie. I have scant interest in trying to free the animals . . . when I can't even free myself," she added under her breath. She sighed, and William noticed for the first time that day how tired she looked. He was uncomfortable with the sensation her drained face awoke in him, just as he had been with the sight of her panic. He looked away so he wouldn't have to see it anymore.

⚜ W ⚜

Later that day, Emily stood with her violin under her chin and bow poised above the strings. The library's double French doors leading out to the garden fanned open, inviting in unusually warm autumn weather. She loved it when the outdoor world joined her violin practice sessions. Sunlight filtering through the trees on Fifth Avenue danced over the top of the grand piano. The de Koningh pianoforte, curving gracefully just inside the curtains, was usually alive with Emily's husband's playing, but silent now with only the sun to warm its surface. The top was closed and locked over the keys and had been for over a month since Corey left with his father to help with the reconstruction of the de Koningh textile business after the war.

The library in the de Koningh mansion offered the peaceful refuge Emily had yearned for ever since the adventure at the bear's cage in the park. The long walk home afterward up Fifth Avenue would usually have given her an energy boost, but that day, for some reason, it had drained her already diminished reserves. She knew the solitude of a half-empty home was not exactly the ideal prescription for happiness, but she was torn between the loneliness of being the only adult in the family household while her husband and his father were away on business in the South, and plenty of freedom for practice and learning new music. The violin took a total commitment, however, leaving little room for administering to the needs of a large establishment with many more servants than Emily thought necessary. She had to admit she recognized a sense of resentment rising in her throat all too often these days, a bitterness at finding she was in fact bringing up her sons virtually on her own, while also losing the closeness and benefits of relationships with their father and grandfather.

Connie sat now against the cushions of the deep couch opposite the piano, a stack of picture books piled around him. An Indian summer breeze rustled the silk curtain liner, brushing it gently against a piano leg just as the cream-colored family cat caressed Emily's shin in passing, a gesture that said, *You're all mine.* She enjoyed watching him leave for an afternoon ramble in the garden, knowing full well it was safe from the dangers of the park inside the wrought-iron gates surrounding his domestic world.

Warming up her mind and fingers with a bright Italian concerto made her feel a glow as if the sun played on her shoulders now instead of the piano's top. Without looking up, she noticed her son William had come in from the garden and tried to ignore him. He paused at the threshold, framed by the French doors and balancing on one foot, while he glanced around.

"What is it, William?" Emily lowered her violin slightly. She had no intention of aborting her practice for her son's intrusion. He knew better than to interrupt her work but had obviously found a way to ignore the imperative; as had Mary, the little housemaid following close behind him with a silver calling-card tray. Emily fought back a sigh that escaped anyway as she eyed her eldest son leading the maid into the room. "William, what do you want? Mary . . . ? Has everyone forgotten the rules in this house?" She held her position, violin raised and bow ready to respond; a clear message that this disturbance should go no further.

"Why is *he* in here, then?" Legs planted solidly apart, William glared at his little brother.

"He's here because he loves to listen. He never interrupts, unlike someone standing before me, *William*." Emily glowered fiercely to penetrate her son's seeming lack of care, but his self-assured stance never changed, nor did his expression pass from casual charm to concern.

"And why . . . ? Mary, is there something you need from me that can't wait until my practice is finished?" Emily's voice cut with an exasperated edge. She felt her palms getting damp and her breath shorten, trapped by resentment which was more of an intrusion than the interruption itself. She knew better than to get lured into William's attention snare. The past few years of traveling on concert tours with two small boys and little domestic help had taught her to deal completely with one challenge at a time.

"Is there something you need me for, Mary?" Emily tried to calm her rising anger. It was so hard to fulfill her responsibilities to both her family and her art. She never felt she did anything well and fully anymore. It had been so much easier when she'd had only her violin to give all her effort to. She took her Guarneri down with her left hand and let it hang along with the bow, relaxed against her skirt, as if waiting patiently for her interrupters to play their parts before coming in again with hers.

"Pardon, ma'am, it's only that there was a visitor here to see you who left a callin' card. He looked just that important, I thought you'd want to know. So, when I saw Master William comin' in through the garden, I followed him." Stepping forward past William, who started to say something and then thought better of it, the maid held out a silver tray with a small white card on it. The significance of a visitor coming to the de Koningh mansion escaped Emily entirely since it was a regular occurrence, but she tried not to let the housemaid see her growing annoyance.

"A visitor?"

"I din'a want to disturb you, ma'am." Mary had worked in the house since before Emily came as a child of thirteen after her mother died. Mary was still here because Klaas de Koningh considered her "family," though she couldn't handle physically taxing work anymore. So, it fell to Emily as the representative head of the household in the absence of Corey and his father to protect Mary from unnecessary burdens. When the de Koningh men came home from their business trip they could take over some of the disciplining of both the boys and the servants, but now it was up to her. She found running a complicated household with children, staff, and numerous social responsibilities more burden than benefit.

Early in her marriage to Corey de Koningh, and even after William was born right after the war ended, with no interest in practical domestic skills Emily had learned to balance her duties as mother and wife with her responsibilities to her music. But adding the requirements of the affluent older generation of the de Koningh household seemed to tip the scale. She tried not to struggle against the constraints but often felt she was losing the battle. Suddenly noticing William's smirk, she knew he must be enjoying the inner struggle amplified in her voice. She turned from him to focus pointedly on the housemaid. "An important visitor, Mary? Someone you felt had to be brought to my attention immediately?"

"Indeed, ma'am. Only, his callin' card ain't as clear as it might be."

Mary leaned in toward her mistress and lowered her voice. "Master William dropped one of his spitballs from the landin', and it melted some of the gentleman's writin' away." She held the silver tray out to Emily with the soggy calling card balanced against the edge to dry.

"William! You promised not to do that anymore. You're much too old for such childish behavior." Emily kept her focus on the card and Mary's outstretched hand in hopes of hiding the smile weakening her resolve, especially as William was obviously not too old for just such a prank.

"That's not fair, Mary!" William railed. "You promised not to tell. And besides, Mother, Mary says you and Father did the same thing when you were young." William stood tall, dark eyes flashing a challenge. Emily was instantly struck by his resemblance to her own father. She hadn't enjoyed the confrontations with Lord William Alden when she was a child any more than she liked standoffs with his grandson now.

"It's Mary's duty to report anything amiss in the running of the household, Willie, and yours not to add to her work." Emily glanced at Mary and saw she, too, was fighting back a smile. "And besides, your father and I had none of the opportunities to play that you do today. We had no Central Park to run around in and we weren't allowed to bounce balls in the courtyard. Our pranks were more about gaining some freedom than causing trouble." A vision of twelve-year-old Corey climbing out onto the roof with her thirteen-year-old self close behind flashed through her mind, causing instant discomfort. She must keep the attic access to the roof locked and hidden from her boys lest they repeat their parents' dangerous misdemeanors, if they hadn't done so already.

"How am I supposed to read this now?" She picked the damp card up gingerly between her thumb and forefinger so as not to smudge what was left of a personal note written on the reverse side.

"It's from Mr. John W. Mackay," William announced. Proud to be delivering the message, he overcame the judged unfairness of the housemaid's betrayal.

"*Mac*-key," Emily corrected, waving the card gently to dry it out faster. "The man we met in Central Park after Connie got stuck in the bear's cage. It's pronounced *Mac*-key, not Mac-*kay*."

"That's not how it's spelled." William had clearly spent time sounding out the card before Mary salvaged it. "How do you know it's pronounced that way, and who is he, anyway?"

"Willie, do you never stop asking questions? We met his wife in Paris . . . or maybe London, when your father and I did a concert tour in Europe. When we saw him in the park at the zoo this morning you could certainly tell he's kept up his robust physique. I gather he was forced to gain extreme prowess in the boxing ring to protect himself as a young immigrant just come to this city."

"Why? Are immigrant children in more danger than others?"

Realizing her son was launched on another long-winded investigation and argument, Emily nodded and smiled to the housemaid. "Thank you, Mary." It seemed best not to include the de Koningh servants in the results of William's investigation. She gave up hope of her violin practice with a small sigh, carefully returning the Guarneri and her bow to the case lying open on top of the desk. She didn't close and fasten it, though, leaving open the possibility of revisiting it before the hour was done. The venerable old violin shone with a patina that could come only from the anointing of a century of caring hands. A luster more beautiful than any applied veneer rose up from it. She rested her hand lightly on the instrument's neck for a moment, a small apology for their premature parting and remembrance of all they'd already shared.

As if he'd been suddenly released by the same light touch, her younger son, Connie, all but forgotten sitting quietly amid his picture books, slid off the couch to the floor accompanied by a few stray volumes. The unspoken message in the violin's return to its case was that practice had ended, at least momentarily. He landed with a muffled thump on the Oriental rug, his books settling around him, pages rustling as they fell. Emily bent to help him up, gathering the picture books together as she did so. She smiled at him gently, resting her hand on his shiny blond head just as she had on the violin. And Connie smiled back, feeling the affection in it without appreciating her nostalgia for a young blond boy who was now his father. She saw that William also noticed her caress and could tell another barrage of questions was about to be launched, so she threw a preemptive strike of her own.

"Now Willie," she said, forcefully, "why so much interest in Mr. Mackay?" She dropped down on the piano bench and slid over, pulling Connie along with her and making room for William to join them. But he chose to stand by the piano, looking at them both at eye level.

"Well he's so tall, maybe as tall as Father, and he looks so strong. I watched him jump down from his carriage in the park without any help, though he's old. Probably as old as you are, Mother."

"That's not so old!" Emily's smile lit up her eyes and deepened the dimples in her cheeks. "I'm not even thirty yet, and I assume Mr. Mackay is only a little older, but that doesn't assign either one of us to the rubbish heap. Although from your perspective I can see why you might disagree," she added, almost under her breath. "From what I've read of him in the press, Mr. Mackay started his life building ships and fighting in the streets," she explained. "He came from Ireland as a child and had an extremely hard beginning here. I think he's never forgotten that, which is why he keeps himself so fit, even though he no longer needs to protect himself or his family with his fists." Emily tightened her arm around Connie involuntarily and pulled him up on her lap.

William frowned and narrowed his eyes. "I thought he was very important and rich."

"He is now," Emily said, "but that doesn't mean he always was.

Many men in this country start out poor and end up rich. It seldom happens in Europe, but that's the way it is here."

"How could an Irish immigrant be so rich now?"

"Because he's as wealthy as a sultan and has been for a long time, Willie. Not all the Irish are servants. He discovered a silver mine in Nevada called the Comstock Lode, and now he owns railroads and telegraph companies . . ."

"Then why does he live in a hotel?"

"I don't know that he does," Emily said, but she caught William glancing down at the puckered calling card resting on the piano top and sensed he knew something she didn't. Picking the card up, she turned it over and read the blurred handwritten message out loud: *Request your musical skills for an American concert. Please contact me at my hotel or club, both listed here. Look forward to seeing you again.*

"Your father and I have already accepted as many concerts as we can handle right now," Emily muttered out loud, slipping the card into her side-seam skirt pocket just as William took a breath and started to speak. "That's enough, Willie," his mother interrupted. Sometimes she talked with William just to hear her own thoughts out loud, but even knowing he was still curious about her elegant admirer, she had no interest in sharing gossip about John Mackay with her son.

She'd heard in Paris that Mrs. Mackay lived only in European palaces with their children. Her husband had apparently rejected his wife's grand ways. Some women, Emily knew from the papers' gossip columns, had intimated that he was unhappy with her pretensions and now spent most of his time in the United States, living in hotels and clubs, but that was none of her business. She had enough trouble of her own without worrying about someone else's. "Willie, didn't you have vocabulary words to copy for school?" Connie started to squirm in her lap. "And, Connie . . ." She hugged her young son. "I can feel there's something *you'd* like to say. It's your turn to ask a question before I send you both down to the kitchen, so I can finish practicing." She looked at Connie's still plump baby face and nodded encouragement.

Wide-eyed, Connie asked, "Why were you and Papa married when you were children?"

Emily flinched. "We weren't," she said. "What made you think that?"

"You said you were playing here together when you were children and dropping spitballs from the landing like William."

"Oh, Connie dear! We both lived here because your grandfather Alden didn't want to leave me alone in London after my mother died. Grandpa Klaas was his friend, so he asked if I could come for a while to live with him and his family. Your father and I were best friends right from the start, but we weren't married until many years later, after the war. Now that's enough from both of you," she announced, sliding off the piano bench with Connie and putting him down on his stout little legs. "Willie, please take Connie to the kitchen for some milk and cookies. Your own music lesson will start in just an hour, and I need to get back to mine."

Satisfied that she'd paid the necessary attention to both children, she took a freer breath and started to steer them for the library door to the hall when Connie let out a howl. It gained volume insistently, rising to fill the whole room with no warning. Emily froze in place, dropping down to her younger son's level with a look of panic on her face. "Connie! What's wrong?"

"I don't want you to die and leave me alone, just like your mother did," the little boy wept. His pain contorted his face and he made no attempt to cover it up.

"Good Lord, Connie. I'm not going anywhere and would never leave you. Besides, you have a wonderful family that loves you, and there will always be people around. You'll never be alone. Let's talk about this another time," she added, gently. "It's a big topic for a little boy, but I can assure you right now that I'm not going away or leaving you alone. I just want to play my violin," she added, with a little smile as she wiped the tears from his cheeks. "Could you take a deep breath, go with William to get a cookie from Mary, and let me have a little time to myself to practice? I'll see you before Professor Haussmann comes for William's piano lesson. All right?"

He nodded and turned to put his hand in his big brother's, but a few small sniffles escaped as he left the library, trailing slightly behind. Emily's shoulders sank as she watched them go, wondering where she'd find the reserves she needed now to practice the Schubert Fantasy in C. Traveling more often than in the past to perform a few nights and afternoons each week, more repertoire had to be learned and the de Koninghs found it easier if Europe was left off their schedule. It hadn't occurred to her before she'd had her first child that more than just her time and energy would be drained away by a young family. Pieces of her heart also seemed to go with them never to be returned if she had to leave her boys behind, as many of their past European performances had forced her to do. She felt often she was missing important changes as they grew and knew well how it hurt a child to fear being left alone. But while it was easier to leave them at the de Koningh mansion when she performed closer to home, it also meant she had to leave them behind, something she now refused to do when traveling in Europe. There didn't seem to be an ideal solution to the dilemma of needing to be just herself and wanting to be their mother as well. She knew it was a struggle few women would understand. But having lost her own mother as a child, Emily felt a different pull to her children than most mothers of her day.

She picked the Guarneri up out of its case again and lifted its partner, the bow. She'd hoped to practice with Corey on the piano but had to trust he was practicing on his own during his trip down south with his father. Certainly, Klaas would give him every encouragement to do so. She knew in a few minutes she'd be pressing her cheek onto the beautiful old instrument to feel the vibration passed from it to her, and from her to anyone who wanted to listen. The communion was deeper even than what she shared with her family, but the guilty thought passed quickly as she took a deep, calming breath and prepared to leave the dailiness of her domestic life behind.

Emily knew how lucky she was, and said so, often. Some people couldn't escape the confines of their personal worlds, no matter where they were, but she had a magic passkey to open whatever enclosure she was in, and she always carried it with her. She only wished now for more energy and strength to affect her escape. She wasn't used to being abandoned by her body, and the headaches, nausea, and exhaustion she'd experienced recently reminded her of the life she sometimes wanted to forget. She looked back at the music on the stand, counting silently through the opening bars of ephemeral notes for the piano and then to where the violin entered. She touched her bow to the strings so gently and with such reverence and respect she hoped both the long-gone composer and God would hear and appreciate it.

CHAPTER TWO

"BESSIE'S COMING!" Connie rocketed off the window seat at the top of the de Koningh mansion's first-floor landing. "I can see her carriage at the corner. She's almost here!" His chubby four-year-old legs punched down the stairs; short, reflexive pistons ricocheting from step to step in a desperate effort to make them disappear faster. "Bessie, Bessie, Bessie . . ." His shrieks mimicked a steam engine announcing its arrival.

Anyone watching his clattering descent would have held their breath—his mother certainly did—fearing he'd reach the bottom in a mound of childish rubble. Choking down her panic, Emily watched his body gain momentum seemingly beyond its control as her youngest son tried to make up for the hindrance of his short legs when he was in a hurry. She breathed a silent prayer until he bounced to a halt at her feet at the bottom landing. She couldn't help grabbing him and hugging him against her knees, relief washing away all the reserve she'd worked for. She bent down to give him a kiss.

"Philip Cornelius de Koningh," she crooned against his tangled mop of curls, "you promised to slow down and take these stairs one at a time. It scares me to see you attack them like a whirlwind!" She hugged him again, more for herself than for him. "I don't suppose you're expecting some of Bessie's sugar cookies to materialize in a box with your name on it, are you?" She kissed the top of his head and let him go with a pat on his bottom, hoping the familiar touch would mask her fading terror. There was certainly no reason to make him fearful of the natural joys of childhood because his mother saw them as the true perils they were. "Go on to the kitchen and see what Bessie has for you," Emily added, sure there would be a treat for Connie, as always.

"Why doesn't she come in the front door? It would be so much faster," Connie said, skipping backward across the marble entrance floor.

"Mind how you go, Connie. Turn around so you can see the door to the kitchen," Emily warned. "Bessie's coming to do us a service, and she's not a guest, or family, Connie." She started to follow him to join in the welcome.

"She's not a servant, either." His eyes crinkled with glee.

"A service, not a servant, Con. She's a seamstress and she's coming to make me some new dresses for my concert tour."

"How did she learn to do that?" he asked. "Maybe I could be a seamstress someday. Then I could go with you to every one of your performances." He slipped his hand in Emily's and together they walked quickly to the door under the stairs. She pushed it open and they could both see William already standing below the back stairs, bouncing his rubber ball on the kitchen floor. It made a smack each time it hit the floor and he counted them in succession. He was getting close to the mixing table in the middle of the room and ignoring the annoyed glances coming from Mary, and Emma, the cook.

"Hello, Mother." He never looked up or stopped bouncing the ball. "Bessie's coming. I could see her carriage from the courtyard when I was playing. I was going to tell you."

"Really? What prevented you?" Emily asked, eyeing him with as much annoyance as the cook did. "William, please don't bounce that inside. You belong out in the courtyard with it. William . . ." Her voice rose in warning, but he was unresponsive.

"How did Bessie learn seamstressing?" Connie asked again, tugging on her skirt to regain her attention.

"She said her mother taught her. Her mother came over on a ship to the customs port of Sag Harbor at the end of Long Island. She was a slave to a whaling captain's wife."

"But Bessie's white, Mother. She can't have been a slave." William grabbed the ball in midair and held it suspended while he stared at Emily.

"I didn't say Bessie was a slave, William. I said her mother was. And there were white slaves long before there were African ones, and Chinese ones and Turkish ones, too. In the country I was born in, England, they used to grab people right off the streets who had no homes or no way of taking care of themselves, and just send them away on ships as slaves to the captains. They were poor and helpless. Color makes no difference where cruelty and power are concerned."

"True!" Mary nodded. "The Scots had it worst of all. The judges of Edinburgh ordered that any lost soul makin' life unpleasant for the British high-class be enslaved and shipped to the colonies. We Irish know all about that, too." She looked at Emily. William stood with the ball in the middle of the kitchen, staring from one to the other.

"Slavery has existed in every empire on earth," Emily said, ignoring Mary's jab at her aristocratic British ancestors. "Our recent civil war in America brought that to everyone's attention, but we should always be aware without the spotlight of war . . . do you both understand?" She looked from William to Connie and back again to William, who in fact had started the difficult questioning. They looked overwhelmed. It was a topic she'd revisit at another time.

"Mary, could you open the back door, please, and help Bessie with whatever she's carrying. You too, boys. I'm going up to my room to get ready for her, so when you've said your greetings, please bring her up to me." She smiled at both boys and Mary, indicating the slavery lesson was over, and left them all together in the kitchen, the excitement of Bessie's arrival hanging in the air. Emily wondered briefly what her husband and father-in-law's explanations would have been to the questions about slavery she'd barely touched on, what with their connections to the South.

Ordinarily Emily would have joined the boys to wait for Bessie's arrival, but she suddenly felt too tired for the commotion. A few moments' rest on the bed was a definite possibility since Bessie's homemade cookies would slow her departure from the kitchen and arrival upstairs. Emily might have as much as ten minutes with her eyes shut.

❧☙ ❧☙

Emily's eyes flew open, wide but unseeing, until Bessie's curly gray hair came into focus. The kind blue eyes locked onto hers, pulling her back to full consciousness against her will.

"Bessie! What . . . ?"

"You were taking a little nap," Bessie said, one hand on Emily's shoulder nudging her back down to the pillow. "Rest a minute more. I'm sorry I woke you." Emily stared back up at her seamstress, hearing her musical voice but not fully comprehending the words.

"A nap . . . rest . . . ?" Emily narrowed her vision and focused on the seamstress's blue silk ribbon with the small gold locket around her neck. Nothing was more of a talisman for Bessie than that locket with a picture of her mother in it. "You didn't disturb me. I have no idea why I dropped off that way. I've been practicing my violin late at night because the days are too full. Maybe I'm not getting enough sleep." Emily pushed herself up off the bed, trying to look alert and move purposefully, but feeling drugged and slightly ill.

"Late at night!" Bessie shook her head and scowled her disapproval. "You'll have to stop that. It'll make you sick. Why don't you tell the children they have to keep themselves busy so you can have your practice time back? Couldn't Mary or someone look after them long enough for you to get time for yourself and your work?"

"Oh, it's not the children's fault. It's . . . I can't seem to do anything very well anymore, Bessie." Emily sank back down as if someone had punched her behind the knees. "I used to be good at everything and now I'm good at nothing." She heard the break in her voice and was shaken by it. "Could you pull the balcony door open a little so we can get some fresh air?"

Bessie pushed the draperies and inner mesh curtains aside and opened half of the French door to the bedroom balcony just a crack. There didn't seem any noticeable change in the atmosphere of the room, but Emily thought she felt better just watching the curtains move a little in the air currents flowing from Central Park across Fifth Avenue. Bessie sat down on the bed, slipping one arm around Emily's shoulders and holding the other hand in Emily's lap. She squeezed it for reassurance, warmth, friendship, or some inexplicably welcome feminine empathy.

"You're exhausted and doing too much," Bessie said.

That simple fact was indisputable, but somehow hearing it from the calm, competent seamstress made it more real. Emily looked up at Bessie, taking in the soft lines in her forehead and around her eyes and mouth, outlines hinting at a full but not always easy life. Quite a bit taller than Emily, she often appeared to be passing her judgment and support to her client easily and naturally, and Emily accepted both with the same comfort of a natural relationship born of mutual respect. She'd never noted that Bessie was the closest and only female friend in her life, or at least the only one she had time for or cared to connect with.

Emily nodded, and wiped an unexpected tear off her cheek with her other hand. Bessie gently pushed Emily's head down on her shoulder and rocked her slightly. "It takes a lot to make you cry," she said, her voice soft. "I'll bet you're lonely, too. This big old house can't be much fun for a woman to run. And the sole company of children and staff with no men around probably isn't what you expected when you chose married life—though life's seldom what we expect, is it?" She smiled at Emily a little, suggesting that disappointment wasn't the end of the world, either.

"It's time your husband and father-in-law came home, Mrs. de Koningh. When are they due back?" She looked at Emily almost cheerfully, as if this was the solution to all her problems rather than the problem itself.

"I have no idea, Bessie. I'm worried because I have some concerts I've agreed to do with my husband, and we haven't rehearsed for them. But all I can do is be as prepared as I can be, and that's where you come in." Emily pushed up from the bed again and tried to arrange her expression into its most purposeful aspect. "I need some new formal performance dresses. I got much too fat after Connie was born, and somehow I was able to ignore it until I tried to get into my old evening clothes. You'll have to take all new measurements, but it will be worthwhile since I'll need at least three new ones. Shall we get started?" She hoped she sounded cheered by the expectation of her new clothes, but really it discouraged her more than ever. Losing the body she'd assumed would always be hers seemed the final injustice at a time when nothing was fair. Her vulnerability had been well hidden until she could no longer pretend neither she nor her life had changed.

"Wonderful!" Bessie seemed to glow with the delight of her assignment. "I'll start measuring while you tell me what you need and how you picture the dresses." She slipped Emily's robe off so only a thin cotton slip was between the tape and Emily's body. "I assume we still have to keep some coverage on the arms?" Bessie moved over to the sitting area at the end of the big double bed, placing her bag of supplies down on the sewing table next to a small sofa and opening it wide to expose the contents. Mass-produced pins, measuring tape, a paper journal, and flat lead pencil appeared as if magically summoned. She steered Emily to the mirror on the back of the closet door and put the pencil and notebook with Mrs. Adriaan de Koningh written on it, next to each other on the table. Taking Emily's measurements with a reassuring professionalism, she turned her client gently when a different angle was needed. Emily allowed herself to be moved at Bessie's will with no contribution on her part.

"So what kind of dresses have you been picturing?" Bessie turned Emily around and stretched the measuring tape from the base of Emily's neck to the bottom of her waist at her back. She wrote the results down in the notebook. "I know these are to be formal but still for the stage," Bessie said, "so undoubtedly the shoulders must be covered, but not restricted." Emily nodded absently. "And the waist, I remember, can't hamper your movement," Bessie continued. "Nothing so tight you can't lift your arms freely." Emily nodded again, seemingly too distracted by her own image in the mirror to willingly join in designing her dresses. "Mrs. de Koningh, could you help me please?" Bessie shook her head in exasperation.

Emily started and looked over her shoulder. "I'm sorry, Bessie. Do you need me to turn?"

"No, just talk to me. Thinking of three new evening gowns should give you pleasure, not put you to sleep."

"Of course, Bessie. I was elsewhere. This is a pleasure, and they're going to be very important to my performances, so of course I want to help." Emily fixed her eyes on the reflection of her body in the mirror. A squarer, more solid woman than she remembered stared back at her, a distant relative of the long-waisted, deceptively delicate-looking Emily who once would have met her gaze.

"Good," Bessie said, with an emphatic bob of her curly gray head. "Now you can turn." She circled Emily's waist with the tape, looked at it a little longer than Emily thought necessary, and wrote the results in the notebook. "Heavens, you have put on some inches since the last dress!" She glanced up at Emily where she stood eyeing herself in the mirror. "But of course, that one was a few years ago." Bessie went back with the tape and started measuring around Emily's hips.

"This will be disastrous too, I'm sure," Emily sighed.

"Not much change," Bessie assured her. "Now the rib cage and then we're done."

"Is there a way to design a dress in two pieces so the waist will move with me?" Emily could feel what little enthusiasm she'd had for the idea of the new dresses drying up and shrinking like a sponge without water.

"Of course, but what's most important is to be sure we accentuate your virtues and hide the flaws. It's really quite easy to trick the eye of the beholder into staring at your shoulders, neck, and bust, ignoring your waist completely."

"Oh Bessie, I never used to have any flaws. What's happened to me?" Emily collapsed down on the love seat next to her seamstress, who was beginning to sketch in the notebook.

"Don't waste energy on those thoughts. Everybody has flaws." Bessie glanced for a minute at Emily slumped beside her and then went back to her drawing. "Now sit up and look at this." She placed the notebook on Emily's lap. "This is the latest two-piece style with a long waist, pointed at the bottom to make it appear even longer. It tricks the eye into seeing the midriff as inches smaller than it is; positively willowy." She smiled at Emily and gave her a conspiratorial nudge.

"No, Bessie," Emily said firmly. "I can't wear that long waist even if it is a two-piece. I'm too thick in the middle now. I'll need the higher waist and you'll just have to design something decorative to make it look . . . better." She stared past Bessie to the embroidered carpet, losing herself in the scrolls of silk thread decorating the border. How nice it was to have a father-in-law in the textile business. Furnishings for the grand old house were always new and vibrant, thanks to the access he had to thread and cloth from all over the world. But Emily was hard-pressed to be enthusiastic about cloth of any kind for herself. She understood her husband's lack of interest in his father's textile business. Her interests had always been elsewhere, but it was lucky that her husband at least had a discerning eye for fashion so he could advise her performance wardrobe.

"Bessie," she exclaimed, as if suddenly waking up, "I want the other two dresses to have Empire waists with loose fabric falling right from my rib cage to the floor. That way I'll be able to move as much as I like with complete freedom and comfort, and they'll hide a multitude of sins."

"Good Lord, no, Mrs. de Koningh." Bessie's eyes were as big as if she'd seen a ghost. "That style was in fashion in our mothers' day. We're way beyond that now! You can't wear an Empire waist!" She looked genuinely horrified and sounded as if she was in shock.

"Not my mother, Bessie. She didn't live long enough. And anyway, you can just call it Regency or À La Grecque, and if it's been that long then it's time to bring them back. That's what I want, and I know you can do it. We can just make the bodices special and modern, and the fabrics and decorative threads can be distinctive, too, thanks to my husband's father. He has access to notions most people have never seen, and I have every faith in you, Bessie," she added, smiling with much more enthusiasm than she felt. Bessie stared at her. Suddenly Emily felt as if the room was swimming around her and she was sinking in a whirlpool. "Bessie," she gasped, "could you open the hall door a little, so we get more cross-draft from the balcony, please. I'm feeling strange."

Bessie looked at Emily harder and moved over to the ornate, heavy wooden door, turning the handle and tugging it open. Much to the surprise of both women, a small, round creature tumbled into the room, rolling into a ball like a fuzzy caterpillar and coming to a stop at Emily's feet. As caterpillars will do when surprised, this one stayed in his tight circle for a few seconds, assessing the possibility of danger and acclimating to his surroundings. Slowly a blond head with curls and big brown eyes unwound itself and looked up at the women.

"Cornelius de Koningh! Where did you come from and what were you doing at the door?" It was all Emily could do to keep a straight face. The expression in Connie's eyes showed he was undoubtedly far more surprised than they had been by his sudden arrival.

"Don't call me Cornelius. Call me Connie dear," he begged. "Don't be mad at me, Mama. I was just resting against the door so I could be near you and Bessie. I didn't mean anything." His quivering lower lip showed he was alarmingly close to tears.

"Connie . . . dear," Emily added, smiling down at him, "you have to knock if you want to come in. The only rule is that you must respect people's privacy. That's all." She put her hand on Connie's curls heaped all over his forehead and looked at her seamstress.

"Bessie, would it be all right with you if Connie joined us as long as he'll be very quiet and lets us work uninterrupted?"

"Certainly." Bessie nodded. "I wish I had more cookies, but I gave them all to the boys when I came in. Connie, would you like to draw for a while?"

"Yes! But I don't really know how and I've nothing to draw with," he sniffed.

"What do you use for your art lessons?"

"Don't have art lessons. Just music sometimes with William and Professor Haussmann," Connie moaned. "But I don't like music very much."

"Really?" Bessie's eyebrows shot up and she looked at Emily with obvious misgivings. Connie saw her expression and prolonged eye contact with his mother.

"Oh, I like to listen to music, especially when Mama practices. But I don't like to make it myself. I really want to draw things the way you do, Bessie." He looked at her journal with his mother's name on it, studying one of the dress sketches Bessie had left it open to.

"Then if you want drawing lessons when I come back next time, we can get you some paper and graphite pencils cased in wood to work with and keep for your own. A cabinetmaker in New England cuts pencils now so we don't have to order them all the way from Germany." She winked at him, conspiratorially. "I'll try to get some for you. Does that sound good?"

"Yes! Mama, will you get me what Bessie says I need? Will you?" Emily nodded and helped him to his feet, guiding him to the open floor in front of the French doors to the balcony.

"I don't have anything extra today," Bessie said. "You can use a clean page at the back of the journal." She carried her workbook and pencil over and let them both drop down on the rug in front of him.

"Here are some fabric swatches, too," she said, pulling two chain rings out of her skirt pocket and tossing them gently down next to the journal. "You can fan the colors and textures out and let them give you ideas." Connie stared at the silk and velvet squares spread in a rainbow of hues, their edges cut in jagged points with pinking shears so they wouldn't unravel.

"Be very careful with that pencil, Con," Emily warned. She tilted his face up to her eyes with her index finger under his chin. "Don't touch the graphite to anything but the paper. Don't be careless in any way with it because it will mark everything. Promise me, Con? It's important." She held his eyes with hers, fastening his attention with her soft insistence.

"I will be careful, Mama. I'm just going to copy Bessie's picture so I can be a seamstress too." He flopped down on the floor with the swatches and Bessie's journal and pencil and set to work. Emily was used to his quiet concentration when they were in a room together and turned back to Bessie without another thought for their intruder.

"Now Bessie, here's what I'm thinking." She put her hands up high on her rib cage just under her bust and turned slightly sideways. "I want the skirt to fall straight from here. You said yourself the rib cage hadn't changed much, so emphasizing that virtue will be good. The skirt can be a solid color without being fussy, no pleats or flounces of any kind. But then the top of the dress can be cut low and have some special embroidery, maybe gold thread or something. And the sleeves should be just enough to cap the shoulder." She brushed her shoulders lightly with her fingers and lifted her arms gracefully in a gesture mimicking the way she held her violin and bow. "You see," she laughed, "I've been listening to you all along. Cut the top low and decorate the bodice and sleeves with something special so my matronly waist will no longer be an issue."

"I suppose . . . if that's what you want . . . it's your performance after all." Bessie frowned and looked down at her notebook. "Let me see that a minute, Connie." She put her hand out for the journal and he handed it to her reluctantly. "I'll sketch a sleeve and bodice for you," she said to Emily, putting her hand down for the pencil Connie also relinquished, but not without a sigh. "The bodice can be very low and catch up right at the edge of the shoulder, capped by a puffy little sleeve they call a 'beetle wing.'" She sketched the sweep of fabric ending in the gathered sleeve. "See how the arm is essentially bare, as is the shoulder? Yet there's nothing tasteless or spare about it." Bessie continued to sketch as Emily watched.

"'Beetle wing'! What do you take me for, Bessie? I have no interest in looking like a bug!" she joked. Bessie kept sketching without dignifying her attempt at humor.

"It's just a fashion term. Look. Doesn't this look pretty?" Bessie said, holding the sketch up for Emily to see. "All but the skirt. I don't like that. It has no movement hanging straight from your rib cage, although I understand the need for as little extra fabric and weight as possible." They both glared at the sketch as if it was a dead end.

"Look!" Connie yelled, peeking out from behind the gauze liner curtain next to the balcony. Both women jumped from surprise at the sound of his voice. "Look at me," he called out. "Can you see me?"

"Yes, of course." Emily tried to keep her annoyance down. He was only four after all, and he'd been very quiet and unnoticed, just as he'd promised. "We see you through the curtain, but not really clearly," she added. "Now please settle down a little longer while Bessie and I finish our work." Emily turned back to Bessie, but Connie couldn't be silenced.

"You can wear this," he crowed. "She can put a skirt like this over the top of the other one. You can see the underneath one right through." He held the gauze curtain up to his face and grinned at Emily and Bessie, who looked at his beaming smile and started to laugh. Bessie moved toward him.

"Master de Koningh, I do believe you've just designed your mother's new dress. The overskirt can be a light mesh with an occasional embroidered flower to match the design on the bodice and sleeves, while the underskirt can be a solid color working as a layered background. Little Connie, you're a wonder!" She unwrapped him from the curtain and gave him a big hug and kiss. He turned a warm shade of pink from his neck to his forehead under the mass of curls.

"Can I go now?" he asked. "I want to tell Mary what I've just done." He squirmed out of her embrace and skipped over to the oak door, pulling it open a little wider to slip through. Both women chuckled watching his chubby legs disappear as quickly as they'd arrived.

"He's a gift, Mrs. de Koningh. Truly, a gift," Bessie said. "And his idea's a good one. Out of the mouths of babes," she chuckled. "I'm going to work on it at home in muslin so you can see just what it would look like before I start." She began to put her tape, journal, pencil, and swatches back in the sewing bag. "You get some rest if you can," she added maternally, nodding at Emily as she closed her bag and picked it up to leave. "I'm hoping you'll hear some good news about the return of the de Koningh men by the time I see you again." She smiled reassurance as if to say, of course you will.

"That would be nice, Bessie, but I'm not sure it would make things any easier. Thank you for putting up with my complaints. I know how lucky I am. I've really never wanted for much of anything;

just a family, and some freedom now and then." She waved as her seamstress retreated down the hall. The last thing Emily saw of her friend was a glint on her mother's gold locket as she stopped and turned to share her parting wave.

❧ ⚘ ❧

Mist formed from cooler temperatures at the top of the mountain range softened the edge of the Alleghenies as far as Corey de Koningh could see from his seat on the train. Insistent rocking confirming their continuous movement blurred grass and trees through the window, yet his view of the mountains in the distance never altered; all a matter of time, he knew. Worn low and smooth over millennia, the topography had actually been changing endlessly. Cool air hanging onto the higher elevations lured many southern families escaping from sweltering summers at lower altitudes. But now it was fall, and Corey worried that his father might find the change too much. Older people seemed more susceptible to cold. Klaas's health had never returned fully after the end of the Civil War, and Corey feared that advancing age had also attacked and stolen his father's energy. He hoped this trip to take the waters at the famous White Sulphur Springs would bring some healing. His father had suggested the trip himself, so perhaps he, too, finally acknowledged the need for a cure. Only his general state of health could be affected, of course. There was no remedy for depression and old age.

Corey rose to walk the length of the train's four cars to stretch his long legs, something he couldn't do riding in a horse-drawn coach, and another reason why he preferred to travel by rail whenever possible. Moving around was important to a man of his height if his knees, hips, and back were to work with the suppleness his youth demanded. He wondered now how he'd ever been able to stand the carriage trips from New York to Boston in his school days. When he was a child, he hadn't had to deal with the extra inches of spine and leg acquired in a two-year growth spurt when he was seventeen. That had been an exhausting time, trying to catch up and deal with his body, always tired without understanding why. He'd annoyed himself as well as everyone around him with depression and instantaneous rages, only to learn, once he'd exceeded his new height of six feet, that they'd all been part of a natural change.

He'd have to remember those passions, so out of control, when his own sons reached that age. Empathy on the part of a parent could go a long way; a lesson he'd learned from his father when he'd feared a lack of understanding about his desire for a career in music. He'd assumed, apparently in error, that his father wanted him to join the family textile business in spite of Corey's lack of interest and his passion for playing the piano and composing music. Families were often complicated mysteries. There were many similarities between the generations, yet so many differences, as well, that he often wondered if there was anything inherited from one group to the next other than names and fortunes. His own boys were such a mix of characteristics their looks and personalities seemed almost haphazard to him, and yet to be honest, at their young ages they changed too fast to pin down. Each time he was away from them performing with Emily, or on business to aid his father with his work down south, he felt he hardly knew them when he returned home. This trip had only been a few weeks so far, and it didn't seem as challenging from the point of view of his parental duties; all of which he knew he must take very seriously, as most men raised in Dutch households would. He'd missed his younger son's fourth birthday, but in the meantime, Emily had plenty of help around the mansion on Fifth Avenue, and the antics of two little boys would keep her cheerful company while he was away.

He smiled, picturing the comforts of the house in New York as he looked around his temporary home, the interior of the passenger car. It was the only one devoted to carrying tourists from the North to southern health spas like the one at White Sulphur Springs in West

Virginia. He'd noted with each trip south that the rise in tourism after the war had been swift. It benefited the crushed southern economy, as well as northerners wanting to experience the beauty of the land they felt largely responsible for decimating. Of course, West Virginia had never been part of the rebel South during the war, but most northerners lumped everything below Washington, D.C., together, and guilt was a strong stimulus! To be sure, the hotels weren't up to the traffic yet, but he usually didn't have to stay in them, so he didn't worry about the lack of luxury and even basic comfort. Relief at finding his father alive after the war had also been a powerful motivator, so Corey was now joining him on his business trips to the reconstructed plantations of friends and clients three or four times a year. No lack of comfort there. Every effort was taken to make them feel welcome and relaxed, thanks undoubtedly to Klaas's lifelong connections with southern families and dealing with their cotton crops for his export business.

Their land, and particularly their houses, gracious and generous in every way, reflected the refinement of the people, and especially the beautiful southern women who lived solely to carry out their domestic duties. There could be no doubt these ladies were different from their northern counterparts, like Corey's wife, who seemed to have tired of her traditional role as a spouse and mother. But his Emily was a case unto herself of course, being a musician and performer as well; very different. Her insistence in her youth on discarding the heavy clothing and restrictive undergarments of her generation of women, on learning and playing a masculine instrument like the violin from an early age, and her determination to have a performance career of her own all pointed to a woman who assumed many freedoms for herself unimagined by others of her day.

There was no doubt that southern women knew how to take care of men, and even less doubt that they enjoyed it. Actually, he'd never felt northern women were particularly inviting, even in his college years. Emily had always been the only one he'd ever found enticing from the first moment he'd met her. But they'd come a long way since their childhood together and much had changed. Work, parenting, and perhaps even his wife's increasing fame, if he was to be totally honest, all challenged the appeal she'd had for him at the age of thirteen. Maybe his diminished importance to her career had also affected her interest in him. Either way, the early years of their marriage had certainly brought changes to the way they saw and appreciated each other. A sudden vision of the morning sun warming the shoulders of their lovely southern hostess yesterday as she poured a cup of coffee for him disrupted his memories of home. His father had barely looked up from the paper where he read it at the table as the young woman swept into the dining room in her mimosa-colored dress with the huge skirt and tiny waist, but everyone else noticed. How could one not? Emily had always had just such a waist in her youth, but child-bearing and the lack of emphasis provided by corsets of the day had changed it, and he hadn't realized he cared until he'd unknowingly compared the women of the South, who clearly also cared.

He took his seat on the train again and closed his eyes. His knees rose up above his waist, but he was used to seats made to fit much shorter bodies. Still, with no one else sitting next to him, he could spread his legs wide for support and lay his hands on them. He sighed and rested his head on the seat back. The clattering, uneven rhythm on the newly repaired rail tracks, not yet modernized as some of the northern-financed ones were, rocked his legs against the sway of his torso. He enjoyed the rhythm, wondering if he could use it in a piano piece in the future. The fingers of his right hand tapped out the faster, syncopated clacking as his left detailed the steady, repetitive bass of the rocking. He played around with his right hand until he had a varied and complicated beat in duple meter, two beats to the measure, displacing a note now and then as if a wheel had missed. A broad smile spread across his face as the bockety syncopation grew.

"You a piano man?" A boy's voice broke through Corey's compos-ing daydream. He opened his eyes to see a train conductor no older than fifteen dressed in a loose railroad uniform that almost swal-lowed him up. He'd rolled up the sleeves and pants in a vain attempt to make it fit. Some of the new railroads were training professional employees at last, obviously a step this train hadn't taken yet. He was a pretty boy, dark-haired and brown-eyed, reminding Corey of his own son William. The lad's southern drawl made him sound some-what exotic to Corey's musical ear.

"A piano man . . . ," Corey repeated, lifting his head from the seat back. "Yes, I suppose I am. What made you think so?" He smiled his warmest greeting, eyes shining through a shock of blond hair slipping over his forehead as he rested.

"Yo' hands," the boy said, "you was playin' a mighty tune with 'em." He grinned back at Corey, who glanced down at his long fingers spread out on his legs.

"How did you like that rhythm?" he asked the boy with a wink.

"Fine!" the boy answered. "But it got pretty wild—reckon it'd be hard to dance to."

"Not really," Corey said. "I've seen people do it in saloons down here, though they don't know about it yet up north."

"What do you call that music?" The boy attached himself to the edge of Corey's seat, with one hand at the back and a leg pressed against the armrest. He looked like a piece of seaweed attached to a rock, swaying in the tidal flow of the train's onward rush. Corey smiled at the improbability of having a talk about piano music on a train.

"It's not really called anything," he explained, sitting up straighter yet still relaxed against the seat back, buttressed by splayed legs and arms. "The ragged, messy part is the misplaced beat you noticed up at the top," he said, tapping out a catchy percussion on his knee with his right hand. "Then the bottom has to be steady." He played the rhythmic, even bass with his left hand on his left knee. "The bass acts like a drum, keeping everything grounded while the treble"—he played with his right hand on his knee again—"the treble teases and taunts you until you go almost mad. But you never lose your way completely if the bass keeps going. You always have something steady to bring you back home again." Corey smiled at the boy while he kept playing his knees.

The boy's eyes narrowed. "Can you play it for real?" he asked Corey.

"You bet I can," Corey assured him with a smile. "I can play anything in the world on a piano. But I don't think I'd get much call for a ragged piece where I come from. Takes so long for some things to change you can hardly wait." Corey looked out the window at the mountains in the distance slowly slipping by.

"Where's that you come from?" the boy asked. Corey had finally figured out his new friend was lonely and hungry for talk. He didn't mind obliging the boy when the conversation was about music. He put his long right index finger to his lips and shook his head in warning as the youthful conductor looked at Klaas de Koningh sleeping against the window in the seat across the aisle. "Looks like your father," the boy said softly, studying Klaas.

Corey nodded, but he had no intention of discussing the similarity in his and his father's looks. He couldn't imagine two more dissimilar men, but apparently the young conductor could see something Corey couldn't, or wouldn't. "Oh, mostly I play in concert halls in the big cities all over the world," he told his young friend. "Very different music from what you have down here," Corey added. "But I must say I've come to love your mountain people's tunes and the minstrels' songs I hear in the saloons."

"Why did you come to listen to our music?" the boy asked. He seemed mesmerized by Corey's voice and showed no inclination to move away.

"My father buys cotton for his business," Corey said. "But I spend most of my time here selling pianos for a manufacturer from the

North, and writing down the music I hear, just for my own pleasure. I love getting away from the music of all the European composers I grew up playing. But why are you so interested?" He'd never known a boy who didn't want to talk about himself and figured it was time this one had his chance.

"I wanted to go to music school . . . would have, too, if the war hadn't come . . . so my father was killed and all my brothers . . . my school shut down. Now it's just me and my sisters," he said, looking out the train's window as if he could see his whole family there. "My mother died of fright, we figure. I played a fiddle once. Never thought I'd be working on a train, though. But you do what you have to do."

"I'm sorry," Corey whispered. He wanted to reach out and touch the boy's shoulder, but something told him not to. He understood the bitter ache of losing a father, even though his own had finally come home.

"Not your fault," the boy said, pulling his back up straight.

"Oh, but I think it is," Corey said. "Maybe everyone's at fault in the North."

"Naw," the boy scoffed. "Too much happened to be anyone's fault." His eyes shifted to his left hand resting on the back of the seat. Corey followed his gaze and saw in a sudden rush of horror the boy had lost a middle finger down to the first knuckle. The young conductor saw him looking at it before he could turn his eyes away.

"What happened there?" Corey asked. Caught looking at the altered hand, he knew confronting the truth was his only choice.

"Ain't no one who's been railroading a while who hasn't lost at least part of a finger or worse," the boy said, taking his hand off the seat and looking at it. "The link and pin couplers are tough. A switchman has to go between the cars to connect 'em himself. They used to send the smallest children to do it since they fit better."

Corey winced. "So, you got stuck between the cars somehow?"

"Nope. Never was a switchman. Brakeman's just as bad, though.

Have to ride on top of the car to set the brakes, and then jump to the next car to spin a wheel for them on that one. Easy to slip and fall."

"Good Lord! You must be happy to be in here now instead of out there." Corey glanced out the window and saw the tops of some of the cars bobbing up and down as the train started around a curve. He'd decided it was time to change the subject. He'd heard enough about railroading. But the boy didn't pick up on the finality in his change of tone.

"I'm happy to be out of the cab, which is where they put me after the accident," he went on. "Those things are freezin' in winter, boilin' in summer, so rough your insides could fall out, and you can't see nothin' in the rear of the locomotive like that. Engineer has to look out the side window to see the track right in front on right-hand curves. Rest of the time he's blind."

"What? That can't be safe!" Corey's anxiety had moved from his face to his voice. The boy heard it at last and tried to make amends.

"New trains have brakes inside and knuckle couplers, so no one'll have to connect the cars anymore. Some of those rich men up in the North started buyin' these railroads and layin' track for new trains." He smiled at Corey for reassurance, but Corey could stand no more.

"So, you used to play the fiddle. Do you still?"

"Not with this hand," the boy said, frowning as if the question's futility made him mad.

"Well sure, it's too bad it wasn't the right hand that was injured . . . Sorry, I didn't mean any injury would be better than another, but the bow wouldn't have been hard to handle with the loss of the finger."

"That's right, sir. But I can't handle the fingerin'." The boy avoided Corey's eyes and looked down instead at the long, graceful pianist's hands resting on his knees.

"Well, no, not the way you used to. But you could adjust and do it differently. There are so many ways to get at the notes. I'll bet if you wanted to you could figure something out that would work."

"You're a piano man, sir. Don't mean no disrespect, but you don't know nothin' about playin' the fiddle. It's hard enough with all yo' fingers."

"Oh yes, I know," Corey said, feeling as if he could finally talk with some authority. It was a great relief. "My wife plays the fiddle. I've watched her change fingering to suit herself. She has strong hands but they're not big. She's found ways." He grinned at the young conductor. "You might still get to music school someday," he said.

"No, sir. That won't happen. No one wants a fiddler with three fingers who can't pay his way." The boy sighed almost imperceptibly and dropped his head for a second.

"What's your name, boy?" Corey asked, turning in his seat to hold the young man's eyes with his. In five years, his own son would be almost the same age. How would life treat him?

"Augustus, sir. Augustus Hardwick, that is. Family's everythin', right? So, can't forget the Hardwick. Nice talkin' with you, but sure wish I'd heard you play that raggedy-time on a piano." With that, he nodded and pushed off the seat to bump his way down the aisle, ricocheting off the other seats as he went.

Corey shook his head as he watched him go. Turning to gaze at his father sleeping, Corey was suddenly aware of a tether between them, a pull reaching across the aisle. It was invisible, but somehow the young conductor who was particularly sensitive to family had seen it anyway.

CHAPTER THREE

𝄞 KLAAS DE KONINGH GREETED HIS SON on the sweeping front porch of The Old White, the popular moniker for the Grand Central Hotel at the White Sulphur Springs resort. *I don't know which of us is older or whiter,* Klaas quipped when they'd registered at the front desk. "You should dress for dinner, Corey. There's plenty of time," his father said.

From the minute Corey stepped over the threshold—or even sooner, right from his first sight of the sweeping grounds and long, curved driveway up to the huge pillared porch—he understood they were entering a world of calm, dignified grace, and peace. It seemed as if The Old White was an iconic symbol of reconciliation. The fact that White Sulphur Springs was a part of West Virginia, the only state born from the Confederacy in its protesting secession from the Union, made its blend of North and South ideal for joining the two worlds.

WELCOME TO 'THE OLD WHITE', a sign read on the wall next to huge French double doors at the entrance, and Corey couldn't help feeling that everything about this place was welcoming. He'd worried the West Virginia resort would be a stilted southern-gentlemen's club, but the message in every open vista and room was anything but stiff. The joining of the natural environment with the exquisite hotel, cottages, stables, and spa nestled in the Allegheny Mountains produced a magical effect, lifting the spirits and slowing the pulse at the same time. It was the perfect tonic for war-weary nerves.

One week of deep sleep every night in the cool, fresh mountain air and daytime walks over the miles of beautiful grounds, to say nothing of the restorative daily tonics of the smelly sulfur spring water, had brought some vitality and color back to Klaas's cheeks. Occasionally a shadow of some former worry crossed his face and the old pain seemed to return, but for the most part, Corey felt his father's mental and physical health was improving. "We have time for a stroll before dinner, don't we?" he asked, looking up at his father from the bottom step of the veranda and lifting his hand both in greeting and invitation.

"We do," Klaas replied, "if you'd rather do that than change for dinner. Where would you like to go?" He started down the steps of the porch toward Corey's outstretched arm, slipping slightly off the middle riser as he reached its edge. Corey slid his arm further forward to reach his father's chest, and Klaas ended up gripping Corey's upper arm. He leaned against his son for a moment, unaware he'd been lifted to the bottom step in one safe, smooth move. "Oh dear," he breathed. "Moving too fast, I guess. Thank you." Corey nodded with a vague smile as if he hadn't even noticed his father slip, and together they started off slowly around the long, curved driveway.

"Where would *you* like to go?" he asked Klaas, and pushed his hair, always a little too long, off his forehead. He noticed how fresh, neat, and perfectly proportioned his father looked, in sharp contrast to his much-too-tall son. "How about a walk to the springhouse," Corey suggested, raising his head and lifting himself another inch. "I can see the green copper dome of its roof from here. I think we can get there and back in time for dinner."

"Oh, no! I don't think I can handle that sulfur smell of rotten eggs more than once a day." Klaas wrinkled his nose and turned down his mouth, his opinion of the daily dose of spring water made clear. "I can't understand how so many believe they'll live forever if they swallow that stuff."

Corey chuckled, clearly appreciating the irony of his father's objection to taking his medicine while his son tried to cajole him into it. "It's been proven, Father. It's good for strengthening bones, warding off kidney stones, improving joint function, increasing energy, and ensuring alertness . . . among other things. It's virtually a wonder medicine!" Klaas wrinkled his nose again and shook his head. "And if you don't like to drink it, you can bathe in it to let it relax and purify you!" Corey grinned at his father now, in full agreement with his rejection of the putrid water for bathing purposes.

"How about going down through the garden instead?" Klaas suggested. "And if there's time, we could see a little of the croquet at the bottom of the hill. I must admit it's pleasant watching the ladies beating their male counterparts at a game that doesn't require anything but guile and skill. A much more even match of natural abilities," he said, with a wink. Klaas's good humor sparkled from his pale blue eyes, and Corey nodded.

"It's pleasant observing southern ladies do everything," Corey said, tucking his strong arm under his father's frail one. He had to stoop to compensate for their height discrepancy, working hard not to show it for his father's sake as they started to move. Corey noticed how often they'd switched roles recently, he now the parent and Klaas the child. It made him acutely uncomfortable. He had young sons of his own and didn't need any more responsibilities.

Panicked during the war by the thought that the father he needed and loved might have been captured and killed behind Confederate lines, Corey was overjoyed by the miracle of Klaas's return home, but dismayed to find his father had new needs of his own. The years of detention in the South during the war had taken a serious toll on the old gentleman's health. Corey could see that there were still sufferings that hadn't been fully assimilated or forgotten, making his father vulnerable in ways his son couldn't understand.

Two men in fashionable waistcoats and top hats and an older lady with a parasol gave them sidelong glances. Corey and Klaas sat down near them, discussing the flowering fall foliage in the garden they'd just passed. There was certainly no mistaking their northern accents, blunt and hard-edged even to their own ears in comparison with the local languorous vowels.

A gentlemanly southern threesome rose from a table nearby and departed, casting narrow looks in the de Koninghs' direction as they passed. They left their drinks and biscuits sitting unfinished, seemingly in a hurry to avoid contact with the northern intruders. "That insolence is the only thing that could ruin our stay," Corey muttered. The de Koningh men were often unprepared for the sometimes-frosty reception they got in postwar southern society. They'd traveled widely since the end of the fighting, as Klaas had returned to New York after his years as a hostage with no visible change in his attitude of congeniality toward the southern cotton planters. Almost before his health had improved, he was eager to start traveling throughout the South again, and Corey had often joined him to keep him close. The past six years of private meetings with friendly business colleagues acclimated Corey to the way of southern living his father so admired, also increasing his appreciation for the femininity of the women who seemed so unlike any he'd known up north.

"Reconciliation is still a dream, not a reality," Klaas muttered. "Though every time the two societies come together, there seems to be less bitterness." Klaas sighed as he sat forward to signal a waiter. "Don't let it bother you," he said, more firmly than Corey had heard him in a long while. "Someday, it will be gone. Imagine how the Negroes must feel. We're in a similar position as we represent the enemy who forced their masters' defeat."

"Father, I'm not sure I understand your benevolence after what you went through at the hands of these people during the war." Corey nodded to the black waiter who stood poised to flee as he interpreted the subject of their raised voices. "Please, some tea here if you will. No biscuits, though. It's too close to dinner," Corey added, with a reassuring smile. The young man bowed his head briefly and smiled at both men before he turned to fulfill their request. "Well, he's a good deal friendlier than some others around here," Corey muttered. "I guess you're right. He recognizes a commonality in the disgust these people have for both of us."

"Oh, for heaven's sake, Corey, don't be peevish. We've had a wonderful time, and a few understandably bitter southerners shouldn't ruin it." Klaas turned slowly in his seat as he spoke. "Well, well . . . now just look at that."

Corey turned also to see a couple of elderly men moving past the croquet court with a crowd of people following them. Men, women, and even small children tagged along like flotsam in the wake of a ship. The men stopped for a moment to talk, and the crowd parted long enough for one of the men to nod slightly toward Klaas de Koningh. "Who are they, Father? Do you know them?" Corey whispered from the side of his mouth.

"I believe I do." Klaas smiled slightly and then bowed back toward the two figures on the hill. "I recognize George Peabody, most certainly," he said, watching the men start walking again. "He's probably the best-known philanthropist in America. I met him a long time ago, when we were both young, which I guess only confirms that it was a long time ago. Look at us now!"

"Did he recognize you, Father?"

"I doubt it. We've both changed too much. It was just the polite greeting of a courteous gentleman." Klaas chuckled at the irony of the connection through time.

"What's he doing here and why such a fuss?" Corey asked.

"He's probably taking the waters, just as we are," Klaas answered, pretending not to notice Corey's disgruntled tone. "I've read he's set up a fund to advance public education in the South. It's truly astounding that West Virginia started a public school for Negroes during the war, when it was illegal in the rest of the South for a slave to be educated at all, much less taught to read."

"I wonder if that learning includes music education. Probably not," Corey muttered.

"What are you grumbling about now?" Klaas asked, leaning forward to hear better.

"I was just wondering if a man like Peabody would consider music a necessary part of the public education he's funding. Then I said, *probably not*." His father looked puzzled. "I met a young man on our way down here on the train when you were sleeping," Corey explained. "He wanted to go to a music conservatory but couldn't afford it, as his father was killed in the war and the family had no wage earners other than himself. I'll bet there are lots of young people with similar needs, both white and black, that lost fathers in the war. I wish educators would see music as part of a school's legacy. Why is it only the wealthy families who understand it as a necessity?"

Klaas looked in the direction of the crowd again. "Peabody's probably the most revered man in Dixie right now, except perhaps the man he's walking with. I assume he's causing as much of the fuss as Peabody."

Corey turned again to look, but the group closed around the two as they moved off. "Who is it?" Corey muttered, losing sight of the men.

"General Lee, I believe. I've never met him in person, but he looks like the few portraits I've seen of him, and his meeting with someone of Peabody's renown would make sense." A strange shadow brushed across Klaas's face as if the Blue Ridge Mountains and the general who'd fought the great battles for the Confederacy were affecting his memory. He shook himself and managed a small smile. "Lee's the president of Washington College in Lexington, and I'm sure they're planning ways to strengthen education down here. If so, they're right. No better way to rebuild the South." Klaas tapped his son's hand as if to emphasize his point.

"Of course," Corey said. "Who could argue with that? But just let them study music in the saloons, then—learn a few drinking songs and some ragged-time. There's an education there, too." Corey turned to watch the crowd move off. "So, Peabody's more famous than the general?"

"In the North he is, most definitely. Although in the South, Lee still enjoys hero worship, as you can see." Klaas's eyes followed the entourage over Corey's shoulder as it disappeared on the horizon. Corey watched his father surveilling the two famous old men but refused to show any real interest of his own. He doubted anyone would remember either one of them a few decades into the future.

Father and son looked back as someone approached their table. A soft beauty of feminine southern perfection stood beside them, cream silk parasol closed and held in both hands in front of her peach-colored skirt. Her skin matched the parasol perfectly, and burnished copper hair, swept up off her neck and piled on her head, glowed in the late-day warmth of the sun. "Good afternoon, gentlemen," she said, drawing out each syllable to make a spoken music Corey was learning to love. He glanced at his father, who smiled back with his eyes.

"I'm Marcella Bond," the young woman announced, as both men rose to their feet in unison. "Mr. Peabody noted your isolation and worried you might not be feeling the warmth of southern hospitality as you should. General Lee suggested some of us might try to rectify that sad situation, and I offered to come over to meet you . . ." She smiled again, lowering her lashes as she looked from one de Koningh to the other. ". . . for the general, of course. Most of my friends call me Marcy, and I do hope I'll be able to count on you both to do the same."

Both men stared at her silently, seemingly incredulous at having been singled out for her special and appealing attention. Klaas was the first to recover. "How kind of you, Miss Bond, and so thoughtful of the general. I am Klaas de Koningh and this is my son, Adriaan. Would you like to join us for tea? We just ordered for ourselves, but another cup should be easy to come by." She smiled but shook her head.

"So, you're our southern angel," Corey said. "How amazing. Does the general make a habit of hiding his resentment toward the North with gifts of your caliber?"

"I've asked him about that," Marcy said, without a pause to consider his rudeness.

"And what's his reply?" Corey asked. He hadn't moved to relax his stance, and his narrow gaze seemed to slice through the air between them. His intense focus kept him from noticing the waiter quietly laying out their tea service.

"He's said that looking into his own heart and in the presence of his God, he's never known a moment of cynicism or hatred toward the people of the North." She looked from one man to the other with an ease suggesting she was comfortable with her reply.

"Really! And you believe him?" Corey's voice had a small waver to it.

"I most certainly do," she said evenly, as if she hadn't noticed any faltering on his part. She smiled at him with warmth that could have melted the early morning frost in the valley, which was always considerable. They both stared at each other, her gaze frank and open, and his tense and closed. Suddenly Corey shifted uncomfortably to his other foot as if his body had just recognized its distress. "Well in that case, I hope you'll call me Corey, Miss Bond. All my friends do." He bowed a little. It was safer and easier than trying to move his long legs from behind the table.

"Delighted, Corey, I'm sure, if you'll call me Marcy. Mr. de Koningh, is there a chance I could tempt you two to join my aunt Sarah Stovall and me for dinner in the formal dining room tonight? We're here alone and would be pleased to share the company of two such charming gentlemen. Perhaps we can make up for whatever discomfort others may have caused while you were visiting the South this time. Nothing would make us happier."

"Our pleasure, Miss . . . Marcy. Eight o'clock at the dining room? And if you see them first, please thank Mr. Peabody and the general for their concern on our behalf. I doubt I could ever repay them in kind." Klaas chuckled, with a twinkle in his eye that not even the imperturbable Marcy could miss. "What an unexpected but pleasant turn of events," he said to Corey, as their new acquaintance disappeared into the late-afternoon haze as softly and suddenly as she'd arrived.

"Father, what are you thinking?" Corey groaned. "The aunt is probably a crashing bore who looks like a marzipan sweet, and laughs like a sticky confection, too. Not a brain in those southern heads, you know; just feathers, flowers, and bumblebees."

"Oh, come on," Klaas chided, sitting down, and reaching for the teapot that neither one of them had noticed until that moment. "You know it will be a relief to have someone other than your old father to talk to at dinner for once." He winked at Corey and poured him some tea and milk without asking. "Drink up, my boy. We have more satisfying beverages awaiting our attention in the bar very soon." He let the soft, cool mountain air start to settle around them without further comment as he sipped his own infusion. He seemed to know when to leave his son to his own thoughts.

Suddenly Corey put his cup down and looked directly at Klaas. "Father, why did you insist on coming here to White Sulphur Springs? I sense there's more to it than a desire to *take the waters.*"

A silence followed his question and grew between them. Finally, Klaas focused on Corey's face. "I've been here before," he said quietly. "I wanted to see if it had changed or if my feelings about it had, before I got too old."

"When were you here before?" Corey prompted, unable to stop himself to let his father finish at his own pace.

His father shook his head and looked a long way out over the distant ridge of the mountain range. "I suppose I could tell you now," he sighed, "now that it's done."

꙳꙳ ꙳ꙏ꙳

The bar at The Old White was just below entry level as the ground behind the building fell off rather sharply, and the building's architect had chosen to use that change in topography to his advantage. Small, narrow windows placed high across the back added to its air of privacy and mystery, as if the bar's patrons wanted to hide their whereabouts. There was a masculine solemnity and heft to it, making Corey feel more comfortable than he had since the intrusion of the intrepid Marcella Bond. Occasionally he found the extreme femininity of southern women made him uneasy, while at the same time appreciating it immensely. He was becoming aware of the conflicts about women that seemed to live within him.

Those strange gender power struggles he'd watched long ago, as all children do, had left him suspicious of hidden schemes and distrusting of anything he couldn't immediately figure out. Women were usually no exception to the things that confused him, thanks to his difficult, reflexively angry mother. She'd taken every opportunity to exact punishment for his father's inability to duplicate her own family for her, and eventually had only Corey to interact with, as Klaas de Koningh had despaired of ever communicating with her. As everyone including Corey loved the gentle, thoughtful Klaas, Corey had spent most of his childhood totally unable to understand his parents' relationship, or lack of it. His father finally explained his mother's averseness to leaving her home and her own father, something he'd understood too late, alas, to avoid the quagmire he got into by marrying her. He'd been so sure, he told Corey once before he'd disappeared during the war, that he could make his mother happy just by bringing her to the de Koningh family home in New York. He'd clearly been wrong.

Corey once felt he understood his own wife perfectly but realized now how much easier it had been when they were both children. In many ways, he felt lucky to have grown up with the girl whom he'd eventually married. There was nothing they didn't know about each other. With Emily, what you saw was what you got. There was no weakness under her strength and no selfishness motivating her generosity. Neither one of them controlled the other. She was his friend and professional partner, and he suddenly realized he missed her mightily while at the same time reveling in his freedom. The sooner he could get his father past whatever he was going through, the better his chances of getting home, a fact that both cheered and frightened him. Certainly, the early years of his marriage had been challenging, with two children arriving to complicate the living almost immediately. In truth, he and Emily were little more than children themselves when they'd commandeered the Presbyterian minister in West Chester to marry them, with only their early music teacher and Corey's best friend from college to witness it.

The absence of family had magnified the importance of starting one of their own for Emily, he knew. Estranged at the time from her father and losing her mother at the age of thirteen left her with only Robert Haussmann, her violin teacher, to *give her away*. Corey had many people he could have turned to for his best man when his father had been captured by Confederates and held until the end of the war. But having his young friend Bill stand up with him somehow closed the circle in a logical way they all seemed comfortable with. All except Bill, perhaps, who Corey knew had such a deep attachment to him he worried about a natural jealousy where Emily was concerned, just as he had about Robert giving her away in marriage when he might have preferred to marry her himself. It had been complicated, as all human relationships were, but he and Emily were in a hurry to form their family before the war could break it apart, and thus they'd possibly made a mistake in their haste, yet just as possibly done the smartest thing possible. Only time would answer that question. And if most women were no exception to what Corey didn't understand, southern women were always the rule, a fact that confounded and enticed him simultaneously.

He thanked the bartender for the drinks and turned with them to the small table in the corner, stopping for a second to watch his father sitting quietly, enjoying the peace the discreet bar seemed to guarantee. Was his father's reclusiveness now a result of his age, or the impact their northern accents seemed to be having on the southern guests? A film had dropped over his father's eyes when Corey asked about his previous trip to White Sulphur Springs. The explanation needed to be over with to open Klaas up again. They could talk alone here before the onslaught of southern femininity in the dining room. Corey was still curious about Klaas's experiences during the war, because his father seemed resistant, which made Corey hesitant, too. He didn't know if it was common for all fathers and sons, but he was aware that he was just as afraid of the answers as he was of not hearing them.

"You want to know about my first trip here," Klaas began, as Corey approached the table, "and I want to tell you." He looked as if something tight was lodged in his chest. He massaged it, pressing it absentmindedly with the heel of his hand.

"Father, if it's too difficult or just none of my business, then don't tell me." The potential for escape was almost irresistible.

"No. I want to tell you . . . want you to know. It was during the Civil War," Klaas said. "Right in the middle and up to the end of it."

Corey stared at him. "How could that be, Father? This place was shut down during the war. The brochure we got the first day we arrived said so. It didn't reopen until months after the surrender."

"Yes, and all the time it was shut down, I was here." Klaas lifted his glass to take a drink. There was a slight tremor in his thin, blue-veined hand as it pressed the glass to his lips. Corey suddenly wished with all his heart he'd never asked about the trip, hadn't forced the conversation, and could somehow take it all back. But it was too late. Klaas lowered the glass to the table and tried to begin again. "I'm sorry, Father," Corey interrupted. "I see how hard this is for you." He put one of his young, strong hands over his father's gaunt, delicate ones.

"It's all right," Klaas assured him. "I want to talk about it. If not to you, to whom, then?"

Corey drew his hand back, resting it around the base of his glass to give it something to do. "I won't interrupt again," he assured his father. "Please, go on."

Klaas let out a deep sigh and started over. "The Old White was closed to the public at the start of the war, but opened as a hospital for Confederate soldiers," he said. "Did you know that? *I* know," he went on, without waiting for a response, "because I was one of its earliest patients."

Now he paused, but when no question came, he continued. "I was injured in an attack on one of the plantations I often stayed at for business." He swept on past Corey's sharp intake of breath. "The home was spared, although the cotton crop was burned and most of the food stores, horses, and family treasures were looted. They offered to take me with them, but I was clearly in no condition to travel with a fast-moving cavalry and no medical attention. I judged my southern friends to be right when they said they could take better care of me themselves, and so I stayed with them, assuming I'd find my own way home once I felt well again. But my leg was taking a long time to heal as wounds do when one gets older, and the family I was staying with finally had to escape to relatives in Philadelphia, leaving me with a Confederate regiment now bivouacked on their plantation." Corey held the breath he'd taken while Klaas talked. "When the regiment had to move out, they delivered me to the hospital—here, in West Virginia. You can imagine the gratitude I felt for the family and those soldiers who took care of me."

Corey's voice rose sharply on the tight breath he still held. "Do you mean to say they had no idea of your involvement leading slaves to the Underground Railroad?"

"They never did."

"So you were never a Confederate prisoner?"

"I was behind the lines, but never a prisoner of the Confederate army—a friend of a southern family and patient in a Confederate hospital, but never a prisoner—until our own army finally came marching into this valley, captured the hospital, and burned the place to the ground."

"My God!" Corey's eyes darted to his father, then up at the ceiling in the bar, and around the room in a frantic attempt to catch up with the visions in his head. "Burned to the ground, you say. Yes, it did mention that in the brochure, but when you feel no personal connection to the place it's just another fact. Were you caught in the fire? I used to have nightmares about fire when I first came to Virginia! I wonder if they could have been concurrent with your experience." He stared at his father in horror, beginning to imagine a much bigger fright for the old gentleman than he'd ever considered once he was back home safely. "I had no idea," he murmured.

"How could you?" Klaas responded. "I never told you or anyone else about that time, partly because it took me a while to assimilate it myself; but also, because I felt guilty. I often lay awake at night, first at the plantation and then in the hospital, wondering what would happen to you if I didn't get home alive. I knew you'd essentially be an orphan, as your mother would never be able to contribute to your happiness, and I had no awareness of Emily's return to your life at that time. I often fell asleep weeping over my selfishness and lack of responsibility for my family in deciding to continue my work with the Underground Railroad at such a dangerous time. It was all of my emotional distress that caused my slow recovery and weight loss, I fear, not the injury on its own." He picked up his glass and moved it to his lips, but put it back down again without drinking. "When we have children, they must come first," he said, "even before our duty to the larger social institutions that govern our lives." He looked at Corey directly for the first time, picking up his glass again and finally taking a long drink from it.

Corey moved uncomfortably in his chair, but never stopped looking at Klaas. "But why did we never hear any of this once you were home and found yourself safe with all the people you love around you? You must have felt relieved to realize Emily was back in our lives. I know how special she's been to you ever since she was a child when she first came to live with us. And soon, even the war ended. By then you had grandchildren to give you hope, and even Mother's decision to live with her relatives in Schenectady must have been a relief of sorts.

"We all wondered what had happened and assumed the trauma had been so great you couldn't speak of it. I know that's so with many soldiers. But how could it have been that the story never came out some other way, if not through you? Why have I never heard any of it from the southern friends of yours we've visited for your work over the past five or six years? Why was it all kept so secret? Did you never think the truth would connect us all to each other in an important way? That we, as a family, all deserved that kind of bond?" He looked at his father almost angrily, although Klaas heard in his son's voice the same kind of tension relief a parent feels for a lost child once found.

He smiled, a small, faint upturn in the thin line of his compressed lips. "It's more unnerving to deal with a parent's secrets than the stories behind them," he admitted, a bit of color finally coming back to his cheeks. "And there's often more to a story than the facts that get related after it's over. Stories change with the retelling, and unknowns get filled in to make sense of them. The confusion of events near the end of the war could only be untangled by those who lived the nightmare. Some are best left alone, but I understand your need to know." Klaas seemed much calmer, the tremor gone in his hand and his expression no longer guarded. The change affected Corey the same way. He realized he'd always been pulled into the emotional tension around his parents' lives and failed marriage, but now his father's quieter mood helped his as well. They were sharing secrets with each other that no one else had heard.

"It's just a selfish need to understand your past . . . as it relates to mine," Corey said. "There was a lot of pain for us all during the war. Not knowing where you were was the worst of it. If I could connect what I know with what I don't, I think I could put that whole time to rest." He was surprised to see his father shaking his head.

"There's no way any of us will ever put that whole time to rest," Klaas muttered. "It will be the singular trauma this nation has to deal with, I'm sure. It will affect the way we all view each other in this country for hundreds of years, if not forever. But I do understand a son wanting to know his father's story to make sense of his own. What I've already told you is most of what you need to hear. There's not much more to it." Klaas smiled gently, and Corey realized the sharing would have its limits, albeit acceptable ones for them both. He resisted the urge to fill the space between them now with his own voice.

"There were natural threats from exhausted soldiers on both sides at the end of the war," Klaas picked up his narrative again. "There was no resolution to the dilemma of being on both sides of the war at the same time, as some like me were. The Confederacy didn't trust my involvement with the South once cotton exports were banned, and the Union wanted more and more commitment from me, while I'm sure they worried I might be a double agent. Each side threatened me numerous times, but I've never had a problem talking my way out of trouble, as you know." Klaas's eyes twinkled, and Corey could picture his father charming the Confederate army's commanding officer, while he simultaneously reassured the president that the

Underground Railroad would stay open. No wonder he'd survived. His air of quiet decency elicited trust and respect from everyone. Except, perhaps, his own son. It was clear to Corey that his father had indeed been a double agent when he was wounded behind enemy lines, and also just as clear that there were parts of the story he would never hear.

He recognized there had been more guilt to carry beyond Klaas's fear for his family. "You came back to us, which is all that matters. Your health has returned, your business is improving again, and your family has grown, thanks to the addition of my children. This story has ended well," Corey said. He picked his glass up and drained it, hoping Klaas would see that no more raking over of painful memories was necessary.

"Oh, I sincerely hope the story hasn't ended," Klaas replied, his eyes dancing with that same light that had finally returned during their talk. "I'm so looking forward to dinner with our lovely new female friends. Speaking of which, why don't we go and meet them now. Even though everyone seems to be late to everything in the South, I hate to keep them waiting." He left his glass on the table and started to push himself up. Corey noticed the effort was greater than it would have been a few years ago.

"Would you mind if I joined you a little later?" Corey asked, as he too unwound his long legs and stood quickly to help Klaas up. "I want to find the telegraph room and send word home of our delayed return. I'm a little worried about the performance schedule Emily was working on when I left. She'll need to know just when I can join her again. Can you handle the aunt and her beautiful niece without me for a while?" Klaas nodded and straightened his back with some effort, a little sigh escaping unwittingly, which his son nevertheless heard. But Corey's sympathies had already turned in on his own regrets, and more time away from home was one of them now.

He slipped his hand under his father's arm, perhaps a little too quickly, to guide him out of the bar and toward the dining room, sending him off in one direction as Corey went in the other. He moved off to the front door of the entrance lobby as his father passed through the opening to the formal dining room on the other side, looking for all the world like the handsome, courtly gentleman he once was. It seemed the prospect of dinner with the ladies had picked up his spirits.

Corey returned his thoughts to his telegraph message for home. Cold night mountain air, always a surprise when the southern afternoon had been so balmy, cleared his head and narrowed his focus to the task at hand. He stopped for a moment, shoving his chilled hands deep in his pockets, taking a full, delicious breath of the night. What magic happened up here in the mountains to change an involuntary thing like breathing into a luxury? A purple swath traced the ridge of closer hills already deep in evening shadows, but a surprising scarlet burst like a flash of fire sprang from the west side of the mountains in the distance, reminding him of the time he'd spent at the university in Virginia during the war, and of Emily there with him.

DEAR EMI stop TRIP EXTENDED THROUGH WEEKEND stop FATHER'S HEALTH IMPROVING stop HOPE FAMILY IS WELL AND REHEARSAL CAN WAIT stop MISS YOU ALL stop LOVE COREY stop

Yes, stop. He hadn't even offered a reason for their delay, because he didn't have one, and the words had a hollow ring. It was time his own family came first. He turned his collar up against the cold, heading east across the lawn into darkness.

"Lovely dinner. I don't know when I've enjoyed an evening so much," Klaas said, dabbing his lips with his napkin and folding it

carefully to put it beside his dish. Corey savored the last piece of his peach dessert with whipped cream, letting the pregnant sweetness of the spectacular fruit grown at The Old White, and most evocative of the Deep South, blanket his taste buds. He knew the warmth he felt came as much from the delightful sour mash whiskey he'd nursed through his meal in lieu of the French wine the others drank. It might have been the food, or the rosy décor of the dining room, or even the pleasant company of their feminine dinner companions. But it was hard to distinguish the different elements of the glow at this time of night. Just watching the lift in his father's expression and voice was enough to warm his spirits.

"You ladies are primarily responsible for the success of this evening," his father said. Corey nodded vaguely, and Klaas jumped in to cover his occasionally distracted behavior before the ladies noticed. "It goes without saying," Klaas added, with a slight lean toward Sarah Stovall on his left, "that the grace and charm of southern women is unparalleled, and you two ladies are prime examples of the best of your gender. I've always said the South shines when it comes to the domestic arts, and one of those is putting a man at complete ease."

He smiled graciously at the dark-haired, pleasingly plump Mrs. Stovall, whose artfully arranged curls and jet earrings surrounded by pearls gleamed in the soft light of the candles, which were positioned carefully on the table, and turned just perfectly to leave the lines of sight open for all the diners. Klaas slid his gaze to Corey, encouraging him to join the conversation. Corey smiled back and settled in his chair, wiping his mouth with the oversized white damask dinner napkin and then tossing it down carelessly beside his empty dish. His relaxed posture seemed a direct challenge to his father's particular formality. "Southern women certainly do work hard," Corey said. "But I wonder if the height of the pedestal to which men from the North have raised them isn't more about nostalgia."

"For what?" his father queried, his voice wavering slightly.

"For the long-lost Victorian supremacy afforded all men in our society." Corey looked around at their two dinner companions, who showed no reaction on their lovely faces, and then to his father, who looked horrified. Corey was instantly sorry for diminishing the pleasure Klaas had been enjoying during their dinner with General Lee's feminine diplomats. Sarah Stovall, a war widow they'd been told, and her beautiful niece had been nothing if not attentive and thoroughly enjoyable throughout their meal together. What made him want to ruin his father's amusement? He suddenly hoped the widow's beautiful niece would come to his father's rescue where his own son had failed.

"How rewarding to have new acquaintances recognize our accomplishments with such . . . appreciation," Marcy Bond said. "Women in the South do work hard . . . at *everything*," she added, as if she wanted there to be no mistake about her point of reference and where it differed from Corey's. "But that's quite enough praise for us, gentlemen. Young Mr. de Koningh, where do your interests lie, sir?" She cocked her head to the left and lifted her chin without moving in her seat, sending a look of defiance directly at Corey. What made her so appealing? There was nothing specifically unusual about her looks that he hadn't seen in other women he'd known. Rather she seemed a metaphor representing all the beauty and grace of refined domestic comfort. Perhaps it was her voice and the way she moved, or her unwavering attention . . .

"Interests?" he muttered, noticing the smooth curve of her shoulder before her capped, melon-colored taffeta sleeve hid the top of her arm.

"Yes, Mr. de Koningh. You are occupied with something, are you not, sir?"

"Indeed!" Klaas injected quickly, springing to his son's defense, obviously eager to make amends for what he judged to be Corey's impertinence. "Corey is an accomplished concert pianist and com-poser! Tell them, Corey. Tell the ladies about your music." He looked as if his pride and frustration, both working in tandem where his son was concerned, might overcome him and make him speechless.

"A pianist!" Marcella Bond turned more toward Corey. "Talk about expanding one's sphere of influence! Well . . . how interesting."

"I don't follow you, Miss Bond. What sphere of influence?" Corey had the distinct impression she understood his guilt at ruining his father's evening and was meting out her version of justice. He had to admit she was much more interesting with the flash of an avenging angel than she had been as a pastel table decoration.

"Playing at the piano has always belonged to the woman of the household, has it not? At least that is so in the South. It seems a strange occupation for a man of substance." Her voice modulated to a low, throbbing purr, reminding Corey of the marmalade cat who'd visited him and his father every morning of their stay at The Old White, rubbing aggressively against their ankles as they ate breakfast on their porch and reminding him of the de Koningh family cat in New York. "The piano has always been every well-brought-up woman's suitable skill for entertainment, but I can't say it's exactly a manly art, or even an acceptable way for a true gentleman to earn a living. Is that what life up north has come to?" She held Corey's gaze for a few silent seconds, suddenly cutting the air with a laugh like the lightness of chimes on the breeze, winking at her aunt as if to say, *this game is over.* The widow dropped her eyes to her lap to hide the smile that all could nonetheless see.

Thoughts of the giants of music like Mozart, Schumann, Brahms, and the mighty Bach flew through Corey's head. Did those men know it was not a "manly art," or have any doubts about supporting their families with their unmanly gains? But a lifetime of growing up with his own Emily's challenges had taught Corey to play for higher stakes than the ego-crushing risks these ladies were flirting with. It was his turn to spar. "I assume that means you and your aunt," he bowed his head in the Widow Stovall's direction, "both play the piano yourselves with some level of skill?" Both women nodded.

"And who were your teachers? You must have had some professional instruction. There are very few self-taught piano virtuosi in the world, and I think I've heard of all those men."

"Miss Bond's musical education was handled by my sister, Anne, Mr. de Koningh. She taught the middle grades in our local school and considered it her duty to include the musical arts as part of a proper lady's upbringing. And mine was passed to me by my dear mother. It's common in a southern family for the arts to be perpetuated by those who uphold the culture."

"I see . . . yes . . . well . . . perhaps that explains your attitude about the acceptability of playing the pianoforte as a profession." He looked out around the dining room slowly, almost lazily, as if the talk at his own table was too tame to hold his attention.

"I don't follow you, sir," Marcella drawled. Corey shook himself a little as if to focus on the conversation at hand, but truly to lessen the impact her liquid accent had on his sensitive ear.

"Oh, I just meant my study of the piano was handled by a European maestro, and my later training in the vocal arts at university as well. There's a different quality of skill on the continent. I'm sure growing up on a plantation surrounded by family responsibilities requires other skills, from both men and women—athleticism and domesticity, for example. It's a good thing I have none of those, ladies. As you can see, there are very few muscles on this stretched-out body of mine and I prefer travel to being home whenever the opportunity presents itself." He laughed easily at his own self-deprecation, avoiding his father's eyes for fear he'd collapse under the weight of Klaas's assumed and understandable censure. He controlled his breathing through the silence that followed, while he could see the Widow Stovall rising slowly to fill her seat like a bowl of leavening bread. What had caused him to lash out at his dinner companions with such vitriol?

"I always thought you Yankees believed southern men were emasculated by an overly feminized Dixie," she said. "I'm delighted to find there's no lack of love for us up north. But I'm confused . . . if, as you say, the European musical esthetic has been your motivation, then why, sir, are you here?" The Widow Stovall had delivered the longest speech of her entire evening's discourse, seemingly overcome by curiosity. Her niece still eyed Corey with something giving away her developing distrust. He turned slowly in his seat toward her aunt.

"I'm here to accompany my father in his travels for his work, and for folk music, Mrs. Stovall. Studying the melodies and rhythms of the South is my prime directive for being here. My father's business needed attention, and I recognized an opportunity to enjoy each other's company and conduct my research at the same time. The improvement in travel by rail was another stimulus, with this wonderful old hotel and spa the perfect draw at the end of a long trip." Corey picked up the silver demitasse spoon next to his coffee cup, slowly stirring the dark, syrupy contents, enjoying the muted ring of bone china as his spoon traced its delicate circle. He hoped his feminine interrogators would be too busy digesting his treatise on folk music to notice the fact that he'd left his coffee black, so his diversionary stirring motions, in fact, were unnecessary.

"Folk music," Sarah Stovall muttered. "Why would a serious, concert-trained musician have any interest in . . . folk music?" Corey looked up to see more than confusion on the widow's face. Something more like a form of disgust had taken its place.

"Folk songs and dances are really the soul of all music; the very beginning," Corey said patiently, as if instructing a student who had no knowledge as a base to rise from. "You might be surprised by the number of famous classical European composers who study and use the form in their work; like Schumann, Brahms, and Dvorak . . . even Mozart; all composers of . . . substance." He looked over at his father and met his eyes, seeing something like a grudging acceptance. It made him relax, so he put down his spoon and drank from the coffee cup. He could feel the stage was still his and his audience expected something more from him.

"I can't imagine a better way to unify this country of ours than through the music of its people," he continued. Smiling at each one of his dinner companions in turn, he noticed that Marcella Bond's dark eyes had a different light, and he brought his own back to hers again without quite knowing why. She took a deep breath and caught his gaze, holding it for a minute before she spoke. He noted how perfect her timing was, focusing attention on her next phrase better than any loud proclamation could. He was, nonetheless, totally unprepared for what came next.

"Would you entertain us on the piano while you're here, Corey?" Her voice had somehow moved up from the depth of her feline purr to a bird-like trill in her throat. He was surprised and delighted to find she could play so many parts without revealing the transitions.

"Do you sing, Miss Bond?" he asked. She nodded slightly. "You have an unusually well-developed vocal range, and I'd be delighted to accompany you," Corey said, unable to hide his admiration for how her speech had modulated in a matter of seconds.

"The stage is no place for a woman of culture," she laughed, "but I do enjoy a private song in a chamber, now and then. Perhaps you could play for me at one of our parties." She lowered her eyes, and then slowly raised them to his again. "We have one planned next week here at the hotel, and my aunt and I would be honored if you'd both join us for it. Wouldn't we, Aunt Sarah?" She turned to see the Widow Stovall nodding vigorously, and Corey sensed his father beaming with equal enthusiasm.

"How wonderful of you to include us, ladies. Of course, Corey will play for you. He also teaches and leads choral groups, so I'm sure he'd join you in singing, Miss Bond."

"Oh, I'm afraid that won't be possible. Father, no! We must go home, ladies, I'm sorry to say. I, we, thank you, but can't accept your invitation." He knew he sounded scattered, but one look at the crushed hopes on his father's face warned him that winning this battle would take a high personal toll—one he probably couldn't afford.

✦✦✦

Work delay here. Corey read his notes to his father for a new telegram. *Taking train to New York next week. Please send full performance schedule including repertoire. Suggest Robert accompany you pre-Chicago. Love to you and boys.*

"Anything else, Father? Did I leave anything out?" Father and son sat together in the Old White bar again, ostensibly enjoying a digestive after their rich meal with the ladies, but in fact to discuss their unusual evening.

"Should you give Emily a date for our return?" Klaas asked, a sound of concern creeping in through the hesitancy in his voice.

"I don't want to add another disappointment. It's worse to promise something and then not deliver it. Something seems to get in the way too often lately. I think this will be enough, and I hope it's the last telegraph I must send. Once the Stovall's entertainment is over, we can't let anything keep us from returning to New York." Corey eased the sheet of paper he'd been writing on from the telegraph pad, but it wasn't the decisive rip of an unbreakable ultimatum.

Klaas noticed, and knew it was the best time to present his next surprise to his son. "Well, perhaps it's wise not to be too specific, Corey, because there is one other thing that we should try to do while we're down here. It would be a shame to miss such a wonderful opportunity when we've come so far."

"What are you talking about, Father? What opportunity?" Corey asked, slowly rising and leaving his glass of port untouched on the table.

Klaas sat up straight, beaming. "To sell one of Mr. Steinway's grand pianos to the Widow Stovall! In fact, I believe you could sell more than one. Possibly a few uprights will be needed. You get a substantial commission for those sales, and it can only increase your value to Mr. Steinway and the whole music community in New York; I mean, when you bring them customers they have no access to."

Corey stepped back as if he needed space to focus on what his father was saying. "When did all this come up, Father? I had no idea the Stovalls needed a piano."

"I just mentioned to Sarah in passing, and it seems theirs were all burned or ruined during the war. It's such a loss for a lady down here, Corey, to have no piano to play. They have no way to shine in polite society. It's not our idea of a necessity but this is a different culture I know well, and you'd be doing them an enormous favor if you'd come with me to see the spaces they have in mind for the replacement instruments." It suddenly dawned on Corey that his father's business skills for identifying opportunities were still in full force. Then Klaas added unexpectedly, "And . . . I'd so love to see their mansion. I hear it's absolutely beautiful . . . such a flattering invitation . . . they do seem genuine in wanting us to come." His father's pleading tone brought sadness with it that Corey was unprepared for.

"All right, Father," Corey sighed. "But this is the last delay. I've made a performance commitment to Emily and she has every right to count on it. I've been away from her and the boys much too long as it is." He folded the paper he'd written his telegram on and tore it in half.

"Wonderful!" Klaas cried, pushing up from the table with a sparkle in his eyes. "The Stovalls will be so delighted to hear this. And you know the ladies will do everything in their power to entertain us royally."

"I have no doubt, Father," Corey sighed. "Entertainment seems to be one of their greatest strengths."

CHAPTER FOUR

ROBERT HAUSSMANN could see the front of the de Koningh mansion from two blocks away on Fifth Avenue. It always gave him a private smile to find such European architecture in this, the most Dutch of American cities. The six-story building looked like an early French Renaissance castle. He could see the entire frontage as he got closer, one hundred feet of it along Fifth Avenue, with half of that occupied by the house and the other a side lawn fifty feet across. He loved looking out on that well-tended grass with the gardens placed geometrically, all visible from inside the library when he taught his young charges music there.

Usually Robert walked over the four blocks from his own home between Lexington and Third Avenues. He'd spent more than half his life making this pilgrimage to give children of the de Koningh household piano lessons, and then of course he'd also supported Emily in her exploration of the violin at an early age. He was in his fifties now and well past middle age but remembered her when she was thirteen as if they'd been working together on those early lessons just last month. But that was an old memory. Her first son, William, was already past his infancy and showing much of his mother's stubbornness with little of her passion. The piano was an intellectual conquest for him, but nothing more. And his little brother, Connie, was also no longer a baby, but too young to do much more than play games at the keyboard. He also showed little interest in music, though his sweet smile blossomed when he had a drawing pencil and paper in front of him.

"Professor Haussmann, welcome!" The stooped, aging front hall maid waved to him from the steps as she poked vainly with a broom at some brittle brown leaves curled in defiance of the chill fall wind. "Mrs. de Koningh's waiting for you in the library, as usual. She's practicing," Mary added.

Robert nodded to the maid he'd known since her arrival off the boat from Ireland as not much more than an adolescent, patting her on the shoulder as he passed. Funny. He remembered how stiff he'd been with the servants when he'd first come to the mansion over thirty years ago. The rules of polite society in America were all so new to him then, and he hadn't been sure where he fit in, if at all, or just how polite he had to be. A music teacher was certainly not one of the new American sovereigns, but not exactly a servant, either.

Now everything had changed, as things do. His maturity, the Civil War, Emily and Corey's marriage, the almost immediate arrival of their first child, and even the economic and political makeup of New York City itself had all worked to adjust his lifestyle and role in the culture of this new age. He had to admit he was a bit suspicious of the unrestricted growth of money and industry after the war, as well as the rosy outlook of most Americans that there would never be a reversal to the upward trajectory, but that was possibly his age and his European roots talking. He'd seen it all before. And Robert hated to admit how fearful he was that America would be plunged into war again, whether one of its own making or those of other nations, all the conflicts he'd fled from in Europe when he'd originally left home. He occasionally acknowledged a sickening suspicion that he might be tangled in the tentacles of his own history and would never get free. Perhaps everyone always was, but he hoped the freshness of the American form of democracy and capitalism would prove his anxiety wrong.

Moving through the vast entrance foyer and past the massive staircase, he walked straight to the library, the scene of all the most important and meaningful interactions he'd had with the de Koningh family of pupils over the years. He'd spent almost all his time at the mansion, a few hours every day, in that room. He stopped outside the closed oak door to be sure he wouldn't interrupt Emily's practice at a crucial phrase. Listening carefully, he realized something was different so stayed poised to knock on the door yet held back. One gray-gloved fist hovered to rap on the wood molding just as the door swung open.

"Robert . . . what a surprise." Emily stood frozen, violin and bow in hand. She looked tired. Her face had a strained expression he wasn't familiar with.

"I didn't want to disturb your practice," he said, watching her carefully to see if he could read something in her drained color and tight mouth.

"Oh, I've had enough," she said, with a dispirited drop of her shoulders.

"Having some trouble?" he asked. He'd seldom seen her abuse herself with self-doubt or criticism. She looked down at her instrument and bow hanging in her left hand, and then back up at Robert. Something flipped over in his chest when he saw the inflamed edge around her eyes and realized she'd undoubtedly been crying.

"No trouble," she said, "just no good."

"Do you want to talk about it?" He dropped his voice to meet hers.

"Not really," she said, with a little more of the strength of spirit he was used to. "Were you coming in for lessons with William?" Robert nodded. "Come on in, then. He's finishing up some schoolwork. He'll be down in ten minutes." She sighed with a diffidence that broke his heart. He wanted to catch her and set her on her feet again.

"Emily!" he suddenly exclaimed. "Where did my painting go?" He stepped back to stare at the wall beside the library door. "It's always been there and now it's gone!"

Emily broke into a grin and chuckled. "You mean the Philip de Koninck landscape that was worth a small fortune?" He smiled and nodded. What a relief it was to see her eyes light up and hear her laugh. "Well, as it was a family heirloom, it's been returned to the family in Schuylerville. They claimed Corey's mother promised it to them when his father sent her up there during the war. After she died, he didn't have the heart to bicker with the relatives over it. I'm surprised you haven't noted its absence before."

"I guess I've been in too much of a hurry of late. But when I stopped in the hall just now, I felt it was missing. Which suggests that we haven't had a talk lately, either. If William's going to be tied up for a while, why don't we use the time to catch up?" He smiled as casually as he could, moving forward into the room and forcing her to step aside without protest. He pushed the door shut with a quick shove, trying to make the movement look natural. Every instinct told him to keep the atmosphere around them as easy as possible. Emily could close herself down quickly if she wanted to, and then he knew he'd never solve the mystery of her tears.

"What have you been working on?" he asked, pulling his gloves off and placing them on the desk with his leather briefcase. Pretending not to notice she was still mute, he strode to the piano as if it was an expected continuum into the room. "What's this for?" he asked, bending over to look at the sheet music on the piano bench. "César Franck! Oh my, Emily, such a modern composer!" He hoped to provoke her and pull her out of herself. "Difficult work. Is this an experiment?"

"Not so modern, Robert. A lot of modulation and a clear respect for the music. I think you two would get along famously! It's for a performance in Chicago," Emily added, putting her violin and bow in the case left open on top of the piano. The reverence she had for her instrument was obvious in the care she took to lower it gently to the red velvet lining. It was his instrument, loaned to her in perpetuity.

"But there may not be a performance at all if Corey doesn't come back very soon," she added, with a little sigh and maybe just a catch in her throat.

"Where is he? Does he know about the booking?"

"Just what do you think, Robert?" Emily asked with an edge to her voice. "Could I make a booking for us without telling Corey?" Her annoyance was out of proportion to his question, but he didn't let himself get pulled down in her irritation.

"Can I help? Would you like me to get word to him somehow?"

"Absolutely not. He knows the performance schedule, and what his part is. It's his choice to come home or not. But if we must cancel Chicago at the last minute, I fear it will ruin both of our careers."

"Emily, that's neither likely nor fair. A brash, young western town like Chicago is not a pivotal venue for classical music, so your careers are certainly not at stake, and I'm sure Corey won't disappoint you, anyway." Robert shut the sheet music and moved it off the piano bench to the desk so he could sit down. "Come," he said, placing his hand on the bench beside him. "Tell me what's really bothering you. There must be more to it."

Emily looked at the seat and then at Robert, her first violin teacher, mentor, and earliest musical ally other than Corey, realizing she hadn't paid attention to him in an exceptionally long while. She steadied her thoughts to focus directly on Robert at the piano, noticing all that made him who he was now, not who she remembered him to have been. She was surprised to see her memory and the reality were closely aligned. The young teacher collaborating with the child who wanted to play the violin was now a middle-aged man who looked almost unchanged, except for his manner. And the willful child was now a determined, mature female violinist, still struggling. Not much change in her, either, at least not in her musical inclinations, though the rest of her was unfamiliar to herself. Her life had become complicated in comparison with those early years of clarity and focus. Even the things she longed for had been simple and obvious. Now, she knew very well she was never satisfied and always at odds with herself, though she wasn't sure why.

Robert's red hair was a little darker and duller, but still full and healthy, with just a light brushstroke of gray at the temples. His prodigious red mustache and beard were as they always had been, dense and well-trimmed. His forehead showed the tender skin expected with his redhead's coloring, and his widow's peak gave him the look of a poet. Reddish-brown brows arched over soft blue eyes, seemingly shy and unsure, almost reluctant to view the painful things of the world. Pale eyelashes disappeared in the light, adding to his impression of vulnerability.

His bottom lip was visible through the dense beard and mustache, moving slightly as he played and softly curving, as if tasting the music most people only heard. She looked down at the hands resting on his knees, never having noticed before how different they were from Corey's. You'd think pianists would share certain characteristics, but Corey's hands were exceptionally long and thin, giving him a crucial reach of twelve keys, while Robert's strong, square hands didn't seem so remarkable. But it was his wrists that held her attention. The delicate bone and shape of the forearm where they joined his hands seemed to suggest that a flexible wrist might indeed be the secret to beautiful music.

Startled by the chime of the desk clock, Emily realized she'd been silent too long. Lifting her dark eyes in her pale face to his, she murmured, "I can't tell you what's wrong, Robert, because I don't know myself. If I figure it out, I promise you'll be the second to know." She signed with a deep private regret.

"Who will be the first?" he asked her.

"What's an ulster?"

William lay on his back on the library carpet, legs bent, feet resting on the couch. Both arms stretched up straight holding a newspaper over his head. He'd started mimicking his grandfather de Koningh's obsession with the news since he'd become a prolific reader at such an early age.

"Ulcer?" Emily looked down at her son, remembering how often she'd draped herself over the couch the same way as a child while Corey played the piano; only the paper roof she'd held then had musical notes instead of letters. William shook his head without looking at her. "What's the context, then?" Emily tried her best to keep irritation out of her voice. She was sitting at the desk working on the adjusted repertoire for her Chicago performance, and praying for peace in the library by herself, already a lost cause. Her mind paced. "Read the sentence to me," she said, slowing her breathing to dull the edge of her annoyance. She liked practicing breath control for performance. It had the most profound effect at so many levels. Changing one's physicality moved the music, too.

"It's not a sentence. It's in an advertisement for a sale at S. P. Teasdel. It reads: straw hats, white shirts, gents' underwear, ladies' Ulsters . . . I want to know if Ulsters means ladies' underwear."

"William, please take your shoes off the couch." Again, Emily noticed the struggle to keep her voice buoyant. It would never do to let her older son know he'd gotten under her skin. Without acknowledging her or her directive, William pulled his feet back off the cushion, clearly preparing a new onslaught of trivia. Apparently, he could tell she was upset. He tucked his shoes under the couch's upholstered skirt.

"So, is it some kind of ladies' underwear?" he asked.

"No, William, it's an overcoat for winter, usually made from very dense wool so it's waterproof. Your father has one. It's that herringbone with the gray and brown checks. It has a cape over the shoulders, so the snow and rain won't seep through." William looked disappointed, secretly pleasing Emily.

"But this is the dumbest advertisement then, Mother. One minute they're selling winter coats and shirts, and the next they offer straw hats and bathing costumes. It's almost winter. Why would any store be selling all those now?"

"You said it was a sale, Willie. That probably means they have stock they want to get rid of. But the way people travel today, you never know who'll need a bathing costume one minute and overcoat the next." Emily pulled a piece of sheet music toward her and crossed something off. She shook her head, flipping through the pages before pushing it away.

"What's this say?" William asked, undeterred by Emily's lack of enthusiasm and attention.

"A China cork hat," she read, and stifled a sigh. "I assume it's made of cork from a China oak. They're the trees most wine corks come from." Noticing William was listening at last she decided to go on, pretending to care. "Cork hats are wonderfully light and cool, like straw. Good heavens, that really is an odd list," she said, glancing up from her work. "Let me have a look at it. That kind of a sale might actually be worth going to." She joined William on the floor, propped up against the couch with her back straight and feet out in front of her. William flashed a smile unexpectedly, pleased he'd brought his mother down to his level at last. He slid the newspaper over so she could see it better.

"What do you think? Should we go find out what else they have?" He tried to sound grown-up, a full collaborator in the plan to go shopping for bargains.

"Children's linen suits," she read. "And boys' underwear of all ages," she sang out, suddenly laughing. "What are all ages—the boys, or the underwear?" She winked at William and he started to giggle. Emily nudged him a little and he rolled over. She started to fold the paper, stopping when something caught her eye.

"Well look at this! My friend Jacques Offenbach is coming here from France for the opening of one of his operettas. We should go!"

Her familiar dimples flashed for a moment at each corner of her mouth.

"Who's he, Mother? Another violinist?" William rolled back on his stomach next to her to look at the picture of the fashionably dressed gentleman in a top hat.

Emily suddenly felt more energetic than she had in weeks. "Good Lord, no. He's a composer of wonderful light operettas. I saw his first one in Paris when I was studying there with Professor Haussmann before you were born." William stared at her, as if the idea of anything happening before he was born was preposterous.

"He's become very popular since then; all over the world, not just in France." She peered around William's shoulder, so she could see better. "It says that picture you're looking at was taken in Philadelphia before the opening of one of his works that's going to be performed here, too." She leaned down over the paper with William, two shiny dark heads touching in support of each other and discovery.

"I wonder if Robert would like to come with us," she muttered, almost to herself. "Of course, he would. And you should come, too," she said, bumping William's head with her own for emphasis. "There's no better introduction to the world of opera for someone young than Monsieur Offenbach's!" She straightened up so fast she knocked William's chin with her skull. Both groaned and laughed.

"Why don't I tell Professor Haussmann," William announced. It was not a question. He jumped to his feet leaving Emily propped against the couch with the paper next to her. "He's with Mary and Emma in the kitchen, so I'll meet him there."

"Indeed. There might just be some cookies in the kitchen for you when you take him the good tidings," Emily said to his retreating back. He was gone out the door before he could have heard her, pulling it closed behind him with a wild tug announcing his intention to greet his music teacher alone. Emily sighed and smiled to herself. Had she known it would be so easy to secure her solitude she'd have bribed him with cookies much sooner.

Looking back down at the paper, Emily noticed a four-column article running down the middle of the page and bordered by the advertisements William had taken such delight in. It was a commentary by Samuel L. Clemens, as if everyone didn't know who Mark Twain was, about the appropriateness of using civilians instead of trained soldiers to plan military strategy. A quick glance revealed the usual Clemens wit, tongue-in-cheek, as he described his own half-hour visit to the Military Academy at West Point. He announced it prepared him for war as fully as the years of study America's leaders put in. Even with the article's wry humor, she was repulsed and exhausted by the constant references to war. Was it all an attempt to demean their new President Grant as he tried to grow past his years as a general? Or was it prompted by the victor's guilt northern men couldn't seem to rid themselves of? She was so tired of all the blame. It was claustrophobic and confining when everyone should be waking to opportunities after the war.

Emily looked up over the piano to the garden running along Fifth Avenue. It was still vibrant with the burnished red and gold of autumn. In this day and age . . . her father would say, prefacing the description of a change in manners or custom much like a change of season. This was truly a new day and age, as industry exploded all over the country and everything was different, though not always for the better, she had to admit.

Looking back down at the article, Emily remembered Clemens had coined the phrase the Gilded Age. Yes, he was right. This age was truly just gilt and not pure gold after all. Anyone taking the time could see the tarnish already spreading. Mr. Clemens was good at pointing that out indirectly. There it was again, that word "guilt," or "gilt"—gold-plated remorse—that's what the North offered the South. She smiled at the nuance just one less letter could suggest, like the addition or subtraction of an eighth note on a score. The Gilded Age was nothing more than an overdose of guilt.

What did any of them have to feel guilty about, least of all her husband and his father, who'd both suffered in their own ways during the war? Why were they down south yet again, trying to make up for something they hadn't been responsible for? Inadvertently her hand slipped into her skirt pocket to feel the telegram from Corey. She slipped it out and unfolded it, hopeful she might have misunderstood its message.

WORK DELAY HERE stop TAKING TRAIN TO NEW YORK NEXT WEEK stop PLEASE SEND FULL PERFORMANCE SCHEDULE INCLUDING REPERTOIRE stop SUGGEST ROBERT ACCOMPANY YOU stop

She folded the paper just as the library door swung open. Robert Haussmann leaned into the room from the hall outside the library, held back by the massive oak door standing open at a slight angle. William was nowhere in sight, undoubtedly stalling his entry for lessons with another application of Emma's cookies. "Am I disturbing you?" Robert asked, making Emily realize she probably had a scowl on her face.

"Not at all, Robert. Please, come in." She didn't have to try to smile, cheered by the break offered by his interruption. "I was just thinking of you." She struggled to her feet, pushing herself up with the couch as leverage, surprised at the effort it took. She must have been sitting too long, the circulation in her legs cut off by idleness. He moved quickly across the room, reaching out to help her up. "Thanks," she whispered under her breath. "My advancing years are beginning to be an embarrassment." She smiled at him, brushing a few dark wisps of hair off her forehead.

"Never," he said with a smile softening his bottom lip. But she could still see concern in his eyes under the auburn brows. "What's that you have there?" He pointed to the telegram. She understood his true question to be, what does it say?

She looked directly at him. "Robert, would you come to Chicago with me?"

"What—why?" he asked, those same red brows drawn together.

"Because I don't want to change the program, and I can't perform it without an accompanist. You're the only one who can play with me, other than Corey, and I can't wait for him any longer. We have a week to rehearse together before we have to get on the train. Will you do it, Robert, please?" She watched shadows move across his face so fast she was tempted to look for the changing light source responsible. They both stood quite still, neither one sure of what the other was thinking. Finally, Robert looked away, out to the garden and then down at the carpet before coming back up to meet Emily's eyes.

"All right," he said, "I'll go. But you must let Corey and his father know. It might make a difference to their travel plans," he added, as if an excuse for the disclosure was part of his bargain.

"They don't need a pretext to stay down south longer," she said, putting the telegram into his hand. "Read it. The delays go on and on, without appreciation for our life up here that must also advance." She saw him glance down at the telegram. "Go ahead," she said with a nod. "Read it. You need to understand what I've been dealing with these last few months." She moved away toward her desk with a disgusted toss of her head, but Robert still held the telegram in his hand without looking at it.

"I don't need to," he muttered. "It's enough that you find it upsetting. Your music comes first, so of course I'll come if you want me to."

He followed her to the desk, putting the telegram down. Finally, she picked it up and stuffed it back in her pocket, shoving it down so deep it seemed her skirt might tear.

Robert Haussmann did not often seem distraught, but for the last two days he'd agonized over Emily's request for him to accompany her on her next concert tour and sitting at the piano in her library brought the dilemma back to him with crushing reality. He'd just finished giving a lesson to William, and little had been accomplished. It was desperately frustrating to teach those who didn't care about music. He was also anxious about taking Emily's husband's place as her accompanist, even for a short time. His presence with her might well be the stuff of gossip. His life as one of the foremost teachers of the pianoforte had been shaped long ago in a familiar design prescribed by Old New York's high society. Their patterns of living were totally predictable, making his job much easier, the measures of his life suited perfectly to their societal rhythms. He had, in truth, become more like one of them than an inhabitant of that middle world where foreigners and artists dwell, suspended in a limbo of belonging but not quite fitting in, neither a domestic servant nor a full master. He was grateful for his European background, which these wealthy Americans deeply valued with an esteem he hadn't fully appreciated at first as a young man new to the city.

His acceptance had been gradual, and so he realized now it had come upon him long before he'd acknowledged the change. Teaching the children of old-moneyed Manhattan had certainly aided his access—a toe, or even a whole foot, across the thresholds along Fifth Avenue. But it was an exceedingly long and sometimes perilous way up the silken ladder, La Scala di Seta, to finally find oneself in the oak-paneled libraries of high society like this one of the de Koninghs'. Rossini's operatic farce embodied the process in the hard work on stage made to look like a relaxed romp. He too had worked extremely hard to get where he was, and he deserved the trust and appreciation of his wealthy clientele. But that was, of course, not to his credit in this world. Working hard at anything was not meant to be a gentleman's objective.

Robert's typical posture on the piano bench gave the impression of readiness: upright and still but relaxed, leaning slightly forward toward the music on the stand as if it held a magnetic attraction. He reached up to touch Emily's unfamiliar score on the piano rack now, pulling it slightly closer as if to introduce himself. He could never change the fact of not being born to this gentleman's life, but that fact had lessened greatly in importance over the years. Many of the families he'd worked with (he no longer said "for" even to himself) had been forced to rent their mansions here and in Newport. After the Civil War shrank America's currency, they had no choice but to live in Europe for extended periods until their fortunes were rebuilt, along with their country. When the ruling families had returned, he'd noticed they had a different appreciation for the depth of culture and broader viewpoint older societies offered—in truth a realization of New York's provincialism from the very people who'd formerly protected the citadel.

Reverence for all things European had already displaced the old society here, and that had certainly helped him rise in their eyes as well. He'd lost his German accent long ago, his musical ear affording him sympathy for the nuances of the language of his adopted country. He certainly still had a hint of something unusual in his speech, but Americans thought him British, then French when he denied the Anglican connection, and eventually nodded when he claimed Vienna as his birthplace. It wasn't, but the small village in the mountains he'd come from would have meant nothing, and he'd quickly understood Old New York's distrust of places unknown. He'd always been confused by the irony of the Americans' struggle for political autonomy as it clung to the culture of the patriarchs they'd fought for independence from. It reminded him of the caged animals in the zoo who'd wandered around aimlessly after being mistakenly freed, only to return to whatever cages were still standing open to them.

He slipped the score off the piano rack, bringing it down to the keyboard where he could study it at a more comfortable distance. The de Koningh family leather binder had been slipped around the score for protection and to add extra support in the upright position. Being embraced by the de Koninghs to teach Corey almost from the start of his career had undoubtedly smoothed Robert's way up the career and social ladder, although the added unexpected benefit of teaching Lord Alden's daughter had been a boon of a different sort. The treasure tucked away inside the mansion on Fifth Avenue took the form of a young motherless girl who'd come to live with the de Koninghs soon after her mother's death. Her spirit, looks, intellect, and musical talent had inspired and tormented Robert all their years together. He'd been graced and fulfilled by her connection as a musician, and possibly with their personal relationship as well, although that was a perplexing situation he was never sure of as time went by.

That was not to say twelve-year-old Corey de Koningh hadn't been a challenging and rewarding student himself. A quick learner devoted to his piano studies, he'd always had a bent for composition, and both proclivities were enhanced by a lovely singing voice. An unusual sparkle in his eye accompanied his continuous torrent of questions, assuring Robert's pleasure with the opportunity to offer him classical training. But Corey's crystal-clear soprano voice had eventually changed to the depth of an amber baritone along with the change of his tiny body to a lofty six-foot height. The commitment to classical music and composition had also altered into a connection to popular music and light singing of glee club fare as a young adult. Although he'd continued to tour with Emily, as her accompanist after the war, his heart was clearly not in the mission of their musical team. He was her accompanist out of duty and habit, but perhaps nothing more. Still, it was possible Corey's old music teacher was judging his former student too harshly.

Robert looked down at the score and saw some of Emily's notations in the margins. He couldn't read them, but then he'd never
been able to. They were in her own shorthand. And why not? She
played alone, the solo violin part, with other musicians behind her.
There was no reason her notes should be shared with others. She was
a virtuoso violinist just as she'd promised she would be from the
start. Denied the right to play the instrument by the rules of feminine modesty, she'd hidden it in bed with her at night, reading sheet
music to herself as bedtime stories, and eventually making her way
to Robert's house, ostensibly to learn the piano, but in truth to study
the violin with him. Where teaching Corey had been merely challenging, Emily had been provocative in the extreme. The fire for the
sound of bow on string burned deep within her and she'd left no
obstacles standing. Robert had bowed to her will, at first out of
surprise and self-preservation, but soon with a profound admiration
for her talent.

He looked down at her symbols again, seeing her familiar small,
strong hands moving the pencil, a look of unreserved determination
on her face. Her shiny dark child's ringlets brushed her shoulders
when he'd first known her, and he'd memorized the angle of her neck
as she'd grown, hair finally swept up even though it revealed the
brownish bruise under her chin on the left side. A violinist's beauty
mark, he'd assured her, that proved her partnership with the instrument. He was there at the very time she'd needed nurturing and
attention the most, and her talent flourished like a hibiscus bloom-
ing. He realized he was rubbing the notations on the score lightly. He
pulled his hand up, uncomfortable with the associated memories.
For all the years she'd been away in finishing school he'd had only
those remembrances of her, while she'd moved on in her musical life,
which meant of course she'd moved on in her daily life as well,
without him.

How could he not have fallen in love with Emily Alden? Everyone
did. She'd been an irresistible amateur violinist, for what was the

true definition of amateur but a lover of something? And now she was an alluring professional, pulling all who heard her under the spell cast by the depth of her art, fighting the prejudice against women performing on the public stage. Her name secured the bookings and assured a full audience at each musical venue. The public knew her as Emily de Koningh, but Emily Alden had been the one who visited all the biggest concert houses of Europe with Robert as her tutor. That Emily was the one who continually took center stage in his interior vision. She'd always known who she was, while he had never really understood. That very incendiary nature he so admired had also upset his balance, both then and now.

So now . . . here he was again, about to embark on a mission in support of Emily's music, but in truth, more to sustain the dreams of the woman he had no right to. Yes, again. He ran the fingers of his right hand over the keys, playing a little reminder of the adagio movement of the Brahms violin concerto. That had been her biggest emotional stumbling block on their first European tour together. Well, maybe not her biggest. He had to admit his rejected proposal of marriage had probably been even bigger. After all, he'd been her teacher, mentor, and guide on that trip at her father's request, and he was fifteen years her senior. He could hardly believe now, looking back all those years, that he'd lost his hard-won reserve and displayed his heart on his sleeve so improperly. But her rejection at the time had certainly been his biggest stumbling block, so hard to get over even with her deft handling of what was a terrible embarrassment for them both. He bent forward over the keyboard, bowing his head. His eyes closed, and he could see the first time he'd met with Emily's father in his gentlemen's club on Fifth Avenue. He'd been seduced then by Lord Alden's rationale, appealing to Robert's obvious concern for Emily's musical career, and to both their hidden anxieties over losing her forever. And he'd been aware of it then. It did no good to pretend he hadn't.

Her father had appointed him her mentor, tutor, and chaperone on a grand tour through Europe to displace young Corey de Koningh from her life, and Robert had gone along with the plan in desperation, convincing himself his devotion to Emily's skill was his only motive. He smiled at himself inwardly. She'd taken charge of her life herself eventually, as she always did, and married Corey de Koningh after all. They'd both been overeager to have a family of their own, and their first child had arrived uncomfortably early, but they'd seemed happy for a while. Their two sons were special and yet so like their parents in many ways. Robert had done his best to stay close to these boys, to carry on the legacy of culture and music begun in this same library when their own parents were not so much older than William and Connie were now. And he'd had to stay close to Emily.

He opened his eyes and raised his head, straightening his back. Lowering the carved, ebony fall over the piano keys, he rested his fingers there in mute homage to the historical memory of lessons past. He moved his gaze around the room, taking in the oak paneling, the paintings from the de Koningh family collection in Amsterdam, the thickly carpeted floor and warm fabric upholstery, all so familiar to him over the years of teaching music here to two generations of de Koningh children, and Emily.

The walls of books opposite the piano had never attracted him, though they added to the room's wonderful acoustics, and he turned slowly to look at the shelves of sheet music behind him, all old friends of over twenty years. He'd appropriated some of them for Emily from that collection when she was a child, emphasizing the possibilities offered by all the female composers starting in the 1500s. She'd been more interested in news of the few women performers of the day, petitioning for word of pianist Clara Schumann's conquests on stages around the world.

But there had been few female violinists to serve as her inspiration, and news of those pioneers had never risen to the top of the public consciousness in America, so the men had been her beacons, Joseph Joachim prime among them. Robert had taken her to a series of Joachim's concerts in England before their return to New York that year. He remembered giving in to her wish to return home early to further her education directly after those concerts. He knew she'd seen the Civil War in America as possibly her only chance to attend a formerly all-male university, the war having decimated the male student population. But the discomfort of his precluded marriage proposal to Emily Alden over a decade ago remained.

Now Robert was yet again bowing to Emily's wishes in the name of music, and again stepping into Corey's place in her life at a time and circumstance just as inappropriate as the first had been. Perhaps it was unworthy of him in so many ways, but she needed him, and he couldn't turn away. Or so he told himself.

A sound at the French doors leading to the garden on Fifth Avenue made him jump. Spinning around on the bench, he saw Emily struggling to pull the heavy glass casement shut and secure the curved brass handle. "Emily! What . . ."

"William shouldn't go out this way. I've told him so many times. He's not strong enough to close it properly and one gust of wind from across Central Park will smash it for good."

Robert heard the tall case clock in the entrance hall outside the library strike four. "Emily," he snapped, "you're late. William is always tardy, and just left with little accomplished. If you can't be disciplined about our rehearsals, we must start meeting at my house. You wouldn't have distractions there. I don't have forever to wait for you, you know."

The stunned look on Emily's face told him he'd overdone it. He saw the shock turn into something more like hurt, and he also noticed how tired and strained she seemed, making him more ashamed of lashing out at her. The flash of his temper was unexpected, and in fact he knew she'd probably never experienced this

degree of severity in all the years they'd known each other. It surprised him as well. There'd been minor rebukes from him before
over her flippancy and teasing, both habits unbecoming a lady of her
position and performer of her stature. He'd certainly grown tired of
her constant challenge response to every suggestion he'd ever
offered as her teacher. But Robert Haussmann understood this
explosion was different, and that for some reason he'd become
extremely distraught.

CHAPTER FIVE

"Come with me," Marcy said. Corey tried to pretend he hadn't been watching her slow, sensuous walk flow toward him up the old brick path between the magnolias. He moved a little, as if he'd only just recognized some sound distracting him from his reading. He left the book about counterpoint lying on his lap, one hand holding his place open as if to take himself back immediately once the disturbance she'd created had passed. He enjoyed the balancing act of two hands, two themes, or two harmonies in his music, but had somehow missed the irony of doing the same in his life.

"Where?" he asked, vaguely. "Where are you going?" He noticed she was dressed more casually than usual, a simple cotton skirt meeting a plain white bodice at her tiny waist, greatly accentuating the curves of her womanly figure above and below the divide. It didn't quite look natural, certainly not like his wife's body without the special undergarments she'd rejected years ago. But he didn't mind if it was all about creating an illusion. It was a pleasant deception. It seemed southern women were still intent on pleasing men, something he'd begun to question in their northern counterparts.

"What did you say?" he asked again, trying to suggest whatever it was hadn't been important enough to warrant his attention. With the green eyes Corey hadn't allowed himself to take note of the night before, Marcy Bond stood looking up at him now from just below the first step to the veranda. Her burnished copper highlights weaving through her hair, and head cocked slightly to one side as if questioning his sincerity—as well she might—she was an impossible combination of perfect physical beauty. There was an intensity about the way he exchanged looks with her from his rocking chair, making the indifference he pretended quite ridiculous.

"Oh come now, Corey," she laughed. "I called and waved from the gate." She tucked a loose curl back under her hair gathered at the top of her head by a green ribbon. Corey noticed the lock drop disobediently back down, settling at the nape of her neck. "I said I'm going to hear some wonderful musicians perform and asked if you'd like to come," she added, lowering her eyelashes as if to protect herself from the sun. He continued to stare at her, but his look was now tinged with discomfort.

"Join me. You'll be glad you did," she said again, a sweet smile lighting a warm, welcoming spark in her eyes that suddenly seemed to have shifted to the shimmering topaz of an angora cat. Corey didn't move, the book still lifeless on his lap with his hand on top. "I won't bite, you know," Marcy said. "Come with me." He watched as she raised her arm with confidence, reaching out to him with the assurance he'd follow her example and reach back. But he didn't. Just hearing her ask that question again, *why don't you come with me*, he could feel the solid ground slipping away underneath him and was afraid of what might slide with it. What in heaven's name could she see in him to be interested in? Her aunt had described a decimated southern male population and scant opportunity for a young woman to enjoy herself of late. Was that all it was? Just a need to practice her skills on a man, any man, so she wouldn't lose them.

Slowing his breathing in and out, he found he was feeling more normal, as he'd taken time to settle the odd feeling in his chest (a sensation not unlike stage fright, which he was certainly used to) and realized he could find his voice. "Did you say what kind of music you're going to hear? Maybe I just didn't catch it."

He seemed to be regaining some of his composure, closing the book on his lap and propping it under one arm as if preparing to leave the comfort of his rocker, and possibly the company of his young hostess; or also possibly to join her wherever she was going.

"Of course I didn't. If you couldn't hear me call from the gate you certainly wouldn't have heard a dissertation on tonight's performers." She put both hands on her hips, stating a challenge in purely physical terms and accentuating her astounding figure even more than her clothing could alone. Her voice was still draped in the polite, soothing tones of her southern accent he'd come to expect, and almost crave, as one would an addiction to a sweet. Corey couldn't take his eyes off her, fingering the spine of his book as he stalled for time in hopes of coming up with a reason to send her away. She made him tremendously uncomfortable, and as he stared at her in silence, he realized the scene was reminiscent of another not so very long ago.

Were men and women always draping themselves flirtatiously around verandas in the South? The last time, during his first trip south during the war, he'd been on the steps and Emily had held the high ground of the porch. He'd felt no disquiet then, and realized he'd never been uncomfortable anywhere around Emily at any time. This overt sensual assault from his southern hostess was outside his experience, and he had no idea how to defend himself. He weighed his resistance to this beautiful young woman; Emily had always reminded him of what he already knew about life: the radiance of music, the saving grace of intellect, the strange loneliness of family that wasn't there, the privilege of a society they both took for granted. They'd always understood each other without ever saying so. How could they not have become man and wife? Marcy reminded him of all the things in life he'd never known or experienced and had never even considered. That's what scared him about her. And something in his gut told him she would threaten all his certainties and turn them into doubts. She made him feel a bit foolish and extremely naïve, though a husband and father who'd contributed to the Union effort during the War between the States should have felt a maturity, confidence, and assurance around a young woman of the South, one would think.

"I'll take your silence for considered interest," Marcy said, climbing up two more steps. "But why do you have so much trouble connecting with women your own age? If the way you treat me is any example of your social skills, I'm surprised you ever got married." He couldn't tell if she was deadly serious or teasing him again, but that was perhaps no different from the way she handled all social interaction.

"I don't know why you'd be interested in having a connection with me," he said, "but I don't recall having any trouble when I was in college. Though I can't say I can remember any of the young lovelies well who draped themselves over me; maybe that's because there were too many of them, and perhaps none were notable." He grinned at her, assuming she'd take his jocular tone in the foolish spirit he'd intended.

"That's not what I meant by *socializing*," Marcy laughed, a light ringing sound that reminded him of crystals bumping into each other. "It's one thing to be followed around as if you were the master and they the dogs, and quite another to share equally in an intellectual partnership and attraction of equal measure. Is that what you had with your wife?" He couldn't miss the reference to his marriage in the past tense and stiffened involuntarily. He nodded.

"We always knew we'd be married someday," he said, remembering his childhood with Emily. "We met when we were thirteen and the future together was decided for us."

"An arranged marriage when you were so young?" Her eyes grew wide with feigned shock.

He wouldn't give in to her disingenuous surprise. "Of sorts, I suppose, but not the kind you mean. Our parents were not in favor at the start and actually worked quite hard to send us in other directions, but we're both stubborn and we resisted." He smiled, remembering the ups and downs of his and Emily's early relationship and how their friendship had solidified from the first day they'd met. "If our marriage was arranged, then it was we who arranged it." Marcy was silent for once, apparently digesting what he'd said. She took a deep breath, and then let it out, lifting her chin as if to mark a change of direction.

"The slaves around here used to play music together once a week in one of the bigger cabins," she said, as if he'd never told her about his life before they'd met. "When I was a child, my nurse took me to hear them all the time." Corey could feel himself start to pay attention to what she was saying rather than what she looked like. Suddenly he wasn't afraid to let her see she had his interest.

"My father told me how decimated the plantations were after the war," Corey said, "but they don't look nearly as bad as I expected." Marcy nodded.

"We didn't have as many big plantations as they had in the Confederate states, which is why we also had fewer slaves. But the wealthiest Virginians, like the Washingtons and Shephers, moved here generations ago and just re-created what they'd had in Virginia, so while there was less obvious destruction, I believe that was because there was less to ruin." Corey watched his hostess carefully, suddenly aware of a slight uneasiness as she spoke of the war. "The Negroes helped put many of the homes back together and restored the land to some semblance of its former order." Her smile spread easily, as if there'd never been any upset in her narrative.

"Really? That can't have been a pleasant task: helping the people who exploited them," Corey said, aware he was working to keep the conversation focused on anything but himself. He noticed he was doing better at holding off Marcy's taunts.

"Oh, I think they've always considered the land partly theirs because of all the work they put in on it, and I know they didn't want to see the only homes they'd ever known in ruin. Like many of our neighbors, we used to rent our slaves to owners farther south to work bigger plantations, but we never sold them or let them go. We also felt they were part of the land up here." Corey looked slightly pained, a small frown clouding his eyes as he watched Marcy talk, but he said nothing. The silence spread a little further than Marcy was apparently comfortable with, so she started to draw a small circle with the toe of her delicate boot. "They've also started to organize and run social events for each other," she went on, "so they have dances and even sometimes give lessons on the fiddle and upright. And sometimes," she continued when Corey said nothing, "they even show off on instruments they brought from Africa."

"Some kind of drums?" Corey asked, leaning forward a little. He was fighting the impulse to jump up from his seat and move off. Marcy smiled easily, coming up the last three steps and sitting down in the empty wicker chair next to his, making his escape less likely.

"Yes!" she announced breathlessly, seemingly excited to have him holding up his end of the conversation at last. "It's round and has strings stretched across the hide of the drum, and when the strings are plucked, they resonate in the most unusual way. I really can't describe it. You'd have to hear it to understand. It's called a banjo."

"I know the sound," Corey interrupted, a small smile pulling at the corners of his mouth as he remembered the marvelous syncopation of the banjos he'd heard in the bars and honky-tonks throughout the South. He liked to think of it as a tool of rebellion.

"Well, I go mostly just to hear that," she said, obviously delighted to have Corey engaged at last and sitting so near without running away. "It always feels to me as if the banjo carries all the others like a cantering colt. I know you've heard a lot of folk music from Europe, as you told us at dinner last week, but this is folk music from America! You'd love it."

He smiled at her with a relaxed grin she hadn't seen since he'd first introduced himself back at the Grand Central Hotel. He realized she would probably misinterpret it as a warming of his attitude toward her, when he was sure it was only the pleasure of learning he could hear skilled banjo players perform nearby. But he'd begun to feel as if he was getting his bearings and stopped caring what she thought of him. The idea of a roomful of musicians had brought him down to earth.

"Perhaps you're right," he said, thoughtfully. "I'm used to such a different kind of musical partnership, although there are similarities. The interaction, the camaraderie . . . I think it's important to join in music that's totally unfamiliar. Maybe that's the only way we really hear each other and ourselves. We need a new environment to make us sit up and take notice." Marcy Bond looked with wonder and perhaps a little too much admiration at him, as if she couldn't believe the torrent of words and ideas now coming from her formerly silent companion. She was clearly happy about the way his eyes and face lit up when she talked about music. But she only paused for a moment, then leapt up from her chair, alight with obvious pleasure and dynamic physical tension.

"Let's go, then," she cried, "but you might want to leave your jacket. It's a little formal for the venue and I think you'll be too hot once the dancing starts." Also pausing only momentarily, he pushed up out of his chair, dropping his book and taking off his jacket to dump it on the seat behind him. He started rolling up the sleeves of his white shirt, his long and unusually strong forearms, formed by a lifetime of practice on the piano, now exposed to the clearly appreciative view of his young hostess. "That's better," Marcy said, smiling with a nod of approval. "Now, let's go. We have quite an evening ahead of us."

⁕⟡⟡⟡⁕

Following his enticing southern guide, Corey found himself drawn to a well-worn path through the trees, twisting through ferns and tiny wild yellow orchids peeking up between the rocks. The trail had clearly been formed over years of human use leading somewhere people wanted to go. He had trouble keeping up with Marcy's sure-footed guidance, but his long legs made up for what his coordination lacked. His nerves were still attacking him, but somewhat reassured by the clarity of the path's direction, he repeated the mantra in his head that he could always stop and return to the plantation if he wanted to. He was sure he could find his own way back.

Suddenly and without warning, the trees separated in front of them, and one more step took them from forest to clearing. Corey straightened up, happy to catch his breath but a little off balance with the change in topography and light. It seemed to herald a new phase of their adventure, perhaps making his flight more difficult.

"Well, here we are," Marcy announced, her copper-colored curls escaping from the ribbon tying them out of her face in a most appealing way. "Almost; we're not quite where we're going to end up yet."

Corey was a little out of breath from either the mountain goat run he'd made following his hostess, or the nerves in his stomach, or both. "Where are we?" he asked, standing beside Marcy now as she looked out over the clearing in front of them and the group of small, neat cabins encircling the grass with an open gazebo in the middle. A smile spread up at the corners of his mouth as he brushed his ever-unruly hair out of his eyes. "One could almost believe we've come upon a fairy ring," he muttered under his breath.

"They're some of the old slave quarters," Marcy said, looking around the circle of neat white bungalows with the same pleasure he had. "You can see there aren't very many, but we've renovated them since the war, updated and, in some cases, added onto them, so the Negroes who stayed to work for us could have better living conditions. There actually used to be more of them, but with the drop in our already small former slave population it seemed to make sense to get rid of the ones we didn't need. They were just a reminder of times we'd rather forget." She reached up to tuck some of her recalcitrant curls under the ribbon meant to control them.

"Times we'd all rather forget," Corey said, watching her attempts at taming her hair with more consideration than he probably should have, or that was required by the distraction.

"It's a difficult situation," she said, looking at him pointedly.

"Why? Surely one can live with the discomfort of guilt without missing out on the joys of life as they come along." Looking at her standing next to him now he wondered how he'd gone so long in his life without meeting someone like her, a concentrated energy directed fully and singularly at him for his sole attention and pleasure. This was very different from the challenging spirit Emily had leveled at him from the age of thirteen, and he realized it was rather nice not to have to work so hard for her interest.

"Those who sided with the confederacy in West Virginia, like my family, have been barred from voting until now; second-class citizens, you might say," she added, taking a step back until she stood beside him. "Reconstruction has turned out to be about more than rebuilding a way of life," she said, gazing very far away over the cabins to somewhere else. "It seems we all need a lot of help putting ourselves back together." She looked sad for the first time since he'd met her.

He began to feel a sympathy for her he'd have not thought possible a few days before. "It's hard to tell how much pain lives inside each one of us until you go way below the surface," she said, dropping her eyes as if turning her own gaze inward, and then leaning lightly against his arm and glancing up into his eyes without letting him go. Finally, he nodded, as much to break her hold on him as to be compassionate. There was no doubt he was feeling a great deal of emotion as she rested lightly against him for sympathy, but he knew full well it was up to him to decide what support he might offer.

"I know," he said, quietly. "Repairing social fabric is much harder than renovating cabins." He looked up at the clearing again. "Are we going over there? Is this our destination?" People were beginning to walk around the meadow now, some sitting on benches at the edges of the grass and a few others moving into the gazebo with musical instruments. One family with four children started to spread a quilt out on the lawn. "Is this where the concert's going to be?" He started forward ahead of Marcy without thinking of what he was doing or waiting for her affirmation.

"Yes, it looks that way," she nodded. "Though it's usually inside the Negro emporium this time of year," she called from behind. "I guess it's so warm for fall they decided it would be more fun outside. West Virginia's a strange mix of hot and cold, thanks to the split personality of the Ohio River. But we're always looking for ways to enjoy the warmth while it lasts. It seems I may have led you astray," she said, cheerfully. "You could have used your jacket after all."

Corey stopped and turned to look at her. "I hope that's all you've led me astray about," he said, a slight narrowing of his eyes the only indication that he might be serious. Marcy ignored the warning and pushed past him with a jump over a stone in the way. She lost her balance on landing in her soft leather slippers and wobbled against the loose rock, threatening an unhappy outcome. She reached out for him and Corey caught her before her delicate ankle gave up its support. He looked at her while he held her, knowing full well her accident had most likely been planned, and not caring. "That would have been a bad start to a potentially happy evening," he said, still holding on to her. He realized he'd reached a point of needing to find out more about what lay inside her beautiful skin, as well.

Putting weight on her foot to test the ankle's resilience, Marcy attempted to tuck in her white shirtwaist that hadn't actually come out in her hike or fall, giving Corey plenty of time to watch her close up, marveling at her ability to envelop his senses in a most intoxicating way, even though he appreciated that she was also proud of her artifice. It was a game of seduction she'd obviously practiced often and knew she excelled at, and he found he was happy she did.

"Shall we go?" she asked, as if it had been Corey delaying their progress toward the clearing and impending concert, instead of her.

"After you," he answered, watching her move forward. "Don't let me slow you down," he added, following with his eyes as she headed for one of the benches at the edge of the bushes nearest the gazebo. He started after her toward the musicians, suddenly feeling more at home than he had in weeks. Understanding her unwritten language made him feel newly confident, aware that she'd targeted him as her prey for a reason: because she wanted him; which he found agreeably flattering.

She was already seated alone when he caught up, accepting a cup of fermented peach juice offered by a young man passing a tray of drinks. She put it on the bench by her side. Obviously too early for most of the audience to arrive, the musicians were just beginning to gather and unpack their instruments. Corey could hardly resist going into the gazebo with them, but reminding himself that this was not his performance, he sat down next to Marcy and her drink, close enough to talk but leaving enough space not to appear too familiar or allow her to infringe on his enjoyment of the performance. Even she had to take a lesser position to the music. More and more, he was beginning to feel as if he was setting his feet back on his own ground. "Who organized these concerts?" he asked, unable to take his eyes off the musicians as they smiled and chatted with each other, some already tuning their instruments, and others searching for wayward accessories like picks and bows.

"They're really not *concerts*," Marcy said, her voice bringing him back to the present role he played as an audience member. "The slaves have come together informally as long as anyone can remember to share music, stories really, passed from one to another; and dances. After the war, they started calling them *socials*." She smiled and nodded at a few of the couples passing by, taking on the mantle of a charming hostess. "There are town proctors who are meant to keep them organized and watch over their behavior, although that's just to make some of the uncomfortable white folks happy. The Negroes don't need proctors to socialize!" She looked over at the gazebo, sitting up straighter to wave at a white-haired man unpacking an instrument Corey recognized as a banjo.

"That's Old Black Charlie," she said, eyes dancing as they had when she'd first invited Corey on the veranda to join her. "He's my favorite. He almost brought me up because I spent so much time sitting at his feet. Just wait until he gets his fingers flying on those strings!" She rocked a little on her seat in anticipation. "You won't believe what you see and hear!"

Focusing first on Charlie with his muted red neck scarf and deep blue cotton shirt, Corey turned to face the slowly expanding group in the gazebo. Each one stroked his instrument in a playful, intimate way, as if getting reacquainted with it while connecting with his fellow musicians at the same time. A cheerful banter flowed naturally between them, carrying the camaraderie with jokes and comments shared only by their happy group. Corey knew well how important the release of pre-performance nerves was but wondered if this seemingly casual and disjointed band of players could come together musically in a way that would carry the audience with them. He recognized the ritual, but this one was so different from the onstage preparations an orchestra or even chamber music group would practice. He admitted to doubts about Marcy's ragtag performers warming up now to do *something*; he wasn't sure what.

Glancing quickly around the square as a young mulatto woman bent to light candles in the lanterns, he realized the audience had been expanding continuously and now started to spill out beyond the benches to the tree line. Excitement in the air was building, and the flickering lanterns gave the scene a feel of firefly magic in the trees; a romantic atmosphere enhancing Corey's sense of illusoriness. He was uniquely tuned to the tremor that went through an audience just before the conductor breezed through the silent, seated musicians awaiting his arrival in an orchestra pit; but this was nothing like that.

Everything about his own training perpetuated the European myth that musical royalty and its appreciative subjects must remain separate to foster the required respect. But these men purposely presented a kind of egalitarian connection to their audience that fascinated him. The sense of closeness they fostered seemed to join an electric current running from themselves throughout the varied crowd. Could they possibly produce anything of worth, musically speaking, with such a devil-may-care boldness?

Suddenly, as if his thoughts had been amplified and shared with everyone, he heard the banjo gather itself together, gain momentum, and start to move into a rollicking theme he was unfamiliar with. He recognized the *clawhammer* technique he'd seen before on other trips down south. Charlie moved his thumb and forefinger or middle finger in a down-picking motion, producing a powerful rhythm. He knew some players had discarded this technique, using a finger-picking reminding him of the way acoustic guitars were played. But who knew what would happen next? Lifted and collected by the banjo's merriment, the other instruments began to speak up as well, with the fiddle taking the first step forward in a way that made the refrains of the music sing out clear and strong accompanying the banjo's tuning. Corey could tell Charlie's instrument was modified to the mandolin and fiddle. He liked the way these men adjusted their instruments in different ways, making the players and audience listen differently, too. Joining in a rolling participation that seemed both carefully planned and entirely free at the same time, the guitar, harmonica, and small African drum began to play with Charlie's motif until everyone supported different parts of the same music with a joy and expressiveness Corey thought he'd never heard before.

"It's so different now that they're all free men," Marcy whispered in his ear. He jumped at the feel of her breath, having forgotten her there beside him in the excitement of the opening notes. He left his head close to her lips, delighting in the presence of her warmth.

"Different how?" he asked, looking straight ahead, and wondering if she'd noticed his reaction to her closeness. The musicians were winding down their short first number and latecomers rustled around on the grass trying to settle down for the next piece. Smiles spread throughout the audience, which seemed to have an invisible bond with the men and their instruments in the gazebo. Corey finally turned toward Marcy, their faces just inches apart.

"They're just freer," she whispered. "I think the duty of carrying the slave community's hope for survival weighed them down. Now they perform for sheer pleasure," she said, never moving away. He pulled back slowly, still unable to take his eyes off her lips.

"Sheer pleasure . . . ," he repeated. "I never thought about performing music as a mission of mercy, or of how freedom would affect the playing. But why would I?" he mused, softly. "I've always been utterly at liberty to do anything I want. Or have I?" He ran his tongue over his lower lip, leaning down to reach for the cup of the fermented peach juice. He took a slow sip, swallowing only after letting the warm, sweet liquor roll around on his tongue. He put the cup back on the bench, thinking he'd never tasted anything as strong that was still as soft and pleasing, much like the southern woman sitting beside him now. He could tell he was sinking into the inebriation of his drink and his hostess.

Suddenly he sprang from the bench, gesturing to a young Negro mother with two small children clinging to her skirts, and holding a baby. "Please, take my seat," he called to her. "I need to stand closer to the gazebo." He smiled and bowed his head slightly, stepping over beside her and motioning to his empty place on the bench again. She looked doubtful, but he nodded and smiled, and she finally thanked him and moved to sit with one child on each side and the baby on her lap. Marcy had already gotten up herself, ostensibly to make more room. She and Corey wove their way around the edge of the now packed lawn, careful to avoid stepping on any outspread tablecloths or blankets. But instead of stopping just short of the front line of the onlookers, Marcy continued to the gazebo.

"Hey there, Miss Marcy," Charlie called, rubbing his banjo strings lightly as if to retain a necessary contact before the next song.

"Hello, Charlie," she said, flashing the elderly Negro one of her beautiful smiles. "Y'all sound great tonight, but where's Pickin' Pete?" Corey grinned as if he'd been in on the conversation from the start. He wanted to be a part of their family.

"They have a banjo picker," he said, nodding at Charlie. "Why would they need another?" Marcy looked confused for a moment, then laughed her light tinkling sound.

"No, he's not called Pickin' Pete because of his expertise with a banjo. He plays the piano. The Pickin's for his skill in the cotton fields. He was our most popular hire for other plantation owners further south." The skinny elderly harmonica player nodded vigorously.

Charlie shrugged and smiled at the other men, raising his bushy white eyebrows in the direction of the empty piano. "No idea where he is now," he chuckled, "though if I had to guess, I'd say drinkin' whiskey at a bar somewhere. We'll do fine. Just have to leave out the rags," he added.

"Oh no, Charlie. Everyone here's counting on dancing, and the rags are the best for that!"

"We'll make up for it some other way," one of the men chimed in. They all seemed very comfortable having a relaxed conversation with Corey's gorgeous hostess, something he himself had not yet mastered.

"Charlie, my friend Corey here is a pianist from up north. I'm sure he could help with the rags. He says he's been learning some of them during his travels. Could he play with you?" She turned to Corey with a wink of her almond-shaped eye, and then back to fix Charlie with her most dazzling smile.

"Love to have the help. C'mon over here, young man," Charlie drawled. "Any friend of Miss Marcy is a friend of ours."

"I couldn't possibly," Corey said, eyes wide with shock and surprise he had no intention of hiding. "I'd only get in your way. I know none of the music you're playing, but I love it."

"That's all that matters," Charlie chuckled. "Loving it's the price of entry! Join us, young Corey. You can listen to the themes in the next piece first and then just come in with us when you feel good. C'mon, now," he said, tossing his white head in the direction of the upright piano standing behind them. "We need all the help we can get." And at that, he started plucking the strings of the banjo, nodding at the guitarist and Corey at the same time. Without knowing exactly how it happened, Corey found himself stepping into the gazebo and starting over to sit on the empty piano bench. He thought he'd felt a shove from behind, possibly from Marcy before she stepped back to the line of listeners, but he couldn't be sure.

What followed was to be the most unusual experience Corey had ever had at the piano. He did exactly as Charlie suggested, sitting still at first to listen to the instruments come in one by one. Then they held their own individual themes as they joined together in a marvelous brew of intoxicating sound and rhythm. Suddenly, he felt as if they were calling him, especially the fiddle with its clear, predominant line so easy to pick up. He jumped in and let his fingers fly, loose and relaxed like the sounds all around him. It felt like a ride through the clouds if such a thing were possible. Dripping perspiration partway through one of the next pieces, he wiped his forehead with his rolled-up sleeve, noting how glad he was not to have a jacket on. The musicians were all grinning at him from ear to ear, and he grinned back, tossing his hair out of his eyes and laughing softly.

There seemed no pauses anymore between the pieces, momentum building to the first rag they seemed eager to try without Pickin' Pete. Charlie started the melody, strumming slowly and clearly, and Corey realized he recognized it from one of his trips to Virginia. He hadn't considered that the music might be circulating more now that the musicians were free to live and travel where they pleased. Enormously grateful for the chance to join them all at last as a full collaborator instead of a struggling follower, Corey let his upper hand play the melody loud and clear, while his left hand started to beat out the syncopated rhythm he loved so well. Charlie bowed his head to him, and the others all picked up the faster beat Corey was accelerating with his right hand again.

Able to relax better riding the wave of a melody Corey finally knew, he looked out at the early evening congregants on the green, watching the moving concentric circles of dancers holding hands and swaying back and forth. He could see Marcy moving with small swings of her hips as she accentuated the beat of the music where she stood. She caught his eyes with hers and held them as long as he'd let her, but he broke away so he could look from one musician to the next while they each moved together and apart, much like the dancers. He had no idea how long they'd all been playing or how he knew when they were done, but the language they spoke together was completely clear to him. Finally, they all smiled at each other and let their hands drop to their sides. The audience hooted and clapped, but he could hardly hear the sound they made as he watched them jumping to their feet, crying out and waving to the musicians in the gazebo. He got up slowly, bowing with the other musicians repeatedly and finally searching with his eyes for Marcy at the front of the audience.

He couldn't imagine a more rewarding way to entertain, and wondered why it was so foreign to him, even with all his years of training in his own home and practice at school and later with his wife. For some reason he didn't analyze, thinking of Emily and their time together in lessons, on stage in concert halls, or simply practicing for future performances raised no discomfort or feeling of any kind. They were all just facts of his everyday existence. But from somewhere seemingly far off, he heard Marcy saying, "Why didn't you tell me you were such a star, Corey? You were wonderful! You can't be appreciated fully back home, or else you'd be prouder of your accomplishments." He looked at her standing next to Charlie as he packed up his banjo, an air of happy exhaustion permeating everything around the gazebo. She was responsible for bringing him here, exposing him to these men and this music, and, most importantly, to himself. It was time for him to let her know he understood what she'd given him.

"Thanks, Corey. You were indeed just what we needed," Charlie was saying. "I hope you'll take some of our music with you when you head back home. Miss Marcy," he said, hugging her and kissing her copper curls now plastered in wild profusion to her forehead in the heat of the dancing that had brought them there in the first place, "are you able to find your way to the plantation now that it's dark, or would you want us to take you with a lantern?"

Marcy shook her head. "Thanks to you all." She smiled and nodded in the direction of the group of men packing up their instruments. "But I brought Corey over on the path, and I think we can find our way back, even in the dark." She took hold of Corey's hand and said, "We'll just hold on to each other and I'm sure we'll be fine." She turned to leave, and Corey followed without hesitation.

Charlie nodded. "I'm sure *you* will be," he said, smiling as he watched them walk toward the path in the woods. "But will *he*?" The musicians nodded and smiled back in unison.

⁕⸻⁂⸻⁕

A cool far-off mist had settled over the small valley at some point in the night. It hugged the hills like gray velvet, a beautiful fabric clinging to the shape of its wearer and softening the outlines of peaks in the distance. Corey and Klaas sat together in silence at the Widow Stovall's breakfast table. The father seemed mesmerized by the quiet beauty of the scene beyond their curved bay window, fingering the delicate Limoges handle of his teacup distractedly as it sat in front of him. The son sipped from his cup, apparently focusing with severe intensity on some inner turmoil demanding his attention.

Klaas moved in his seat, bringing his thoughts back to the breakfast he was sharing with Corey, if in fact he'd ever really been away from it at all. Corey had felt his father's scrutiny from the moment he'd sat down at the table even though their eyes barely met long enough to say "good morning."

"I received a letter from home yesterday," Klaas said, reaching inside his waistcoat and bringing out a white envelope. "It was addressed to both of us, as you'll see there . . ." He put it gently on the table between them and picked up his cup. "You were off with Miss Bond at the time it was delivered, so I opened it for us. You should read it, now that you're back."

"Really. What does it say?" Corey asked, eyeing the letter sideways.

"Pick it up. It won't bite, you know," Klaas said, with a small, mirthless laugh. He took a sip from his cup and let the silence between them expand before he put the cup down and started to speak again. "It's from Emily. It says there's much preparation necessary before the performance in Chicago you both agreed to do for the inauguration of the new concert hall. She feels too pressed because the time is getting short and she doesn't know when we'll return, so she commandeered Robert Haussmann to work with her and fill the role of accompanist." He paused, clearly watching for a reaction from Corey, which didn't come.

"They leave for Chicago together soon," he went on, "traveling to arrive before rehearsals in the music hall." Klaas put down his cup carefully, resting his hand with the fine bones and long, delicate fingers on the tablecloth. He watched Corey with a penetrating quietness. "I have a responsibility for keeping you away so long." Klaas shifted uncomfortably in his chair, looking away and through the dining room for the first time since he'd started speaking. He nudged the letter closer to Corey, who reached out at last to take it, tucking it inside his own jacket without looking at it. "The children need you; your work needs you; and Emily obviously needs you most of all. The fault is mine," said Klaas. "It was selfish of me to ask you to stay for this extended period away from home. The time has come for our departure; in fact, it's almost past. I'll let our hostesses know this morning and we'll make arrangements to get back to New York."

"We can't possibly get home before they leave for Chicago," Corey said, sounding like a recalcitrant child. "And you've been having such a good time here, I think you should have more opportunities to enjoy the Widow Stovall's hospitality."

"Perhaps we can't get home before they go," Klaas answered, with more strength than Corey had heard in his voice for a long time. "But if not, we'll be there for the children and staff left behind. They're more than enough reason to get back as quickly as possible."

"What's that you're saying?" Mrs. Stovall had entered the room unnoticed behind Klaas's chair. "Oh, please say I heard you mistakenly!" she intoned. "It would break my heart to lose the company of you two gentlemen when we've only just introduced you to our West Virginian way of life. Must you really go so soon?" She brushed the back of Klaas's jacket as she passed his chair, and he looked up at her, a warm appreciation showing clearly on his face that he made no effort to restrain.

"Indeed we must, madame," Klaas said. "But that doesn't diminish the pleasure we've had thanks entirely to your hospitality. I hope we can return the favor someday." He smiled warmly at her, clearly speaking out of conviction rather than courtesy.

"But sir . . . ," the widow began as she slipped into the chair next to Klaas's with a rustle of wide skirts and a whiff of tastefully applied perfume.

". . . no buts," Klaas responded quickly, allowing no space for disagreement. "We have much to attend to at home and we must be on our way, alas."

The widow seemed greatly disappointed yet was clearly too polite to argue when a gentleman had made up his mind. "Good heavens," she exclaimed, rising slightly in her chair to look through the dining room opening to the front hall, "I can't imagine why Marcy is sleeping so late this morning. I'll have the maid alert her to your early departure so she can be sure to see you off with me. I know she's quite taken with your son's friendship," she smiled at Corey, "and it's been a long time since she's had anyone . . . any young men her own age around." Klaas raised one eyebrow and looked at Corey over his own teacup.

The widow rang a small brass bell at her place, turning to speak with the maid when she came in. Having smoothly accepted her fresh orange juice, tea, and toast, she started to eat her breakfast calmly, as if business as usual was the only possible option after Klaas's surprising announcement. "Indeed, you will both be missed, gentlemen," she added, a bright smile lighting her face as she looked from one to the other. Corey's mouth turned up slightly and he bowed his head, but Klaas sat back in his chair and took a breath.

"Actually, there is a question I have," he said, looking from Corey to the widow and back again. "Are there any bears in West Virginia? I thought I might have seen a couple early this morning."

Sarah Stovall gasped, putting her teacup down too quickly. "Oh my, yes, indeed there are," she exclaimed, "but I do hope you're wrong about seeing them. They aren't usually brazen enough anymore to come around humans. Are you sure? Where were they?" She looked quite worried, and Corey eyed his father with a raised eyebrow of his own. Something about the tone of Klaas's voice made him worry as well, but undoubtedly for a different reason than Mrs. Stovall.

Klaas looked directly at Corey as he said, "The animals were right here on your veranda, madame. I'd gotten up early to enjoy the day just before dawn, as I often do, and came out to look to the horizon where the light begins to glow at the top of the hills. Suddenly, I saw two big bears in the dark on the veranda, hugging each other, or something to that effect."

"Good heavens!" the widow exclaimed again, her eyes opening wide. "It sounds as if they were in a fight of some kind."

"I think not," Klaas said slowly, seemingly considering her suggestion with great care. "The embrace looked more amorous than antagonistic. But either way, it's time for us city folk to get back to the safety of New York where there are no bears to wrestle with. Don't you agree, Corey?" The silence was so loud Corey could hear it ringing in his ears.

"I'm not sure I do," he said, finally, holding his father's eyes with his. "Being here has reminded me that we have to get out of our own well-worn, comfortable cycle of life. But now, madame," he said, turning to the Widow Stovall, "I must excuse myself to pack for our departure. I came early to breakfast, so now need to get organized for our trip home." He stood, nodding his head slightly to no one in particular, and turned to leave the dining room.

"I do hope you're not too worried about the bears, sir," the Widow Stovall said as she inclined toward Klaas. "I wouldn't want anything to mar your memories of this time we've had together, and I assure you we're quite safe here."

"Oh I'm sure you are, as well; quite safe," Klaas exclaimed, dabbing his mouth with his napkin and then folding it before placing it carefully by his teacup. "But I'm not so sure my son is," he added. "And like most parents, I will do anything to keep him out of harm's way."

CHAPTER SIX

THE STAIRCASE IN THE DE KONINGH MANSION curved out of sight with a seductive invitation to follow. Rising from the entry hall to the first-floor landing with a fluid grace surprising in something so large in its mantle of creamy Maryland marble, the stairs' languorous turns were carved all in one piece. No seams disturbed its pristine surface. Imagine the surprise to guests in the mansion's early days! Visiting Europeans must have been amazed that the young heathen land had the natural resources and skills to sculpt such a work of art. Weaving intricate patterns of wreathes connected by festoons or family crests of some kind, the wrought-iron baluster offered enough contrast to assure balance. Its broad mahogany handrail ended in a gently curled newel, perfect for a delightful slide from top to bottom. It was an enticement the de Koningh children and their friends had been unable to pass up over the years. Riding the wave of the rail to the shore of the entrance hall floor had been a favorite pastime for young Corey and Emily, as well.

Now little Connie de Koningh peered through the iron scroll-work of the banister unseen. A sweep of polished stone at the top concealed the first landing from those entering at street level; designed for privacy, it also forced someone on the stairs down a few risers if a clear view of the front door was the goal. Connie had learned to sit on the penultimate step to spy on arriving guests. His older brother William jeered that he was mistaken if he thought he was hidden, but Connie knew dinner guests were too distracted to look up as they removed coats and hats and prepared to be received by their hosts. He sat with his knees tucked up under his chin, flannel pajamas and soft-soled leather slippers branding him an after-bedtime escapee. Wrapping his arms under his thighs so not even a stray finger would show through the grillwork, he narrowed his big brown eyes to focus clearly on the expected arrivals.

His mother passed through the entrance hall on her way to check the library before her friends arrived for dinner. She seldom entertained when his father was away, but this time Corey's absence had been so prolonged she felt the need to connect in particular with other artists. Emily was lonely, and she thought it might be affecting her health. Was estrangement strictly a female condition? Her husband didn't seem to suffer from the same malady, or at least his few letters home didn't indicate so.

Their scheduled performance in Chicago loomed closer by the day, but Emily decided there was nothing to be gained from putting off dinner with her friends any longer; travel and performances would only make getting together less likely in the near future. A dinner with like-minded adults was just the stimulus she needed. Loving them dearly, she had nonetheless grown tired of her sons' childish chatter of late. It made her wonder if she was fashioned to be a mother at all. Her secret suspicion was—probably not. After all, she'd had no mother of her own to learn the skills from, but that's why it was so important for her to do what she was best at once in a while to feel less a failure. What a fine line it was, almost translucent, between satisfying her natural instincts to nurture her children fully and preserve something of herself just for her own sanity.

She stopped across from the staircase to check the tall case clock standing in the shell alcove, smiling as she remembered Robert's Austrian horologist friend who'd brought it to her. Insisting it was "the clock of the grand*mother*" when he'd installed it in the alcove, Herr Kronenberger explained it had a distinctly feminine personality and delicacy, so must not be referred to as a *grandfather* clock. Emily had been surprised to find only one of those in the de Koningh house when she'd first moved in at the age of thirteen. Every landing in her father's home in London had had its own clock. She'd always felt the big timepieces produced a deeply grounding effect. Like a healthy heartbeat, they'd given her a sense of dependability, and she'd missed the rhythm of their weights in the de Koningh home and said so . . . often.

No one had taken her longing for the familiar seriously except Robert, who'd eventually surprised her with this gift of a clock of the grand*mother* on the birth of her first son, William, who was fascinated with the sound of the old bell striking the hour and mesmerized by the shining brass pendulum swinging back and forth. Emily took secret delight in the fact that it was the female of the clock family that was keeping an eye on her and her children, since there were no other women in the household. Although it wasn't really in scale with the rest of the entrance hall—not imposing or grand enough, neither formal nor big enough to be of note to important guests—it soothed and pleased her as it kept its steady vigil.

Tonight she noted the clock was a little slow, but that was the fault of whoever had set it, and easily remedied. She reached up to open the wood-framed glass protecting the face. Slightly above her head, even if it wasn't as big as its male counterpart, she could see a biased view of herself reflected in the brass of the clock face behind it. Her new performance dress with its beetle-wing sleeves off her shoulders, low scooped neckline, and Empire waist cut a fetching silhouette as she raised her arms to change the one and only hand of the clock just short of seven. She smiled at the ease of movement the dress's style provided, and pushed one of the sleeves a little farther off her shoulder. Pleased with what she saw of her always shapely neck reflected in the clock face, she pushed the other sleeve lower as well and paused, distracted by the glow of light reflected from a blond head of curls at the top of the stairs behind her. She could see the last step before it reached the upper landing and her youngest son doubled up to rest his head on his knees. She almost turned to frown at him, but stopped herself in time to allow him the joy of ignoring a bedtime rule without censure. Breaking the rules now and then was an important part of living.

Pushing the glass front closed gently, she turned the small, old key to secure the frame in place. There were many little rituals associated with winding the clock, all of them pleasantly reassuring. She looked back up at the graceful hour hand hovering just before seven. These simple country clocks were designed without fanfare. No need for a minute hand on the farm. But the tide of human events could get just as mangled between the minutes as the hours, days, weeks, and years. What was the movement of time other than a human construct anyway? Was one hand less complicated than two? It all depended on what went on in your head and heart.

She looked back once more at her reflection in the clock window. It didn't even mark her changes over time. Bells had originally been rung to call people and priests together for community prayer or social alliance. That was their purpose. This one would call her friends together for dinner. She stepped away toward the library in hopes of avoiding the sound of the clock striking the hour so close. She knew its old misshapen bell's clang could be disturbingly dissonant, depending on one's mood, and didn't want it to jar her well-being, too tenuous these days to put at risk just before her first dinner party in months. She slipped silently into the library to enjoy the quiet before the gathering began.

"What do you think you're doing?" William whispered over his brother's head. "You were supposed to be in bed an hour ago." The sarcastic, accusatory tone said the answer to his question was not in doubt.

"Want to know who's coming for dinner," Connie muttered into his kneecap, hoping William hadn't seen the involuntary twitch of shock at his voice.

"Ask me," William said.

"Wanted to see myself," Connie mumbled against his leg again, without looking at William. Why his brother always pretended to know everything was a mystery and huge annoyance to the little boy. Was it a requisite of being older, or just of being William?

"Why? You don't know any of them except Professor Haussmann," William said, with a sneer that made Connie shiver, as much for its rising intensity as its tone. He doubted William would want to attract attention to himself before one of his mother's dinner parties, but you could never be sure. Possibly the pleasure of getting Connie in trouble would be enough motivation for his big brother to risk exposure.

Connie lifted his head, turning back slightly toward William to send his voice away from the staircase, but keeping his eyes focused on the front door below. "Want to see how they're dressed, not who they are," he said, in a low, emphatic whisper just as the doorbell rang. Edward, the footman, moved softly across the marble foyer below them to open it.

"That's the man we saw in the park the day I got my knee stuck, isn't it?" Connie asked, lifting up a little with excitement. "See how straight he stands with his shoulders back and his head up. It makes his clothes look fine—the way he stands, I mean."

"Yes, that's Mr. Mackay, *the silver king*," William whispered as he slipped down on a step near to his brother, a little too loud for Connie's comfort. William had to sit three steps below to see clearly through the baluster.

"He was a boxer once, I think, before he found all that money. I wonder why he dresses so simply when he could afford diamonds instead of buttons," William went on.

"I like the way he looks," Connie whispered. "Shhh . . . someone's coming in."

"That's Mr. Dunne, one of mother's friends; an editor at the *Times*. He looks young, but he can't be. Mother's known him since before she was married. I wonder why she has only men friends. I've asked her but she doesn't say." William's tone was unusually conversational. Connie was unsettled by it, accustomed as he was to being held at arm's length by his brother, like a specimen worthy only of prodding or torture. But he was also upset by the inference that there was something wrong with his mother's friends, so since she wasn't there to speak for herself, he did.

"She doesn't," Connie hissed back at William. "Bessie's her friend, and there are lots of other ladies she knows from . . . other places, too," he added. "But there aren't many lady musicians, and I don't think she finds the others very much fun."

"Bessie works for her. She can't be a friend, dummy. And friends aren't for fun, anyway. They're to help you belong and get ahead. You really don't know anything, do you?" William looked at his brother and shook his head with a snort of disgust. "I have friends from school, like the Stuyvesant brothers, and you have a friend or two from other families we know, like Theo and his little sister Edith. But Edward and Bessie can't be your friends," William said, nodding toward the footman in the hall below them.

Connie said nothing and kept his eyes on the door. Suddenly he lifted his chin off his knees and took a long breath. A man in a silk top hat with a brocade waistcoat showing under a black velvet cape had just stepped into the hall. The cape undulated behind him like a midnight sea. An elegant lady swept in on his arm. She rustled with a promise of rich fabric, a green satin skirt peeking out under her gray velvet cape lined with scarlet silk.

"That's Monsieur Offenbach. He's a composer," William announced. "I met him at the opera with Mother and Professor Haussmann. They were friends in Paris years ago when Mother was studying with the professor there. And that must be the opera singer Mother said he was bringing with him, but she doesn't look much like a painted woman of the stage, does she?"

"If she's an opera singer, she's not an actress," Connie muttered. "She's a musician."

William narrowed his eyes and shot the short, dark-haired woman on Monsieur Offenbach's arm a frigid look. "Mother says there's nothing wrong with being an actress, unless of course you want to be accepted in society. Then there's everything wrong with it."

"Mother wouldn't say that," Connie hissed. He'd forgotten the importance of his camouflage behind the iron curlicues.

"But she did. Or maybe just the part about nothing being wrong. I don't remember," William sighed, as if the boredom of the discussion had brought on a lethargy he was unable to resist.

"Oh look!" Connie breathed, grabbing his brother's arm. "Here comes Professor Haussmann. I've never seen him in dinner clothes, have you?"

"Of course." William exhaled with the full power of disdain he'd held back with such difficulty until then. "He always wears white tie to perform or to escort Mother to the theater. I suppose you've been asleep too early to see them go out together."

"He looks *fine*," Connie breathed.

"He should. It's a uniform for a performer so he'd better stand out in it."

"No, not like that. He looks as if he likes being dressed up." Connie wiggled a little and sat up even straighter, almost as if he expected to greet his music teacher. Then realizing what he'd done, he glanced at his brother to be sure he hadn't noticed and curled up in a tighter ball than ever. "I wish Father was here, too," he whispered.

"Don't worry. Professor Haussmann will take his place at the table," William assured him. "And Mother can handle the rest of the evening on her own. That's all the guests now." He nodded, pushing up and leaving as silently as he'd arrived twenty minutes before.

"That's not what I meant," Connie whispered to himself. "I just miss Father." He unwound his chubby frame from its cramped position and stepped slowly back on the top step to the landing. He'd suddenly lost interest in the dinner party, wanting to get away from it and his brother, too.

Glancing at his reflection in the clock face as he passed it, Robert Haussmann caught sight of the youngest de Koningh standing at the top of the stairs and flinched, unsure if he should deal with the disobedience that had brought the boy out of bed to spy on his mother's party. He was undoubtedly the only male authority figure in the child's life now. But Connie's disappearance beyond the landing and his likely retreat to bed saved Robert the decision.

"Robert, you're here too, and looking very distinguished, if I do say so; and I do!" He started a little, turning to be instantly caught by Emily's sparkling eyes and mischievous smile. "Come, do join us all in the library. Edward will bring your hat and walking stick in to sit beside you if you'd prefer. But we have plenty of human accessories to keep you company." He thought he saw a shadow cross her face but couldn't tell if he'd imagined it. Was she missing the de Koningh men as she stepped forward alone to play multiple roles on this home stage of her own making? She lifted her arm as if expecting his support and turned with a coquettish tilt of her head to reenter the library. He couldn't understand how she accelerated her moods so fast, exchanging one for another before he could catch up. But the mystery of Emily no longer upset him. He couldn't resist the invitation. Placing his hat and walking stick on the bench and losing his irritation at her teasing when she caught him looking at himself in the face of the clock, he lifted his right arm and offered it to her, feeling buoyant as she slipped her arm through his and smiled a warm welcome.

"We'll have fun tonight, Robert," she said, giving his arm an affectionate squeeze. "It's been too long since we've had a meeting of artistic minds in this house. By the way, do you know anything about Jacques Offenbach's leading-lady friend?" She stopped short before coming to the half-open door to the library to lower her voice. "I'm wondering about their relationship." She cocked her head to one side and looked Robert in the eye, raising one eyebrow in disconcertingly expressive emphasis.

"Emily, please behave tonight," he answered with a small sigh. "Your guests are all very accomplished and well-established professionals, to say nothing of their wealth and social status. They aren't used to being assaulted with impertinent questions." His tone of exasperation must have told her she'd shaken him, just as she'd intended.

"On the contrary, Robert!" Her dimples deepened as she lifted her voice and head simultaneously. "I think my guests thrive on inquisitive controversy. They all enjoy breaking the rules or they wouldn't be as creative and successful as they are. Isn't that so, Jacques?" She smiled at her notoriously nonconformist friend as she applied an almost imperceptible pressure through Robert's dinner jacket with her hand on his arm, propelling him forward and into the room involuntarily. He assumed no one noticed the startled look on his face, as they were all drawn to Emily's assured and implied welcome and saw only her sheen.

Jacques Offenbach turned to meet her with an impish grin of his own, bowing his head and reaching for her right hand. His long wavy hair brushed his shoulders in contrast to his receding hairline, and pince-nez balanced over the bridge of his nose added to his air of drama. Two deep lines curved around his mouth, seemingly cut from a lifetime of smiles, and in fact his long, thin face shone with an expression of perpetual humor, as if he lived with a private joke playing in his mind at all times. "I missed the point of your question, madame, as you were just entering when you made your comment. But whatever it was, I agree with you wholeheartedly. You've long been one of my favorite muses and I wouldn't consider contradicting you." He raised her hand to his lips as he bowed over it again.

"Then you disappoint me mightily, sir," Emily said to the top of his balding head. "I was counting on a good deal more stimulation tonight than can be offered by abject agreement." She could feel Robert shift uncomfortably under her left arm where she'd admittedly forgotten him.

"Edward!" She released both men and turned slightly to address the footman. "Would you please take everyone's drink requests and then let the cook know we'll be ready for dinner within the hour?" She moved away from the door to open the room to her footman, stopping next to Monsieur Offenbach's leading-lady friend. "We haven't met formally, madame, or is it mademoiselle?" she said. Having no idea if the lady was married or single, she'd assumed safety in the universal label for female opera singers of the greatest acclaim. "I look forward to hearing of your collaboration with my old friend Jacques. We can compare notes on his idiosyncrasies."

Offenbach's breath escaped in a short, explosive laugh, while Robert's face fell in an expression of *Oh Emily, will you never learn?* But he was surprised to see a look of affection on Monsieur Offenbach's face, as he joined his dinner partner's and Emily's hands together in both of his. "At last, my two favorite women together in the same place: Marie Garnier and Madame de Koningh."

"Are you sure you don't mean 'two of your many favorite women'?" Emily asked. "As I recall, all your operas feature your ladies—La belle Hélène, La Grande-Duchesse, La Périchole . . ."

"How could I not favor you all?" he answered, with a wink.

"A wise deferral, monsieur," his leading lady quipped. "The theater, and Grand Opera in particular, breed such adroit politicians. It's hard to believe they're not wasted on the stage when governments are so bereft of talent."

"Musicians are much too smart to be wasted on politics," Emily chuckled. Everyone nodded, except Robert, whose abstention wasn't noticed, obscured as he was behind his hostess.

⚜

"Wonderful dinner, my dear. The food was d-delicious and the company d-d-delightful," John Mackay stuttered slightly in his thick Irish brogue. Standing in the French doors leading to the library's garden, he stretched his lower back out a little with a hand buttressed on each hip. Taking a deep breath, he pulled the pungent outdoor aroma of fallen leaves all the way through his expansive boxer's chest to his toes. "Can't say when I've enjoyed a meal with an intimate group in a private home so much," he added, smiling a little as he exhaled slowly with obvious pleasure. "But then, I haven't eaten at a home with an intimate group in a long time," he admitted, to no one in particular.

"You live at the Windsor Hotel when you're here in New York, Mr. Mackay?" Emily knew his compliments about the dinner were meant for her ears.

"I do, Mrs. de Koningh. It's convenient but not very . . . ," he paused, ". . . f-familial," he finished, satisfied he'd found just the right word.

Emily noted how handsome and fit the blond, Celtic silver mine king looked as his features relaxed, maybe for the first time in a long while away from the challenges of his businesses. The newspapers were constantly filled with stories of his enterprises, so much so that they made her tired just to read about them. The thought that anyone could survive the pressures of that life seemed out of the question. "I'm so glad you found the setting tonight the right blend of domesticity and haute cuisine." Emily smiled with the intent to comfort. "But it seems to me you and I are in the same position, living so long apart from our spouses," she added unexpectedly. Mr. Mackay turned to look at her in some surprise. His expression suggested he no longer thought much about his chosen lifestyle, a necessity with a wife who had no interest in living in America with him even though she'd been born there.

"I suppose . . . quite the same," he agreed slowly. "I assume we're both people of strong will and commitment to our work. Without loosening any of our obligations to family, we nonetheless are driven to travel and live in disagreeable public places alone in order to fulfill our dreams for ourselves. I'd say you're correct: we are a very great deal alike." He pulled himself up even straighter to display his strong build with assurance, leaving no room for discussion. But Emily had learned to make room for herself where there was none.

"Maybe not, sir, but I think it a very different matter for a man to choose a singular professional path," she said, looking at him with the narrowed vision of close scrutiny. "You have no idea the penalty a woman pays for such a decision."

"We all pay for our choices," he responded without pause, "men as well as women. But in truth, that's why I find women who move in their own sphere so interesting. I'm drawn to bravery under all circumstances." His smile was so genuine, eyes so alight with the pleasure of adventure, that she hoped she was seeing her own sons as the men they might be in the future.

"Would you enjoy an after-dinner drink and cigar on the patio tonight?" she asked, taking John Mackay's arm and turning to include her other guests just arriving in the library from the dining room. "It's an unusually sultry evening for fall in New York," she added, with a smile in Robert's direction. She knew he'd be remembering the year they'd had snow in October, interrupting an outdoor concert for the neighborhood children who'd preferred to go sledding rather than listening to a Schumann Fantasie in the garden.

"I hardly think s-sultry d-describes an evening of such energy and promise," John Mackay exclaimed, with a laugh.

"Oh, I think it does, sir. There's something a little provocative in the air combined with wet leaves and warm temperatures," Emily said, her smile as open and genuine as ever.

"For heaven's sake, Emily. Every suggestion doesn't have to be treated as a contest," Robert whispered at her elbow. She pretended not to hear, although everyone else had.

"She said 'sultry,' Professor Haussmann, not 'lazy,'" Johnny Dunne broke in as he moved up to join them. His mane of healthy hair and suntanned face made him look a little out of place, like a wild animal found wandering by mistake in a domestic garden.

"That's why it's necessary to have a man of letters with us at all times," Emily laughed, nodding her head in Johnny's direction. "Where the musicians quibble about the significance of the notes, or even the silences between notes, the literary artisans clarify the spoken language for us in a way the rest of us can't."

Robert dropped back a few paces and the others followed Emily to the French doors separating the library from the patio and garden on Fifth Avenue. The doors already stood open, and sheer silk curtains lining the yellow brocade draperies on either side of the opening fluttered and whispered in the unexpectedly warm night air. *Come along,* they seemed to call. *Why stay inside on a night such as this?*

"Come along, Robert," Emily was saying, as she turned to look for him once she was outside with the other guests. He started a little and pulled himself together to join them, wondering how such an eclectic and seemingly disparate group of people could enjoy each other so much, moving together almost as a tidal flow carrying each other along.

"Will you ladies be leaving us now for a while? I can tell Edward to pass the cigars, if you like." Robert looked hard at Emily, hinting too broadly for her comfort that she'd forgotten her duties as a hostess, leaving Monsieur Offenbach's friend, Marie Garnier, adrift in a sea of male carnivores when she needed the respite of Emily's private rooms upstairs to recover her composure after dinner. Emily looked out over the hedge of fall-blooming clematis along the Fifth Avenue wall to stave off her defensiveness, thankful she could see its tiny white blossoms reflecting the light of the gibbous moon. No need to look at Robert's eyes, undoubtedly dark with rebuke.

"No, thank you, Robert," she said quietly to the warm night air. "Madame Garnier and I have no need to escape such engaging company." She turned to catch the smile on that lady's face, just in time to nod at her. "Madame will feel free, I'm sure, to excuse herself if necessary, but we're both enjoying ourselves enormously and I wouldn't miss a minute of the conversation right here. Unless . . . ," she added, slowly turning in place to look at the others, "you men would prefer it." Her dimples deepened though her smile was hardly perceptible.

"You see!" Jacques Offenbach cheered. "This is exactly why we find female artists so enticing. There's a spirit . . . of some kind . . ." He waved his hand in small circles as if to indicate an ongoing list of artistic energies he was at a loss to describe further.

"A way of connecting outward instead of d-drawing in, as so many l-ladies do." John Mackay finished the thought for him, and took Emily's elbow to escort her down the steps. "By all means let's enjoy the garden while we can," the silver king nodded, looking at each of the guests briefly and starting to move. "And if being outdoors means the ladies can put up with our smoking cigars, then b-by all means let's have them," he added cheerfully, looking directly at Robert as if cigars had always been the crux of the dilemma.

"Good idea." Emily gave John Mackay a grateful nod and led the group down the second tier of marble steps to the lower patio.

Turning to invite them all to be seated on the surprisingly comfortable cast-iron furniture, Emily realized the men were waiting for her to choose her seat first. "Please find a chair or bench you can relax on," she said. "I'm going to get myself a shawl and will take a seat wherever there's one left when I return. Please, sit."

"I'll go, Emily," Robert offered. "I'll ask Mary for one of your shawls when I find Edward with the cigars. You stay with your guests." He bowed slightly and turned to go, too fast for her to protest, and leaving her wondering if she had somehow hurt him again when it was she who'd been upset about his reproach of her after-dinner protocol. How was it she was always straining against the very hand that offered her support, and always had? Noticing they were still all waiting for her to be seated first, Emily moved forward to one of the side chairs to Monsieur Offenbach's left. She'd noted how much easier the higher seat would be to get up from later, a calculation she'd found herself making more often lately.

"Please sit with me here, monsieur, and we'll save this chair on my left for Robert when he returns. Now please, make yourselves comfortable."

"This evening has been delightful and invigorating, Mrs. de Koningh." Marie Garnier sank down on a chaise with an ottoman, her huge green satin puff of skirt rising up around her and settling again in a waft of French perfume. She reminded Emily of an elegant night-blooming moon flower, finally releasing its intoxicating reminder, and Emily said so.

"Yes, Mrs. de Koningh is right. You've added a wonderful, exotic atmosphere to our salon, madame," Monsieur Offenbach assured her. "But now that we're outside in this moonlight, I'm sure you'll open up to an even fuller loveliness. Actresses, flowers, and all performers," he added with an afterthought, "are so well tuned to the night air."

"Indeed we are," his leading lady assured them all, resting her small, shiny dark head against the chair's high back to study the night sky. "Moon flowers come by their names honestly," she mused. "The flowers open unfailingly in the evening and last the entire night." She seemed to be speaking to the heavens. "They close when the sunlight touches their petals, though, just like us," she added with a laugh, lifting her head to look directly at Emily.

"Oh, how I wish that were true for me," Emily replied. "Two young boys and a household to care for demands an early rise with the dawn. It makes for an overload of exhaustion much of the time. Tomorrow, for instance, I have to pack for an imminent departure by train to Chicago for a performance with Robert next week. It makes me tired just to think of all the work I still have to accomplish before I go." She tried to let her breath out slowly so it wouldn't be heard as a sigh, but the extra control only made her tenser. She was relieved to see Edward arriving with her father-in-law's gilded box full of his finest Cuban cigars. Her silk-lined cashmere shawl was draped over his left arm, giving her a chance to push up from her seat to relieve her tension. Robert stepped from behind Edward to assist her, but too late to be of any real help. Emily seemed not to notice.

"I do wish there were more women in our profession, madame," Emily said, in an attempt to turn the talk in a general direction, as she reached for her shawl before Edward passed the cigars.

"But surely, the changes coming now in your field must be heartening to you," John Mackay said, rolling one of the cigars between his thumb and forefingers and sniffing the tobacco as his pressure released some of the oils. "There are some wonderful female pianists performing all over the world. . . ." He looked at Robert for affirmation, which he barely got in a small nod. "And even that divine composer . . . the F-French woman who's published hundreds of pieces already. . . ." He looked over at Jacques Offenbach for help this time.

"Cécile Chaminade," Marie Garnier chimed in, but Mackay spoke over her suggestion.

"Truly a bird of paradise!"

Emily had noticed that John Mackay spoke right past or through the opera singer more than once during dinner. "A *caged* bird, I'm quite sure," Emily said, each word heavily weighted. "Meant to be pretty to look at and listen to, but always restrained. No breaking out and flying around the room."

"Not at all!" Jacques Offenbach objected cheerfully, sitting forward off his seat to command the attention of everyone in the circle. "It's true Cécile Chaminade's father never approved of her music education, but she got it anyway, thanks to her mother, studying with the best teachers for piano and violin and finally with Benjamin Godard in music composition." He nodded at Robert and Madame Garnier in quick succession. "Her published work is very popular in France. Why, my colleague Ambroise Thomas has said she's 'not a woman who composes, but a composer who is a woman.' This is a bird who has flown free for a very long time, Mrs. de Koningh." He settled back in his seat, shaking his head when Edward offered him the box of cigars. "When you come to France next, I'll be sure to have you both meet her," he said to Emily and Robert together, as the footman moved past him and started back into the house. "You will be bringing Mrs. de Koningh back to Paris soon, Professor Haussmann?"

Robert stiffened, glancing at Emily. "I'm not Emily's usual accompanist," he said, his voice sounding tighter and his now-indeterminate European accent more pronounced. "I'm only performing with her in Chicago while her husband is with his father on business." His spine stayed erect, head slightly forward in preparation for any challenge.

"I only meant . . . the first time we met in Paris you were her . . . caretaker, I believe. But perhaps I choose the wrong word. My English is not as perfect as I like to think sometimes."

"I, too, thought you were her manager," Johnny Dunne said. "Perhaps a better word, Professor Haussmann. Wasn't that your role when we first met at the *New York Times* headquarters so many years ago?" Dunne's voice seemed to float out from the darkness on a puff of smoke. Emily knew his eyes must be closed since neither the light from the house nor the outdoor wall sconces reflected back from them.

"No, indeed it wasn't," Emily said quickly, announcing her readiness to come to Robert's defense. "We were there at the same time quite by chance, Johnny." She turned to face the direction the reporter's voice had come from when she felt Robert relaxing slightly. "We were both there in search of information about the de Koningh family's whereabouts. My father-in-law had gone missing during the war, and Professor Haussmann and I spent much time and energy trying to locate him and his son, who was to become my husband a little later."

"Apparently an ongoing endeavor," Johnny Dunne replied quietly. "I mean the need to locate them. I believe both gentlemen are still missing?" Neither Emily nor Robert could miss the flash of his eyes opening in the candlelight from the large sconces flanking the French doors.

Emily ignored the implication and continued, "Where did that come from, Johnny? You've been unusually quiet this evening until now. No, they aren't missing. But my father-in-law struggles with the reconstruction of his cotton business in the South, and is leaning more heavily than he used to on my husband to get that done. I believe my husband is torn between his duties to his family here and his father down there. So between the two of them, the de Koningh household and the people up north can find no way of attracting my husband's attention."

Johnny released the cigar's smoke from his mouth slowly and evenly, with the relish of a man who appreciates superior tobacco. "I'm always quiet, Emily. Listening is my business," he said in a slow, sure voice. "I can't hear people's stories if I do all the talking." His voice was heavy, like the night air. "Listening in a group setting can bring new insights. For example, I've never heard you discuss life in a cage before, and I've known you a few years, now."

"Why would I have talked about it with you when I was released a long time ago? Thanks in great measure to Robert Haussmann." She spoke to the darkness in his direction. "Robert has always been a *caregiver*, not a *taker*, as Monsieur Offenbach suggested. It was Professor Haussmann who freed me as a child, and also my husband, from conventions and rules that would have trapped us in very different, nonmusical lives. Although I must say my husband is playing strange things these days that neither Robert nor I can understand or appreciate entirely. Perhaps it isn't music at all."

"Truly, Mrs. de Koningh? But isn't that just his way of breaking out of another cage?" John Mackay rubbed his cigar out gently in the ashtray next to him even though it was only half finished. Emily was relieved, understanding he was preparing to end the conversation. She was suddenly very tired and ready to be alone again. "It seems to me," Mackay went on, "that *once* out of the cage isn't enough to secure freedom. One has to repeat the escape often. I've seen it in horses out West. When they've been corralled too long they can't believe they're finally free, and then in fact need to keep testing the gate even when it's open." Emily felt whatever flippant retort had risen in her throat die out, a burning sensation in her core its only physical manifestation. "But you forget, my dear," Mackay went on, "that I have heard you play the violin in Paris. As an amateur cellist myself, I could tell that the music had already freed you. You didn't need someone else to throw the doors open. You're already at liberty."

"Yes, free to succeed and fail as well," she muttered, almost under her breath. A stunned silence told Emily she'd allowed her expanding depression to touch the others, too. She knew John Mackay was right. "Enough of this topic of breaking things—rules, restraints, or anything else. An evening as perfect as this one is all about building things." She smiled warmly even though few could see her clearly because she knew her change of tempo would be felt with just the tilt of her head. She helped end the evening and discussion by reminding them, however, of her impending trip to Chicago to perform, and how she needed an early rise to prepare in the morning. They all understood her plea, each saying their goodnights and thanks as they left the foyer in coats and hats to return home to their beds. The last carriage pulled slowly away from the driveway to head down Fifth Avenue in the fall evening fog, lacquered sides shining in halos of light from the glow of the streetlamps. Emily waved them all off until she could barely see a speck in the distance or hear the hollow ring of the horses' hooves.

"A lovely dinner party, Emily," Robert said quietly in the hall behind her. "I hope it wasn't too much for you, though. You have so much weighing on you right now. Could we talk a few minutes? I'm worried about you."

"Then I'm sure you'll understand the thing I need most right now is rest, not talk. Thank you for your support tonight, Robert. It was much appreciated. But it's time now for you to go and for me to retire." And with that she smiled slightly, nodded goodnight to both Robert and Edward as he appeared inexplicably again from the lower staircase to move silently to the front door. Robert reached for his hat and walking stick on the bench, took one last look at Emily's back as she moved slowly up the stairs, nodded slightly to Edward, and moved through the front door and out onto the street without a word. He had his thoughts for company on his walk home.

Unfortunately, little Connie de Koningh, woken up by the sound of laughter from the departing dinner guests, had left his bed to return to his spot on the staircase. He overheard his mother's news of her trip to Chicago with Professor Haussmann, and realized he was being left behind again. With no father at home and not even Professor Haussmann to connect his days in some way to his mother's life,

Connie feared he might lose her forever. His puffy, tear-stained eyes greeted Emily as she reached the top of the stairs, the rise of elation she'd gotten from her friends fully deflated. Sitting down on the polished marble next to her youngest son, the pressure against her abdomen of her newly recognized unborn child reminded her that the cage door was swinging shut again, just as it often had for her, and probably would again unless she hurried to get through it.

CHAPTER SEVEN

SCREECHING, ROCKING, AND THRUSTING FORWARD with a speed unmatched by any other form of transportation, Emily felt this train trip to Chicago as an attack from a modern assailant. She'd never been attracted by the allure of passenger trains. The transition from travel by horse and carriage to steam locomotives had started in Great Britain long before it arrived in other countries, but she'd not been allowed to ride on them as a child, the dirt, noise, and vibration all considered unhealthy for the very young or elderly.

She remembered being bounced out of the carriage once as an infant riding with her mother, or maybe she'd just heard of it so often she thought she could recall it. She had landed on her head but luckily hadn't broken any bones; there'd been much anxiety over her potential injuries, while her father arrived unscathed on his train from London. So much for the inherent safety or danger of travel! But her returns from America to Europe on tour, first for her musical education and then later to perform, had forced the new machinery on her without restraint. She hadn't paid much attention to it. All that mattered was getting where she had to go with her violin, so she usually concentrated on the scores to be performed rather than the scenes racing by or the assault to her senses. But this time, however, it seemed different, and harder to lose her thoughts of home for visions of her music and where she was headed.

She stared out the window while the scenery melted into a blur. Tired of trying to distinguish one racing form from another, she felt a strange panic at the swiftness of the movement tearing her away from her home and children. Glancing over at Robert, she saw he seemed imperturbable, sitting up quite straight against the back of the seat and rocking slightly with the convulsive movement of the locomotive. She could almost imagine him running through a score in his head, envisioning the rhythm and changes from one passage to another with no thought or care for anything else. She understood the train was also bringing her closer to the world of music and her performance in Chicago, pushing and pulling at the same time, depending on your point of view. She feared she might split between the two. The speed only made the conflict worse. Why was she here? *Because she needed to share her love of music.* Why hadn't she come here sooner? *Because her family had needed her.*

"Isn't that Mr. de Koningh's daughter?" An aging doyenne's voice projected up from her ample bosom and over the conversation in the dining car. Her husband glanced from the menu he was reading to follow the direction of her gaze, which was not hard to do. She looked like a great blue heron on point.

"Daughter-in-law," he muttered, glancing down again to study the unusual dinner options intended to outdo the competition on other trains from New York to the Midwest.

"What?" the woman at the end of the car cried, causing Emily to jump, and pulling her attention back from the window. The outraged female glared at her husband, her flashing eye and jutting jaw just as clear to him as they were to the rest of the diners. All but Emily. She looked down at her plate loaded with too much food and too little appeal, aware only that it represented an overwhelming responsibility she didn't want. She hated waste but had no appetite up to the task of eating a meal whole careening across the country.

Robert Haussmann sighed imperceptibly, trying to pretend his overly sensitive musical ear hadn't detected the verbal cymbal clashing of the creature behind him. Emily knew he liked it when appreciative music lovers recognized her in public, but the voice from the woman at the end of the car addressed Emily's social status rather than her prominence as a world-class performer. Emily guessed he could feel what was coming next, just as he could always predict the resolution of a passage of music before he'd even heard it. Alas, he was seldom wrong.

"It's the de Koningh girl, all right," the matron assured her husband, puffing out her formidable chest like a triumphant jay. Even though Robert couldn't see her, there was no mistaking the glee in her voice as she shared her pronouncement with everyone else in the Pullman car. Now truly annoyed, her husband responded in kind, his voice rising in volume.

"She's married to the de Koningh son. *There is no daughter.*" Emphasizing each word with irritation, he glared at his wife over his pince-nez without putting his menu down. "And please, lower your voice. The entire dining car can hear you."

His wife rearranged herself on the plush red velvet chair, now the image of a satisfied mourning dove settled back down in her nest. She'd intentionally included the other passengers in the conversation because her husband was so unresponsive. "Ah, but of course," she breathed. "Now I realize you are quite right." Her feigned acceptance was muttered through lace finery ruffled around her neck. "But then, I wonder who that is she's traveling and dining with? He certainly bears no resemblance of any kind to her husband!" This last statement was offered at twice the intensity of her first, causing a number of people to turn away from their meals and toward Emily and Robert at the last table in the dining car. They sat along the side reserved for settings of two instead of four. It pleased the matriarch to see her narrative had been followed all along.

Robert's sharp intake of breath showed he could no longer ignore the dissonance from the society matron's perch. He glanced over at

Emily, surprised to see her staring out the window, apparently unaware or just unconcerned with the spicy scenario suggested by the female magpie.

"In Europe, a mature woman traveling with a man not her husband wouldn't merit a second glance. More important, Europeans would no doubt recognize the great female violinist Emily de Koningh; Americans are still so backward about a lot of things." Robert let the last of his sigh out, but Emily heard it and turned suddenly from the window.

"What's the matter, Robert? Not happy with your braised duck? It looks delectable to me." He had the impression she was more aware of the anxiety in the dining car than she let on. There was an air of strain about her, though he couldn't place the cause exactly so assumed it must be the fault of the gossip floating down the aisle.

"It seems the woman at the end has recognized you as a de Koningh, but is uncomfortable that I, not your husband, accompany you for dinner . . . and as your travel companion," he added testily. "She's sharing that fact with the entire restaurant car, as well. Apparently she has no intention of letting any of us dine in peace." Emily thought how young Robert looked. The reflection from the overhead chandeliers burnished his cinnamon hair and beard with a copper glow. In a stark contrast, the disgruntled tone of his voice reminded her of a grumpy old man who'd been kept from his supper too long.

"Which one is she?" Emily elevated her voice and leaned around Robert to peer down the aisle. He shook his head at her imperceptibly, but his displeasure forced her out of her seat. For some reason she always found Robert's reticence a challenge she couldn't resist. "The woman all the way down?" she asked him, in a still louder voice. He couldn't ignore her anymore, so turned slightly to see the matron glowering in their direction, shoulders back and bosom thrust forward in preparation for a fight. She could not be missed.

"I believe so," he breathed weakly, but Emily had already pushed her seat back and started toward her accuser without waiting for

Robert's confirmation. "Oh Emily," he moaned under his breath. "Please . . . ," but she was already three-quarters of the way down the car, touching the backs of the other chairs lightly along the way to correct her balance as the train rushed toward Chicago.

He was appalled and enthralled at the same time, both too much to look away. Dread for what might come next held him hostage in his seat along with all the other passengers. Not even the waiters could move, each stationed along the sides between the tables for instantaneous service. The armies were lined up along the walls of the car holding their collective breath while the combatants faced each other. Farther and farther Emily advanced down the aisle toward the stalwart woman who sat erect and still, a monument of implacable resolve in her voluntary self-righteousness.

Watching Emily move forward, her shiny dark hair piled on her head glistening in the overhead chandeliers like a royal crown, Robert felt as if time was standing painfully still. But the piece of braised duckling balanced on the end of his fork found its way into his mouth, its warmth reminding him no time had passed at all. Chewing and swallowing the start of his entrée calmed him, making him aware that it was important to appear as undisturbed and natural as Emily did. He'd seen her respond to public censure so well, so often. She seemed impervious to the disapproving glares from men and women in the first rows of the audience when she walked on stage. Only the beauty of the music mattered to her. He picked up his glass of wine, continuing with his meal to contribute to Emily's appearance of nonchalance. He heard her say in a bold, clear voice, "Good evening, madame. Do we know each other?"

Robert would never forget the negotiation that followed. Visibly shocked by Emily's public intrusion, the matron found herself speechless, giving Emily a momentary advantage. She grabbed it by apologizing for not recognizing the woman, as the professor traveling with her as her accompanist had overheard a suggestion that she

was a friend of Emily's father-in-law. Having been assured that the
couple were not acquaintances of Mr. de Koningh, Sr., and that she
had committed no offense, Emily offered them both free tickets to
her performance at Crosby's Opera House in Chicago. She promised
them that this once-in-a-lifetime opportunity to hear the great
Robert Haussmann, foremost proponent of the pianoforte who
would be playing with her, should not be missed. Both the woman
and her husband gushed their thanks, suggesting that Emily and
Robert join them at their table for dinner, as they were seated at one
of the tables for four but were dining alone. She turned down their
offer graciously, explaining she and the professor were almost
through dinner and still had work to do before retiring, separately.
Maybe another time . . .

". . . But most definitely not!" she muttered to herself, on her way
back to Robert at their table.

The rows of diners sitting horizontally along the length of the
dining car swam before her. She assumed the train's unpredictable
lurching caused the young couple with children to tip dangerously in
their seats as she passed. Or was it she who'd lost her balance? The
couple seemed to call silently after her, *where are your children*. Or did
they? She thought the middle-aged man reading the arts section of a
newspaper looked up with curiosity as she passed, but then saw his
wife beside him smile shyly at her. It was clearly a look of recognition
for an artist of some renown. Or was it? Maybe it was derisive—a
judgment for traveling so far from home to entertain strangers under
hot lights for pay. Women had no business doing so—but why didn't
they?

The thoughts weakened her knees and she felt suddenly
exhausted by the effort she'd made; aware she was aching in all her
joints as if a great stone weight had been placed on her shoulders. She
had so little stamina these days. Expecting her third child was not
the easy process she'd enjoyed with the other two. Slipping back into

her seat, she could feel the blood draining from her face and knew she must look beaten instead of exhilarated by her victory. A waiter appeared from nowhere, unfurling her napkin onto her lap. Surprised by both the waiter and the snap of the huge white cloth in her face, she sat down too hard and let out a small gasp.

"Emily, are you ill?" A look of deep concern crossed Robert's face. "Your color is quite poor, and you seem distressed." She tried to brighten her expression and sit up straighter. It took every ounce of energy she had.

"I'm quite well, Robert. There's nothing to worry about. I just find train travel a little difficult—claustrophobic, I think. It tires me out more than I expected, and the altercation with that couple was probably something I should have avoided. It was unnecessarily enervating. I should have listened to you." She smiled wanly, frightened because she was truly beginning to feel sick.

"On the contrary," Robert announced brightly. "I thought you were spectacular! You put those two where they belonged and promoted our performance for all to hear. You were brilliant!" Always proud of how Emily dealt with opposition to a woman performing in public, Robert enthusiastically drained his wineglass and nodded to the waiter for a refill. "You've given me the incentive to read through our entire program tonight after dinner. Shall we do it together?" He beamed at her like a childish cohort planning an exciting project, all concern for her fatigue apparently forgotten.

"Not tonight, Robert. Not tonight . . ." Her voice drifted off as she poked at the food on her plate with the huge silver fork she felt she could hardly lift. "I have to write Connie that letter I promised him. Remember, I said *every day and every new stop along the way* he'd hear from me with a description of where we are. I'll take the letter to the postal car and they'll get it off tomorrow when we stop in Cleveland."

She didn't tell Robert she not only had no intention of reading her music that night, but also had no interest in performing next week.

She hoped when they arrived at the Palmer House Hotel on State Street she'd feel better with a room of her own and more space to move around in. Everything would be better in Chicago. She hated the sight of the drought-ridden countryside all along the route and knew it would be less obvious where buildings took the place of trees and grass. She wanted to escape—the drought, the pressure in her lower back, the pain in her head—and Robert.

Imagining the borders of Ohio slipping past their dark train window that night as she lay propped up in her sleeper birth, Emily realized getting into bed had calmed her panic and lessened her pain. The doctor had warned against being overtired. She'd write the children again tomorrow when they stopped somewhere in Illinois She knew Connie would be tracing the route as he got her letters one by one, and somehow thinking of him opening and reading them also soothed her, as if she could keep her hand on his head even this far away. She closed her eyes and listened to Bach playing in her mind. After all, this is what she was born to do—play the violin— and also worry about her children. That too was her commitment. She fell asleep, rocked with the even beat of the big wheels of the modern railroad on newly laid tracks, taking her toward another bend in the road, and hopefully on to another successful performance. After all, nothing creative could exist without change.

Robert sat in the straight-backed chair in his berth, allowing himself to rest against the upholstery with his sheet music open on his lap. A surprising lurch of the train sent the score flying to the floor, but he let it lie there as he listened to the music in his mind. He wished he'd been able to convince Emily to choose the Schumann, but she'd been fixated on the program she'd chosen with Corey. He had no doubt she could enchant any audience, as long as she projected her usual energy and warmth. But she'd been so distracted lately, so torn between her children and her music. He worried, for the first time, about her ability to choose her artistic calling over her domestic diversions. Most would assume it went the other way: her music the diversion and motherhood her calling. But Robert knew otherwise, and choose she must, at some point soon. He shut his eyes and swayed in his seat to the music in his head. He could see Emily standing at his piano with the Guarneri violin cradled under her chin while their shared love of the music filled the space between the notes. He was determined to make the vision a reality again.

❧ ⁂ ☙

Corey couldn't believe he'd almost reached Philadelphia already. Usually the scenery and changing landscape would have captured his attention, making him very much aware of the country the train passed through and changes wrought by the movement of the earth's surface over the millennia. Ordinarily he loved the speed of the new trains, the excitement of the undeniable possibilities waiting just beyond the horizon. But this trip he'd noticed nothing—either through the train car's window or in the different towns they'd stopped at while picking up passengers and cargo. He had no idea where they were and cared only in so much as he prayed it was nowhere near New York yet. Most of the time, Corey chose train travel because he liked having more space to stretch out in than the carriage allowed, and he loved the onward rush to arrive at a destination, seemingly almost before he'd left the departure point; or so it was in comparison to horse, carriage, or boat.

But this day, he had a screaming need inside to slow down, everything, from the travel north to his eventual return at least a week before his father in his carriage. Why hadn't Corey offered to accompany Klaas home to be sure he was well taken care of? That way their arrival back at the de Koningh mansion could have been delayed beyond Emily and Robert's departure for their performance. Corey's hasty retreat from the Widow Stovall's West Virginia plantation was supposedly driven by the need to return home in such a timely manner that he'd be able to join Emily in the trip to Chicago and the performance to open the new concert hall. But the thought of coming home to the suffocation of all the familiar faces, only to turn around again immediately to travel alone with Emily on a train to Chicago, would be excruciating; an ever closing noose around his neck, choking off his oxygen.

He could literally feel the weight of Emily's letter, sent to him and his father, as an isolated drag on the inside pocket of his waistcoat. He still hadn't looked at it. There was really little reason to, as his father had told him of its contents at breakfast the other morning. Sitting in the Widow Stovall's dining room then, he'd felt the same belligerent rejection of the literal call home, as he did now fingering the edges of the envelope in his pocket without removing it from the dark depths of its burial in his coat. In the same space, he'd also slipped a note from Marcy Bond, the smell of gardenia hovering over it, and presented to him by Mrs. Stovall's housemaid as he lifted his leather satchel up to the carriage taking him to the train station.

The intrepid Marcy had been nowhere in sight, nor did she reappear in person to say goodbye, which was probably a good thing. But why, if she was so fearless, did she not find a way to reconnoiter the results of her night with him before his leaving?

He had a feeling she would never explain, yet the pull to find out what lay in her perfumed missive of sensory delight was much stronger than his need to understand Emily's message from home. Both envelopes sat side by side on his chest, and one had every right to be there, yet he didn't want it, while the other had none, yet he cherished the fact of its existence. He knew they were enemies of a very real and dangerous moral discrepancy, and if they remained together in his left vest pocket he'd be allowing something very dark to fester too close to his heart. He didn't know how he'd gotten in the complex predicament he found himself in, but nonetheless he knew he was fully responsible for it, and what he wanted most now was some kind of transparency and accountability. That way his guilt and the illness he felt creeping through his system could be stopped from spreading. Yet he wasn't ready to face Emily with the kind of honesty that would bring the relief he needed. Time away from her and her many admirers and supporters would help. He needed to catch his breath. The way the train was barreling along he'd be in New York almost before he'd left West Virginia, and that wouldn't give him time to work out his feelings.

He pulled both envelopes out of his pocket slowly, separating them with one in each hand so they wouldn't have to touch each other. He placed Emily's letter next to the right of him on the seat, pushed back far enough to keep it from falling onto the floor when the train lurched around corners. The ragged edge at the top where Klaas had opened it was visible, making Corey feel as if it was a conspiracy of disapproval, an accusatory reckoning that had placed the letter in his pocket in the first place. The letter from Marcy Bond looked smooth and pristine, untouched and beautifully personal. He didn't have to know what was inside, because he could feel its acceptance and lighthearted pleasure. He held it in his hand, lifting it to smell the heady aroma of gardenia that seemed to say almost everything he wanted to hear. Yet still, his curiosity overcame his sensory intoxication and the letter's contents became his only essential objective.

Eyeing the soft ivory stationery he still held in his hand, enjoying the sweep of the feminine handwriting that moved smoothly across the face of the envelope, he felt closer to its owner than he ever had when they were together. Somehow the letter was the most private manifestation for him of a relationship that hadn't existed until a few days ago. Suddenly a hand reached over his shoulder holding a pocketknife. He started, looking back and up to see a gentleman passenger reaching the knife out to him with a smile.

"Please, allow me," the gentleman said. "I've watched you contemplating that letter for the past half hour and can stand it no longer. I guess you've lost your own knife, so please use mine to slit the envelope." He smiled again, nodding encouragement and pushing the knife closer to Corey's shoulder. Corey smiled a little, nodded, and took the knife without comment. He unfolded the blade and slipped its thin, silver, razor-sharp edge between the flap and the envelope. The quality of the instrument made short work of slitting the paper, leaving almost as clean an edge as before it was opened.

"Thank you," Corey said quietly, folding the blade back into its case and handing the knife to its owner. He was half afraid the man would sit down and watch him pull the letter out to read it, wondering if his benefactor was somehow linked to a collusion to keep Corey from enjoying Marcy's message in private. But the man nodded back at him, slipped the knife away, and turned to go.

"I hope it's good news," he said, turning back slightly toward Corey before he left. *Ah yes, Marcy was always good news, depending on how you understood her.* He unfolded the two sheets of stationery and started to read, enjoying the intimacy of her hand directed solely at him. The uniqueness of the style in soft, swirling curls pleased him so much, especially in the spelling of his own name, that he forgot to pay attention to anything the words actually meant.

By the end of the second page, he suddenly realized something unexpected was happening, because he saw the phrase *we can always remain friends*, and then, *goodbye.* He reread both pages twice, trying to metabolize the contents. There was no question that Marcy had thought better of her night with him and wanted to reposition herself properly with her home and family. She felt he would only be a complication toward her end of a peaceful and joyful relationship with her aunt. After the horrors of the war, peace was all she wanted. She said she knew they'd be friends always, or hoped so. Corey slipped the pages back in their envelope and slid it into his pocket. Then he picked up Emily's letter and read it, concentrating on its tone rather than meaning, as he already knew what had been said. Clearly, she was exasperated, angry, hurt, and despairing. All that and she didn't even know about what had caused the great black hole in his soul that would probably devastate their family.

Corey picked his head up to stare out the window, just as the conductor came through the car calling out, *Brief stop in Pennsylvania*. He realized he was almost home, but nothing looked familiar. Where was home? He thought of his best friend from school who lived in Philadelphia, wishing he could get off the train and go to him—go anywhere but home. He knew he wanted that unconditional acceptance for who he was today, but wondered if even his friends would be able to stand him when they knew he wanted to abandon his family and run away.

"It's beautiful country, isn't it?" said the elderly gentleman who'd loaned him his knife. He stood in the aisle with his satchel next to Corey's seat, apparently preparing to disembark at the next stop. Corey looked out at fields and farms slipping fast away, and a deep blue sky with stacks of white clouds that were always in the same spot, if you only looked up and had no fixed point to judge them by. "Whatever's bothering you, young man, I can assure you it won't last forever," the gentleman said. "You just have to take a deep breath and let things settle on their own a bit. That may be an old man's perspective, but I can tell you it works."

"What I've done will last forever," Corey said, staring out the window again.

"That's what they all say," his visitor announced, "but that's just romantic nonsense. Change is inevitable."

Corey shifted in his seat. "I think the good things don't last, but the bad ones do," he said. "And whether it's forever or just a moment doesn't matter when you carry the weight of guilt with you."

The old gentleman frowned. "I'm sorry, young man," he said, softly. "I hope you can get someone to help lift that weight from your shoulders."

❦ ❦ ❦

A steady stream of scenery slipped past Klaas's coach window, constant and predictable. He liked its measured pace. In fact, that's why he'd chosen to return to New York by carriage instead of by train. Yes, he was one of the luckier ones who could afford the expense of travel by locomotive, yet he found many of those entitlements more limitations than luxuries. He certainly didn't object to travel by rail when his son was with him, the speed matching the urgency of young blood. But when given a choice, he preferred to absorb the changes in topography and culture gradually, and for that he needed a horse and carriage, not a steam engine.

Perhaps he also wanted to say goodbye to the inns and their keepers who'd become home and family, respectively, over the many years he'd traveled down south. There was so much change occurring now: profound alterations to the country and its people that would give his grandsons a vastly different world from his. He wasn't opposed to it, just a little nostalgic. In fact, his slow progress north was designed to help him assimilate subtle changes in the countryside and its inhabitants instead of rejecting them out of surprise and intolerance. As long as it didn't come too fast, he could handle the new. His carriage tilted around a bend in the road, allowing an open view straight to Samuel Washburn's Tavern in the distance. On the outskirts of Philadelphia. It would be the penultimate stopover before arriving in New York.

Klaas had traveled often throughout his long career in textile export and manufacturing. The numerous places he'd stayed and people who'd greeted him ran through his mind. Even when he hadn't been working, traveling to Albany to see his late wife's family had produced the same familiarity with lodgings and the characters who owned them. She'd always insisted on Dutch lineage for the proprietors, and that hadn't been hard to supply as they'd moved farther upstate toward her childhood home in Schuylerville.

His thin lips, completing the long, clean-edged facial geometry of his Dutch descent, twitched up at the corners remembering those bimonthly visits to the inn in Peekskill. It was owned by Jan Peek, the town's namesake, and former owner of a tavern in New York City. The proprietor eventually lost his license because so many of the patrons were "drunk and disorderly" and also because it was said that Jan "tapped" during church hours. Peek's land in upstate New York had a lovely stream winding through it and he'd built the new tavern right next to it. Klaas chuckled at the irony of his wife's comfort staying in the roadhouse on Jan Peek's kill while she ignored "the worthy's" stained reputation purely because he was Dutch. Prejudice took so many different forms!

Klaas caught sight of the Washburn's white clapboard siding and green shutters as the coach pulled into the courtyard to stop just past the outdoor pump. "Washburn's, Mr. de Koningh," the stagecoach driver called out. "'Cept it ain't Washburn's no more. It's Cap'n Storm's!"

"When did that happen?" Klaas handed the lap robe back to the driver as he held one arm out for it and the other for Klaas to lean on.

"Last year. Guess you haven't been back this way for a while."

"I took the train down with my son and I've been a few months in the South on business. But I had no idea Mr. Washburn had sold. Do you know where he is now?"

"Just wanted some new life, don't ya know. A change, he told me." The driver looked uncertain about whether to help the frail old man with an iron will to the door of the inn. "Can ya make it on your own?" he asked. Klaas assured him he was stiff from sitting so long, but capable. Fleeting pride caught him hoping the driver wasn't comparing his agility to last year's.

"Change," Klaas muttered. "Yes of course. Why not? Change is inevitable."

"Well if you've got all your things from the coach, I'll be on my way then. Hope to see you next trip, Mr. de Koningh, that is, if you don't take the train down again."

"This will have to be goodbye, my good man." Klaas straightened up with effort, putting enormous integrity into his long back and lift of his chin. He wanted the coachman to remember him well, standing tall. "I probably won't be back this way," he added, putting out his bare hand to take the coachman's gloved one.

"How's that, sir?" The driver looked startled, imagining a disclosure he hadn't expected and didn't want. "You bin comin' here so long," he offered, almost apologetically.

"That's just the point," Klaas said, still holding the driver's hand. He let it go when he started to speak again. "I'm selling my business. It *has* been a long time, and it's time for me to change, too."

"Good luck then, sir. I'm sure it takes courage and all to do that at your age." The coachman tipped his hat and turned back to his carriage. Klaas watched him go, wondering if everyone was going to express the same assumption when they heard about his decision— or at least think it, if words failed them. He was taking on a new business endeavor, if that was the right way to describe a collaboration like the one he and the Widow Stovall were about to embark on.

"Seems to me it's more frightening to do nothing," he said aloud. "Why shouldn't someone my age start anew?" he muttered, under his breath. But he had to admit, he was going to be taking on a lot of change all at once, truly a whole new life. Most people his age wouldn't do it, but he'd decided it was the best way to feel alive. Since he'd made it through the war he might as well enjoy his time going forward as completely as possible.

"What was that, sir?" He turned to see a young boy of about ten years old picking up his suitcase delivered to the front porch by the carriage driver.

"Here now, boy, that will be too heavy for you." Klaas brushed the air as if cleaning away cobwebs. But the boy had already lifted the case with surprising ease, scattering Klaas's objection to the winds.

"No one else to carry it, sir, so it better not be." The unruly-haired lad crinkled his nose at Klaas and smiled. "Yesterday I was carrying water at the farm and today I'm carrying suitcases." It was neither rude nor angry, but his familiar expression seemed to wake Klaas up.

"So now they have children doing men's work here," Klaas said to the boy's back, watching him march off to the desk with it. Everyone had to adjust to the changes the war had wrought. There weren't enough men to keep things going so the boys had to step in.

"Since the new owner took over the inn. Immigrant, I think, the new owner, I mean." One of the passengers Klaas recognized from the coach muttered under his breath as he passed. He was obviously uncomfortable with both the new owner and his ethnicity, whatever it was, to say nothing of the boy's youth. Klaas wondered at the animosity of his informant's tone. Was it that he'd had some difficult personal experience coloring his outlook? *Immigrants*, he'd said. Of course. That's where so much of the transformation of society was coming from.

"In Philadelphia, too? Not just New York, then," Klaas asked the traveler. But he got no conversation back, as if everyone was aware of the poison *immigrants* were spreading everywhere and the horrid fact of it wasn't worthy of discussion.

What an amazing assortment of choices and adjustments. Sometimes the options exhausted Klaas and other times they energized him. He let his muscles release his shoulders as he eyed the boy lugging his case. He seemed every bit as efficient as his adult counterparts had been in the past, putting down the heavy suitcase carefully, picking up a key for Klaas from the desk, and motioning for him to sign in at the register.

Yesterday the farmhouse and today the inn. The child's broad smile announced his pleasure at being where he was right now. Interesting how people viewed the same alterations so differently. Everyone looked out from the middle of their own world, where they were of course the very center of everything. One had to understand that each experience would be judged from that divergent central vantage point. The boy's view was so different from the carriage driver's, which was different from the other passengers' and yet again from Klaas's. Did that make it harder to accept? It depended on who was at the center looking out.

Klaas wondered if his own family would be able to adjust to the changes he was about to bring to their lives as well as this farm boy had accepted his. There would still need to be letters of confirmation, discussions back and forth of the pros and cons to moving a long way from home, and in particular, a very different society, even though the North and South weren't so far apart anymore as one might imagine, especially in West Virginia. One might almost think that state had a split personality, rending its politics, topography, and economy in a way that could take centuries to bring together again. Until then, that lovely lady would do better moving north to a smoother, more established way of life, bringing her wealth and her niece with her. Klaas would welcome the companionship of a woman trained to join her husband in his pursuit of happiness. And surely Sarah Stovall was just such a woman if there ever was one.

CHAPTER EIGHT

"QUITE GRAND!" ROBERT EXCLAIMED, climbing down from the carriage after Emily at Chicago's Palmer House Hotel. They both paused for a moment to look up through the streetlamps at a sign marked LADIES' ENTRANCE. He'd never taken much notice of the separate doors for women in hotels before, but suddenly that fact, and the actual fact of them, embarrassed him.

"This way, please." The doorman who'd helped Emily out of the carriage motioned to the main doorway just to their left. A long line of hacks blocked theirs from the front of the building.

"Is Mrs. de Koningh not required to go in that way?" Robert looked worried, apparently torn between the two massive entries flanked by Greek pillars and decorative cornices.

"Now that would be a waste of time, Robert," Emily laughed. "A law restricting women from entering a building with men wouldn't last long." Robert pulled the collar of his coat up a little. "Although I suppose polite society's just protecting women on their own from undesirables," she murmured to herself, with a small smile.

"There are social laws, Emily. They exist for a reason." Robert took Emily's elbow as if to steer her through dangerous waters.

"Yes, Robert, I know," she said. "But I think some of those rules tend to cause more trouble than they could possibly dispel."

"The ladies' entrance is only required when ladies travel alone," the doorman explained, in a voice colored with mixed European accents rivaling Robert's own for mystery of origin.

Emily shook her head and looked to the darkening sky. "What lady worthy of the name would ever travel alone?" she queried, her smile spreading to the corners of her mouth and her ever-ready dimples. Robert looked straight ahead with a pained expression and gestured for her to follow close behind the doorman. She moved past him smoothly into the hotel's grand foyer. "Wicked Emily," she said under her breath. Sighing softly, she stopped just before reaching the front desk, perfectly happy to let Robert take over the administration of their reservations, as she was suddenly very tired. She could feel without looking in a mirror that her coloring had gone sallow and her hair lost its luster. The end of another exhausting day. At least she was finally going to spend the night on solid ground going nowhere.

"Feeling better?" Robert asked, then nodded as if he'd answered his own question, and turning to the clerk at the registration desk, missed her shrug.

"It's certainly good to get off that train," she said to the clerk and Robert simultaneously. "I don't think I'll ever get used to the noise and speed of them."

"Finally getting your balance." Robert nodded again without looking up. He glanced at the clerk, seeking reassurance that the huge numbers printed at the top of the page he was signing were correct. But the clerk was gazing appreciatively at Emily, apparently unconcerned with the rooms' cost or the length of time Robert took to sign.

"My lord! This is a palace in the plains." Emily moved her eyes slowly around the glorious lobby of marble and plaster highlighted with gold leaf. "There's nothing like this in New York."

"The Palmer welcomes you." The clerk bowed slightly at the waist. "We're very proud of our hotel, Madame de Koningh. We've only been open twelve days, you know. All of Chicago's dignitaries are staying here, as well as Mr. and Mrs. Palmer. We hope your stay is a pleasant one, and that your performance will be all the better for the comfort of our first-class hotel."

"I'm sure we'll be a lot more than comfortable," Emily responded, with a hint of her usual spark showing in her voice. "I wonder, sir, if you could tell us how close we are to Crosby's Opera House. We're to meet Mr. Uranus Crosby tomorrow morning for rehearsals, and I hope we don't have to get up too early."

"It's quite close by, madame. You'll be able to relax in your rooms . . . ," he glanced down at the big brass keys in his hand, ". . . 508 and 512. You can sleep late, and have a leisurely breakfast." Emily's gaze rose to the intricately painted ceiling, praising the architectural heavens for that piece of good news, when a loud voice interrupted her thoughts.

"Did I hear my name? You're not planning to move my room, are you? Because I won't stand for it!" A tall, heavily bearded man in a narrow top hat and formal waistcoat drew himself up to his full height, glowering down at the desk clerk. Emily was startled by the thought that he could be Robert's relative, the resemblance was so striking; or perhaps it was mannerisms rather than features completing the simile. He must be Prussian. Even that narrow top hat looked like a German helmet! She couldn't help grinning at the man in what she'd have warned her own children might be unacceptably rude behavior.

The clerk bowed at the waist. "Madame de Koningh, this is Mr. Uranus Crosby," the clerk announced. "Mr. Crosby refers to the fact that all the rooms at the Palmer are uniquely decorated, Madame de Koningh. No two are alike."

Mr. Crosby eyed his new acquaintance. "Oh indeed they are," he said to no one in particular. "Number 508 is paneled in redwood and lined with weighty drapes. It has the gloomiest aspect you can imagine. While 510 has California laurel overlaid with maroon satin, an English marble fireplace, French chandeliers, a Persian bedspread, and Turkish carpets—a veritable smorgasbord! Still, it's much less funereal so I'm satisfied with it. Did you say this lovely lady is appearing at my opera house?" Emily was intrigued and a bit confused by his performance, but realized her exhaustion was making it hard to follow the conversation.

"I did, Mr. Crosby. She will play for your opening tomorrow."

Not wanting to appear as lost as she was beginning to feel, Emily jumped back into the introduction the clerk had begun. "My goodness, how fortuitous!" She beamed at the bearded older version of Robert, and held out her hand to shake his. He took it, bowing over it stiffly and noting the violin case resting at her feet, a familiar, familial connection to the tool of her trade identifying her in a way no formal introduction could. He was well used to musicians, and therefore the symbiosis between them and their instruments.

She covered up her surprise at his American name in light of his heavy German accent, saying only, "Mr. Crosby, I'm delighted to meet you at last. I would not have expected to find a gentleman of such clearly European background in Chicago with your American name."

"Discovered!" He leaned toward her, raising his eyebrows to look at her face more closely, and then straightened up. "Uranus Crosby is more palatable out here than Conreid Erklentz would be."

"Yes, I see. Erklentz's Opera House would be harder to sell." She knew the difficulty of bringing orchestral music to the West but hadn't considered the challenges to others who wanted to champion that cause. She'd only appreciated the obstacles from her own point of view.

Taking no offense, he smiled through his dark beard and serious brown mustache. "Prejudice is a shame, and you Americans know that all too well," he offered, replacing his top hat on his head as he spoke. "But I've found the best way to combat it for myself is in word and deed . . . and a change of costume, as it were."

"Hence Crosby!" she chuckled. "Give people another way to view something and hope they'll start to see with their inner eye as well. Exactly what we musicians do, and in fact, all artists, I suppose. A purposeful creation, Mr. Crosby." They bowed slightly to each other, acknowledging an unspoken agreement of great complexity.

"Ridiculous," Robert muttered, finally unable to contain his rising discomfort.

"And you are . . . ?" Crosby turned slightly to look at Robert, finally accepting his presence that he'd denied until that moment.

"May I present Professor Robert Haussmann, Mr. Crosby, my accompanist, and foremost proponent of the pianoforte in New York City."

"Ah." Crosby exhaled. "You're the gentleman I communicated with over the past few weeks, then. But, my dear Madame de Koningh," he dropped his noncommittal acknowledgment of Robert and returned to Emily. "I won't have you taking that ghastly room 508! I haven't unpacked yet, so please remove my luggage from 510 and reposition it in 508, sir," he ordered the clerk. "The two of you can have 510 and 512," he said, nodding in Robert's direction." The clerk looked confused for the first time.

"Oh good heavens no! I'm not concerned with décor, Mr. Crosby. I assure you I'm too tired to see or appreciate it," Emily objected.

"I'll not have my artist-performers treated as if their emotional health doesn't matter. Take my luggage out of 510 immediately," he said to the clerk, then turned back to Emily. "I look forward to seeing you at rehearsal tomorrow, Madame de Koningh. My hack will wait for you after breakfast and take you to the new opera house with me." He pulled himself up, growing a few inches before their eyes, and clicked his heels. Barely nodding in Robert's direction, he was gone before Emily could utter another word.

"What an unusual individual," she said, staring at the space he'd just vacated.

"Outrageous," Robert muttered, a flush spreading from his red beard to his cheekbones, suggesting to Emily he'd recognized his shared ancestry in Mr. Crosby, born Erklentz.

"And by the way," she turned back to her initial view across the expanse of the marble-tiled lobby, "are there any photographs for sale of this amazing place? We have a couple of hotels in New York, even one huge monstrosity it's going to take many more years to build, but nothing now to hold a candle to this. I'd like to send my children a picture so they won't think I'm hallucinating."

"I know what you mean, madame. I do believe we have photographs of the hotel. It's hard to believe it's real even when you're standing in it! Have you seen the silver dollars set in the floor of the barbershop over there?" He gestured across the lobby.

"I don't often seek out barbershops," she laughed. "But I'm sure Professor Haussmann will visit it while we're here and he can describe the floor pattern to me." She hoped the reference to Robert would put an end to his study of the rate card and move him on to the rooms. She straightened her back with a small groan.

"I think you may have to go yourself," the clerk chuckled, lowering his voice as he ducked his head toward her. "The professor looks as if he may have had a fight with his barber." Emily cast a surprised glance Robert's way, noticing his hair and beard did indeed look more profuse and redder than usual, their copper highlights more obvious the longer they got. She realized she'd been monopolizing all his personal time for rehearsals in New York, and then snatched him almost off his feet to make the train when she'd met him with her carriage a few days ago. She hadn't considered the inconvenience to him and any personal plans he might have had for himself.

"I'll see to it he gets to the barbershop here," she said, raising her voice so that Robert would overhear. "We wouldn't want to frighten the audience away." Robert had finally finished signing for the rooms and returned the pen carefully and precisely to the inkwell on the desk. She smiled with relief at the clerk who nodded back at her and rang for a bellhop, gesturing toward their bags.

Robert put his free hand at the small of her back with a forward pressure that couldn't be mistaken for anything but impatience. Emily stumbled a little in surprise, and then pulled herself up with the purposeful poise of the trained performer she was. "What's the matter, Robert? You're the one who's kept us waiting with all that fuss over the rooms." She stopped where she was, planting herself firmly to make her point.

"Emily." He tugged on her arm with a force that surprised them both. "We won't have time for pictures home to the children or any other nostalgic indulgences. We're here to work, to deliver on a contractual obligation, and we have much to do before that can happen."

"Really, Robert! That's all this performance is to you, just a 'contractual obligation'?" She'd snatched her jacket's trim out of his hand. "I believe we owe the audience a lot more than our presence and a well-rehearsed performance."

Robert noted the flash in her dark eyes: a blaze of something he recognized from long ago. "Why do hotels bring out the worst in you, Emily?"

"The worst in me . . . ?"

"The combative Emily, I meant to say." He let her arm slip from his hand.

"Oh, don't give up that easily, Robert. What do you mean they bring out the combatant in me?"

"I was just remembering . . . in Vienna . . . it was a long time ago."

"You must not have much to think about if you're still mulling over some hotel stay over a decade ago." He looked at her raised chin and flinched at the glint in her eye when he saw it close up. "But if it's so vivid in your mind perhaps you'd clarify it for me."

"I shouldn't have mentioned it. We need to stay focused. Here's the elevator, at last. Please, Emily . . ." He motioned twice toward the retreating back of the bellhop carrying their hand luggage into the elevator.

"I hate these contraptions, but I'm not walking up today," she muttered, stepping decisively onto the red and gold carpet of the cab and turning to face the front. Three fully mirrored walls reflected her image back at Robert; three dimensions of willful determination assured him he was surrounded.

"You have only a few hours to collect yourself before we need to get to work," Robert said, his voice filled with quiet command as they rode up the rest of the way to the fifth floor. As the bellhop led them out of the elevator and down the long hall, neither one spoke, nor did they look at each other. "Madame's room," the bellhop said, putting down the bags and unlocking the door. Emily followed him across the threshold, and then stopped. Mr. Crosby's luggage had, thankfully, already been removed, so there would be no more disturbances. "I'll try to get a rest, unpack, order dinner, and write the letters to the boys before my 'few hours' are up," she said with special emphasis, still looking straight ahead at the bellhop's uniform.

"Emily, there isn't time for that. The boys' communications can wait. You need to practice!" Robert's exasperation couldn't be contained, and he slapped his hat on his thigh to punctuate the importance of his statement. He knew he'd made a mistake when he saw Emily stiffen and spin around to face him, so close she almost knocked him over.

"My boys come first, Robert, before everything."

"Better not tell Mr. Crosby that, Emily."

"Oh, indeed I will, if he asks."

"Then he'll think he has every right to make this the last time he offers you a contract. That's why women make professional relationships impossible. They can't decide what they want in life and the skill and training lose out to feminine emotion. Don't be greedy. You can't have both, Emily." He was met with an amplified silence while the flash in her eye reminded him of well-honed steel.

"You're wrong," she said. "Or at least, I hope you are, because if you're not then my career as a violinist is over, because . . ." She held his eyes with hers, allowing no relief from the threat she knew would wound him most deeply. But he looked so frightened she couldn't go on. Plenty of time to tell him her news later, when he'd calmed down. "Don't worry, Robert. Luckily you are wrong, and I intend to have both my music and my family, no matter how hard it is to accomplish that."

She was surprised to see he didn't look in the least relieved, and she stood in the open door watching him retreat to his room with the beleaguered bellhop. She was chagrined by the young man's inclusion in their argument. "Oh Lord, what's got into Robert now?" she muttered to herself, shutting her door quietly. "Corey, how could you have put me in such a spot? A sulky, unresponsive accompanist and aching back are not what I need right now. Nor is another child."

She sighed, shutting her eyes for a minute to regain some stability, but as the room seemed to be spinning in ever-widening circles, Emily collapsed on the couch, her head coming to rest on the overstuffed maroon satin throw pillow. Nudging the Guarneri's case with the toe of her shoe to be sure it was still beside the couch, she let her muscles release in total relaxation. She had a vague perception before drifting off that she should thank Mr. Crosby for something.

❧ 𝕎 ☙

As Emily napped, Robert paced the floor of his sitting area, leaving a trail of loose wool fluff to mark his progress as the hotel's brand-new carpet covered his polished shoes with blue flotsam. What was he doing wrong? How could he refocus Emily on the concert in Chicago and away from her domestic life in New York?

Had he really lost track of the person she'd become over the last few years, not spending enough time alone with her to understand the profound changes that had stolen her away? That wasn't possible. He'd been in her home, around her children, absorbed the essence of who she was in relation to them and to her work, and to him. There had to be something he'd missed on this trip, and perhaps even before now that he thought of it. She'd seemed changed for a while at home, too, rudderless, and without energy and direction. The de Koningh men had been away too long. That was not his fault; it was theirs, and Emily didn't know who she was anymore. There was only one way to win her sovereignty back without them: through her music.

He stopped pacing and tore off his waistcoat. Tossing it on a chair, pouring himself a straight shot of whiskey from the cut crystal tumbler on the side table. It was always the American preference, but it was there, and it would do. It was not his habit to drink before bed, in fact he seldom drank at all when he was working, but he had no trouble believing in the medicinal powers of the elixir winking at him in the gaslight coming through the huge window. Looking out on Chicago's East Monroe Street, he rubbed the glass between his fingers as he watched the people below moving purposefully back and forth and allowing the heat of the scotch to burn down his throat. It sought out the tension in his body and penetrated each fiber with its molten flow. Soon it seemed as if his mind was moving calmly straight ahead instead of in circles, and he wondered how many of the people he saw on the street would be affected by the performances he and Emily were to give in Chicago that week. Maybe most of them, in which case Madame de Koningh and her accompanist had better be exceptionally good.

The only way to assure success would be to bring Emily back; back to him and the music of her violin. He'd given her the power to do it before and he could do it again. He put his glass down too hard on the table by the bed, spilling some of the scotch on his hand and shirt cuff. Realizing he'd need a fresh change of clothes in the morning anyway, he put down the music he'd just collected and moved to the steamer trunk standing at the foot of the bed with his clean shirts and suits.

A large armoire faced him from the opposite wall, inviting him to unpack his clothes to preserve their freshness. The suit and shirts he'd traveled in would obviously need to be cleaned, so he pushed the electronic call button by his bed meant to summon a member of the hotel's large and attentive staff. The army of bellhops, waiters, and watchmen patrolling the halls was impressive, signaling with their own electric buttons as they passed various points on their rounds. It was still hard to believe these systems were so effectively integrated, but it made one feel safe. He'd order some dinner then too, so he could work the rest of the night without interruption, as there was no doubt Emily wouldn't be joining him to rehearse. Some mental manipulation of the performance material for the next day would be particularly useful before bed.

After a young bellhop removed Robert's suit and shirt soiled during train travel, and taken his order for room service, he laid his two clean suits out on a chair along with his bathrobe and concentrated on transferring his shirts to the armoire. He'd go through three of them each day. One to rehearse in, one to perform in, and one for the reception afterward, another kind of performance but just as important in its own way. Pleased that he'd brought all twelve of the new Parisian hand-tailored silk shirts with him, he decided his hurried preparation in New York for this trip now afforded him the right to relax and rest for a while. There was really nothing he'd left undone, except perhaps his personal toilette. But he could visit the barbershop early tomorrow morning, and for now, he'd take a nap with no worry about anything. The relief of rest without movement and noise enveloped him.

The next thing he knew he was awoken by a horrific clanging coming from everywhere and nowhere at once. Ceiling, floor, and walls all vibrated. He shot up on the bed, heart throbbing in his throat. He saw that he'd slept past midnight and felt instantly guilty for losing the time he'd congratulated himself on saving a few hours before. Sliding slowly to the floor, he stood in the middle of the rich new rug, running his hands through his disheveled hair to wake himself up faster. His first thought was to blame the whiskey for his passing out but noticing the half-full glass still beside his bed, he moved across to the window to see where the noise might be coming from. The sight that now greeted him was astounding, making him feel as if he'd been transported to some unknown planet.

He stood staring in amazement at the way the people below had suddenly become a confusion of ants, all moving over, through, and around each other as they ran seemingly in every direction at once. Had he only imagined the purposeful, civilized humanity strolling the thoroughfare of East Monroe Street before? Or had the whiskey disguised the fact that they were really just the overwrought, disorganized hive of unrefined riffraff one expected to find crowding a young western city? The light-headedness from the drink he'd found so delightfully disorienting before had worn off, so he couldn't understand what he was seeing in the street below. He moved to the call button by his bed, but as he pressed it, he was assaulted by the clanging again, even louder than before. Surely this could no longer be the effects of a glass of whiskey. The sharp sound was developing into an unmistakable roar, and Robert knew enough about his incomparable ear to trust that what he heard was coming to him in real sound waves, not hallucinations.

His hand froze on the call button when he heard a crash from the room above sounding like a collapsing wall. Out of the corner of his eye, he saw something move. It was the armoire. Doing a strange dance across the floor, the massive piece of furniture vibrated with a hideous shudder before it collapsed facedown. It hit with an unearthly silence, because in the wailing of what he realized were sirens, he couldn't hear any other sound as the massive piece of furniture fell. Annihilating his standing wardrobe trunk as it collapsed, the armoire lay in a pile of random pieces of wood and decorative metal. Robert stared in horror at the crushed shirts trapped beneath the rubble. His voice stuck in his throat when he tried to cry out for help. Inching around the devastation on his floor, he snaked his way past the debris to the door, ripping it open with a strange force born of panic, but the sight of fleeing humanity in the hall sent him reeling backward. He'd surely have fallen had he not been clutching the door handle like a drowning man holding on to a life raft in a roiling sea.

⊱⋆⋅☆⋅⋆⊰

Emily had intended to dine early in her room before going to bed. Fully aware that her physical endurance was always tested by full-length solo recitals, she accepted that the added strain of carrying a baby while she performed on her feet under hot lights for more than an hour would be monumental. She'd done it before of course, twice, but somehow this child seemed more difficult. The doctor had been fully accepting of her performance schedule, warning her that the only threat to her or her child lay in overextending herself. Getting too tired would be more dangerous than a fall or exposure to travel on rough roads. With that admonition in mind, she'd allowed herself to sink into a blissful sleep without even finishing her dinner.

The thin wail of a siren much like the cry of a newborn child invaded her dreams, waking her easily, since she hadn't been sleeping deeply or comfortably over the past few weeks. She lay in bed staring at the ceiling, trying to get her bearings and listening for any other recognizable sounds. The escalating alarms, strange roaring sounds, shuffle of many feet in the hall, and voices bouncing off walls in that confined space finally forced her up out of bed. Snatching her dressing gown from the chair, she flung it on without paying attention to its order of fastening and ripped the door open just as she saw

Robert retreating into his own room next door, looking as if he'd slept in his clothes. One of the many watchmen stood in the middle of the hall waving his arms and directing traffic as if he was standing in the middle of Times Square instead of the Palmer Hotel.

"Pardon me, everyone, but I regret to inform you that the hotel is on fire," he called up and down the hall like a town crier, forcing Emily back in her room gasping to fill her lungs. She glanced in panic around her sitting area, hoping something would occur to her, but she could see nothing of importance. Her breathing became more difficult, and she was aware of losing the struggle to force oxygen into her lungs. Could she smell smoke or was she imagining it? Were people actually fleeing from the fire into the streets? "You must hurry!" the same watchman called through her open door as he passed. "Get out of here, fast!"

"I can't move," she whispered.

Robert rolled up his two suits inside his bathrobe, wrapping its sash around them all and tying it tight. He tucked the clothing under his arm and glanced for a moment at the crushed wardrobe trunk with his silk shirts underneath. Spotting his sheet music on the table next to the tumbler of whiskey, he threw his head back and swallowed what was left in the glass and grabbed the music. Slipping it inside the roll of clothing under his arm, he glanced around the room one more time and noticed his wallet lying on the bed where he'd tossed it before his nap.

Perhaps it was foolish to think of money at such a time, but he forced it into his trouser pocket anyway. No reason to let a possible fire consume dollars that could be put to better use. He knew Chicago was used to fires. An industrial city built entirely of wood, now in the midst of a drought, had better be. He'd heard on the train about a large fire just the night before they'd arrived, and it had been put out with practiced expertise, so he assumed this threat would also be dealt with in short order. Grabbing the wallet made him feel foolish, yet who knew what element of opportunist would be wandering the halls with access to the rooms when all the guests were out in the street obeying the fire siren. He took the cash with him.

And his shirts, what of those beautiful shirts? He couldn't get them out now, anyway. The violin! What of the Guarneri? Had Emily thought to take it when the alarm was raised? Emily! And what of Emily? He turned instinctively to look out the door and saw hers standing open with no sign of her. Where was she? Why hadn't she come to get him before she left? Angry that she'd gone without him he ran next door to look into room 510, and saw Emily standing still in the middle of her sitting area. "Emily, come!" he called out to her. "We have to leave right now." He held out his free hand and she looked at it in dull surprise.

"I can't move," she said.

"Of course you can. What's wrong?" he asked.

"I don't know."

"You're in danger, Emily. We have to leave. Where's the Guarneri?"

Emily looked over at the violin in its case at the edge of the couch. "Get it," Robert hissed. "Now!"

She walked slowly to the violin and, bending down stiffly, picked it up and cradled it in her arms, hugging it close to her body. He could see there were tears in her eyes.

"Good, Emily. You see you can move. Now we'll take it out of the hotel to safety. Come with me." She moved back across the Turkish carpet to his side and looked at him questioningly. "Yes, that's right. We have to save the violin, Emily. Let's go." He nudged her gently with his shoulder and she started out the door to the hall.

"Save the Guarneri," she muttered. "Save my child."

Robert watched her clutch the case to her body as she continued to move with increasing speed down the hall to the stairs next to the elevator. He ignored the other people pouring from their rooms without stopping to dress, many men with bare chests and women in nightgowns. No one seemed to notice or care. He saw only Emily in front of him, cradling the violin as if it were human. She'd always felt so close to it; as a child she'd even slept with it herself. Of course she'd treat it as if it was indeed her own child now. He steadied her at the top of the stairs with his free hand, holding her against his hip when he realized she had no way to hold the banister with her arms around the violin.

The flow of people seemed to frighten her, so he turned his body into a splint to steady her descent, holding her with each step down the five-floor escape. At the bottom he felt a rush of relief. It increased as they passed through the lobby and past the barbershop with its silver-dollar floor. Moving slower toward the entrance in the crush of other guests, he noticed most of them had ashen faces and a look of pain. It didn't seem to be anything physical as they were all moving steadily, but more as if their sensibilities had been injured, as if a trusted friend had betrayed them. The hotel was meant to protect them and last forever, but instead it now threatened them with death and its own annihilation. And it was brand new.

His relief disappeared completely when he stepped outside the entrance onto the street, for the sight that greeted them there could not have been dreamed up by a medieval artist painting the damnation of hell. Fallen cornices littered the ground and sizzling telegraph wires whipped around the debris in an unearthly howling wind. A blizzard of red ash fell all around the fleeing hotel guests, reminding him of the snowfall of his native Austria without the peace of its white blanket. These flakes were collecting fast on the wooden sidewalks, sparking new fires every few feet and reminding him of both the wooden city's vulnerability and of his own helplessness. Emily stopped suddenly in front of him, and he assumed her fear of the furnace around them had frozen her in place again.

"Keep moving," he yelled in her ear.

"I'm only in a dressing gown," she moaned. "I can't be out here like this." He pulled her behind an abandoned horseless hack.

"Give me the violin," he ordered. She did so. "Now untie this roll of clothes. You'll see a suit inside. Pull on the trousers and jacket. You'll feel more covered."

Dressed in Robert's trousers and waistcoat, Emily emerged from behind the hack, tucking the trousers up as best she could to avoid tripping. "You'll need shoes of some kind. Those slippers with heels won't last long," he told her. Somehow they'd pulled away from the main flow of traffic enough to be heard without screaming at each other. The change helped calm Robert's nerves. But he knew they'd be tested again in some way he didn't want to imagine. It reminded him of the brief interlude in a powerful score, lulling the audience and making it more vulnerable to what came next.

He feared the severe water shortage and dry conditions because of the drought would spread the fire from house to house and then block to block until it devoured whole neighborhoods. The fire was clearly out of control, advancing toward total destruction of the city. Watching the blazing sky and crashing buildings, there could be no other conclusion. He repositioned the sash around his clothes, grabbing at the fluttering sheet music shaken loose when Emily unrolled the suits, and stuffing it back in the middle of the now smaller bundle. She watched in a trance.

"Come with me," he encouraged, gently. "We need to get you some shoes with solid soles and no heels." Clutching the violin to her stomach again, she stumbled along, tripping on the trousers that were too long and debris scattered everywhere. The hot air burned Robert's lungs, but Emily only coughed slightly now and then, apparently not breathing deeply enough to notice the furnace stealing her oxygen. They stopped to rest for a while on a bench by the side of the road. Robert told Emily to close her eyes for a minute when she put her head on his shoulder, but the nightmare red sky and huge explosions shaking the ground brought her head up instantly again.

"What was that?" she cried out, panic obviously back in full measure.

"Dynamite, miss," a young man answered as he struggled down the street, climbing over rubble with two small children in tow. "They're settin' it off to surround the fires, but it's turnin' the city into a battlefield."

"Let's go, Emily," Robert whispered in her ear. The thought of being chased by dynamite encouraged him to keep moving, even though he had no idea where to move to.

"I can go no further," she whispered back. "I'm too tired. My feet are torn now, and I'm . . . not well. If we can't get help . . . find some transportation . . . I won't make it." She clutched the violin tightly and started to rock back and forth.

Feeling a panic worse than anything he'd experienced so far, Robert jumped up. "Stay right here, then," he ordered. "I'll find you a ride somehow. Don't move." Spotting some carts plodding slowly through the smoke along the street down a hill, he took off after them. Almost immediately he was engulfed in a taupe blanket of air hiding all landmarks, leaving nothing to orient himself with. He saw nothing ahead or behind, and his eyes played tricks on him, making him wonder if he was still upright. His only hope was that gravity was still in force, although his exhaustion and fear worked to make him doubt that as well.

Suddenly a sound of unearthly beauty floated through the haze behind him, making him stand still to locate and identify it. He'd always been able to separate all the instruments playing at once with his incomparable musical ear, and now in the din that surrounded them, he heard a familiar sound. Better for him than a beacon at sea, the beauty of it drew a lifeline from where he'd been, giving him the courage to continue straight to where he must go. He didn't need his eyes anymore; he had his ears, and they had never let him down. But the recognizable beauty of the music was what saved him: the Bach partita, with all its melancholy truth of the human condition and hope for the future seeped into his soul. Of course he recognized it instantly. It was Bach, after all; Bach, the Guarneri, and Emily. She was speaking to him in the language they would share for eternity. And much as he feared leaving her alone on that bench, he dreaded the obvious consequences of not finding her an escape more. So, on he went, with the wavering music encouraging him in the sure knowledge it would lead him back to her again.

⁕⸕🙶͛

An old man, one of the Italian construction workers who'd helped with renovations to the Crosby Opera House, struggled through piles of debris on his way to his escape over the Randolph Street Bridge. He spotted a mound of humanity on a bench in Lincoln Park. He thought he'd heard the reedy sound of a violin piercing the gloom, and realizing it was coming from the direction of the bench, he stopped in front of it to listen.

Such a sorry sight the poor creature made: a gray lump of ill-fitting, cast-off clothes. His heart went out to the homeless beggar, as it always did when he saw an unfortunate soul worse off than himself. These lost people were always the ones who suffered most in times of crisis in the city, and this one's vacant look suggested a sickness of the mind was also likely. He reached out to touch it on the shoulder.

She paused her playing and glanced up, looking him directly in the eye. The shock of connection caught his breath and pulled him back a step. "How did you get here?" he asked, counting on the eye contact they'd had to penetrate her mental fog. She shrugged and started playing again. "Over the bridge? Do you know where you are now?" She shrugged again and kept on playing. So he was right. She was destitute, touched in the head, and came from nowhere but the street to begin with. No one would care for her, and no one would ever ask these people what they remembered about the great fire of Chicago if they lived to speak of it. No one would ask what they were doing when the fire broke out or how their lives were affected by it. No one would ask and no one would care.

He reached into his pocket to find some coins for her, a useless gesture he knew, but one he hoped she'd recognize as kind. Then he remembered he'd put them all on his bureau before he'd gone to bed. In his hasty escape, he'd left them there. Reaching into his other pocket out of habit, he found a handful of lemon drops, and pulling them out, tossed a few into the open violin case at the creature's feet. Realizing she might be hungry and thirsty, he bent down to retrieve one of the candies. A picture of the Palmer House hotel lay in the bottom of the case and a worn photograph labeled "Niccolò Paganini" was taped to the inside of the open top. He recognized the great violinist, a fellow Italian, and wondered at the delusions of grandeur these sad, homeless waifs had. Perhaps it gave them the courage to face each day. The poor woman looked up at him again as she played. He slipped the lemon drop from his fingers gently into her mouth and turned to go, but not before he thought he saw her smile, with two dimples briefly showing at each corner of her dry, cracked lips.

CHAPTER NINE

"I CAN'T TAKE YOU, MISTER. I'll lose my job."

"Lose your job? If you don't take us we'll lose our lives," the man carrying a violin case yelled from the middle of the road.

The little cart's driver and exhausted horse stared at the charred, filthy clothes and red hair and beard of the strange assailant. The color made his head seem to be on fire, too. The driver shuddered. There were no other vehicles moving now. All the other animals were either dead or being held out of the city in safety. "It's starting to rain and the fire's already burning itself out," the driver muttered. "You'll be able to go back home soon." He turned to continue leading the animal pulling his cart, picking through debris to collect whatever valuables might be salvaged.

"No, we won't . . . ," Robert choked. "We don't live here. We're visitors. Look, the woman is so sick," Robert pleaded, with both arms outstretched toward Emily on the bench. "See? She can't sit up anymore. She was preparing for the opening concert at Crosby's Opera House when the fire broke out, and now *look* at her." Robert waved his arms toward the heap of gray clothes. "One of the world's great violinists and that's all that's left." His voice cracked. The fire's heat had robbed his vocal cords and soul of something essential.

"Wait!" he barked, swinging his hands up to the driver's face to stop the cart even though it hadn't moved. The search for valuables had finally reached his consciousness. "I have money. Cash! You can have it all!" He shoved his right hand into his pocket and pulled out a wad of bills. No way to tell how much money was there, but it looked like a great deal in its plentiful disorder. Robert shook it in his fist in front of the man's face.

"Why didn't you say so right off? Chicago's the cash capital of the world right now. Everything's possible with money. Bring her up here." The driver snapped his head toward the bench with its heap, though he wondered what sort of woman might be lurking there.

Without putting the violin down, the red-bearded man ran to gather the pile of rags in his other arm and moved with it slowly to the truck. The driver was too worn to watch their progress, nor had he any energy to assist. It wasn't required since he was doing them such a favor. "Hurry up," he growled once, as they seemed to be dragging. "We need to get going before the rain turns everything to slag."

The red-bearded man settled himself in the middle with the pile of rags on his other side by the door. He finally let go of the violin case, balancing it on top of his feet braced against the floor of the cab. The driver thought he heard a weak cry coming from the rags, and saw the man pick up the case and put it in two arms appearing from the pile of clothes. They pulled the violin in close, hugging it tight.

"Wa-a-ait a minute," the driver breathed. "Did you say she was going to perform at Crosby's?" He looked at the man, and the rags supposed to be a woman, more carefully. The man nodded his head. "Well I'll be . . . Crosby had messengers running all over the city trying to find his performers. Two runners stopped me an hour ago to warn me to be on the lookout."

"Why?" The red-bearded man sounded apprehensive, but then everyone was fearful after twenty-four hours in hell.

"Why, because Crosby's got a string of train cars to get his performers out of the city."

"How? The station . . ."

"Under a constant stream of water to save it. Crosby's a magician.

He's Prussian, you know. Good thing. Very efficient. Got a special section of the Overland Limited to leave for New York tonight. He won't take off until everyone's accounted for . . . one way or another."

Robert stared at him as if he didn't understand, but a twitch of his mouth looked almost like a smile. The driver put out his hand. "Cash," he said. Robert dug into his pocket, pulling out the wad of bills again and crushing it into the driver's palm. He was still staring dazed when the truck lurched forward with the driver's muttered order, "Let's go." The rain started to fall hard and straight, as if some high-spirited god had lost interest in his game of hot rage and reversed tactics to see what would happen.

❦ ⚘ ❦

"Everyone's here." Uranus Crosby nodded many times, relief and satisfaction giving more emphasis to his simple statement than necessary, but no one objected. *Truly, it's a miracle,* they all said of Crosby's painstaking rescue of twelve performers and four opera house staff, and his own wife, of course. "First class, too," he joked to his assistant concert master as they huddled together in the rain, watching the best car the Overland had to offer being coupled to the engine down the track. "Though I don't suppose anyone would have minded if we'd had to scrimp a bit on comfort. Still, I've always said, only the best for my artists' sensitive souls. Though they've all proven their mettle this day. There can be no doubt." With the affection and protective instinct of a father, he watched the last stragglers being lifted aboard the train. All here and all safe at last, including Emily de Koningh.

"Should I run a final check on them once the train gets going?" his assistant asked.

"I'll do it with you," Crosby nodded. "I want to have a good idea of what condition they're in before I telegraph their relatives when we get to Cincinnati, and that assurance can only come from personal knowledge. A commander must review his troops."

He moved forward to follow the last cluster boarding the train. The assistant watched the tall, straight back of his manager closing in on the tattered little group on the platform, wondering what leap of imagination brought him to view them as a fighting force. Then of course he saw it in a flash. They were all a type of natural wartime refugees and Uranus Crosby took care of his people. It was perhaps a good thing he had them to worry about now, because the Great Chicago Fire had top billing as the final performer at Crosby's Opera House. The assistant had seen the devastation himself. There was nothing left of the brand-new architectural beauty but smoldering rubble, just like the rest of the city, including the brand-new Palmer Hotel.

Inside the dining car, Crosby and his assistant moved slowly from table to table, stopping often to ask if there was anything else the performers needed. Ushers and staff from the opera house moved about quietly bringing food and water, as well as stiffer libations to those who wanted it. His friend at the Overland Limited had been doubtful about rounding up waiters and cooks on short notice in the wake of the tragedy, so Uranus assured him he could handle the staffing himself. And he had. He took a childish delight in looking over the car filled with dark suits and men in derby hats, women in big skirts and straw boaters or bonnets with plumes. How had they survived with costumes intact, he wondered. There would be many strange stories told about this day in the months to come. But now, there seemed a brave, almost cheerful holiday mood his performers were in since their safety seemed assured; no doubt it was the numbness of aftershock.

One of his staff offered a woman a glass of champagne to match the mood of the aftershock, but she laughed in disgust, explaining they'd been offered nothing but champagne as they escaped along their route out of the city with drinking water nonexistent.

Apparently many homes had stocked up on the effervescent wine in preparation for the celebrations to come with the opening of so many new and beautiful institutions. "I was afraid we'd all reignite the flames just from our breath," she informed him, asking for the only thing she truly craved, which was water.

Watching an articulate peacock feather sweeping back and forth as one woman moved her head to talk, Crosby marveled at the foolish things people clung to in times of stress. Like that piano teacher accompanying Mrs. de Koningh, mourning the loss of his twelve handmade silk shirts from Paris; which reminded Uranus that he hadn't seen Haussmann or Mrs. de Koningh in a long time. He didn't think they'd even come to dinner in the dining car. He asked his assistant, sitting at the last table making notes next to each name on their list, if he'd seen the violinist and her accompanist. He shook his head. "Her berth number?" Uranus asked. "I'll see if there's a problem."

Moving off quickly in the direction his assistant indicated, he couldn't help feeling a foreboding, making no sense under the happy circumstance of their successful escape to the East and safety. But he wasn't a man to give in to feelings, especially negative or fearful ones. So Crosby pushed himself resolutely forward in search of Emily de Koningh and her pianist. He paused for only a second outside her door, then raised his hand to knock but stopped for a moment. Ominous doubt he was normally a stranger to held his hand in midair. He shook his head to free the misgivings and knocked. "It's Uranus Crosby," he announced quietly.

"Don't answer, Robert, please!" he heard quite plainly through the door. Then nothing.

"Mrs. de Koningh, I wonder if you need anything. I'd hoped you'd join us in the dining car. There's such relief and camaraderie, it would do you good." He waited with his head bowed, but still heard nothing. Then suddenly, the pocket door slid sideways, and Robert Haussmann stood before him in his shirt and a pair of fresh trousers, his face ashen and eyes fevered. Uranus Crosby stiffened in shock.

"My God, sir, what's the matter?" Robert stepped back to open the view into the compartment beyond, revealing a mound of covers on the opened cot with Emily de Koningh wrapped up to her chin. "Is she ill? Or wounded?" He looked at Robert who looked back as if lost for words as well as solutions.

"Neither, Mr. Crosby. I can answer for myself," Emily replied. "But I am in a great deal of pain."

"But what is the cause, madame? Please tell me and I'll help any way I can." Emily groaned from the bed. Crosby looked back at Robert and then at Emily, and back again at Robert. "What's going on?" he asked, more sternly this time. "Tell me, please."

"He can't, Mr. Crosby. I've forbade him to. But I'd like to see your wife if you'd send her to me."

"My wife?"

"Yes, I'll talk with no one else." She cried out again, in obvious pain, and Uranus Crosby could tell his only recourse was to do as she demanded. His wife was not someone he considered a good alternative to himself in times of trouble, but she was indeed a woman. So if that was Mrs. de Koningh's only solace, then get her he would. "Right away," he said, turning to go. He heard Emily talking again before the door slid shut.

"When she comes, Robert, I want you out of here, too . . . please."

✦⟶ ⟶✦ ⟋⟍ ✦⟵ ⟵✦

The train platform in the Cincinnati station was bare of travelers, desolate and quiet in the cold early morning air. The trip from Chicago to Cincinnati had taken over three days, but the rescue overnight sleeper's stop was unscheduled. The passengers and crew were clearly exhausted, yet there was an odd energy surrounding the platform and single train car, undoubtedly emanating from the group of newspaper reporters filing into the stationary car like a procession of determined ants.

"She can't be taken out while all the reporters are on the train," Uranus Crosby said with a quiet determination. But Robert Haussmann had a wild manner the opera house manager didn't trust. The pianist looked as if he might break down in tears at any moment, and that would clearly get Mrs. de Koningh nowhere. "Leave her behind the curtains of her cot," Mr. Crosby whispered. "As soon as the last reporter is off the train and out of sight, we'll transport her to the hospital immediately. I have a covered ambulance waiting. You can accompany her as well," he added with a squeeze of the pianist's arm. He truly had no sympathy for weakness, but he knew the man would be less trouble if he wasn't so upset. Calming him was the best strategy.

"She's in agony, Mr. Crosby. I'm afraid she'll die on this train if she stays one more minute. Waiting for these performers to tell their stories to twenty reporters is *ludicrous*!" Robert fairly shouted, proving Crosby right about the need for a quieting influence.

"There's nothing absurd about it, Professor Haussmann. She is not dying on this train. Mrs. de Koningh has gained strength with every hour she's been here, and her voice is a clear indication that she's not giving up. My wife assures me that although she's in great pain, it will undoubtedly be resolved at the hospital. So whatever female ailment she's afflicted with will be dealt with as soon as we can get her there." Seeing Robert was collecting himself to protest again, Uranus Crosby put both hands on his shoulders as if to give him stability, strength, and a clear message he was going nowhere.

"My wife informs me Mrs. de Koningh's ailment is not to be discussed in public, and that an airing in the press would mortify her and her family greatly, to say nothing of possibly ruining her career." He could feel Robert deflate between his two hands, causing him to tighten his grip in order to hold him up. "Buck up, sir. All will be well. Uranus Crosby takes care of everything if you give him time. Now go back to Mrs. de Koningh and prepare yourself to accompany her to the hospital, if you want to. Go on now." He gave Robert a gentle push to send him on his way.

Robert stumbled backward a few steps before regaining his balance and moving off down the hall, glancing at a group of reporters milling around outside the train. Suddenly he stopped, stooping to get a better look through the low, double-hung windows, his breath catching in his throat. "Mr. Crosby," he called out. "I recognize one of them. He knows Mrs. de Koningh well. In fact, he's probably here to interview her. We have to get her out and away to the hospital without him seeing her."

"Can't be done," the opera house manager assured him. "Try that and they'll all see her for sure. If he's a friend, the best strategy would be to bring him on and secure his confidence. Then perhaps he can help distract the others while we get her out behind those curtains and onto the coach. Which one is he? Show me. There's no time to lose, sir."

"There—the brown suit and fedora, shaggy mane of sandy hair. Can I tell Mrs. de Koningh that Mr. Dunne is coming to talk with her?" Robert asked.

"Of course. Her cooperation is the most essential necessity of all. Go do it, sir, and I'll pull Mr. Dunne off from the group." He watched Robert move down the aisle of the train car, stricken as if he was shell-shocked, as indeed he was.

Johnny Dunne stood outside the train with both hands in his pockets. The weather was suddenly turning colder, and the chill had a bone-penetrating dampness to it. He muttered monosyllabic answers to questions from his fellow reporters, deeply frustrated to stand outside the train knowing Emily was inside just a few yards away. But that was also why he could wait—knowing she was safe now.

He'd never forget reading the first news of the fire as it came across the tape in his office at the *New York Times*. Then firsthand witness reports had come in by telegraph. The horror expanded with every new revelation about the growing devastation, bad enough on its own without the news of the fall of the new Palmer House Hotel and its neighbor to the north, the Crosby Opera House. That strike had sparked recognition that Emily de Koningh had gone to Chicago and booked into that very hotel they'd discussed at her dinner party only a few weeks prior. She was there. He knew it.

Without a second thought, Johnny took the assignment to cover the Great Chicago Fire away from his head reporter, telling Ben it was undoubtedly going to be the biggest disaster of the nineteenth century in America, and Johnny would handle the initial coverage himself meeting the refugees' train in Cincinnati from the failed opera house opening. Ben had assumed he'd be accompanying Johnny, but Ben's sense of importance was satisfied with sharing the byline while Johnny traveled alone. So the sole representative of the *New York Times* at the train station in Cincinnati had no intention whatsoever of looking for stories or interviewing either the opera house manager or eleven of the twelve performers who escaped with their lives. Only one, Emily de Koningh, was of any interest to him.

"Mr. Dunne?" Johnny looked up at a tall, bushy-haired, and heavily bearded man. He nodded. "Come with me over here, please, so we can talk in private." He followed the man to the back of the train car, slowly, so as not to arouse the interest of other reporters. They'd all started talking animatedly together, forgetting Johnny almost from the start of their vigil, as they'd deemed him unpleasant and noncommunicative; full of himself, they'd decided.

"You're a friend of Mrs. de Koningh, is that right?" the man asked him. "Professor Haussmann spotted you and suggested I bring you in alone. Mrs. de Koningh is not well. It's imperative we get her to the hospital without being seen by the others." He glanced over at the group of reporters and back at Johnny. "Can you help with that?" Johnny narrowed his vision as he stared at the manager and set his jaw.

"I can," he said, leaving Uranus Crosby with the impression that his responsibility for the beleaguered Mrs. de Koningh was about to end. Uranus was, in fact, relieved. Feminine maladies he couldn't and didn't want to understand were not his usual assignment. But she was of course one of his performers, and now he felt released from the strain of her pain knowing someone else was taking over her care.

He had the ambulance carriage brought around to the opposite side of the train, as instructed by Mr. Dunne, saw Mrs. de Koningh safely off the train and on her way without the knowledge of the reporters who were fully engaged now with the other survivors inside the train. An early word to the artists from Uranus Crosby to spare no detail of their harrowing stories when talking with the press assured their complete attention inside when Emily was being removed from the car. When the train finally left its siding for New York again, no one knew she was missing from her berth except the doctor who'd secretly boarded the train to attend her, the reporter with her, her accompanist, and of course, Uranus Crosby.

News of the hardy band of artists and the opera house manager who saved them reached the public within days. The papers reported that all had survived without incident, except poor Emily de Koningh. Stories were invented to fill the vacuum thus created. Some said Emily was the only one who couldn't withstand the shock. Others said she was injured in the fire and the "wounded violinist" was being treated to ensure she'd be able to perform the next week in New York. Others said she was on the verge of a nervous breakdown, so she was taken to the hospital where an operation was performed, though no one knew what kind of operation would cure a nervous breakdown. As was often true with such reports, they did nothing to edify those who knew her personally but seemed to satisfy the public's curiosity.

Uranus Crosby took to the telegraphs to reassure relatives and friends of the performers that they were well, paying special attention to the one for the de Koningh mansion. There he assured the household that Emily was alive and recovering, most certainly in the hospital, but that the danger had passed, and she was being tended by the best doctors in Cincinnati as well as two of her friends, Mr. J. R. Dunne and her accompanist, Professor Haussmann. He told them she'd be brought home to New York by a private rail car that he, Uranus Crosby, had rented for the purpose. He reassured them there was nothing to worry about, and that the professor would explain everything once they returned home, which would most likely be in a week's time. He could imagine the uproar her household must be in but was unaware of the true horror of a home with two children and no adult relatives. No one had remembered to inform him of the de Koningh men's absence from home.

Robert Haussmann spent his time in Cincinnati fending off interviews with reporters in the hospital. He'd finally been told of the loss of Emily's child, but not by Emily herself or her doctor. The revelation came from Johnny Dunne, a shock Robert found profoundly unnerving because of his sudden adjustment to a different relationship to both Emily and the journalist. Had he not found a way to save both her and her violin from the fire in Chicago? Why then was he now relegated to the status of onlooker and Johnny to her trusted collaborator? He knew well not to speak of the specifics of such an event with anyone in public, and so struggled with the parameters of his new role as something less than a caretaker.

Understanding Robert's discomfort with his exclusion, Johnny stayed out of his way, appearing only once when he was assured of Emily's recovery, and then seemingly melting back into the mass of his colleagues returning to New York as if he'd never left them. "It's ridiculous to think you can't talk about a pregnancy," Johnny had scoffed when first told to hold his tongue. "Where do people think we'd all be without them?" But Emily had sworn him to silence at the advice of both her attorney and Mr. Crosby, and so he complied.

"You don't understand," she'd wailed at him when he'd objected.

"I know how the public will censure me. *A pregnant woman shouldn't travel, shouldn't expose her pregnancy to the world, shouldn't leave her children at home without her* . . . You don't, and never will. You're a *man!*" He'd found no cogent argument to refute her accusation, and so finally left Cincinnati as quietly as he'd come, though with a much lighter spirit. It never occurred to him that Emily's true trials might not be over, but only just beginning, no doubt because he was a man.

Robert pushed open the door of Emily's bedroom on Fifth Avenue very slowly so as not to wake her. They'd only arrived home the day before, and she was now resting around the clock until ancient Dr. Anderson said it was safe for her to get up for a while. The sight of her under the soft satin puff, her dark hair on the pillow spread around her like a floating sea star, sent him back to those early days when she'd been barely a teenager. She looked comfortable, safe, and protected as she was, but there was still some kind of tension as she lay there, just as always. He knew Emily had always been wired differently no matter where she was.

Bessie, Emily's companion and seamstress, had greeted them upon arrival at the mansion. She hadn't left Emily's side since then. Pulling on the curtains a little, Bessie checked to be sure the sun wasn't falling across Emily's pale face, disturbing at a time when she needed sleep. Connie sat beside his mother, happily joined together along his left side and her right. Leaning back on her pillows with his chubby little legs stretched out on top of the duvet, he let his shoeless feet play a game of hide-and-seek with each other under the cashmere throw pulled halfway up. Robert could hear Connie's high voice pattering in response to Emily's low murmurs, the duet adding an unexpected and welcome cheer to her sickroom. No one noticed when Robert pushed the door opened softly, so they continued on with their attentions without looking up.

"It was very beautiful, Mama. The photo you sent from the hotel looked like a magic palace." She nodded. "And the one of the opera house with those elegant ladies and gentlemen in their cloaks and hats . . . Awful that everything's ruined!"

"The whole city is ravaged, Con. Not just a few pretty buildings. Everything is gone. People's businesses, their homes, their schools . . . everything." Her voice sounded dull to Robert at a distance.

"Were there many people hurt, Mama? William was reading about it in the paper, but he wouldn't let me see." Connie turned his curly blond head on the pillow so he could look directly at Emily, but she didn't open her eyes.

"Yes, Con. Very many were hurt or killed. The whole city is nothing but death and destruction." Her eyes were still closed, so Robert could tell she wasn't watching the dark cloud spreading over her young son's face. He took an agitated step into the room, looking at Bessie to catch her reaction to the discussion on the bed. Her eyebrows drew together in concern matching his own. They both felt Emily's lack of connection to the boy's distress was at once uncharacteristic and upsetting.

"You could have been killed too, Mama. Then I'd never have seen you again." He struggled to hold back tears, but they were already showing, squeezing just around his eyelashes. Emily didn't open hers.

"But I wasn't, Connie. I'm right here, though I don't know that will do anyone any good."

Unable to hold back any longer, Robert moved deliberately across the carpet to the right side of the bed where Connie lay. Touching him on the shoulder so as not to surprise him, he leaned over and touched Emily's shoulder as well with his other hand. "We were very lucky, Connie," he went on, as if he'd been there all along. "We got help when we needed it and so were able to escape the fire ourselves. Some things are just meant to be, and obviously we're meant to be right here with you now, as we are." He patted the child's shoulder again and straightened up. "And you know, I've heard that something almost like a miracle is taking place there."

Connie wiped his eyes and looked at Robert fully for the first time. He knew a miracle had something to do with magic, and so his curiosity had started to grow. Emily opened her eyes, too. Encouraged by this new turn, Robert pulled a chair over from the bedside table and sat down with a smile.

"A . . . a miracle?" The boy turned toward his music teacher now to get the full import of what was coming.

"Yes, Connie. Apparently the city is already being rebuilt. In fact, that very hotel you saw in the postcard, which was so beautiful, is already rising from the ashes. The very next day, in fact, its owner obtained a huge loan and began rebuilding immediately. That's happening everywhere, all over Chicago. It's even said both the hotel and the city itself might be more beautiful and better and safer because of the fire. Sometimes you have to lose something to get something better in its place." He saw Emily stir a little.

"So soon?" she asked, letting her eyes flutter shut.

Reluctant to lose her again to the locked place somewhere deep within where they couldn't follow, Robert fought to hold her attention. He said to Connie, "I've just heard from your mother's friend Johnny Dunne that many of her artist colleagues have rallied to help the people of Chicago in her name!" Robert was relieved to see her eyelids float open and her gaze back on him. He nodded at her.

"Mr. Dunne has rallied the *Times* to pay back all the people who bought tickets to the opening night concert. It's over $100,000! That will leave the opera house manager financially whole and free to start again." Emily moved a little in bed and let out a small sigh, encouraging Robert to go on. "John Mackay is giving huge sums of money to rebuild the concert hall." Her eyes flickered. "And Jacques Offenbach is planning a benefit performance in Paris to raise money to replace the performers' instruments destroyed in the fire." Robert glanced over at the Guarneri in its protective case, sitting next to

Emily's settee as if it had never left. "And Monsieur Offenbach's leading ladies have come together to collect costumes and clothing for all the citizens of Chicago who lost their belongings in the fire."

Connie sat up straight. "Even silks and satins?" he asked.

"And ostrich feathers!" Robert saw a tiny smile at the corner of Emily's mouth.

"I think your mama needs to rest now." Bessie's calm voice came over Robert's shoulder. "I brought cookies for you, Connie. Mary has them in the kitchen." Connie slipped off the bed to the carpet so fast Robert couldn't push his chair back in time, catching the little boy against his shins.

"You, too, Professor Haussmann," he giggled, as Robert scooped him off his legs and onto his own stocking feet.

"I'll be down in a few minutes, if you'll save one for me."

Nodding vigorously and shoving his hand into Bessie's outstretched palm, Connie scuffed into his shoes by the bed and danced out of the room. Bessie turned to wink at Robert, a contented partner in the unspoken plan to warm the room's atmosphere. They were both pleased to see the shadow of a smile on Emily's mouth. The heavy door shut silently, and Robert leaned over the bed toward her again.

"I have more good news." Her eyes were open, though expressionless. He wanted to put some kind of spirit back in them again.

"Corey and his father are coming home tomorrow," Robert announced. He smiled with the assurance that this would be the necessary catalyst to bring her back to life.

She turned her head away from him, closing her eyes again. "I don't want to see him," she said. Her mouth was set in a determined line he knew well. The layers of hurt had built up so thick on her face Robert didn't know how they'd ever be removed.

"Emily, you can't blame Corey for your loss!" She said nothing, but the line of her mouth deepened. "You mustn't. He's not responsible. No one is. Why, if anyone could be blamed for your miscarriage it would be me." She rocked her head back and forth, "no" escaping from the line of her pursed lips. "Well surely you can't blame yourself! Nothing could have prevented this from happening. Emily . . perhaps it was a blessing disguised as a tragedy."

She turned on her left side, presenting her back to Robert seated in his chair. Her outline under the duvet looked stiff making him wonder if her recent trauma was threatening her with fearful images of fire and pain. She must just need rest. She'd get over it all with a good sleep. He rose slowly, touching her shoulder and saying, "Rest, then." Watching her breath rise and fall, he thought perhaps she was finally dozing off. He tiptoed toward the closed door, but stopped by the settee when he spotted the Guarneri in its case. Picking it up, he turned back and placed the violin next to Emily just where her son had lain a few minutes before. Remembering her fondness for sleeping with her instrument as a child, and her protection of it all through their escape from the fire, he felt she'd get comfort from its closeness now. He'd worked hard to clean and polish the outside of the case the day before. It had reeked of smoke, but now only of saddle soap and polish. The inside of the case and its cherished cargo looked virtually untouched. Perhaps the fact that it had already been well-used contributed to its stability now.

"You can rest, Emily," he whispered, patting the Guarneri beside her gently. "The worst is over." He rose to leave, unaware of the tears he'd left behind that wet her lashes.

CHAPTER TEN

"OH MY, IT'S SNOWING!" William glowered at the few random flakes floating past the window. Apparently threatened by his dour expression, the reticent crystals seemed to hesitate before multiplying in defiance.

"Does that mean we can't go out?" Connie crawled up next to him on the window seat in the library to stare at the cold gray sky and bare trees lining Fifth Avenue. "I don't see much snow, William," he declared. He turned his head sideways just enough to read his brother's expression, hoping to ward off the bait-and-switch tactics he'd become so familiar with.

But William's implacable gaze was directed across at the park and not at his younger brother. "Lord, I hope not," William muttered. "I'm so bored." The viscidity of his brother's ever-present discontent filled Connie with a dread he'd long struggled to get away from. The four-year-old hopped down from his perch at the window and started off toward the library door in search of escape.

Corey de Koningh came in from the hall just as his youngest son reached the threshold, wrapping himself around his father's shins with a tether hug that could have easily upended his unprepared parent had he not been quick to bend down to return his attacker's hold. "Where are you off to, little man? Are you ready to go downtown with me?" Father and son held on to each other for a minute, before Corey unwound the little boy's arms from his legs.

"Yes, yes, yes!" Connie shrieked, delighted. "Is William coming?"

"I suppose," his father said distractedly, "if you want him to . . ." Corey had begun to look across the library to the window, as if he was seeing something well beyond the room and his children.

"I think he should come. He's bored. He needs to get happy," Connie whispered, loudly.

"Really? William, is that so? You're bored today? Well, so am I, if you must know," Corey added with a sigh. William's sullen frown moved from Corey to Connie, and back to the scene outside without comment. Corey glanced down at the boy still standing at his knees, sharing a raised eyebrow with him. He noticed Connie looked almost frightened. "William's bad mood is hardly your fault, little man," he assured Connie with a squeeze. "Come on, William, there's no excuse for boredom at your age. That's a sign of a lazy imagination." Corey smiled at his obdurate offspring. "Let's go, boys. We're heading down to see the Christmas windows and Santa Claus. Apparently, they've found a way to make the decorations move on their own. It sounds like magic; the perfect antidote for ennui." He held out his hand as if to pull William to his side across the expanse of library carpet, which had the desired effect. William slipped off the window seat to join his father and brother at the library door.

All three left the room together, and Corey recognized with surprise how much he enjoyed having one hand on William's shoulder and the other filled with Connie's chubby palm. He was unsettled to find he'd missed both boys during his long stay down south with his father. He'd rushed back to New York without Klaas, whose aversion to fast trains had been reason enough for Corey to return alone while his father meandered back in greater comfort at a pace commensurate with his advancing years. But Corey was upset to find himself even less comfortable in the de Koningh mansion on Fifth Avenue than he'd expected. The house and family relied on Klaas's quiet, yet elegant presence as a landmark. Emily, too, had mentioned missing his father greatly; perhaps even more than she'd

missed Corey, he now thought, possibly due to the paternal role
Klaas had played in her upbringing. He knew his own time down
south was also responsible for his unaccustomed discomfort at
home. He wished he'd had more time to settle in before having to
deal with family. The children seemed an unwanted distraction from
his own troubles much of the time.

Corey forced himself not to cast a longing look at the piano as he
and his boys left the library, even though he'd hoped for more time
to practice this afternoon. He'd leave the room to Emily so she could
be with Robert and her violin. She needed it more than he did, and
he needed his boys more than she did, or so she'd said. He wasn't at
all sure she was right. Their argument, not more than a few hours
after he'd returned home, did not bode well for their reunion. Emily
blamed him for ignoring their contractual obligations, both personal
and professional, and Corey blamed her for discounting the importance of her role as a wife and mother and told her so. He was angry
to find he'd raced home to an uncommunicative and unappreciative
wife, and she was mad that he had no empathy for what she'd been
through while he was away, and for exposing her guilt over letting
down her family and children. Why the loss of an unexpected and
largely unwanted child had let anyone down he couldn't fathom, but
it had robbed her of all concern, if any was left, for him and his
unhappiness. He told her he needed time back home to figure out
the value, if any, of what he'd left behind. And she admitted she was
irritated all the time but couldn't explain why or at what. He'd
decided that was a good place to end a conversation that wasn't
leading anywhere productive, and she'd agreed.

Needing to stay on schedule for his planned meeting with Johnny
Dunne at Macy's, he collected the pile of winter clothing, a tangle of
wool scarves, gloves, and coats, from the hall closet, much to the
chagrin of the footman whose job it was to dress them all better than
Corey could. He found he wasn't enjoying all the special intricacies

of fatherhood, including organizing the jumble of dressing and undressing before and after going outdoors, and he wasn't very good at it. He had to admit he hadn't missed the layered clothing often necessary in New York's climate. The weather down south was more forgiving, which helped to lessen his discomfort when thinking about his stay at the Widow Stovall's. Other than his vague unease at being in this house again, there was almost nothing specific that displeased him about his return home, except that Emily was miserable—miserable and angry with everyone and everything around her, and with herself as well. In fact, he thought, mostly with herself.

He'd had a long talk with Robert Haussmann as soon as he'd returned. The emergency telegram had come, however, from Emily's friend Johnny Dunne, at the *New York Times*. But Robert was the one poised at the foot of Emily's bed, as he had been in her childhood, watching her recover as if her well-being was his only care in the world. He and the violin had always kept a vigil, easing Corey's worry when he'd been unable to help her himself. Hovering just out of sight so as not to intrude, Robert had made it clear he was going nowhere until he knew no one in the de Koningh household needed him, especially Emily. That meant he was always within earshot of Corey's most immediate questions and ready to answer them in any way he could.

Yet there really were no answers to the most obvious questions: Why had Emily become so unreachable? Why had she closed herself off from everyone and everything? And why did she blame herself for the loss of her child? Old Dr. Anderson explained the phenomenon of grief over something that had never been. He'd said it was common in the case of miscarriage for a mother to lament the forfeit of a child even when she hadn't welcomed its coming in the first place. That of course didn't apply to Emily directly, but it certainly explained to Corey why she seemed so miserable now: it was simply in a woman's nature. That was clear. He wondered if she understood or cared how he felt about losing the child he hadn't even known they were having. But then, there hadn't been a chance to ask her that yet. Maybe he never would.

"I can't breathe, Papa," Connie squealed, wiggling to get free from Corey's grasp. He'd wrapped the scarf so many times around Connie's little neck that the boy looked like a caricature of a snowman adorned with a human wardrobe. He watched his two sons careen out the front door to the waiting carriage and wondered at their childish laughter. Even William seemed to be swept along by the prevailing atmosphere of adventure. Corey wished he could shed his bad moods as easily as his son had.

"All for one and one for all," William shouted, swinging back and forth on the carriage door. The horse stopped stamping to keep her feet warm and tossed her head up and down, apparently in full agreement with William's decree. Corey smiled to think how Monsieur Dumas's historical novel had become beloved in its English translation as an adventure story for his son. He and Emily had been captured in their youth by Charles Dickens in much the same way. He smiled again and the horse nodded her head again, her bridle bells jangling in a sudden reprise of affirmation. Her hot equine breath hanging on the cold damp air, the mare made it clear every fiber of her powerful body was prepared to transport the de Koningh children and their father downtown or anywhere else they wanted to go.

"We're off!" Corey called out, tapping the coachman on the shoulder and simultaneously swinging his long torso through the door and onto the seat between his sons. The carriage started with a lurch, reminding him of many excursions long ago that had started just the same way. The only thing missing now was . . . Emily. They'd always shared their adventures together as children, and as young adults. Now where was she?

The ride from Ninety-Fourth Street and Fifth Avenue to Fourteenth Street and Sixth Avenue was a long one, and the de Koningh men diverted each other by singing sea shanty songs and Christmas carols for the first ten minutes of the trip, rocking on the seats to the music like gimballed holiday toys. Suddenly William sat up tall, and putting his forehead to the glass, groaned in the first note of discontent since they'd started off. "It's still snowing. We'd best turn back for home," he muttered, motioning for his father and brother to join him at the window.

"Oh no, must we, Papa? Is it really so bad?" Connie whimpered like a stray kitten, and Corey silently vowed to get him to Mr. Macy's windows even if a blizzard threatened to close the city.

"No way of knowing yet, Con. But the newspaper said nothing of snow today, so I have a feeling this is just a passing flurry and not a storm."

"How can the newspaper know what the weather is if it hasn't happened yet?" Connie's childish sophistication surprised Corey. He'd forgotten how sharp and wise children could be.

William rolled his eyes in disgust, ostensibly unable to control himself in the wake of his brother's naivete. "They don't *report* the weather, silly; they *predict.* Mother says the weather-watchers send temperature and air pressure readings to the papers so we can be prepared for the worst," William intoned in his most pedantic and snide manner.

"Why is snow the worst?" his brother asked, instantly argumentative because he wasn't happy about the label of *silly.* "I love it. Watching it fall, the way it makes everything quiet so all you can hear is the horse snorting and the hand shovels scraping. If I hear those sounds when I wake up in the morning I know it will be a special day before I even open my eyes! And I love playing in it: sledding, making snow men and forts, and throwing snowballs. I love it." Connie glowed with pleasure.

"I think your brother's talking more about how hard it is to get food and supplies in the city when it snows with over a million people living here." Corey hoped he could remember how to mediate a comfort zone between his two boys, not easy but necessary. He was out of practice.

"Right, Father. And trying to get the carriages around on those silly runners that get stuck in the deep snow is impossible. It's hopeless trying to clear the roads by shoveling snow into the carts and dumping it in the rivers." William looked pleased with himself and his new camaraderie with his father.

"Why hopeless, William? It helps somewhat and gives temporary work to the people who drive the carts. There's always an upside to each new challenge to city living if you'll only look for it." Corey winked at his younger son reassuringly, who didn't seem to feel nearly as silly as he had, now that his father had taken his side against his brother. "Anyway, don't worry about all that," Corey ordered them both. "I think Connie has the right idea in looking forward to fun in the snow instead of some impending doom that isn't here and most likely won't be. You have to learn to enjoy life more, William." Corey realized he'd developed a strange new predilection down south for throwing caution to the winds and didn't mind sharing it with his sons.

"Yes, enjoy life," Connie echoed. He grinned up at his father, delighted with the feeling of being on the grown-up side of an argument.

"Tell *that* to our horse and driver," William grumbled. He jerked his head toward the street view through the carriage window, and all of them could see the snow intensifying. Corey realized Connie was watching him and knew it was an important time to keep a light touch to the discussion about the rest of the afternoon.

"Don't worry, William. We're almost at Fourteenth Street and as soon as we've crossed to Sixth Avenue we can get out and walk. I'll send the carriage home before there can be any more build-up."

"Oh fine! And how will we get home then?" William's sullen glower couldn't be mistaken for anything but rudeness, but Corey refused to let him win the battle for the low ground. He was amazed by how obstinate the boy could be—was that new or had he just forgotten?—and wondered if he'd be able to survive an afternoon around him.

"There's an elevated train right across from Mr. Macy's dry goods store," Corey reminded both boys. "Even if all ground travel is stopped, I'm sure we can get home that way. Come on now, boys, hats and scarves back on so we can enjoy our time looking at the windows before we go in. Your mother tells me Santa Claus is walking around inside to greet all the shoppers, too."

Connie clapped his mittened hands together in silent glee, while William shook his head in disgust. Corey narrowed his eyes, leveling a severe warning at his older son not to spoil his little brother's expectations. "Squeeze every ounce of pleasure out of each day that you can, my friend," he warned, as he held his older son back in the carriage for a moment while the driver carefully lifted Connie down first. "There's already enough unhappiness in the world without adding to it." He squeezed William's shoulder a little harder than necessary, causing him to look up at him to find out why; exactly what he'd wanted, since the boy was insisting on avoiding his eyes while he wallowed in whatever discontent his childish temper was prey to. He reminded Corey of Emily somewhat, and he wondered how that had happened so suddenly since he'd been away.

"Cheer up, William, for all our sakes, and mostly your own." Corey held his son's eyes a moment longer. He stepped from the cab last, and gathering both boys up on the snowy pavement under each arm, he swung them over the small pile of snow already collected at the corner by Mr. Macy's overeager shovelers focused only on their assignment to clear the sidewalk. Even William grinned at the surprise momentary flight through the snowy air and seemed to drop his ill temper on the other side of the mound of snow. He ran with his brother to the windows under the sign flanked by two stars:

☆ R. H. MACY'S & CO. ☆

"Is that the star of Bethlehem?" Connie asked, pointing up at the sign.
"I doubt it," his father chuckled. "Apparently Mr. Macy was a

sailor before he went into the dry goods business, and he has a tattoo on his arm that looks like that."

"How do you know?" William asked.

"I don't," Corey replied. "I've just heard the story and I assume it has some truth to it."

"Oh, look here, Papa!" Connie shouted, pulling Corey toward the windows by the hand with surprising strength. "It's a rocking horse, and it's moving as if an invisible child is riding it. Look how beautiful the coat is, so shiny and brown, and the brass tack and saddle decorations gleam like gold. How does it move? Could I have a horse like that for Christmas?"

"Please, one question at a time, Con," Corey laughed. "I can't see how they've made the horse rock. Maybe it has fishing line attached to pull it back and forth, but I don't know. That's the magic." They both bent down to try to find some clue to the horse's movement but couldn't. "And I don't think we need this particular rocking horse, Con, because we have one back home."

"No, we don't," Connie pouted, surprised his father didn't know more about the nursery toys. "We've never had one, have we, William." Both boys shook their heads in unison, making Corey laugh at the severity of their expressions over the injustice of the deficit.

"Well there should be," he chuckled. "There's one of your grandfather's up in the attic. We'll have a look as soon as we get home and bring it out of retirement. Your mother and I used to play with it." He looked past the boys and Mr. Macy's windows to an attic excursion long ago in his memory that had taken him and Emily to the roof together; dangerous and forbidden territory he'd rather his boys knew nothing of now, but a secret place he was profoundly grateful for then. He pulled himself back just in time to hear the boys arguing over a game of Graces, the hoops and wands considered an appropriate challenge for girls, though boys loved to join in catching the smaller hoops as a lark.

"I think Grandfather Alden is sending us some quoits for

Christmas," William announced to no one in particular. "He told me it's a good game to play inside when the weather's bad, as it usually is in England."

"When did you hear from your grandfather Alden?" Corey asked, surprised to learn there'd been contact with Emily's British father he hadn't known about.

"Oh, sometime when you were away," William muttered vaguely. "Lots of things happened while you were away." His dark, retaliatory look made Corey feel as ostracized as his son obviously meant it to.

Refusing the bait, Corey changed the subject quickly. "Come now, boys, is there anything you see here you'd want to tell Santa Claus about when we write to him? Other than what your grandfather Alden is already giving you, of course," he added, in hopes of warding off another sneer from William over the reality of Santa Claus in a red wool costume inside the store.

"Yes!" piped up Connie, his round pink face glowing with excitement and cold air. "Look there, Papa." He pushed repeatedly on the window glass with his mitten. "What does it say there?"

"Where? Over that doll sitting under the Christmas tree?" Corey asked, confused by the urgency of Connie's directive.

"Yes!"

"That's for girls, you little fool," William sneered. "We don't have any in our family, and mother's too old," he added, as if to handle Connie's deranged mind with care.

"Read me the sign, Papa," Connie begged.

"It says, *Hertwig German Glazed Porcelain China Head Doll with blouse detail*," Corey read out loud. "I think people are supposed to make clothes for her, because the only thing she has on is that simple blouse painted on her porcelain top, and you see there are all those uncut fabrics in the box beside her."

"That's what I want for Christmas, Papa! I want to make her clothes. See how her black hair shines! She looks just like Mama, but her eyes are blue like yours. She's beautiful. If I had a sister, she'd look just like that. I want to take care of her and make her lots of clothes. Ple-e-ase, Papa. Can I ask Santa Claus for the china doll? Ple-e-ease . . ."

"Oh, Jesus!" William groaned, sounding a great deal like Mary the little parlor maid. Corey promised himself he'd have a talk with her about swearing in front of the children.

"Quiet, William," Corey ordered. "Connie, we'll write a private letter to Santa at home so you can explain exactly why you want the doll so much. It will make more sense to him that way." He stroked his younger son's face gently, tucking some of his loose blond curls that had escaped from his wool cap back underneath it where they'd stay dry. "Shall we warm up inside?" he asked with a smile. "We'll see what's going on beyond the windows." He was such a lovable little creature, but Corey wondered if his hours were well spent soothing his baby's nerves. There really wasn't time in the world for all the things one wanted to do, and surely that spent with children got in the way of many other adult relationships one wanted to nurture.

"Father, let's not," William groused in a sour tone. "We've already seen what we came for and I'm getting tired. I didn't want to come in the first place. Can't we find somewhere else to go that would be more interesting?"

"I'm sure we can," said a voice behind them, seemingly out of the crowd of Fourteenth Street shoppers. "What brings the de Koningh men to Ladies' Mile?"

"Are we on Ladies' Mile now?" William asked, spinning around to see where the voice had come from. "Mr. Dunne, is that you?" All three de Koninghs saw energetic Johnny Dunne materializing through the snow, swathed in his long winter overcoat and beaver hat, understanding instinctively that their afternoon was about to take a radical turn.

"Indeed it is, William de Koningh. Ladies' Mile stretches along Broadway from Ninth to Twenty-Third Street and includes Fifth and Sixth Avenues from Fourteenth to Twenty-Fifth Streets. Mr. Macy's store marks the entrance to it. But what brings you here to the Mile with no ladies?" William was delighted, as he knew an escapade was undoubtedly in the wind. Connie was not, as he knew it meant the visit to Macy's was probably coming to a swift end. And Corey was relieved, happy to have his caretaking time with his boys shortened, and glad to have a chance to talk with Emily's friend about the events of the Chicago fire that had caused such lasting upheaval in her life. He'd worried the snowfall might cancel their plan to meet. It was the main reason he'd offered to bring the boys downtown in the first place.

"What a pleasure, Dunne," he said, reaching out for Johnny's gloved hand. "And I might ask the same of you. Where are the ladies with you? Though there seems to be plenty of feminine interest, as usual," he added with a chuckle.

It was true. The crowded shopping district was filled with fashionable women scurrying to and fro, with most of them giving Johnny Dunne an appreciative, appraising glance as they rushed by. Some even slowed slightly for a better look. "I was finishing some shopping for my employee Christmas presents," Johnny explained, "but I've decided I don't want to spend any more time in the shops with a snowstorm in the works. Is your carriage near?"

"I sent it home," Corey announced brightly, hoping to overwhelm William's repeated objections with his own good cheer.

"I suggested it," William announced, looking up at Johnny. "We didn't want our horse and driver to get stuck."

"Excellent foresight!" Johnny exclaimed, putting his hand on William's shoulder as if knighting him with a sword. "But I have the newspaper's hack with me, and if you'd all like to join me we could reconnoiter at the *Times*'s headquarters and avoid the teeth of the storm together. There might even be some coffee and hot chocolate waiting for us."

Both boys launched into a chorus of pleas, obviously feeling the astral pull of Johnny's magnetism. For a moment Corey tried to pretend resistance, but quickly gave in to enjoy the rush to Johnny's cab, all of them laughing with the pleasure of escape. It was just something about Johnny's energy, and Corey felt freer than he had in days.

"How will we get home if the snow gets worse?" he heard William ask Johnny in a good-humored tone totally missing just a few minutes before.

"Why worry about that now?" Johnny laughed. "Perhaps it will have stopped by then, or you can stay the night in the office with me, sleeping on desks with coats thrown over you and under your heads."

"No. I don't want to. Mother would worry about us," Connie whimpered.

"So what? You're almost men now and she'll have to get used to a little worry here and there." He winked at William conspiratorially, but Connie missed the cue as he was so much shorter, and wouldn't have understood if he'd seen it, anyway. He started to sniffle.

"It's okay, Con," Corey assured his son as he picked him up and hugged him. "We'll be going home at least partway by elevated train if the weather thickens, but a *short* stop with Mr. Dunne for hot chocolate would be a good way to fortify us beforehand." He smiled at Johnny, making it clear the parameters of their visit had just been set, though they could be changed at any time if Connie became upset again. But as Connie was now viewing the world from the high vantage point of his father's shoulder, higher than either William or Johnny, his anxiety turned to acquiescence immediately.

"Good, Papa," he chirped. "We'll have hot chocolate and then go home to Mama. She'll not miss us at all."

"Follow me," Johnny announced, putting his arm out for William to hold on to as if they were old acquaintances. Clearly feeling the privilege of friendship with an adult of such importance, William drew himself up and marched off with Johnny, reminding Corey of how often his son invoked the image of Emily's father, both taking themselves too seriously. Visions of the Pied Piper of

Hamelin also crossed his mind as they all traipsed along through the snow to the hack, as if tethered by an invisible silken cord with Johnny in the lead.

The boys poured questions out for the rest of the trip to the *Times*'s building, stopping only once when they arrived to look up for a second at the impressive columns supporting the façade. A small army of men and boys shoveled the path to the building and swept the steps as soon as a few flakes fell where they'd just been cleared. It seemed a hopeless task.

"Is this where you live?" Connie breathed, staring up at the big building devoted entirely to the gathering and dissemination of news.

"Almost," Johnny chuckled. "More often than not."

"I don't think I'd like to live here," Connie said, with a frown.

"Don't be such a baby," William snorted. "He just means he has to work long hours, so he's here a lot. Right, Mr. Dunne?"

"Very perceptive, William," Johnny replied. "However, you're lucky to have a beautiful house to live in, your own bedroom, and a beautiful mother to care for your every wish. I can certainly understand your brother's disquiet over spending even one minute more than necessary away from his home and her side."

"It's just because he's a baby," William scoffed. "You have no idea how dull it is at home, Mr. Dunne. I'd leave in a minute if I could live as you do." William's eyes shone with a fevered light that made Corey uncomfortable. Where had such brashness come from? Was it extant only in the throes of Johnny's charm, or had a plant of slow growth nurtured in a soil of discontent he'd been unaware of in his absence? Had Emily noted it and tried to head it off? Or was there, in fact, a little bit of Emily reflecting in William's assertiveness? Would she then be unable to recognize the trouble that might be brewing just under the surface? Her own unhappiness was perhaps as much a part of her nature as it was a consequence of her miscarriage—Emily just being Emily. He hadn't realized it before, but watching William now made him wonder.

"It's a pretty special building, young de Koninghs. The only one built just for a newspaper. I'm going to show you all around and then I think you'll feel right at home, just as I do."

Johnny helped both boys out of the carriage almost before Corey noticed they'd stopped. He glanced up at the big, sloppy snowflakes falling so thickly they seemed to obstruct breathing as well as vision. A vague guilt brushed past him as he watched Connie struggling through the drifts at the curb. Should a father have headed them for home as soon as the storm intensified? Should his own plan to talk with Johnny have been executed without the boys? He wasn't quite sure how it had happened. He'd just wanted to cover his meeting with the antics of the children. He wasn't used to the constancy of his sons' care. Fatherhood had happened so fast he'd barely had time to adjust, and the importance of it overwhelmed him. He wondered if this was all there was to life, as he'd had no time to see very much else.

"Come on, de Koningh." Johnny swung around with a boy in each hand. "We need to get these young men some hot chocolate with whipped cream. And I know just where to find it."

He grinned as he watched Corey unfold himself out of the carriage. Looking for all the world like a third conspiring child, Johnny shook the snowflakes that hadn't melted yet from his shaggy brown hair. Corey jogged a few long strides to catch up to them and they all continued at a prance up the steps to the building. Just inside the door, Johnny shook his head violently and the snow flew off in every direction. The boys did the same to their arms and legs, and all three cackled with the fun of turning themselves into playful puppies just coming in from a swim. It wasn't possible to miss the change in mood as they mimicked their pied piper host.

Across the marble entry hall, the de Koningh boys followed their leader past the big Christmas tree and on toward the huge staircase. Corey took off his wet coat and shook it, moving off again to be sure he'd stay with them. The boys seemed to have forgotten him. He watched them all chatting happily together, surprised at the ease with which they'd replaced him, how quickly it had happened, wondering if it was because they weren't used to having him around. Three long strides put him back with them, and Connie's little hand slipped easily into his. They looked at each other and smiled.

"We can go now," Connie said, happily. "My papa's here." They all started to climb together, and Corey realized how much better he felt with Connie's hand in his. He was needed.

After a stop on the second floor with Johnny to pick up some of the excellent peppermint-spiced hot chocolate with whipped cream made by one of the secretaries, they moved up one more flight to the editorial floor. A train was set up near the stairs, raised on a tabletop platform so the boys could watch it at eye level. In and out of miniature villages and rural mountain scenes it wound with an eager determination. Corey recognized that the repetitive, clicking rhythm of its little toy wheels on the track was also part of its allure, reminding him of his own travels on its real counterparts. The music of technology was everywhere these days.

"Where did you get this?" William asked. He was trying to appear only vaguely interested, but he couldn't take his eyes off the twists and turns the locomotive and cars were making at breakneck speed.

"Schwarz's Toy Bazaar," Johnny told him. "Did you stop in there before I met you today?"

"No. Where is it?" William asked, still following the train's disappearance under bridges and through groves of pine trees along its route.

"Just on Broadway. They have a complete collection of toys for Christmas and nothing else to get in your way. Old Otto Schwarz really knows how to make children happy!" They all stood mesmerized for three or four revolutions of the track before Corey could tear his attention away.

"We'll have to go there soon," he said, smiling at William and

Connie with a nod. Then turning to Johnny, he said almost apologetically, "I haven't been in the city for a while. I didn't realize Schwarz's had moved."

"Lots of things have changed since you've been here, Father." William kept following the train, beginning to move slowly around the platform on foot to watch from all angles.

"So they have," Corey agreed. "In fact, I'd like to talk with Mr. Dunne about some of them for a while. Could you boys be happy for a few minutes here with the trains?" William never looked up but nodded. Connie saw him and nodded too. "Are you sure, Con? We'll be right . . ." He looked around the room and back to Johnny.

"Right over there where the glass door is," Johnny finished for him. "You can see through it, so you'll know we're there. Come and get us if you need anything, right?" He moved off easily, and Corey found himself again torn between the need to take care of his boys and the lure of easy adult companionship offered by Johnny's hospitality.

"Don't go anywhere else, William, and watch out for your brother, understand?" Corey ordered. William nodded and Corey turned to follow Johnny into his office. He laid his coat down on a chair by the door with the boys' coats and hats while Johnny hung his up to dry on a hat rack in the corner behind his desk. "Can I hang them for you?" Johnny asked, with a nod to the rack. "At least the boys' coats, if you want. They'll be dry then when you're ready to go."

"We won't be here that long," Corey assured him. "Thanks, but this is fine."

"As you wish. So what can I do for you?" Johnny asked. He looked amused, as if he knew what Corey wanted, the cat playing with its mouse.

"Your opinion," Corey said without a pause. "You're an opinion editor, so I assume it should be very easy for you." A quizzical narrowing of Johnny's eyes and lift to his brows was all the reaction Corey saw, so he continued. "You were with my wife when she miscarried after the Great Chicago Fire. For all I know you may have saved her life." Johnny sat back in his chair looking almost relieved and shook his head. Corey continued as if that answer hadn't really been of importance. "You certainly know a great deal about what happened to her during that ordeal then, Dunne, and I'd like to know if you can tell me why she's so horribly upset and angry now. You'd think surviving the fire with both her violin and Professor Haussmann would be cause for great joy instead of sorrow, wouldn't you?"

Johnny rocked forward in his chair to lean on his desk, resting his chin on his tented hands as if to steady his focus on Corey. "I'm hardly Emily's confidant," he said, "but I presume the loss of her child was a very great sorrow." Corey couldn't imagine why the opinion editor of the *New York Times* was being so obtuse, but something held him back from pushing further into unknown territory.

"Do you think, then, that she'd planned to give up her career?" Corey asked, watching Johnny closely. There was some clue in his intuition yet undiscovered, but he'd keep questioning until it was clear.

"No idea. As I said, she's never confided in me about anything. But I'd suspect not a chance. Why should she?"

"She's struggled with only two children. I can only imagine that three would have put an end to her performing. She'd have forgotten the violin and never looked back." Corey knew that was just wishful thinking on his part and held no basis in reality. He couldn't even look at Johnny when he said it, knowing full well how ridiculous it was.

"She's a healthy girl. She can fill the void and have more children anytime she wants. The doctors in Cincinnati made that clear. But she's not putting down the violin, from anything I've seen," Johnny said, looking at Corey with a small frown as if he couldn't believe how lacking in empathy he was.

"Then her upset now isn't because she'd set her heart on giving up music to become a full-time mother?" Again, Corey found himself looking away for fear his disingenuousness would be obvious.

"Of course not. Not in my opinion, anyway. Listen, I'm sure she struggled. Boys aren't easy, are they?" Johnny made a circle with his hand, suggesting he and Corey both were included in the category of difficult boys. "But I think Emily's real battles are professional." Johnny bowed his head a little. "In my opinion, she needs a full-time accompanist who's her support partner. The strain of keeping up her performance schedule without one is doing her in."

"You mean without me," Corey said. Johnny remained expressionless. "But Professor Haussmann fills in for me . . . or do you mean she wants to get rid of me completely?" He was surprised how easily it had come out.

"Nonsense, de Koningh," Johnny interrupted. "She doesn't need some old teacher, or even you, on her *professional* team. She needs someone totally disconnected from her private life. Someone whose job it is to be there always, no matter what, when she's working. Someone who hasn't known her since she was a child, doesn't know her family trials and tribulations, but just knows her music." Corey stared at him, still having trouble moving from the miscarriage to the replacement of Emily's accompanist.

"And you don't need to be tagging along behind your wife either, de Koningh. Emily says you love modern music. You can't be part of the nineteenth century's new music scene if you're steeped in the classical traditions of eighteenth-century Austria. You need your freedom to follow your own sounds. Am I right? Wouldn't that make for a happier family all around?"

Corey stared at Johnny for a few seconds. He was either a maniac or a genius, or maybe a little of both. Finally he started to laugh. "Sounds idyllic, but how can I explore new music and still attend to my family? I've begun to realize that when Emily needs to be away, I should be with the children."

"Okay, not impossible. She told me you'd become enamored of

the southern ragged-time. Is that so?" Johnny stopped to look Corey in the eye as he nodded. "Fine. There are lots of immigrants who are playing it up where the farms used to be in Harlem. You know they've been breaking them all up, like that huge Roosevelt tract, and there are little pubs all over the place filled to the brim with people from other places. You don't have to go south anymore. Reconstruction hasn't delivered on its promises to the South, so the South is coming north!"

Corey smiled back at Johnny's unwavering enthusiasm, not sure it was founded in reality but pleased by it, nonetheless. "And your other suggestion . . . where would Emily find a qualified accompanist at this stage in her career?"

"Oh, good Lord, de Koningh. That's your department; yours and the professor's. Between the two of you there must be plenty of ways to connect her with qualified pianists who could try out for the job. Let her be the judge and choose her own. It might just distract her from her loss enough to turn things around."

Corey gave him a long, rueful glance filled with his guilt over Emily's disappointments in life, all seemingly tied to him somehow. Johnny mistook the look for criticism and pushed his chair back defensively to put more space between them.

"Well you asked for my opinion, my friend. You don't have to take it."

"I know that. And I thank you for it and will do some thinking. You've opened my eyes in ways I wasn't prepared for. And now, I'd better start for home with the boys. This storm could prove an unpleasant challenge, though don't tell William I said so."

Corey pushed up out of his chair, noticing how dark it was now outside the office windows. The partners' clock on Johnny's desk said it was only three, but the snow was forcing an early nightfall on the city, adding a sinister element to what had seemed like fun only a few hours ago. Corey started picking up the sodden mass of clothes on the chair beside him, wishing he'd taken Johnny's offer to hang at least the boys' things up to dry. But before Corey could gather and sort them all, William dashed into the room without knocking. He hung on the door to catch his breath. "Connie's gone, Father," he sputtered. "Completely gone. I've looked everywhere. I don't know what happened. He just vanished!"

⊱⋅☙ ❧⋅⊰

"I've locked all the exits to the building, Mr. Dunne, as you ordered, but I can't keep them closed for long. It's a fire hazard." The security guard looked a little put out, as if the trouble caused by the disappearance of the child was purposeful.

"Just find the boy, Captain O'Rourke, and then we can open them. Do you have people searching every floor?" Johnny took a deep breath, realizing the elderly employee who'd been hired as a favor to a *Times* executive was undoubtedly incapable of moving quickly for any reason.

"I do, sir. We blocked everything, but don't know exactly when he disappeared. There may have been time for him to have gotten out, but we'll have a check of the building completed soon." The aged floor guard looked as if he hadn't absorbed the seriousness of the problem yet. "You say you and the boy's father did an extensive search of your own floor, too. Can I talk with the father to get a full description of the boy?"

"Of course, if you think mine may have been lacking. Just be sure your staff knows where to reach you for questions and updates." Johnny spun around and took off to rejoin Corey and William in his office, his dynamism in direct opposition to the guard's lethargy.

"You and William wait here for Captain O'Rourke. I'll get out on the floor to do some questioning of my own," he ordered, starting for the door but stopping abruptly before he got to it. Moving back to Corey's chair where William stood pressed up against his knee, he put his hand on Corey's shoulder and squeezed. "We'll find him. You stay here," he said, as Corey struggled to his feet. It was virtually impossible to keep a man over six feet tall down in his chair if he didn't want to stay there.

"Please get your secretary to be with William," Corey breathed. "I need to get out there right away. He can see me above everyone else at a distance and that might help." Corey looked like a wild animal about to bolt.

"Stay, in case he comes looking for you both. It's just a matter of a little more time," Johnny assured him. Corey stood frozen to the spot, and Johnny couldn't look at either one of them, feeling both as if the older boy was in shock over the loss of his charge, and possibly able to see inside Johnny and his father to their own fears. But father and son had each other for comfort and that freed Johnny to get out and do something. He'd always found action the cure for most troubles. That's why he'd instinctively known Emily would need to get moving again to deal with her emotional problems, whatever they were. Contemplation would accomplish nothing, allowing fear to seep in and stain everything. They were a lot alike that way. He'd been so focused on her husband and sons he'd all but forgotten her. But he needed to stop the spreading panic here. The only way to do that was to find the boy. He moved out the door without looking back. "In there, Captain," he ordered the floor guard as he left, gesturing toward the two tense forms frozen together. He had his own investigation to conduct.

Racing up and down the stairs, he jogged back and forth on each floor, questioning staff and reporters alike. He knew them all so well, he knew just who to spend time with and who to ignore. Why were there so many conflicting reports sighting Connie de Koningh? Human nature. Johnny shook his head in disgust as he moved from person to person. He wished there was some way to speak to them all instantaneously, but there wasn't, and personal contact was his only option. He found he was grateful for going down the stairs at last, a chance to catch his breath from the headlong dash to find a child who'd gone missing too long ago, he feared. Then just at that moment of darkness, he saw little Connie de Koningh pulling away from one of the secretaries and hanging off her arm like a petulant monkey. "We have him, de Koningh!"

Johnny burst back into his office just as Captain O'Rourke was preparing to leave. "He's okay; completely unaware of how he frightened everyone. Two of my staff are with him now discussing Christmas presents and Santa Claus. They're bringing him here to you and his brother. But before they get here, I'll tell you that one of the secretaries he'd met at the second-floor hot chocolate table seemed to be trying to leave the building with him. The smart little bugger was putting up quite a resistance, and that's what alerted us to his whereabouts. I'll handle her, and if necessary, you can press charges later," he said to Corey. "But that won't actually do much since she didn't actually leave with him."

"I'd drop it all since it turned out to be a false alarm of sorts," Captain O'Rourke muttered, looking at Johnny as if he was the only person there who could understand the facts dispassionately. "Seems there are childless women all over who think little of lifting someone else's youngster to fill their own need," the captain said, nodding his head decisively as if his explanation would dismiss all concern over the incident rather than aggravate it.

"Or perhaps it's about money, or both. The police can determine that later," Johnny added. "This is not the kind of thing to be swept under the rug. We need to be sure it won't happen again with this woman. We'll get back to you with the results of the investigation, de Koningh," he announced, assuming a sense of commitment to a solution would relieve some of Corey's trauma.

Corey shook his head, shooting Johnny a severe warning glance. He slid his eyes toward William and shook his head again. Johnny swallowed his next words and nodded. He was chagrined that he'd ignored William's presence completely in the excitement and relief of being able to report Connie safe. He wondered how Corey had learned the skill of child empathy since he'd shown little concern for his wife or interest in being a father in the past. He wondered if it was an instinct engaged only in times of extreme danger.

Leaving the building immediately as soon as Connie came back with Johnny's secretary, the boys and their father were bundled into one of the newspaper's hacks, tucked in on both sides by two of the staff grinning broadly under their ruddy Irish complexions heightened by the swirling snow. William had said nothing since Connie was found. He stared at his brother, then at the floor of the cab, then out the window, then back at his brother again. Connie piped up quite cheerily now and then, looking around at his father and brother as he did so and obviously unable to understand the tension in the air. But since no one tried to silence him, he kept up his light prattle whenever he felt like it. Corey struggled not to hold on to Connie too tightly, so he hugged him often instead. He was obviously overcome by demons in his head, and Johnny realized he felt worse for the father at that moment than he did for the child.

"I'll come down to see you to discuss this, Dunne, in a day or so," Corey said, as Johnny reached out for his arm through the hack's open door. "Thank you. I don't know how . . ."

"Not necessary, de Koningh." Johnny lowered his voice as Corey leaned partially out the door and closer to him. "I'll come to see you at your home. By then I'll have all the information we'll need to explain this to Emily."

"No! She mustn't know anything about it. At least, not now while she's so . . . sensitive. I don't know what it would do to her. I'll make sure the boys are silent, too."

"You can't be serious." Johnny looked shocked as he started to close the door. "You can't keep this from her." He noticed a dark look of confusion on Corey's face as the hack started to move forward silently on its snow runners.

"I mean it, de Koningh," Johnny said, tapping the door firmly. "Don't do that to her." But he doubted his warning had been heard, either because of the hack's movement away from the curb or Corey's fear of the message. He noticed the window being dropped a little for air from inside and grabbed the opportunity. Jogging alongside the carriage, he nodded toward the boys sitting behind Corey and panted, "They'll tell her anyway."

"No, they won't," Corey muttered back. "De Koningh men take care of their women."

Johnny stood hatless, the snow whirling madly around as if he was centered in a giant snow globe shaken at just that moment by an angry god. "Don't lock her up like a captive bird in a cage," he muttered. He thought of Emily racing after the children's hoop across the square in Vienna where he'd first seen her. Her freedom of movement and spirit had impressed him instantly. He couldn't bear to think of her now, trapped in a life without air and light, controlled by her masters and their prescriptions. Ah well, she'd have to find her own way out. If she wanted it badly enough, she surely would. He turned to go back into the building, brushing the snow out of his hair as he went up the steps.

"Oh, leave it," scolded a pretty young woman as she came up behind him. She was one of the secretaries who were recently swelling the staffing ranks at the paper, and he searched his mind for her name but couldn't come up with it. "Now I know what you'll look like when you're old, white hair and all," she said, clearly adopting the holiday mood the snow was bringing.

"Why would you want to?" He laughed, bowing his bare head slightly. "You have me here right now. Isn't that better?" She smiled back up at him.

CHAPTER ELEVEN

"Good Lord, Johnny! Were you following me?" Emily threw a glare at Johnny Dunne sharp enough to cut a vein, her dark eyes biting into his, a clear sign her energy had returned.

"Yes, I was following you," he admitted, with his usual open grin. He'd been lured by the spring and swing in her step and the sheen of her dark hair when he'd spotted her half a block away this afternoon. It had brought back the memory of her bounding down the sidewalk and into the street in Vienna years ago like a flash of light.

He gasped when she stopped short on Fourteenth Street and spun around so that they were face to face, just as suddenly as they'd been in St. Stephen's Square on that summer day before the Civil War broke out in earnest. Moving always with purpose, he'd watched her thread her way this time through the New York City crowd with that same drive, but now it seemed to him a little more directed and less reckless, though still with the obvious momentum of a forceful spirit. Possibly her change in lifestyle and her maturity, and even her motherhood, tethered her more to the earth. But he couldn't take his eyes off her now, just as then.

"I recognized you in the crowd and was trying to catch up with you. What are you doing here?" he asked.

"Could you rephrase that question? It's a free country, you know." Emily looked annoyed and distracted—not at all like her younger self, whose pleasure at meeting him out of the blue on her first trip to

Europe had seemed to shine from the gold flecks in her eyes. Yes, he remembered challenges in their conversation then, and questions about why he'd been so close when she'd started to fall; but they'd been wrapped in a kind of lightheartedness clearly lacking now. This morning her dark eyes snapped like the shiny fruit on an inkberry bush, the kind with lots of thorns. Johnny tried not to laugh, taking a deep breath as he watched her level head holding his eyes, and he started over more carefully.

"Why, Emily de Koningh! What a pleasure it is to see you here. What brings you to this part of town?"

"Much better," she said, allowing a small smile to play at the corners of her mouth for the first time. "I just left my bow off to have work done on it. I was halfway down the street when I realized I'd left my gloves on the counter, so I'm heading back to the store now. Will you come with me?" Without waiting for his answer, she started down the street again, retracing the steps he'd seen her take a few minutes before. A little annoyed by her assumption he'd tag along, he realized he'd admitted to following her in the first place, so it made sense that he'd continue now. In fact, watching her on the street he was aware of a riptide yanking him through the midtown pedestrians. He was a good enough athlete to understand he'd just have to ride along, not fighting it if he wanted to survive and eventually get free.

She'd interrupted his life twelve years ago in Vienna, pulling him in with her undertow before he knew he was in trouble. He'd resented it then, recognizing a power he was unable to resist. He didn't like being upset by her when he was going along in his own rhythm. He negotiated life with no impediments. He didn't want to be stopped midstream, with all the swirling eddies and debris that get dammed up around an obstacle like that, trapping and holding him there. He remembered how he'd rushed to catch her on that summer day when he'd first seen her in St. Stephen's Square. She'd positively glowed with excitement, though possibly his memory was playing tricks on him. It was unusual for a woman to show her feelings so freely. It was probably wrong for her to have them in the first place, or so most people would think. But for some reason, he liked that about her. Though he wouldn't admit it to Emily or anyone else.

Unnerved by her then, he'd been thankful to find she was soon to leave Vienna, slipping easily back in his old cadence until—there she was again, sweeping into his office and his life in New York a few months later and again, completely unexpectedly. He'd been stuck in all that turmoil of hers, embroiled with her family problems during the war until he'd finally broken free. Or was it she who'd escaped? Then there were many easy years of work and friends, life without her in New York with a new job, and more freedom and collegiality than ever, when suddenly she reappeared, pushing in with her career and fame, and troubles. Always, more complications and passions, and more undertow.

"What happened? Did you break your bow somehow?" Johnny asked the question to show his lack of knowledge of string instrument bows, but also to imply he was following her only to get an answer to his question. He was a journalist after all, and he knew how to suggest rapt attention even when it was lacking.

"Nothing like that." Emily's expression was firm now with the authority he recalled. "I don't remember enough about the night of the fire in Chicago to account for the bow's exposure to heat and fumes, but clearly it was unprotected some of the time, and that's bad for it."

"So this work you're having done is purely prophylactic?" He was striding next to her, easily matching his own energetic step to hers.

"No, I only wish it were. I began to notice I was having trouble turning the screw—the part down by the frog—the handle—that you use to adjust the tension of the hairs. Heat shrinks them, and frankly even noxious vapors can affect them badly."

"No surprise then that you're having trouble with it. I had no idea the bow was so complicated and . . . delicate. Almost human, you might say."

"Anything under tension will eventually lose its resilience, become brittle, and break; people too," she added, looking at him directly. "Usually it happens with the hair of a bow just at the most challenging passage in a performance. There's really no warning and it's devastating, so best to ensure against it if possible."

"Sounds like life," Johnny said, with a chuckle she didn't join in on. Perhaps he'd made light of something too important. "I do know . . . they're very valuable, right?" Emily rolled her eyes and nodded. He recalled the bow was on loan with the violin from Robert Haussmann. "You could always get a new one if this one needs replacing," he said, without looking at her.

She ignored his comment. "Here we are," she announced, stopping in front of a small shop all but hidden between two larger stores, a dry goods and a ladies' dress shop. She reached for the knob to pull the door open, but he got his hand there first, and smiling lightly down at her, pulled the door open and held it for her to pass through. "How about something at the tearoom down the street when you're done here?" he asked, as she passed by him into the shop.

She paused for an imperceptible moment, then nodded. "There are my gloves, right where I left them." He stayed in the door to hold it open and she returned almost instantly, putting a hand on his arm. "Shall we be off then?" she said, with a slight dip of her head. She sounded as if it had been her idea instead of his, but she looked at him questioningly.

"Just down the block," he motioned with a nod.

As they moved quickly along the pavement together, Johnny was aware of how evenly their pace matched even though she was smaller than he. It made him less inclined to hover protectively at her elbow as he might have done, attempting to protect her from the throngs of pedestrians taking up every inch of spare sidewalk. Competitive even in this, he rather liked the way she moved on with a force he could count on. Suddenly she stopped and dropped behind him, almost falling when a large man jolted her as he angled to cross the street. Johnny retraced his steps back to them both just in time to hear the man say, "Sorry, Mrs. de Koningh. Didn't recognize you out here with everyone." He'd taken off before Johnny could censure him for his rudeness. Anyone could see Emily was still shaken and out of breath. She must have been hit quite hard.

"Are you all right?" he asked, putting his hand on her shoulder in an attempt to give her stability. "What was that all about?"

Emily shrugged and started walking again, though she'd slowed down a bit and looked unsure of herself. "He's an old family acquaintance, a man who's been an avid opera fan and involved in writing music reviews in his spare time."

Johnny watched her face and saw a look developing he could only call grim. "Not a very polite or friendly one, I'd say. What's wrong with him?" He slipped his hand lightly to her back and stayed closer in the crowd. He'd have to be more attentive. He bent lower so he could hear her better.

"Oh, there's nothing wrong with him, or at least I'm sure that's the way he sees it. He thinks there's something wrong with me."

"How so?"

"He's one of the many who find the requirements for a wife and musician completely discordant."

"Odd if he's in the music world himself."

"Not at all," she said, avoiding a group of three men moving slowly and fully engrossed in conversation. They took up more room than necessary, as if totally unaware they had to share the street with anyone else. "The music world he's a part of is totally dominated by men," Emily said matter-of-factly, as if describing a foreign culture to Johnny, which in fact she was, to some extent. "In most people's eyes being a female musician automatically dooms me to failure in real life. Each reality makes the other untenable."

"But a fellow musician must surely see a different truth."

"They don't see us as 'fellows.' Quote, a woman, after all, can never be a complete artist. Unquote. I don't remember who said that, but it doesn't matter. It could have been any of them."

"Henry James, I think. Hard to believe when one notes his admiration for all the lady authors of our day."

"Believe it," she snapped. "That man who almost knocked me over has said to me in my own home that when I insisted on becoming a performing violinist I gave up my femininity, and therefore any right to appreciation or love. That's a direct quote. I'm not exaggerating."

"That's a rather thinly veiled damnation, isn't it? Smacks of jealousy, I'd say." Johnny shook his head and steered Emily to the red tearoom awning just ahead of them. Still upset, she didn't seem to notice his guidance. "And why do people go on the attack?" Johnny continued, "when they're insecure." He nodded as he tried to keep up with her enough to hear without stumbling over her at the same time. Encouraged by Johnny's attention, Emily kept on talking.

"Yes, you're right. One of the many reasons male musicians don't want women to be their colleagues is because they're jealous and frightened of the competition, and"—she began to look quite fierce, dark eyebrows knit almost together over her delicately chiseled nose—"also because they're threatened by women who don't fit easily into their accepted standards of femininity." She finished, looking up at Johnny a little sheepishly, possibly aware for the first time that her tirade might have been misconstrued as anger directed at him in some way.

"That's so among writers, too," Johnny agreed, as he opened the tearoom door for her.

"Women accept it to protect their place in society," she said, nodding to him either in thanks or agreement, "but in my opinion that place isn't worth defending. I read recently in *Women of the Age* magazine that someone in the audience was so thrilled by a Camilla

Urso performance in Europe that he cried out, 'She's woman enough to vote!'" She raised her gloved hand and shook it as if the proclamation was her own. Johnny grinned, hidden slightly behind Emily as she moved into the tearoom.

"What a great line," he chuckled. "Wish I'd said it myself."

Emily seemed not to be listening as she hesitated on the threshold of the tearoom entrance, causing him to stop and take in the scene himself so as not to precede her. The dark, slightly worn wood and maroon leather banquettes gave it the look of a men's club, with surly looking waiters who didn't suffer women easily, adding to the feel of a high-class bar. Men were clearly in charge here. Emily's expression showed she hadn't expected it. This was no prim and proper cozy British tearoom with tablecloths on round tables and the feel of a bright, welcoming kitchen. Johnny could tell she'd never been here before. But of course she hadn't. Wives and mothers didn't visit midtown tearooms. Johnny found it a nice oasis in a difficult day, or just a way to share pleasant company away from the office. Yes, of course it was nice, but not possible if you have family commitments in addition to work. He realized Emily led a more complicated life now than he'd been aware of. Following a waiter to one of the leather banquettes meant for four instead of two, he considered how close he could sit next to her without being rude. He needn't have worried.

"Move over here closer next to me," she said, patting the corner seat just to the left of her. "If you won't feel crowded, that is. I don't want to have to shout at you."

"Much better," he agreed, sliding easily around the table. "Now I can not only hear you, but also enjoy your beautiful profile if you don't want to look directly at me." Her eyes widened and brows shot up as she did just that.

"I must say you're looking well . . . healthy," he added, in hopes she'd find his focus on her well-being more comfortable than her beauty. "You've lost that hint of an injured feral cat that was there for a while after Chicago."

Something shut down behind her eyes, so he moved quickly and smoothly away from the subject of her looks to a discussion of the concerts she now had queued up for the rest of the winter and early spring. She'd taken no residual offense to his clumsy comments about her beauty, a fact he considered a benefit of their years of friendship and her increased maturity. Apparently she was no longer at odds with herself and her place in the world, as her run-in with the music critic had shown.

The waiter returned at last to take their order, and Johnny noticed a slight wink when he asked if they were ready. It meant he'd given Johnny time to spend alone with his "lady friend," even though he hadn't asked for it. He knew they made an attractive, well-matched pair, and said he was sure that had been the waiter's mistake after she'd chastised him for leaving them so long to bear their hunger and thirst.

"A well-matched pair," she scoffed. "That's what we call our horses. Why must men always resort to possessive animal metaphors when they talk about women?"

"They don't," he countered. "It was a casual remark, not a demeaning comparison."

"Oh, come now. It's so unoriginal! I'll bet you even use it in your writing. Feral cats, tamed horses—you men are all alike." She removed her wayward gloves and placed them on the empty banquette beside her. He loved looking at her hands—graceful, useful, and strong at the same time, unexpectedly small hands to be able to accomplish so much on the violin strings.

"I resent and deny that," he said with a chuckle. "What men in your life have been denigrating you with comparisons to dependent animals? Certainly not your friends. Remember, I was with you that night at your dinner party and I didn't hear one animal reference all night." He smiled definitively, as if to announce the end of the discussion and start of a new one.

"Then you weren't listening," she said, eyes narrowed as she watched him. She sat in silence, letting it speak far more eloquently than she could.

He smiled at her without moving. "Go on."

"John Mackay," she answered, "whom I admire greatly, by the way, compared me to an unbound horse who couldn't accept its freedom."

"Just a momentary, and perhaps lazy, choice of words." Johnny relaxed against the deep upholstery of the maroon banquette. He enjoyed sparring with Emily.

"Not likely," she countered, sitting up quite straight with a space between her spine and the seat back. "I first met Mr. Mackay at one of his favorite places in New York, the menagerie in Central Park. Many men like to stroll with their lady friends there, and fathers take their sons. Men like the stimulus of power and control over animals they'd be afraid of in their own habitat. They like to show off in front of the caged animals, and their lady friends and children, for that matter."

"That's a little far-fetched, don't you think?" Johnny shook his head in seeming disbelief, although he had to admit he'd often had exactly the same thoughts when he'd walked past those very same cages. The mix of dominance and fear had embarrassed him, specifically keeping him away from walks past the cages with any of his lady friends.

"Not at all," she said. "It took me a while to figure out, but once I saw how upset my boys were at the menagerie, or at least my younger son was, I thought through his reaction and realized he was right: it's all about power and control of creatures reliant on men for their safety and nourishment, just like the women in society." The flush on Emily's cheeks suggested this was a topic she felt strongly about.

The tearoom conversation had taken on an edge he hadn't prepared for. He wanted to steer her back to an easier topic, with her set squarely in the middle. He was more interested in her personal life than her professional or social existences, whatever they might be.

"Did your husband discuss his visit with me at the paper's headquarters in the snowstorm?" Johnny asked, watching her carefully for clues to her level of knowledge about the events of that day. The waiter returned with their tea just in time to hear the reference to her husband. He pouted slightly without looking at Johnny, implying, Johnny knew only too well, that a larger tip might be required if his discretion and deafness were to be counted on.

"He did," she replied, emptying her shot glass of sherry into the tea that had been placed in front of her. The waiter backed off, head down like a shameful dog at odds with his master. You see how restrained and discreet I am, he seemed to be saying. She took no notice. "They all had a wonderful time," she continued. "I thank you for distracting them while the storm was at its worst. The boys loved your train, and there's been enormous pressure brought to bear on their grandfather Alden in England to produce one for their room at home." Her easy smile told him she knew nothing of her younger son's disappearance. Damn her husband. Why did no one in that house show her the respect she deserved?

"Happy to have been of service when needed." Johnny followed her lead with his own shot of rum. "I'm glad both your boys have good memories of their visit. Especially the little one. And did Corey relate our discussion about your accompanist?" he asked, totally unprepared for what followed.

Emily downed most of her tea, shot of rum and all, in one more swallow. Johnny stared at her. "Slow down," he advised. "That's pretty strong. I think the vapors could shrink the strings on that bow of yours right from here."

Emily's eyes narrowed and the hair prickled on the back of Johnny's neck in warning. Her long hard look continued, and he controlled his nervous impulse to down his own rum. Finally, he could stand the silence no longer. "What's the problem?" He put his hand over hers on the table without a thought, a mistake. She withdrew hers from underneath his slowly, as if so disgusted she didn't want to touch any more of him than necessary. She placed it with her other hand in her lap beneath the table. Sitting in profile to focus out across the dining room, she started to speak in a low voice. "The problem, Johnny, is that you tried to push my life in a direction of your choosing without asking me first. Robert Haussmann is one of the best friends I've ever had." She pulled herself up even straighter, seeming to grow inches before his eyes. She took a deep, centering breath, like the ones she used to quiet her mind before starting to play, and turned only her head to look him in the eye.

"He was the one to support my desire to play the violin . . . ," she went on in a slow, rhythmic tone, "to take me seriously and teach me what I needed to know, to encourage my dream to be a performer when no one else would even consider it." Her voice started to rise with increasing intensity. "Without him, I'd still be banging away on the piano, a percussive, angry instrument for which I have no affinity, but the only one acceptable for women as a performance vehicle when I was growing up!" She ended out of breath with a slight toss of her head, reminding him, he was embarrassed to admit, of a young filly.

Johnny feared she had no intention of stopping there, so he reached for his tea with rum and sipped it slowly but steadily, until little was left. She gathered herself in silence. He put the cup down, finally, in hopes that perhaps she'd had time to calm herself. His wish was denied.

"Furthermore," her eyes flashed a warning, "Robert Haussmann taught me generously and unstintingly for many, many years. Musicians often get so used to the daily routine with a teacher and mentor they take them for granted. But the day comes when we've moved on without them, and we suddenly realize how special what they gave us was." Her voice dropped down to a vibration he could feel before he heard it. "I would never want him to get word of what you suggested and think that the plan came from me."

Johnny watched Emily through his lashes as she delivered her monologue. He was bursting. *You can't be serious. That man is nothing but an anchor for you now.* But he held back, waiting to see if something more was coming. She pushed her teacup and saucer a few inches away, clearly an act of closure.

"And as for your suggestion about Corey," she hissed so low again he almost missed it, "you can take it and burn it, or do whatever else you do with your rubbish." Johnny's head snapped back as if he'd been slapped.

"I don't understand," he breathed. "What's upset you so?"

"What's upset me about your suggestion that my husband go gallivanting all over the country seeking out immigrants and wastrels, neglecting his responsibilities to his family and his wife and music partner? You don't think I might find that upsetting?"

"No, I don't, or I wouldn't have suggested it in the first place." He knew he should stop, but he couldn't resist the force of his growing conviction that she'd lost her way. Pushing both their cups and saucers to one side, he leaned closer toward her, both arms resting on the table to support his upper body. To say he was unaware of the intensity of his eyes would have been a lie, and he used them to fix her in her place at last. He knew something about magnetism himself.

"I want to free you, Emily, and Corey as well, so both of you can follow the things you care about. I'm not like most of the men you know, condemning a woman who thinks she can balance a home and career in a man's world. I don't know music as you do, but I know writing, and I assure you the stigma attached to an authoress who dares to consider herself the equal of her male counterpart is damning. Most men would think such a woman unworthy . . . because she admits to appetites they don't allow her." Emily's look of cold fury didn't change, as if she were frozen in place. "I may be partial to your needs, but Corey's matter too if you're to be happy. You may both be among the best in the world at what you do, but neither one of you seem to be loving it, at the moment. There's little pleasure in it for you." He couldn't understand why his tone, expression, and words hadn't brought a warmer reaction from her by now, but as she took a deep breath, he prepared himself for her thanks and apology.

"Pleasure," she snapped like a firecracker pulled apart at both ends, "isn't the main goal in life." He suddenly realized the discussion was out of his control. Taking charge of the conversation herself was the only way she could regain her self-respect. "Fulfilling your responsibilities and giving back to those who've supported and nurtured you, keeping your children and family safe and letting them know they're loved, that's what matters. Can you really pretend that . . ." she started to push herself up from the table as if she could think more clearly on her feet, ". . . turning Corey loose to waste his time in saloons down south or up in the wilds of Harlem would be good for either one of us?" He noticed how small she was for the first time, because he'd never really seen her standing still for long. She had a scarlet flush creeping out from her chest to her dark hairline just visible under the very becoming rolled brim of her beige felt hat. Others nearby noticed her now, too, but she didn't seem to care. He should encourage her to sit back down to minimize the spectacle.

"Emily." He reached for her hand again as it hung by her side, and she let him hold the fingers for a moment without pulling away. "Do you think that either one of you can be all you're capable of, personally or professionally, locked up in that twenty-four-karat-gold monster of a house that doesn't even belong to you?" He glanced furtively at the nearby tables, sure she'd see she no longer spoke in private and lower her voice if she followed his eyes. But she ignored his signals with a steadfast glare.

"It does belong to us, and we to it. It's the only real home I've ever known, and now that Corey's father has returned, I must take care of him, too. He took me in when my own father didn't want me and gave me all the opportunities I enjoy, both in music and life."

Johnny's eyebrows shot up. "Corey's father has come home again?"

She ignored his question, almost as if he weren't there. "You make it sound as if we're all caged animals," she went on with her own agenda. "But you don't understand. We're all safe as long as we have each other and that house. It's an invaluable gift we can give the children if we protect it properly. It's essential to the children's survival that they have an entire family intact: mother, father, grandfather, and a home that's generations old. Most important, though, are their parents. Corey and I have to be there for them, always."

She seemed to be losing a little of her fierceness, so he reached up to her shoulder and gently urged her to sit. "You're wrong about that," he said as commandingly as possible. He knew how to stop an argument over editorial copy, after all, with no more than a confident tone and a look. "It's essential for children to learn self-reliance at an early age to feel really safe. Parents only get in the way of that." She sat back down slowly, but she looked like a loaded spring ready to explode upwards again at any moment.

"How do you know?" A quizzical look finally took the place of her angry defiance.

"Because I was a child once, too, though that may be hard to believe." He smiled his most disarming grin, and then traded it for a seriousness he hadn't shown yet. "I never met my father, and my mother was nothing but trouble. She brought home more dreadful men who were jealous of me than you could count. I eventually went to live with an Episcopalian priest and his family who gave me my education, which was my ticket to self-reliance and freedom." Emily's eyes had grown wider, as if something had suddenly occurred to her.

"But at least you had a mother," she whispered. "That's what matters."

"Oh, she mattered, all right," Johnny laughed, scornfully. "She was nothing but trouble. She'd show up once in a while with uncanny precision, just when things had started to calm down in my life. She'd stir everything up again in her big, selfish way. But I finally learned to rise completely above her disturbances and move on. Parents can bring children down faster than a marksman at a skeet shoot."

Emily stared at him in disbelief. "Your mother must have been a very unhappy person," she said, softly.

"I think you're right," he agreed. "But that's why you need to be happy and fulfilled, as does Corey. If you want to be the best parents you can be, you need to be the happiest people you can be. And that means different things for you than for him!" Johnny was feeling very good about himself at that moment. Emily sat so close he could feel the heat from her body, and she seemed now to be absorbing his advice. "We're a breed apart, you and I," he went on. "Artists must live outside the conventional arrangements. Marriage is an impedi-ment to a free woman with a gift and spirit." He'd finally said what was so obvious she couldn't deny he was right. She stared back at him, eyes wide.

"You're not who I thought you were," Emily said at last. "How sad." But Johnny couldn't, or wouldn't, hear her because he'd gone on in his thoughts. He let her words slip past so he wouldn't get caught in her net. She stood up slowly, bringing him back to his senses.

"And how about you?" he asked, aware he was still holding her hand as she stood above him. "Are you who I think you are? Is this so-called safe home of yours worth giving up your music for?" She stared at him and didn't answer. "Because you may not be able to have both, you know. Who takes care of Emily's needs if she won't take care of herself?"

He pulled her hand a little closer to him, not knowing why. Perhaps he thought it would force her to sit down again or possibly he could brush the fingertips, another mistake. She snatched her hand out of his and stepped into the aisle.

"I'm going now," she said. "I need to get back home to my family."

She turned and moved quickly past the huge brass samovar at the end of the serving table and was gone from view before he knew she wasn't coming back. He looked at the space next to him as if it might offer a clue. How had this ended here? Couldn't she see all he'd wanted for her was the autonomy to choose her own way? How could she accuse him of being no better than all the others who tried to control her when what he sought was the exact opposite?

He shook his head and sighed, not sure for once what his next move should be. Finally he signaled the waiter for the bill and pulled out his wallet, noticing she'd left her gloves behind again. He'd have to return them to the house next week. He could see Corey was right. Emily was strung tighter than that bow of hers she'd left off for repair. And if she wasn't careful about how brittle she'd become, she'd break just as suddenly, but surely and devastatingly. He sighed.

"Not the result you expected," the waiter said, brushing a few nonexistent crumbs off the table to emphasize his usefulness. "Impossible to figure," he sighed. "Just built different."

"Yes," Johnny agreed, as he stood up to leave. "And thank heaven they are. But we must remember to let them alone so they can stay that way."

If she'd looked back, Emily might have noted Johnny's clear blue eyes looked opaque now, as if a film lay between him and the rest of the world; but she didn't. Johnny made sure to tip the waiter exactly what he could expect and not one penny more. After all, it had been Emily who'd provided Johnny with invaluable insight that afternoon, and not the server.

CHAPTER TWELVE

T HE DE KONINGH MANSION seemed to be holding its breath so as not to wake the household. It didn't creak and groan as the Alden house in London had, though those floorboards had probably been much older and weaker. Emily couldn't really remember. She'd been there too long ago, when she was so young—barely older than her William was now. Tiptoeing down the back stairs to the kitchen, she bunched her housecoat in one hand, the other hand on the slim wooden rail to reassure her progress. She stifled a gleeful chuckle at the thought of her feet on the servants' staircase—such fun to go barefoot as one knew one shouldn't. But she'd often snuck down like this as a newcomer to the house, usually with Corey, to raid the kitchen pantry of something forbidden, sweet, and crumbly. Their boys seemed just as enamored of the delights to be discovered there.

I can teach you things about this house even those who built it don't know, Corey announced when she'd first arrived. The stealth probably wasn't necessary anymore. Fewer servants and fewer demands for pre-breakfast fires in every room made her discovery less likely, so descent down the main staircase was probably safer. But it was fun and reassuring to retrace those early years in her then-new home, reminding her to be grateful that she had a warm, safe place where she belonged, then as now.

Instinctively she sidestepped the loose saddle board at the entry-level landing to avoid its loud protest, just as Corey had shown

her to do then, and paused for a glance at her grand*mother* clock in
the foyer alcove. Ticking softly, its steady presence assured her there
was still an hour to sunrise, enough time for a cup of tea and a baking
powder biscuit; plenty of time to let her mind settle back in its
mantle of early morning haze nurtured by the contentment of a
warm brew and flaky crust. This was her kitchen now.

She stopped on the bottom step at the servants' entrance, enjoying the neat, quiet order of the open space with its long table for meal
preparation in the middle. Moving silently across the kitchen floor,
she noted how clean Emma, the cook, kept it even though the
wooden boards suffered continuous daily traffic. Corey had been
proud of those narrow oak floorboards, explaining to her on her first
house tour that it was more difficult to lay many narrow strips than a
few very wide ones, and so the kitchen floor was as evocative of
quality as the rest of the house, even though no one important ever
saw it, he'd said. He'd also pointed out how good the wood felt under
bare toes, a happy discovery she'd made with him that quickly
negated his need for boasting about the quality of the house's
construction, or anything else.

Now, as the bare soles of her feet whispered through the kitchen
to the butler's pantry, she realized the house had become her home in
a way it never had for Corey. Perhaps it was her years here without
him when he'd visited his Dutch relatives upstate, or been sent away
to school, or equally important, her many hours making a home for
their children without him when he'd been off with his father or
musician friends in search of who knew what. Or maybe there was
just something intangible about the soul of a house you couldn't
access without being open to it, having it matter as much or more
than almost anything at some point in your life, making it part of
you and you of it. Maybe the terror of the great fire in Chicago she'd
witnessed too close up, where so many had lost their homes so fast,
had made her more appreciative of what she had now. But she

suspected her gratitude for this house had been part of her most of her life, the trauma of recent loss only making it more poignant.

She arrived in front of the shiny black Sterling wood stove, smaller than the double oven in the main kitchen but for her the *HAS NO EQUAL* printed on its right side was a truth echoing her preference for it. A peekaboo front door, designed so you could open the outer access to see what was cooking without opening the door completely, had always seemed more than practical. It was fun. Mica windows also let one watch biscuits rise without losing all the heat. She'd spent almost all her free time after violin practice using this little stove to hone baking skills almost equal to her musical ones, realizing now as she reached for the small copper kettle nestled at the back of the stove that those cooking lessons had also endeared the house to her and her to it. You belong to a house when you bake in it.

The kettle was still warm. The unique thermal qualities of copper had retained the last late-night heating, or her idea for a dawn cup of tea had seen another earlier precedent. Either way she was pleased to skip the stoking of coals to reheat a cold kettle. A pinch of dry mint leaves rolled between her fingers would give her infusion of black tea a pickup to cheer her morning and the day to come. Lost in her sense of well-being from the warmth of the herbal brew swirling in her cup, she forgot her quest for a baking powder biscuit and returned to the main kitchen to sit at the table.

How well she felt. Her legs were strong, now. How healthy she'd become again, losing her extra weight and no longer a victim of pregnancy or age . . . in fact unable to believe she was on her way to her thirtieth birthday. Though unable to know how her mother might have weathered advancing years, she thought a similarity to her father's heartiness a likely possibility. Looking at least a decade younger than his friend Klaas de Koningh, her father had dark, shiny hair streaked with only a few lines of gray. She hadn't seen him in a long time, but Klaas's recent return home brought her to thoughts of

William Alden now living in Paris, and she smiled. His news of an imminent arrival in New York on business had pleased her with an unfamiliar desire to reconnect with him, perhaps a leftover from her recent trauma in Chicago.

Much of her professional success had begun in France, and even though her father had been too busy smoothing out diplomatic discrepancies after the Civil War to have objections to her early career, he was now mostly retired and seemingly had plenty of time to appreciate what she'd accomplished. Solo performances and contracts a few years in advance impressed him in ways that didn't totally surprise her. He'd always been a staunch supporter of his daughter's strengths, even as a small child, although he'd been equally disconnected from her weaknesses, the desire for a full-time parent among those soft points that needed filling. Her father had initially been delighted with Corey's accompanying her on tour, a belief that her husband, a man of elevated social standing, was exactly the stamp of approval she needed to gain acceptance from the public. She could forgive him that.

But lately she'd detected a discomfort in her father's comments about the appearance of something immature and less than manly about Corey's demeanor on stage, an observation she hadn't tried to deny in her communications with Lord Alden as she'd felt the same uneasiness herself, in their married life as well as in performance. But it had never been discussed between her and Corey, nor had she enlisted Corey's father, the one person she'd turned to in her past when help with the family was necessary and beyond her grasp. Somehow she knew instinctively that Corey needed time to find his own way, and that wasn't something anyone could demand of him or push him into. Truly, her hands were tied. Since his return home to the mansion, she'd wanted to cry out to him that he had to turn his attention to his home, to her and the children, and to work, the music they'd both agreed would nourish them forever going forward. But again, she knew that would mean nothing unless it came from him. So there was no assurance in her life now or tomorrow, and all she could do would be to keep her focus straight ahead, with emotional blinders blocking out all distractions and the children and her violin framed squarely in her view.

Resting her hand on the letter in the pocket of her dressing gown from Jacques Offenbach's friend, she picked up her teacup and took another sip, gazing out the kitchen window across the room, where some shapes in the courtyard outside were slowly forming in the expanding early morning light. Winter was on the cusp of change, and early spring suggested itself in the way the birds had started to chorus. The morning's flush already highlighted a new day promising nothing but good if her current mood was any indicator.

She didn't need to take the letter out of her pocket to see what it said. The words still floated in her mind's eye, a happy reminder that her performance career was more robust than ever.

Mon ami François Goulet wishes you in performance with the New York Philharmonic at Andrew Carnegie's Hall. Je suis sûr you will be the only performer of merit. Jacques had made some comments about her beauty, as expected from a Frenchman, and muttered something deprecatory about the American penchant for filling the stage with "common" contemporary performers, thus distracting from those of classical virtue. It was all puffed-up rhetoric, but she was going to accept the booking.

She'd been performing only in New York lately, and it had served her well. She could see the children every night and staying in the public eye with more appearances and less travel had underlined what a great showcase the city was becoming. Her work was going so much better these days. Reviewers had stopped talking about her "breakdown" (a synonym for miscarriage) and the fire, now praising her intonation and technical grace instead. She was used to the less-than-sophisticated American tastes in string instrument performance standards, and reading some of the most robust praise about her "capabilities" often made her wonder, *Is that all they got from my recital?* But audiences still weren't used to seeing a woman onstage alone with a violin raised under her chin, and the fact that they liked her enough to bring her back so often had to be sufficient satisfaction. She worried it might not be the best way to grow as an artist, but then that was America, too. Give the audiences what they want and is easiest for them to hear, not necessarily what's the most interesting, complex, or worthwhile. The lack of stress was a welcome change she was getting used to and enjoying more with each performance.

A quick rinse of her teacup and saucer, and Emily felt ready to start a day that was building a kind of contentment she'd been missing recently. It was a lovely feeling of peace. So much to be thankful for. She decided against returning up the back stairs as she'd originally come down, feeling impervious to any disapproval of her barefoot adventuring in her own home. Her morning coat mostly covered them anyway, reminding her of the young cellist she'd met recently who rehearsed without shoes, her skirts pulled down over her stockinged feet. Moving across the foyer and hall from the back stairs to the main marble entry, she passed the door to her favorite room, the library. Practice room and sanctuary, she found it beautiful in all illuminations and circumstances, especially ignited with the spectacular reflection of the sunrise on houses across Central Park. Lit by the glow from the east, their windows looked as if they'd burst into flame through the bare branches of the late-winter trees. But the image didn't upset her. Finally, she could tell she had healed. Standing for a moment on the library's threshold, she stared at the sight of that dawn and wondered how some days everything could seem so perfectly beautiful.

"Would you both join me in the library for an after-dinner drink?" Klaas asked, a familiar and familial suggestion at the end of the day.

"My favorite room and my favorite father-in-law," Emily said, unhooking her arm from Klaas's and slipping it around his back in a gesture of physical and moral support. He seemed so much older and frailer to her now that he'd returned, and she wanted to care for him as he had for her when she'd needed it most. She'd had no time to pay attention to anything but Corey and herself just after they'd been married, and their budding careers and children's arrival had possibly gotten in the way of care for Klaas's condition that would have been there in the past. The guilt of that omission weighed heavier on Emily now than she could have imagined a few years before. It was another one of their responsibilities as the middle generation of the family.

"Good!" He smiled down at her with the same affection they'd always shared. "We'll have some old port and new talk together." Did she sense a different tension in his voice and across his cheekbones, or was that just the loss of weight and thinning skin she'd already noted?

"Father, if you're tired you could go to bed and we'll talk in the morning." Corey must have picked up that same shortness of breath she thought she'd heard.

"Not that tired. I have something I want to discuss with you both. Let's go into the library for a while and catch up on each other's lives."

"My, that sounds ambitious, and just when we were all having so much fun." Emily feigned a pout as she looked up at Klaas. "But talking with you has ever been one of the pleasures of my life, so let's do it." Klaas touched the top of her head with his lips, but then moved her gently in front of him and into the room ahead of them all.

A perfect fire burned behind the grate, as it always did, and they waited for Emily to choose a chair before settling themselves around one another and close to the warmth. She accepted their deference with a smile, sinking softly into what had often been one of the men's wing chairs in the past. After all, she was the woman of the house now. It was her responsibility, her refuge and her home, so it was also her turn to make herself comfortable in it. Hard not to feel so in this wonderful room with the oak paneling glowing in the firelight and the huge old piano gleaming from its corner by the French doors to the garden.

Klaas walked past her to the liquor cabinet and started to look for his favorite port while Corey moved past him to the piano, a well-choreographed dance they'd practiced a long time. Raising the lid over the keyboard, he slipped onto the seat and started tapping the ivory with his left hand. Emily noticed how often that happened now that he was working on the syncopated rhythms of the rag-ged-time music he'd heard down south. Still, now his right hand joined his left in a quiet rendition of one of Bach's pieces from *The Well-Tempered Clavier.* Counterpoint had certainly started a long time before the folk music that benefited from it now. She smiled at him. He noticed, and bowed a little.

"Come and join us, Corey," Klaas said tersely, waving a glass of port at him as enticement. "We need to talk."

"But I was talking, Father. Didn't you hear what I was saying?"

Emily nodded, the glow from the port Klaas had poured her lighting a path to her core. She was a little surprised by Klaas's irritability. Surely he was still supportive of his son's playing, espe-cially classical composers of Sebastian Bach's eminence. Apparently Corey had heard it too. He raised an eyebrow in her direction, taking his hands off the piano and closing the cover. She shrugged, but her brows drew together in a dark line denying the casualness of her shoulder movement.

Looking back at Klaas now, his thin, parchment-like skin pulled taut over high cheekbones and blue eyes paler than she could remember under frail lashes, she worried that her dearest old friend might have some bad news to tell—perhaps about his health. Corey hadn't warned her, but perhaps he didn't know, either. An incipient dread started to crawl up from her stomach and she put her glass of port down in case the feeling had originated there. She knew how to control her heartbeat. How many times had she done it before a concert? But this wasn't her performance, it was Klaas's, and so there was nothing she could do to quiet her nerves.

She focused only on her father-in-law sitting directly opposite her, waiting for Corey to settle himself in the chair to her left, farthest away from the fire. This had been such a wonderful day, starting with the sunrise tea in the kitchen, moving on to her fittings for new performance dresses, time with the children in the park, rehearsal and practice with Robert Haussmann, and finally dinner and time after in her library. A perfect day. How could it end any other way?

"Tell me, Emily my dear, is your work progressing?"

"Very well, Klaas." She must have been imagining his discomfort. She heard only congeniality now.

"Do you have performances coming up this spring?"

"I do indeed, Klaas. In fact, I've recently received a contract to perform from a French entrepreneur, a Monsieur Goulet, with the New York Philharmonic." She pulled the letter out of her skirt pocket, pleased to have a pleasant topic to inspire them with. A small smile played at Klaas's lips, so she moved on with it quickly. Anything to cheer him up. "You know solo performing isn't new anymore. Franz Liszt popularized it a long time ago in Europe, but it's still more common in America to have many performers on stage together, so although I'll have a leading role, there will be an orchestra and chorus, apparently. . . ." She stopped, realizing he might not care about the specifics.

"American audiences love spectacle, don't they?" Klaas nodded as if there could be no disagreement. "It's easier, more entertaining, less work for the audience. Think of those Ring operas of Wagner's.

Americans prefer opera now to any other form of musical entertainment. If that isn't spectacle, I don't know what is." He chuckled, swirling the contents in his glass distractedly.

"Musical tastes run in cycles," Emily said. "I'm grateful for the work I have now."

"Is this musical *entrepreneur* part of the Robert Goelet family from New York?"

"*Gou*-let, Father," Corey corrected. "She said *Goulet*, not *Goelet*. Everyone entrepreneurial can't be Dutch, you know. You're showing your tribal stripes again." Corey laughed quietly, picking up his glass of port and waving it under his nose. "Ummm, lovely." He breathed in the vapors, but held it in his hand without drinking, as if he were waiting for something to happen: a sign, a sound, something.

"The Goelets were French too, from La Rochelle." Klaas gave his son the look that said he still had much to learn. "They escaped to Amsterdam for the freedom to practice their religion, like so many others. They were Huguenots, I believe. And I don't think I'm tribal," Klaas retorted. "Perhaps you're thinking of your mother." His eyes snapped a challenge that made them look livelier than Emily had seen for a long while.

"Oh, now there's the truth," Corey laughed. "All those mornings I'd have to read her the newspaper in her room, she'd insist on only news of the clan from the Lowlands. Tribal indeed she was. But you are too, Father. Look how comfortable you've always been with the rituals of the South. You can't call those people anything if not tribal." Emily watched the men in light combat, wondering where the strange subject was leading. Certainly Klaas seemed more animated than he had in a while, and perhaps she'd been wrong about his health and a dire message. She felt herself relax somewhat, and waiting for Klaas's response to Corey's jabs, she picked up her glass of port and took another swallow.

"Actually, I agree with you," Klaas said with a nod. "They are and I am—comfortable with them, I mean. And therein lies my news for you." He looked up at Emily this time. She wondered why, holding on to her glass more tightly.

"News?" she murmured.

"Yes." He shifted his weight to his other hip and moved his legs. "I've decided to retire and stop traveling. I've had enough of the deprivation of living away from home and grown uncomfortable with the way the slave trade is still servicing the cotton business, so I want to get out. Reconstruction is not living up to its promise. Much is as it was, or worse, down south."

"Well, I applaud you for that," Corey said. "But I'm surprised you could call the way you've been served in private southern homes by lovely southern hostesses 'deprivation.'" He winked at Emily, and whether the port had started to anesthetize her, or she was just soothed by the fire's glow, her familiar dimples flashed back at him for a moment, seemingly aware of the tease that was now in progress.

"What lovely news." Emily fairly sparkled with relief. "We'll have you home from now on. It will be so much easier for me to care for you as you deserve, and the house will be a true home with the whole family in it." She looked from Klaas to Corey and back again, surprised Corey hadn't sprung to his feet to congratulate his father. He looked wary, sitting quite still.

"Not quite," Klaas said. He changed position in his chair again as if to relieve some unseen stress, but it didn't work, and he moved back to his original position. Emily knew she'd never forget the way his voice had grown guarded with the weight of what was to come. "Not quite," he said again. "I admit to the deprivation I feel when I'm without the comforts of southern hospitality, and that's for sure. But I've decided to correct the deficiency. I'm tired of being lonely and want to enjoy whatever time I have left on this earth. I've decided to bring a little southern comfort up here and asked the Widow Stovall to marry me. She's done me the honor of accepting my offer." He took a breath as if to continue, but thought better of it apparently, taking a sip of his port instead. The silence spread quickly, enveloping everything but the snapping of the logs in the fireplace, each one punctuating something unsaid between the three people in the room. Corey was the first to break the silence.

"That's . . . wonderful, Father," he said warily, glancing over at Emily who was staring at her lap, "I suppose, if it's what you really want. But when did all this come about? There seemed no hint of it at Mrs. Stovall's plantation." Emily's head snapped up, suddenly aware that the trip to West Virginia may have encompassed much more than she'd originally thought. There'd apparently been something other than cotton at stake.

"We've been corresponding since I left," Klaas said, putting his glass down on the table and folding his hands in his lap, looking to Emily like a witness on the stand in a court of law might appear. "We've agreed that such a partnership would benefit us both; she in so much as her life at the plantation in West Virginia does not seem to offer the benefits it once did, and me in ways too abundant to mention." Emily stared at Corey, her big, dark eyes expanding pools of doubt. He couldn't break away from them even though he spoke to Klaas.

"She has no qualms about the imbalance in her proposed partner's . . . age?" Corey asked, alerting Emily to a feeling of dread at the deeply personal turn the questioning had taken.

"None," Klaas answered, quietly. "That is our agreement. She will make my old age more tolerable and I will make her future years more comfortable with a lifestyle of stability and social vibrancy she now lacks. It is a good arrangement."

"Father," Corey said, sounding as if the familiar title was hard to pronounce. "Have you given any thought to the financial claims the widow will be making on your estate? This move smacks of an imprudence I would never have given you credit for." Emily shuddered a little as if a ghost had crossed her path. As hateful as everything Corey was saying seemed, none of it had escaped her own thoughts.

"Well indeed you're right—about my commitment to fiscal responsibility, that is. Sarah Stovall has a substantial inheritance of her own, both from her family and that of her deceased husband. She just prefers not to sink any more of it into the soil of West Virginia, and so, we'll join financial forces and the de Koninghs will be better off than ever. I know this must come as a great surprise to you both," he went on, "but now that you're moving along with a growing family of your own, I can imagine you'd like some of your own privacy and a house geared more to the youthful exuberance your boys quite naturally want to exhibit all the time." He smiled gently at Emily, apparently totally unaware of the cataclysmic effect his news was having on her. The loss of the home and only family she'd ever known coming all at once created a physical and emotional trauma she was totally unprepared for.

"But the most important fact of all," Klaas said, again unaware of what was in fact most important to his daughter-in-law, "is that I shall no longer live a lonely life, and the widow will fulfill her desire to take care of a home, with a social life and events revolving around a couple rather than a single woman. That is what she feels her calling to be, like so many southern women, and their men are the beneficiaries, one of whom will now be me." He finally stopped talking, smiling calmly at Corey before he reached for his glass again.

Emily heard him and everything else through a long, dark tunnel that echoed so brutally she could hardly make sense of the words. *It's time you moved out*, he was saying now, *have a place of your own. Should have happened long ago*, she heard him add. *It would take a few months, whenever the widow could settle her affairs down south, sell her house, plan to come north with her niece.* Corey was stuck stiffly to his chair back, just as Emily was to hers. He looked increasingly upset, and Emily felt it must be because he, too, was being fledged without warning. *It was a big adjustment for the southern women and would not be easy,* Klaas was saying. *He must not forget what they were giving up . . . to start a new life in this city with him.* And was there no thought for what Emily and Corey were giving up as well? *The house on Fifth Avenue would be so alive again. He was suggesting . . . perhaps it was time they moved out . . . had a place of their own . . . should have happened long ago . . .* Emily felt her head spin. Klaas clearly had no idea of what this house had meant to her, and still did. Maybe he'd never understood and never could. To him it was just a large and expensive roof over his head, but to her . . .

Suddenly, Corey didn't seem to be objecting anymore. He and his father unexpectedly sounded more like collaborators than adversaries. Emily couldn't make sense out of anything that was happening. She gripped the upholstered arm of her wing chair so she wouldn't faint. How had everything come apart so fast when she'd thought the tapestry of her life was so carefully and tightly woven? There they sat, the three of them in the firelight, with the men in her life constructing a wholly new plan for hers from the raveled sleeve of what remained, without consulting her about what they were making.

❦ ❦ ❦

Sir William Alden shook his head and frowned as he stared out of his carriage window at the city streets clogged with traffic. "Look at this mess," he said to his daughter, glumly. "I may not have done you a favor offering you a ride downtown. I hope sight-reading chamber music with your friends is worth the trouble. I don't think I've ever seen New York as congested as it is now. Mind you, London and Paris aren't much better." He and Emily watched the chaotic jumble of delivery carts, horses, and pedestrians all competing for space on the streets and roads in a mad scramble to get somewhere. "You can certainly see why there are so many plans floating around for a mass transportation system—getting people and vehicles off the roads would help so much—putting them underground is probably the best option," he muttered.

"Very funny, Father," Emily chuckled. "Yes, I suppose if you buried everyone the problem would be permanently solved." She kept her violin case secured on her lap. She didn't feel safe carrying the violin on foot through the jostling crowds. It was the only reason she'd been grateful for the offer of a ride and was still holding back from her instinct to jump out of the carriage to walk the remaining blocks. She always had an annoying urge to escape close quarters with her father and run away in fear that she'd lose her autonomy somehow, even though she loved having him around.

"It's nice to have time to visit with you anyway," she said, flashing him the dimpled smile she knew he'd always loved. "We haven't seen each other in so long, since right after Connie was born, and so much has happened since then— Good Lord," she exclaimed, grabbing her violin case tighter with one hand and bracing herself with the other against the carriage wall. A violent lurch sent her father almost to his knees opposite her.

"A man crossed in the middle of the street right in front of our horse," she said, "as they all do these days. I had no time to warn you. He's lucky we didn't hit him. In one instant his life and all those that touch him could have been altered forever. I'm beginning to understand the need for a way to move people around underground. I rather wish it could be invented, even though I admit I don't like all the noisy, dangerous mechanical things they try to foist on us today."

Her father had pushed himself back on the seat, bracing himself with his strong legs stretched out across the carriage floor and against the base of the other seat. He looked unperturbed. Emily noticed, as she often did when they'd been apart for a while, how strong and handsome he still was, and she marveled at the fact that his dark good looks had somehow eluded all the single women in the world who must have been setting their marriage caps for him. "I've missed you," she said. "And you've come this time at an opportune moment. Klaas's marriage plans and my performance commitments have come together to possibly create some changes in our lives."

"I know," he said. "Klaas just told me. That's why I wanted to see you today. I must admit his news was the last thing I expected to hear on this business trip. Changes . . ." he said, ruefully . . . "those things you don't like." He reached over to pat her hand. It was enough to tell her he recognized she'd been struggling but didn't want to overdo the sympathy. It was a good strategy, leaving her feeling attended to without pity. It told her he knew she could get through it, even if it was unsettling. She liked that about him. "Have you thought of what you'll do?" he asked, not in a falsely offhanded way, nor in an overly concerned one. She shrugged, and he patted her hand again, saying, "Well, if I can help, I hope you'll tell me." She nodded and smiled, looking away to the teeming street outside the carriage, which was now firmly stopped in the middle of the jam. Suddenly a grubby little hand with an open palm shoved itself in their window. Looking out and down to see to whom it belonged, Emily caught her breath at the sight of a dirty little girl with matted hair and a torn dress, her huge, dark eyes staring up as if she could see into Emily's soul.

"I need pennies, please . . . just for food, is all . . ." the child said, as if she wasn't begging but merely stating a fact. Emily fumbled with her purse, pulling out a coin and stuffing it into the child's hand, where dirty little fingers curled around it and disappeared. Emily sighed, unsettled by the thought that a little girl could be begging in the middle of the crowded street. She noticed her father had been watching her. He made no comment but appeared to be calculating some unseen balance sheet of possibilities.

Life seemed so chaotic and confusing at that moment that Emily didn't even know how to start thinking about what to do next. In the past, she'd always relied on Klaas de Koningh for advice, but that wasn't viable anymore. Changes. Why were all the people—all the men in her life—always deserting her for their own interests? Was it her own fault? Was that the common thread? Was that always a woman's legacy starting from early childhood? "No," she muttered out loud without realizing it. The male lack of constancy was their own weakness, not hers.

"I'm sorry, what did you say?" her father asked, focusing on her now even more closely. She shook her head, and he went back to silently watching her. "How's Corey adjusting to the changes?" he asked, suddenly. She had no idea where the thought had come from unless it had already been there just waiting to spring. "Is he pleased about his father's re-marriage? That's not such an easy adjustment for a son to accept, and Corey's seemed a little off balance to me since I arrived." Emily instantly felt herself wanting to rise to Corey's defense, but whether to aid his reputation with her father or her own for choosing him as her husband, she couldn't be sure. Their changing relationship left a permanent stain on her heart and closed something up inside, but that was something she would hide from the rest of the world.

"I think Klaas's marriage will actually relieve him when he gets more used to it," Emily said. She was searching for a way to separate the troubled Corey the rest of the world saw from the one she used to know so well. "He's put his own interests and work too much aside to help Klaas with his business down south. That won't be necessary anymore, and even the camaraderie with his father he felt responsible for won't be the same. He naturally worried about Klaas's health after the war and his emotional stability after his wife died, but all that will be solved with this one event."

"I suppose," her father nodded, absently. "But I thought there might be more bothering him than his father's care."

"Perhaps you're right," Emily said, feeling all at once it would be nice to unburden herself entirely in the privacy of their isolation. She and her father had often used carriages for their most important talks, probably because his work as a diplomat kept him on the move.

Maybe that's why she felt so enticed by the opportunity now to expose her shaky marriage to him. "I do think Corey's a little lost—personally and professionally," she blurted out. "I know people usually advise vacations to escape from pressure, but I don't think that would be good for Corey or any of us right now. I think we need to be together, for all our sakes," she added, not wanting a solution just for him. Her whole family needed that solidarity. She had an instinct sometimes hard to explain, but important to bear witness to. She could feel her father accepting her explanation without question and was grateful for it. "Father, why do you suppose we can pick up freshly in our relationship, even when we've not always parted on the best of terms?"

William Alden took his time to answer. His daughter knew he'd learned long ago in his life as a diplomat that listening more and speaking less was the best policy. He'd even tried to teach her that in her youth, but with little success. But she knew he understood she was never satisfied when put off, so he would eventually answer her.

"I think perhaps you and I are both committed to the present rather than the past," he said, without taking his eyes off her. "We pick up with what is now and make that our starting point. I'm not saying we aren't the sum of our past experiences. Of course we are. And yet for our rapport we use the stuff of today rather than yesterday. Don't you agree?"

Emily started nodding before she answered, thinking to herself that they had less of a past to deal with than most families, due to her father's virtual abandonment of her after her mother's death. "I do," she said, knowing she'd grown more like her father rather than less so, all while they lived so far apart. She was convinced it must have been set in their natures years, or perhaps even generations, ago. "We have leitmotifs with variations," she added with a grin, knowing her father's appreciation for music would make him extremely comfortable with the idea of recurring themes in their lives, weaving around and through each other. "I've not always been easy for you," she said, her dimples showing in her cheeks again with the understatement of her comment. "I have enough experience with my own children to recognize how difficult and even annoying my stubbornness must have been when I was a child."

"I'd not deny that." He smiled, a flash of recognition passing between them. "But I wasn't as focused on my role as a father as on my job for the Crown in those years," he added, "so perhaps I didn't answer your needs appropriately. Still, we made it through with what is obviously a mutual respect. I think that's who we are," he added, smiling easily at her while still watching her carefully. She sensed he was assessing something but didn't know what. Finally he said, "I have an idea." She shifted uncomfortably on her carriage seat, both from being too long in one position and worry about her father's intentions. Their last carriage ride of any length had produced his bizarre and outrageous plan to remove her from New York, and her work, and Corey, all under the auspices of a promised music educa-tion in Europe that had not materialized. Robert Haussmann had been somewhat unwittingly brought into the scheme to rob her of her autonomy at the age of eighteen, all of which had ended very badly, with Emily's solo return to America without her father's blessing and her relationship with her teacher and mentor almost irrevocably damaged.

"Hear me out," he said, sensing her discomfort. "Perhaps it could offer you a way through your current dilemma and make your decision about how to move your family life forward easier." He stopped to watch her expression to see if it signaled any warning or resistance. She kept her face composed. "I've been thinking about retiring from public life," he began, his tone quite formal and almost as if he was practicing seeing what the words felt like in his mouth and leaving his tongue.

"You don't mean it!" she exclaimed, too incredulous to wait out his explanation. "What would you do if you retired? You can't just go back to England and wait to die!"

"I said *thinking about retiring*, not actually going into full retreat yet! You of all people should know I never support precipitous adjustments without sampling them first."

"Oh yes, I remember," she said, with a tease in her voice. "You've only been single about twenty-five years now. You wouldn't want to rush into anything." Her suppressed merriment forced her dimples to deepen.

"So right," he answered, giving her a sidelong glance and a smile. "But I'd like to get to know my grandsons at last, and I know I can only do that by spending more time with them. If I cut down my work schedule I'd have more hours in the week for them, and if you came to France this summer, we could rent you a house in the country for the whole family and we'd be near each other even while I'm still working. I know you have concert commitments, and we could test out how well we do together. France would also be a great place for you and Corey to further your musical careers, taking separate roads." He stopped talking, leaving Emily time to digest his suggestion. She well remembered how betrayed she'd felt that time before when she was so flattered he'd noticed her and taken time to talk with her, until she'd realized he was setting a trap she couldn't spring on her own. As if reacting to a signal, their carriage rocked and slowly started to move again, also heralding a possible end to their interminable entrapment in daytime city traffic.

"At last," she breathed. "We may finally be moving on." Her father leaned back, taking off his top hat and resting his head against the seat back. "Father," Emily said, quietly, "why the sudden desire for a change of life from a man who doesn't adjust precipitously? Forgive me, but I'm a bit skeptical."

"No need for doubt of any kind," he said. "Someday you'll understand what it means to a grandparent, needing to figure in his, or her, grandchildren's lives. It becomes oddly affirming. Suddenly time and work spent on the foibles of the outside world lose their value. If there was also a chance to smooth the way a bit for you and Corey, I'd say that would be a winning hand."

Emily looked doubtful, thrown off balance that her father had been able to surprise her after so many years of predictability. "But my recital commitments in France run only through the summer months," she said. "In September that will all be over, and what then?"

He smiled, a long slow grin that eventually lit up his eyes. "Then you could move to London, reopen our old house and make it yours . . . yours and your family's. And when my assignments change, which would happen eventually, I could come to live with you there, if you'd have me. You know that house is big enough and laid out to allow many generations their own privacy." She stared at him with a combination of disbelief and a dawning realization that he was talking with great sense.

"I don't remember the house well, Father," she said.

"Good," he answered immediately. "Then you won't have any expectations and can make it your own now. Just think how happy your mother would have been to know you and your family were living there. She loved that house, for whatever reasons people do."

"Yes, she did. That much I do remember," Emily said. She looked out the carriage window again and saw the shops at the end of the street where her violin maker worked. She'd have to get out soon. Her imminent departure made her less guarded and more desirous of a resolution for both her father and for herself. "I have to admit it would be nice to expose the boys to the other half of their ancestral history," she said. "I can't deny it would please me enormously to show them where you, Mother, and I began. I'd also love to have them know you better. And I can even imagine the excitement for Corey of meeting some of these young musicians Paris is becoming so famous for." She looked out the window again, recognizing the upstairs floors of the building that housed the violin maker's shop just a few doors down.

"Yes of course," Lord Alden said quickly, as if concerned Emily's attention was waning. "Paris is a hive of music activity, and if that's his developing interest, then it could be satisfied fully there. But even back in England he'd find much to make him happy. The British choral tradition is not only alive and well, but growing rapidly. Amateur choirs are thriving and performing much of the continent's music, like Mendelssohn's works." Emily flashed a smile at the mention of the name of one of her favorite composers. "The choral societies have been central throughout Queen Victoria's reign, and Corey would be in an ideal position to become involved in that musical life, maybe just the kind of new career engagement he needs now."

Emily looked at her father and through him, apparently seeing a life she'd not considered before. "Here!" she cried, suddenly. "I need to get out here."

"Stop the cab," William Alden called out as he knocked on the driver's compartment. "My daughter—Mrs. de Koningh needs to disembark here," he added, indicating the carriage should pull over next to the curb.

"Father," she said, waiting for the driver to open the door for her, "you've given me much to consider. Please don't mention any of this to anyone else, though, until I've had time to think on it. Truly, I appreciate both your offer and your thoughtfulness in coming up with it. It's just that I need a little time. I'm not sure yet that a move out of the de Koningh house or this city will be necessary. There's still a chance I can find a way to stop the plan to push us out. I wouldn't want to make any 'precipitous adjustments' without thinking them through first." He looked doubtful, but said nothing and smiled warmly, kissing her lightly on the cheek as she prepared to step down from the carriage with the help of the driver.

Emily turned to watch as the carriage pulled away. Clutching her violin close, she waved to her father even though she could no longer see him. She was troubled again by that past discussion in a carriage with Lord Alden ten years before. He'd manipulated her desire for a formal education to convince her to leave both New York and Corey just as the Civil War was breaking out. She'd been vulnerable then and had been controlled to a point of almost losing her way forever. Yes, it had all turned out well enough, but getting to the ultimate solution had not been easy or pleasant. She'd had to run away—from Robert, her father, and even Corey's father before settling in back in New York with her own inheritance, a new husband, a child on the way, and the de Koningh mansion to finally return to.

Perhaps this was just another way of getting what her father wanted, and Emily would find herself prisoner of someone else's lifestyle and private goals again. It was less likely now, though, as she'd come a long way in those ten years and was very much her own woman. And what, in fact, did her father want for himself? His grandchildren and the time to enjoy them. And how was that so very different from what she wanted, too?

The chance to start fresh in a new life with little left over from the past enticed her more than she cared to admit. It seemed to be what they all wanted. Perhaps her father didn't know her quite as well as he thought he did. Change was something she craved if it came on her own terms. She was an artist, after all, and change was most surely a part of the creative process. She just didn't want to give up what she'd already gained. Still, she couldn't deny she wanted to try new things, in her musical life and her home life as well, and perhaps a move to Europe would free them all to try a way yet unknown.

CHAPTER THIRTEEN

𝄞 DRESSMAKER & SEAMSTRESS BESSIE CARTER
Connie struggled to sound out the letters printed on a sign over the second-story window. His reading wasn't as dependable as his older brother's. "Hand . . . sewing and . . ."

"Finishing," Emily prompted, after waiting a few moments to see if Connie could start the word on his own. The boy and his mother stood side by side, heads thrown back to look up at Bessie's dressmaking shop. Connie was accompanying his mother while she tried on two new concert dresses.

"By . . ."

"Machine," she continued for him, when he couldn't get past the "M-a."

"Est . . . Est . . ."

". . . Established," Emily said, quietly. "Established 1855. She's been in business a long time, and just gets more successful every year." The intricately scrolled white woodwork around the sign reminded Emily of Bessie's hand-crocheted collars and cuffs, lovely frosting decorating her high-quality creations. "I can't believe this is the first time I've brought you with me," Emily said to the top of the little boy's rumpled blond head. "Lord, Connie, you need a haircut. You remind me of your father with that unruly tangle of maize!" She tickled the top of his head, messing his hair up a little more and bringing a smile to his plump pink cheeks.

"What's maize? One of those mixed-up tunnels where you can't get out?

"Different spelling. M-a-i-z-e, not m-a-z-e. Confusing language, English. Just imagine if you were coming from a different country to this city and you had to learn English late in life to survive!" She shuddered slightly. "No, maize is Indian corn—the yellow kind, anyway. And the corn silk is always golden and thick. That's what I meant about your hair."

"Father's hair isn't so gold like mine. It's a little silver. Will Bessie let me help?" The little boy stared at the window above as if afraid he'd miss the start of a magic show if he looked away.

"Now, Con, you have to be very good and not bother Bessie if she's busy. I don't know if she'll have other customers today. If other ladies are here, they might not be pleased to see a little boy in the shop."

"I know. I just want to help her with her work."

Emily smiled at her younger son, knowing it was easy getting him to adjust to a new situation. He was so fundamentally happy that nothing upset him for long, except maybe William. She'd known ever since she'd decided to ask Johnny for help that taking Connie along would offer the perfect cover for her plan. Bessie adored him and would most certainly take care of him for an hour or two, and then she'd have time alone with Johnny at the newspaper. And everyone at home would expect her to spend hours at Bessie's shop getting measured and fitted. "Let's go up," she said to her cheerful child.

"Let's!" He slipped his chubby bare hand in her lean gloved one and tugged gently. "Am I entirely like Father, yellow hair and all?" he asked. He was trying to climb right next to Emily and with barely enough room on the narrow staircase for the two of them, let alone enough leg on Connie to keep up to his mother's stride. But her skirts slowed her down a little, handicapping her to his advantage.

"I never knew your father at the same age you are now," she told him as they climbed, "so I can't really say how like you he might have been. But he had much the same carefree attitude at the age of twelve when I did meet him. I wish I could have had more of that easy outlook myself." And I wish William could have more of it now, she thought, watching Connie's stocky torso as it edged in front of her at the top landing. Funny, the way family traits got so mixed up. He had his father's spirit and hair, but her body, while William had Corey's build but her hair. And perhaps William had more of her and her father's temperament than she liked to admit—a fleeting thought she didn't dwell on. Arriving on the top landing at the same time as her younger child, she had only thoughts of her sons' adventures to come, although they'd be quite different from each other, no doubt.

Together they moved across the landing to the little shop they'd seen only glimpses of from the street below. The door was already slightly ajar, so Emily pushed it open all the way, while Connie clapped his hands together and held them to his lips to stop a cry of delight from escaping. But it did anyway. "Oh, Mama," he squealed, "just look at all the dresses!"

Four headless mannequins stood around the room in various stages of undress. One, Emily noted with some dismay, was entirely naked and sported an enlarged bust and rear where the bustle would be attached under a dress. She glanced at Connie to see if the naked, headless, armless, and outrageously overendowed cloth statue disturbed him, but he'd either ignored it completely in favor of the other mannequins or hadn't seen it. Either way, she could appreciate how his attentions had been lured by the assortment of evening and day dresses positioned around the room on hangers, to say nothing of the silk morning dress with yards of sheer, hand-embroidered lace in a cocoon of diaphanous netting. The ethereal cloak floated seemingly without tether from the morning dress's bare shoulders.

Side tables held yards of colored ribbon wrapped around spools of many different widths, and small, beautifully crafted shoes of fine leather poised cleverly around the floor below or next to mannequins, simulating the effect of a complete outfit. A rose parasol, perched nonchalantly by the side of a silver-blue tea dress with blossom trim and soft beige high-button shoes underneath, reminded Emily of a pair of mourning doves nesting peacefully in preparation for a big day to come. No wonder Connie stood transfixed in the doorway staring at this profusion of haberdashers' delights, each one more enticing and delectable than the next.

"Can we go in, Mama?" he whispered through his hands.

"Of course, Con. That's why we came. Take your hands away from your mouth, dear, and let me hold one." He looked up at her, eyes shining, and together they moved into the room to meet Bessie's welcome. She came through a door at the back, past sewing machines on tables littered with scraps of fabric. Three women sat occupied at the pedals and wheels, industrious clatter the only sound from the room. A man stood beyond the machines working at a mannequin.

Two tape measures fluttered around Bessie's neck and shoulders when she opened her arms wide and bent down to greet Connie. "Welcome, my little man," she said, hugging him. "At last you're here to see how the magic is made."

"I've waited to come for such a long time," he answered, so seriously Emily couldn't help but laugh. The thought of Connie waiting a long time for anything at his age struck her as ironic, until she realized from his point of view even a few days could seem a lifetime. She knew all about waiting for fulfillment of one's dreams and hoped he'd never become as expert at it as she had.

"And now your wish has come true," she said to him. "So let's have Bessie bring out my finished concert gowns so you can see them."

"Would you like me to show you around the shop before we look at the dresses?" Bessie nodded, as if she already knew the answer, as indeed she did. Connie's head was bobbing up and down before she'd finished her question.

"I'll wait for you here," Emily offered. "I don't think you need me getting in your way." She turned to study a short velvet jacket draped over the shoulders of one of the mannequins in an evening gown. It looked like a miniature cape ending at the waistline, but flared all around, dropping from darts at the shoulder seams. Almost any style of dress top could fit under it.

"That would work very well for you," Bessie said, just as Emily reached up to touch the velvet with the same thought. They both smiled at the pleasure of their telepathy, and Emily started to walk around to the other mannequins as Bessie took Connie into the sewing room. "Come with me then," Bessie said to the boy, "and I'll introduce you to my helpers in the back. That's where everything is cut and put together. We're in the middle of three orders right now, so there's a bit of a mess until the day is done, but I know you love fabric, Connie, so you'll enjoy the chaos." They went off together, Connie leading the way as if he knew just where he was going.

Emily looked around, noting how the front area was decorated to resemble a drawing room with a few love seats around the walls and paintings of some of Bessie's customers dressed in her designs displaying the beauty of her work. "This room is lovely, Bessie," Emily called, when her dressmaker and Connie reappeared in the sitting room a few minutes later. "You've created such an elegant space for people to imagine their costumes in."

"It's coming along nicely now, better since I've hung more of the portraits." Turning to Connie just behind her, Bessie asked, "Would you like to see the one I have of your mother?"

"Mother has a picture here?" His eyes grew wider and he nodded his head.

"Yes. Come and see." Bessie led them both to one of the bigger frames with a small demilune console table below it. There were no spools of ribbon or decorative boxes of any kind on the table, making it less likely to be an item of attention, so nothing detracted from the gold-framed picture above of a woman in a cream satin gown, her dark hair piled high and a violin raised to her left shoulder. The bow hung down at her other side as if she'd just ended a performance, and the pleasant smile on her face said it had gone well.

"It *is* you, Mama," he breathed in wonder, staring at the huge portrait that was more than twice as tall as he was. "Just look at all those people in chairs around the room, and even listening out in the hall and up the staircase. Why, they're sitting on the stairs, just as I do sometimes, to listen to you, Mama. They're all dressed up sitting on the stairs. Does William know?"

"Oh Connie!" Emily chuckled at how scandalized he was by the thought of adults doing something children weren't supposed to. "That's because there weren't enough seats in the room that night, so the audience just spilled out onto the stairs. The painter thought it would make a good balance of interest for the picture. I'm sure he didn't think a female violinist was enough to hold the viewer's attention."

"Nothing of the sort," Bessie scoffed, moving back to stand beside Connie and looking at the picture from his perspective. "Your mama's performance was so important they had this painting done to hang in a concert hall. She hasn't told them it's finished yet, so I can keep it here and let all my patrons see what important customers I have, and how beautifully I dress them. You should be very proud of your mama."

"I am, Bessie. I certainly am," Connie assured her. "But I wonder . . ."

"Yes?"

"Who dresses everyone else?"

"Who else? I don't know what you mean."

"The poor people. Who dresses the . . . the ones who come from other countries and don't speak English?" He looked at his mother for help.

"Immigrants," Emily announced. "He means all the immigrants who can't afford your prices, Bessie." Emily was rather proud of her young son's concern, and since he was asking the question of some- one as friendly to him as Bessie, there was no chance of misunderstanding. Bessie's eyebrows shot up, nonetheless, as she threw Emily a questioning glance over Connie's head. When Emily nodded and smiled, Bessie answered him carefully.

"They usually make their own clothes, Connie, with whatever cloth they can beg, borrow, or steal. Sometimes if they need something very standard, like a plain white shirt or blouse, they can buy the ones put together in factories for very little money."

"But are they nice?" Connie looked pensive, sucking a bit on his lower lip, a habit Emily thought she'd long ago forgotten from Corey's youth. How interesting that mannerisms could be inherited just as surely as physical traits.

"Actually, those shirtwaists *are* quite well made. It's just that they're cheaper because the hordes of women who sew them are paid so little money. The fabric's not bad either, just not very special." She smiled down at Connie with an expression that said, *Now that's that.*

"But if your workers need your money to live on, how can the . . . immigrants . . . live on so much less?" Bessie looked back at Emily and shrugged a questioning *Where did this come from?*

"It's hard, Con," Emily said quietly. "There are many different challenges people must face in life, and not enough to live on is just one of them when you come to a new country." She'd never experienced those difficulties herself, coming from England with a small fortune of her own, to the home of one of New York's founding families she'd eventually married into. Moving her family now to a new home or country, as her father had suggested, would be a different kind of challenge, having nothing to do with physical shelter or nourishment and everything to do with emotional trauma.

"And how can they hear your music, Mama?" Connie asked. "Can they go to a concert hall or is there another place for people without money to go?" Bessie and Emily exchanged glances again, while he stared back at the picture of Emily performing before a well-dressed, affluent audience in what appeared to be the ballroom of an elegant private mansion. They were both silent. "I shall ask one of your workers, Bessie," Connie announced, undeterred by the grown-ups' lack of disclosure. And at that, he spun around and started back toward the workroom he'd just left.

"Obviously, he's a little too comfortable here," Emily laughed. "Is it all right for him to go back there?" Bessie nodded and laughed too, both women seeming relieved to have escaped Connie's inquisition. Emily took a breath and straightened her back. "Bessie, I've got another important errand to run downtown. I wonder if Connie could stay here with you for an hour or so. He'd be so upset if I tried to pry him away from your shop now. Would it be too much of an imposition?"

"None," the dressmaker answered. "I have no more customers coming in and there's nothing I'd rather do than train a future star fashion designer. Connie and I are old friends, as well you know. Go on your way and he'll be here with me still picking up fabric swatches and cataloguing them by color and texture when you get back." Emily gave her a grateful hug relieved that Bessie hadn't asked where she was going. "Take your time," Bessie called as Emily's rustling skirts whispered down the staircase.

✶⋆ ⋙ W ⋘ ⋆✶

She hoped Johnny would be in his office, as she was a little earlier than planned. She knew she was luckier than most women, with her best friends being powerful men in exalted places. She'd never spent a minute calculating how she could best use her connections to her advantage, but this was the first time she'd been desperate enough to seek out the kind of help she thought Johnny could give.

"Mrs. de Koningh is waiting for you in your office, Mr. Dunne."

"Who told you to put her there?" Always too quick to act on her own, his new assistant was too proactive for comfort, even though Johnny wasn't one for much formality.

"*She* did . . . , sir. Mrs. de Koningh said she'd wait for you there. It was rather an order."

"I might have known." Johnny sighed. He was in no mood to face Emily's challenges in an already difficult workday. Their last encounter in the tearoom had left a bitter taste he had no interest in experiencing again. As she spun around to meet him, he noticed her rearrange her expression, as if he'd caught her in a mood she wasn't comfortable sharing. Instantly struck by the fact that he'd never seen such a deliberate change of expression, Johnny involuntarily braced himself for some new assault, even knowing it would be emotional rather than physical. He spread his legs apart as if to stabilize himself in an athletic-ready stance.

"Hello, Johnny! I hope this isn't a bad time for you."

He purposely made his eyes look flat, as if he'd locked a door behind them. "As a matter of fact, it is," he replied without emotion. "This has already been a very trying day and I truly have no time to spar with you, Emily." Her seeming sensitivity to the stress of his job put him on guard. He wondered which Emily he was going to get this time, still smarting from her overt aggressiveness in the tearoom.

"I am sorry, Johnny. I found myself downtown running errands and wanted to come by your office to apologize . . . for my behavior at our last meeting . . . and . . ." Her huge dark eyes opened wide as she looked directly at him, pulling his own resistance down and opening his senses to her in a way he'd promised himself he wouldn't allow. "I've come to ask a favor of you," she continued.

He barely heard what she was saying. What a strange, dynamic blend of things she was. How could anyone concentrate watching her with so many provocations coming at them all at once? "A favor . . ." He made it sound more like an accomplished fact than a query, her bad behavior of the other day already forgiven.

"Yes," she announced, but went no further, only continuing to look at him.

He waited. "What favor?" he finally asked, unable to bear her dark, liquid gaze any longer, although he also never wanted it to end. Unfortunately, she turned away so he couldn't see her face. How to get her to turn back for another look? "What favor?" he asked again, more insistently. He could just as well have cried, Turn around!

She did exactly that, moving slowly, as if to delay the impact of her looks and what she had to say next. "Something awful has happened to me, and I need help." He sat down with a jolt in his desk chair, as if her strange announcement had pushed him hard when he was off balance and it was lucky the chair was just beneath him. "You remember that Klaas de Koningh has returned home?" she asked, as if she thought he'd known all along she would say that.

"Please, please sit, if you'd like to . . ." He gestured to the other chair in hopes of covering his surprise. "Yes, I remember you told me the other day that Mr. de Koningh had come home. When we . . ."

". . . had that unfortunate afternoon together at the tearoom," she finished the sentence for him. "I was under enormous strain that day. The fire and . . . and my delicate health . . ." She glanced at the open door to Johnny's office as if afraid of being overheard. There were some things a lady never discussed in public. "Well, let's just say I was not myself," she went on. "I hope you'll forgive any caustic remarks I may have made. You were most kind to me and I never thanked you. I'm truly embarrassed by the memory of that debacle." She looked down at the floor, making Johnny aware of how long she'd been standing and how dark her eyelashes were. He half rose from his own chair and gestured toward the other one.

"Please, Emily, sit down. I want to hear what you have to say. Ask any favor, any . . ." Johnny felt as if he might be speaking a foreign tongue with a complex but familiar vocabulary.

"It's hard," she said, looking down again. She moved sideways to the other chair, her skirts brushing the floor lightly and sighing around her as she settled down on the wooden seat, eyes still cast down, so he had to stare at the gleaming dark head bowed in front of him. With its bright, white part down the middle, he was reminded of a renaissance tapestry of a beautiful supplicant doing penance. He heard her whisper, "Something quite terrible has happened."

Heart in his throat, a voice inside him asked, "What?" not caring what the answer was. He just wanted her to go on talking. He was mesmerized by the stillness he'd never seen nor heard in her before. He should have known. There was always a lull in the weather before a terrible storm. Tell me, he might have cried out, but he wasn't sure he'd spoken at all.

She looked up at him moving only her eyes. "My father-in-law is retiring and selling his business," she said softly.

It was absolutely the last thing he would ever have imagined she'd say. He swallowed with relief. "A smart move," he said, quickly recovering his composure. "The cotton markets are all in decline since the war and most of the southern plantations are dying faster than they can be sold." His voice was firmer. He was on stable ground now.

"It's not about smart business," Emily snapped, with some of the old spark. "It's about self-indulgence. He's elderly now. We just celebrated his sixtieth birthday, but he wants to start all over again."

Johnny detected an edge of scorn he'd never connected to Emily's feelings for Klaas de Koningh before. "You mean, start a new *business?*"

"No, not that. A new *family.*" She stared at Johnny, challenging him to guess, but this time he wasn't falling for the bait. He was feeling stronger and would wait until she told him what she wanted him to know. In the meantime, he'd enjoy looking at her sitting like a beautiful delicacy poised on her chair for his enticement. She lifted her chin to match the level of his eyes.

"A new *life* with a new *wife*. He wants to remarry," she said, her voice stiff with frost, and every word offered separately and carefully as if it might break. "He's become enamored of some southern widow and wants to bring her and her niece to New York to live." She took a deep breath, seemingly for relaxation, but actually for courage. "He wants her to become the new Mrs. de Koningh," she ended, with the weight of finality.

Johnny stared back at Emily. He couldn't figure out if this was the "something terrible" or there was something else he hadn't heard yet. "It's happening a lot now," he said at last, a little cautiously. She didn't move, so he went on. "Many northern men are marrying southern women. It's all the rage." He smiled, his first since he'd entered the office with her. "I admit, he's a little older than most men making that move, and many are doing the opposite—going down south for the weather and opportunity. You have to admire his spirit and determination to live fully at his age!" Instantly, he wished he'd kept quiet. He could feel the tempest gathering under the surface of Emily's calm exterior. He knew he'd made a huge mistake of some kind, but he didn't know what it was, so he couldn't ward off its effects.

"Admire his determination?" He couldn't miss the venom in Emily's voice if he'd wanted to, which he did. "You admire the determination to ruin the family and turn us all out? If that's the kind of purpose you respect, then I've come to the wrong place for help." He watched her rise slowly, mechanically, from her chair, seemingly pulled by unseen cords manipulated by an angry god. "You admire his determination to take *my* home and give it to someone else?" The white of her skin set against black eyes reminded him of the face of a wounded soldier, pools of dark pain sunken above high, fevered cheekbones.

"Why in God's name would he do that, Emily?"

"Because he's besotted and no match for a grasping, desperate charlatan from Dixie." She spat the words out as if they'd stung her tongue.

"I'm sure . . . he's too sophisticated to fall for that, Emily. And besides, why should he turn you and Corey out? There's a family bond between you and the de Koninghs strong enough to make a pride of lions jealous."

Emily clenched both fists by her sides. They were somewhat hidden in the folds of her skirt, but Johnny saw the desperation in those hands. He couldn't make sense of it, or of her, couldn't understand the anger she seemed so overcome by, and couldn't feel her overwhelming fear, but he saw it. "He's making a fool of himself," Emily spat out, "falling for a woman who's after him just for his money and position. And he only cares for himself and proving his ascendency." Johnny watched her carefully. There was still something he was missing.

"Maybe he's just scared and lonely," he offered. "Maybe this is his way of taking care of himself so that you and Corey won't have to. Maybe it's the most caring thing he could possibly do for you. A miserable old man with no one to care for or comfort him is not an asset to his children!" He felt awkward, as if he'd been sitting too long and the nerves in his spine were acting up. "What do you need from me, Emily?" He shifted in his seat almost imperceptibly. The muscles along his jawline ached, too. "I can't imagine how I can help."

Emily's arms straightened at her sides pushing her fists deeper into the folds of her skirt. She leaned forward toward Johnny. "You can help me expose the reputations of those dishonest southern belles," she said.

Johnny stared at her. His eyes narrowed. Head tilted to one side, he eyed her quizzically. "And just how could I help you do that?" he asked. For the second time that afternoon, Johnny Dunne watched Emily de Koningh transform into a whole new character before his eyes. She took a deep breath, visibly releasing her shoulders and shaking out her arms and hands as if to revive her circulation. He realized he'd seen her do that after long, intricate passages when she played her violin onstage. The gesture seemed to mark the end of one movement, with the release to prepare for another. He couldn't help seeing the image of her in the middle of a performance, when she suddenly lifted her chin again and started to speak slowly, in a measured, calm, and deliberate way. Surely she was calming down, yet he had the feeling he'd be foolish to relax his guard for even a moment.

"It's simple," she said with a forced smile. "All you have to do is what you do every day of your working life. Research the stories of these two women and then give the results to your society editor."

"To what end?" Johnny asked.

"To print for the edification of our New York society. You know what a small town this is, Johnny. One whiff of scandal and Klaas's fiancée will be chased out on the broomstick she deserves to be tarred and feathered on."

He stared at her. "What if there is no scandal?"

"Then make one. You and I both know how easy it is for facts to support either side of an argument. Whatever they are, you can twist her reputation into a scrambled wreck."

Johnny stared at her in disbelief. "Why would I want to have anything to do with the private affairs of Klaas de Koningh?"

"For me, Johnny! Your first major success at this very paper came from the story you did on Klaas's capture during the War Between the States. You weren't resistant then to digging for the story when I put you onto it. Why? Because Klaas was one of the wealthiest and most respected patriarchs in New York, so his activities are always of interest to your readers. No, indeed, you weren't so high-and-mighty when it came to benefiting from information about the de Koningh family then."

The flush on her cheekbones had spread up to the edge of her hairline and down her collarbone. Of course she was right about his interest in Klaas and his alleged spying for the North. But she'd been concerned about Corey's father then, and he'd worked harder to find the facts for *her*, eventually uncovering the difficult truth about Klaas's capture and imprisonment. Which, yes, had also sold many,

many papers and pushed the byline of J. R. Dunne to a position of prominence. No argument there. "Why? Why would you do this, Emily?" Johnny couldn't recognize her now as the young woman who'd come to him for help then.

"Because this . . . *southern belle* wants to commit a crime. She wants to steal from me, Johnny. I won't let anyone do that." Gone was the composed, cool exterior. Some primal sound took over Emily's voice as it dropped so low he could hardly recognize it. "I will stop anyone who tries to take away my home or my family—and believe me, Johnny, I know how to fight! I've been doing it all my life for the things I need to keep me whole. I know how to battle for my music, my beliefs, and my family—and I'll win this war, too," her black eyes flashed their warning, "with or without your help!" The verbal gauntlet had been thrown in his face more stingingly than a glove announcing a duel.

He flinched a little with the shock of it. Was he resistant because he didn't want to risk being on the wrong side of friendship with Klaas de Koningh? He knew she'd accuse him of it. "No," he said quietly. "You'll have to get someone else to do your dirty work for you."

She glared back at him for only a second. "I should have known you'd let me down. Men always do," she whispered. "I'll find some-one!" she announced, throwing her chin up. "I won't surrender that easily." Her eyes flashed a warning and her breathing was shallow. He stared at her, realizing he'd never seen her so desperate before.

"I wish you knew when to give up to save yourself," Johnny said, quietly. "You could lose everything if you try to ruin Klaas's chance for happiness." He dropped his voice as he looked up at his open door. "What if you complete this scandalous campaign and he finds out you were the one behind it?"

"I don't care what he finds out. In fact, I hope he does learn that I'm the only one who cares enough about his family, his home, and his reputation to act against these women. I don't think he has a thought for what it would mean, to me . . . and to us all. He's always had everything he wants without question. He thinks nothing of giving away my home—"

"It's Klaas's home, Emily, not yours," Johnny interrupted. "It's a family heirloom—his family's, not yours. It passes through the male heirs. You have no legal rights to the mansion or anything else. It all belongs to the de Koningh men. And Klaas can do anything he wants with the house or his life, including putting you out of it if he wants to start something new." Johnny was completely aware that he should stop, but the truth kept tumbling out once it started.

"Stop! You know *nothing*," Emily cried in a hoarse whisper. "What does this have to do with the law? This is about home and safety and . . . love. It's about responsibility, not about inheritance. With the privilege of owning comes the duty of care. He has an obligation!"

"I'll just bet Klaas sees it as freeing you and your little family to live your own lives at last in a new way. He's flinging open the door to that gilt cage on Fifth Avenue, Emily. He probably feels ashamed that he didn't do it sooner, that he stuck you with the responsibility for that place while he was working down south." Johnny ran out of breath, so he stopped. He leaned back in his chair, more from exhaustion than relief, while Emily stood speechless in front of him, suggesting she might finally be absorbing some of the incontrovertible truth he was offering her. He started to consider the human interest in the story about Klaas de Koningh's second marriage. It would truly be a reconstruction and reconciliation of both the North and the South. He'd have to put one of the more experienced reporters on it immediately.

His thoughts were interrupted by some small sound coming from Emily. Looking at her now, he felt sorry for the lack of support he was able to give her. Still, it was time she faced the world as it really was. "You've been fledged, Emily, that's all. Pushed out to fend for yourselves, at last," he said, almost as if it were an easy fact of life that any mother would understand without argument.

"We'll see about that," Emily hissed, spinning around with the toss of her shiny dark head. And before Johnny knew it, she was gone.

※ ☙ ❧ ※

"I need some exercise, Max," she said, leaning out the carriage window when they stopped to wait for a trolley to pass. "I'm going to get out here and walk. Meet me at the top of the park, please."

"But Mrs. de Koningh . . . ," the driver objected. She'd hoped for a simple nod.

"No buts, Max. I need the fresh air. I'll see you back at Seventy-Ninth Street." Emily slipped quickly out of the carriage, hoping the driver hadn't heard the note of desperation in her voice. She pushed across the street through the miasma of dust rising in the air, stirred up by feet, horses, carriages, and trolleys. She held her breath until she reached the other side of Fifth Avenue, almost running into the park where the wall joined the entrance to the zoo. Letting her breath out fast, she gulped the fresh air in and grabbed the railing leading down the steps. *Out with the bad, in with the good* her mother had always told her as a little girl when they took big breaths of air walking together in Hyde Park. How odd that her mother had come to her now, just when she was feeling the need for family.

Looking at some of the cages of animals along the walkways in the zoo, Emily remembered the day she and the boys visited, and Connie got his knee wedged between the bars in the bear's cage. It had all ended well, because they'd stuck together, and she'd solved the problem herself. That's what family was really for. And when they'd run into John Mackay by chance, she'd turned down his belated offer of assistance because they'd just needed to be alone together, their shared relief making them thankful for each other. She'd always been lucky with the support people had offered her, but the truth was she knew she could do a great deal herself, and always had.

She watched one of the chestnut vendors beside the walkway spooning hot delicacies into paper bags to line them up for sale. No one paid much attention to the disheveled young woman, and the zoo being almost empty on that late afternoon reminded Emily that the work this forlorn girl was doing would not be likely to earn her enough money to buy a meal that night. Many women didn't have families to help them, and it was a terrible truth that most women, regardless of their social status, had very little power to affect their own lives. How could she know and appreciate all the stories? In fact, what did she know about the horrors women of the South had endured in a war of their men's making? What had Mrs. Stovall been through, losing her husband and her whole family except her niece?

She walked back over to the chestnut vendor and pulled a coin from her purse, and then another. Holding them out, she made herself look deep in the girl's eyes rather than looking away as she often did. She left her usual smile with the dimples out too, wanting the girl to know she understood there was little to smile about in her world; but the girl smiled back at her, anyway. She was grateful for the coins and wanted to say so, handing Emily two small brown paper bags.

Turning to continue up the path as she thought back to her first time at the zoo with her boys, Emily stopped for a look at the bear they'd believed was menacing Connie. The animal still seemed dejected, and she wondered how long he could survive such a miserable existence for an animal that was meant to be free. "I'm sorry, my friend," she said to him out loud. "I've probably just lost one of my best friends because I was too scared to think straight. You must be scared all the time, so I wouldn't be surprised if you often lash out. I think now I must work to show my friends the kind of person I really am, when I'm not so frightened I can't make sense. Thank you for reminding me we all belong to each other," she said, tears beginning to roll down her cheeks unchecked. She wiped them dry with her glove and turned to walk with determination along the park's edge.

"I shall share these with Connie," she said, reaching into one of the paper bags and pulling out a scored chestnut to peel and eat as she walked. "And Bessie, and her workers, and Max . . ." She chuckled a little, realizing there weren't enough chestnuts to share with everyone. *It's a good problem to have*, she thought. *So many people I care about.*

✻❦ ⚜ ❦✻

"Oh Bessie, I'm so sorry I took so long. I was walking in the park to get some air and lost track of time! Is Connie okay? Was he any trouble?"

"Trouble, you can't be serious! That little future dress designer is in seventh heaven, and now so exhausted he couldn't bother a soul." Bessie pointed to a chaise longue in the back room and Emily saw her golden-haired child so fast asleep it looked as if he'd gone to another land. Piles of pinked fabric of all colors lay on his lap and all around him.

"I hate to wake him," Emily said, looking with such nurturing delight at her son that Bessie had felt compelled to look away, as if to give her more privacy.

"Good," said Bessie. "Because you forgot that even if we didn't work on the new concert dresses, we had to take in the older ones for the New York appearances. Now that you're back to your slimmer self, they will look like sacks of meal hanging on you."

Emily's late arrival back at Bessie's shop after visiting Johnny at his *New York Times* office had left much dressmaking work undone, but the need to get Connie home soon for his supper appeared obvious. Waking from his nap and unable to revive his former cheerfulness, Emily knew it was time to leave. She asked Bessie to join them in the carriage, suggesting they might finish their work back at the de Koningh mansion, and Emily was grateful for the solution to both dilemmas: a hungry child and unfinished business, both of which were her responsibility. Much had been her fault that day, and the afternoon wasted with Johnny was an embarrassment she would long remember. She knew she must have been desperate to envision such a duplicitous scheme to get rid of the widow and her niece, but attempting to involve Johnny in it was inexcusable, and she prayed silently and repeatedly that she hadn't lost his friendship and trust forever.

The quiet privacy of Emily's sitting room at home gave her time and space to let go of the afternoon's fiasco, and gave Bessie the chance to finish the alterations on Emily's costumes that had to be done on a tight schedule. The dresses needed most of their adjustments at the rib cage, as Emily's miscarriage had added more inches to her torso than the previous pregnancies. Now her body had slipped back almost to its original form, even if her spirit didn't seem to be there yet.

"This is one of my more pleasant tasks," Bessie said, smiling as she continued turning Emily in place to distribute the new darts evenly. "Adjusting a beautiful dress to a healthy, slim, and beautiful Emily is the kind of job I wish I had more of. Arms up," she said to Emily's chest from her position on the stool, "but first, two more pins." Emily pulled them from the pincushion and handed them to Bessie. "And do you think you could stop moving from one leg to the other? It's as if you're impatient with something, and it certainly can't be me because I'm moving as fast as I can without sticking you!"

Emily always felt embarrassed by the full focus on her during a dress fitting and knew Bessie had given her the job of supplying the pins specifically to keep her busy and more relaxed. She did love this dress, designed just before her trip to Chicago, with beetle wing sleeves and a sheer green silk gauze overskirt. Although there were still things that reminded her of the crisis of that period in her life that she never wanted to see again, this dress was not one of them. "I'm just still angry about . . . something . . . and I didn't realize I was reliving the experience while you try to fit my dress. Forgive me,

Bessie." The seamstress looked up from her seat on the footstool with raised eyebrows but said nothing.

"It was just an incident . . . that dreadful man who ran into me on the street the other day."

"Who was he?" Bessie asked, tugging a little on a fold of fabric that wouldn't lie flat.

"Oh, just one of the many critics who love to attack me for performing on the stages of the world. It seems their greatest delight is shining the spotlight of censure on me the minute I come out of hiding. It feels personal, even though I know it's not only me. They're uncomfortable with any woman who extends her sphere of influence outside her family. The only way they give in a little is if they think we're bringing morality and culture to the 'great unwashed heathens' of the world. If I went out West to play for an American Indian tribe, they'd applaud me, but when I present the exact same music to an audience at a concert hall they come after me to run me out of town on a rail. I'm so tired of their vitriol. Sometimes it makes me want to quit the stage completely."

"No need to go overboard," Bessie said, looking up at Emily again, pointedly. "Discretion is always the better part of valor. Is there no way you could beat them at their own game?"

Emily looked down, feeling Bessie's annoyance with the fitting; memories of the critic and Johnny had stolen her usual goodwill toward her seamstress and friend. "What do you mean? How would I do that? They have the public's eye, ear, and heart, and we're all just pawns they can toy with." The irritation in her voice could not be missed.

Bessie saw a bit of Emily's old flashing eye she'd missed since her miscarriage and wondered if she was finally rediscovering the fighting spirit she'd lost then. "I was just thinking you might find a way to make them think you were bending to their edicts, while giving your performances for some of the people who can't go to the places great music is played. Surely there are many children and adults in need of relief in this world." Emily looked down at Bessie with a frown, feeling perhaps everyone had been sucked into the vortex of disapproval around her that day. "In other words," Bessie went on, "you could pick the 'great unwashed' you want to perform for instead of letting the critics do it. There are people in need everywhere. You don't have to go to a Western plain to find them. That way you'd make yourself happy and satisfy the critics, too. It's just a thought."

Emily had always fumed at the idea of bowing to the overwhelming demands society made of women, and this seemed like another capitulation that turned her stomach. She didn't want to discuss it anymore, and realized she'd have to stand very still in order to get the dress fitting over with sooner. She didn't want to find herself in a position to explain how her day had gone again, so she started to count her breaths, in and out, eradicating the risk of slowing Bessie down with too much movement or talk.

"It's funny," Bessie said, leaning back to look at the effect her darts were having on the line of the dress, "how the life of a woman can so often be seen through the progression of fashions she's worn. Maybe it's just because it's my business to remember, but I can see my customers in visions from very young girls to grandmothers by remembering each special dress I've made them at the important moments in their lives." She smiled up at Emily still holding the pincushion. "Raise your arms . . . now put them down," Bessie said

Emily lowered her arms and shook them a little to get the circulation going. It was clear to her that Bessie's customers lived in a rarified stratum permitting them to buy Bessie's gorgeous works of art to adorn themselves and their children with. But as Connie had pointed out at Bessie's shop, there were plenty of women who couldn't afford her designs, just as they couldn't afford to come to concert halls.

"I suppose some don't get to have lives worth remembering," Emily said.

"What?" Bessie turned Emily back to face her.

"Oh, nothing," Emily muttered. She knew she needn't take her impatience out on Bessie. Holding the pincushion at the ready again, she studied the yellow silk embroidery thread used to outline what resembled continents on the green silk ball. The cushion was an unfamiliar addition to Bessie's collection of sewing implements, taking the place of a silver box she'd used to store the originally costly but crudely made pins. Now that they were mass-produced they were widely affordable, and pincushions were just beginning to be sold as trinkets or commemorative gifts. "Where did you get this?" Emily asked, studying it more closely. "It's a clever one," she added, noting there were decorations around the perimeter of the circle as well.

"Mrs. Vanderpool gave it to me," Bessie answered, taking out two pins from the bodice of Emily's dress to reposition them. "Do you see what's around the outside?"

"Little creatures of some kind," Emily said, raising the cushion to look at it better.

"Men," Bessie said. "There are little Chinamen positioned all around, holding up the world made of silk. I believe it represents Mrs. Vanderpool's view of reality."

"Good heavens," Emily exclaimed, holding the bright green cushion closer for a better look. "You're right! But what an odd vision to perpetuate, especially from one woman to another." She continued to stare at the ring of little dolls dressed in various colors of bright silk coats, encircling the globe with their arms, their heads all appearing to be miniature versions of the globe as well.

"Not so odd when you think of what happened to her sister," Bessie said quietly. She shrugged and started to turn Emily slowly in order to get a feeling for the totality of her alterations.

"I know nothing of her sister," Emily said, stopping to face Bessie. "Tell me."

"Well, you know I'm not comfortable with gossip about my customers," Bessie said, looking back at her with a worried look as Emily frowned. "But since it was in the paper when it happened, I guess that takes it out of the realm of rumor and into reality." She dropped her hands to her lap and stared across the room. "After her sister's husband died, his brother apparently moved in to take care of his sister-in-law, but in the end continued to spend her money at an outrageous rate. So Mrs. Vanderpool's sister tried to have him removed from the house. She first called neighbors to help her talk with him and then finally the police, but the next thing you know he had *her* removed instead and committed to an insane asylum!"

"Oh, for heaven's sake, Bessie, surely the Vanderpools came to her rescue. It's the brother-in-law who should be jailed, not her sister."

"Indeed," Bessie sighed. "But you and I both know that's not how it works, Emily. The man was within his rights to have her committed, and the Vanderpools didn't feel they should get involved with a lawsuit. I'm sure the publicity is too unpleasant for most families to take on. I don't think most people care about how unfair the legal system is to women."

"Men . . . holding up the world . . . ," Emily murmured, staring at the pincushion. "You know, Bessie, women always come out badly at the hands of those in power, don't they? We end up bearing the brunt for so much tragedy brought on by male weakness. Insecurity and laziness seems to guide too many men's actions." She shook her head, as if arguing with herself silently.

"I've not been sympathetic at times to women who are really only working for their own survival, but I think I allowed myself to be trapped by many of the male values for success I've been fighting to overcome myself. You may have hit on a great idea," she said, staring at Bessie as if she'd just made an important discovery. "Why couldn't I strike a blow for women and performance at the same time? I'd need help with publicity in order to put the critics where they deserve to be, but I could probably get that from Johnny Dunne . . ." She stopped abruptly, as if that last thought had undone her. "He'd most likely be a lot more willing to help me with this kind of project than the one I misguidedly tried to get him to take on before."

Jumping a little in place, she started to step forward, leaving Bessie with a mess of pins and thread dropping from her lap to the floor. Emily stopped, trying to free herself of her half-pinned dress. "I'm sorry, Bessie," she cried, seeing the look of horror on the seamstress's face as her unfinished project was fast becoming upended. Removing one of the pins that had mistakenly gone through securing the dress to her slip, she handed the dress back to Bessie who had repositioned herself on the footstool in hopes of continuing.

"I need to start doing some work on this," Emily beamed, hugging her on the stool. "Thank you. I know just what I'm going to do. Those critics will be eating out of my hands, and I'll end up performing more than ever. And at the same time, I can attract attention to the plight of women like Mrs. Vanderpool's sister." She bent over to pick up the spilled pins, sticking them around the cushion globe and into each of the little men holding it up. "Beware when Emily de Koningh and her music take on 'culture,'" she said, jabbing the last pin hard into the cushion and winking at Bessie.

"Mama," Connie called out cheerfully as he pushed the door to Emily's sitting room open. "Papa isn't going to be here for dinner again tonight, so could we all eat in the kitchen together? Bessie could stay and we'd have a lovely party of our own!" His big dark eyes glowed with the joy that was so often a part of his outlook on life. "I ran into him leaving and he said he wouldn't be back until very, very late!" The glee he obviously felt at the thought of this new development and the opportunities it opened for him didn't consider how the news might affect the others in the room. Emily froze in place where she stood, holding the pincushion with the little men around it in her hand.

"Yes," she said, slowly. "Why don't you tell Mary so she can adjust the dinner menu. Bessie can eat with you and William if she'll stay, but I should eat later with your grandfather. It isn't right to leave him alone, and I don't think he's ready to eat with you children in the pantry quite yet, as good as he's getting at change." She shook her head ruefully, obviously envisioning Klaas in the middle of the often-raucous scene in the kitchen pantry, sometimes including a song around the table, but never a cocktail before dinner! Connie grinned, spinning around on his heel to dash out the door.

His flapping jacket and tousled curls reminded her suddenly of Corey when she'd first met him, hanging on her bedroom door like a monkey and looking almost just like Connie did now. When she was a thirteen-year-old, she'd thought his capacity for joy might be the very antidote to the darkness in her own life. Would it not still be the right cure for the sadness in her thirty-year-old living? Why was Corey never there for her anymore? She shook herself a little and turned the pincushion in her hand. Bessie was looking at her hard enough to bore a hole.

"How long have these late nights been going on?" Bessie asked. "I know you thought the return of the de Koningh men from the South would solve all your problems at home, but it seems they've caused more trouble rather than less."

Emily dropped down on a chair to change her shoes from the performance heels to a softer, flatter version for home. "I'm too tired to get into this now, Bessie," she said with a sigh. "It would be easier for me if Corey spent more time at home, but he has to further his own career and he's working extremely hard to do that. His patrons and audiences are found in taverns and meeting halls uptown, so he must be out all night even if it exhausts him. I need to be supportive and understanding of that and keep our home together and in order while he's working."

"I'd like to know what career it is he's furthering," Bessie said with a scornful laugh.

"Enough, Bessie!" Emily ordered, jumping up from her chair and starting across the room for her closet. "All is well. Corey just must sacrifice a little. It won't last indefinitely."

"It better not," Bessie muttered. "Or else you'll end up like all the other women who find *they're* actually the sacrifice while the men get what they want." She snatched the pincushion from Emily and returned it to her sewing basket, pushing all the pins in furiously as if to bury them forever.

CHAPTER FOURTEEN

EMILY SENSED THE HINT OF SALT in the air before she'd reached the docks. She and the river had much in common. Trapped between parallel constrictions of land, the East River roiled and plunged headlong toward the freedom of the open sea hovering around the base of Manhattan island. Watching the embattled current as it swept past the shore, Emily recognized the desperation well, the struggle for liberty, pressed by constraints beyond one's control. The river reminded her that limits can create chaos in the natural world as well as in the human soul. But she couldn't deny the momentum of the river paralleled her sense of hope springing from her determination to move herself and her career forward in a new way. Bach came to her mind. The rhythm of the tidal flow represented his music so well, bringing her visions of water and a cleansing self-determination.

She'd taken care to dress very differently today, as a performance at an insane asylum was not an occasion for frivolity. She looked exactly like a widow going out for an airing, extremely subdued in a dark gray skirt and white blouse. A gray cape over her shoulders hung only to her waist. She knew the vibrant, dark hair that matched her eyes seemed duller without the contrast of a colorful hat or the ribbons she usually loved to wind through the coils at the back of her neck. Her serious, simple black bonnet with small brim enhanced her look of gravity. She hoped her friend John Mackay wouldn't find the changes too unpleasant. With her plan for ridding herself of Klaas's unwanted marriage disrupted by Johnny Dunne's angry refusal to get involved, she'd decided to turn to the silver king, one of her most dependable supporters, to take her to the asylum on Blackwell's Island. She'd known he was the natural choice for her mission. Even though his philanthropy was always delivered quietly, most people knew his deep commitment to those in need, like the orphans of New York, Paris, and London, and naturally the Catholic Church nurturing his Irish roots. John William Mackay was always there to speak for misplaced or rejected people in need of help. So, she knew he'd be unlikely to turn away from the women on Blackwell's Island who had no voices of their own.

Arriving at the dock with a jolt, the carriage threw her forward, breaking her thoughts apart. "Are we here?" she called up to the driver, coming out of her daze to look at the clog of vessels crowding the pier jutting out into the water. A flow of people had enveloped the carriage as soon as it stopped. Hordes of sailors, merchants, and noisy children crowded the dock all the way up to the slips. This was truly the center of the world if the circulation at the pier was any indication. "I don't see Mr. Mackay," she called, scanning the crowd nearest her window and tightening her grip on the arm of the upholstered seat. She didn't move. Only her eyes darted from the decrepit pier jutting out in the water to the tangle of masts and sails of the ships mixed in with other vessels of all kinds. She assumed some must be versions of the steamships now used to ferry people and produce to the small islands adjacent to the shore.

"He's meetin' ya on board," the driver called down. "Said to tell ya he'll be there for sure. He used to work down here as a boy, ya know. Has lots of old friends to connect with." Possibly she shouldn't have come. Perhaps she should have dropped the whole idea just as soon as it materialized.

"He promised he'd help me," she whispered. But she didn't move.

"C'mon down," the driver called, holding out his hand. How he'd gotten from his seat to open her door so fast was a mystery. She'd lost track of how long she'd been sitting in the coach staring out at the turmoil on the dock. "I can't leave the horses," the driver grumbled. "I'd take ya to the ship if I could."

She nodded. This had been her idea, after all, and she had to keep moving. "I'm ready," she told him, leaning out on his arm to take the top step from the carriage. There was a time she might have bristled at the suggestion she needed support, but not now. "Wait!" she suddenly cried out. Turning back to the interior of the carriage, she pulled her black violin case toward her and clutched it to her chest.

"I'll take that, ma'am," the driver said, reaching to help her with it.

"No, thank you. I can handle it." She twisted slightly away from him, almost slipping off the coach's stepladder to the ground. She gave a little jump to the dock, her instinct suggesting it would be easier than trying to regain her footing on the narrow carriage step.

"Guess ya *can* handle it!" the driver chuckled. "An' there's Mr. Mackay, jus' as he promised." He pointed to the big, strapping figure of the former Irish boxer, now the silver king, emerging from a crowd of sailors at the edge of the pier.

Emily looked up at him with relief as he reached her side. "This is quite a spot, John," she said. She hoped the hustle and noise of the teeming scene would hide the tremor in her voice.

"Have you never been to the slips down here?" Mackay asked with a smile. "It's not quite time to board yet, so I'll show you around before progress changes it all right before our eyes." He stood watching her silently for a moment. She wondered what he was thinking as she stood still, grasping her violin to her chest like a refugee with a child, an odd stance for a performer of her caliber and a woman of her background. She realized she might look like so many other women John Mackay had watched growing up in his immigrant Irish neighborhood, the reciprocal need of the women obvious in the cocoon of care wrapped around their babies. Yes, of course there was a mother's physical protection for her child, but he must have seen the mother's fear for herself, too. The connection to her infant made a mother feel safe, even in a new, strange, and threatening environment. She knew he'd had a close, caring relationship with his own mother.

Suddenly she felt unsure of who she was and where she belonged, and John Mackay suddenly seemed a stranger, or at least not a friend. She hugged the violin's case tighter, grateful for the affirmation the instrument gave her. Maybe her connection to the Guarneri was unusual, but she thought it a universal connection for musicians that most people simply knew nothing of. No wonder John was looking at her so quizzically.

"Are you quite well, Emily?" he asked, bending toward her as if to keep his question for her ears only. "Have you changed your mind about this? You know, you've passed the point of having to mollify the critics by spreading culture to the poor deprived souls trapped in places without edification or beauty." He waited quietly for her answer, neither assuming he knew it nor pressing her to deliver one. Ordinarily she'd have welcomed the pause to decide, but more time now only seemed to make it worse.

"Yes . . . ," she exhaled with unnecessary force, ". . . and no! I mean I *am* well, and *no*, I haven't changed my mind. I'm not going to the asylum to earn accolades permitting me to perform in public. Society's perception of a woman's role must be of some concern to me, and the socialization of art has always intrigued me. I want to share the emotional relief classical music can bring people who are sad or in pain. My little boy reminded me that we all need that kind of comforting, no matter where or how we live. He put me quite to shame. The time has come to take my blinders off and start noticing others' needs." She'd realized that her opposition to Klaas's marriage was ungrateful and selfish in regard to him and perhaps even the woman he wanted to marry. She didn't like herself much anymore and had vowed to change that. "Where shall we go while we wait?" she asked, noticing with discomfort that John was still studying her closely.

"Did you see the boat I came off?" He didn't pause for her answer this time. "That's mine. Come with me and I'll show you." He stepped up next to her so he could place his hand partway around her back—more protective than controlling. His big, muscular frame sent out a warning for the crowds to keep their distance. Emily found herself accepting the shield and support he offered, the second time that morning she'd been grateful for help. Her growing dependence was a little disquieting. It wasn't a stance she was used to or comfortable with.

As Mackay led Emily to his boat, her usually keen sense of observation seemed dulled by the chaotic movement and intense smell of fish and bodies. A total assault, the chaos on the docks arced from the slips and sidewalks directly to her nerves. She wasn't sure she hadn't made a mistake asking John to meet her here—to escort her to the island—and whatever awaited her on it. He couldn't really help her with what she wanted to do, but somehow his streetwise presence and philanthropic focus on the poor and abandoned creatures in society made him the asset she needed. A different sort of man, a lifelong gentleman whose hands had always been clean and nails always polished, would only be a hindrance, even less capable of dealing with what they were going to see than she was.

"Here we are," John announced with obvious pride. "My lovely *Silver Queen*." He waved at some sailors on the deck of a long white ship.

"My, she looks fast . . . like a clipper." Emily breathed freely now, her first smile in a while lighting up her face. "Beautiful," she said. Her eyes shone with reflection from the water light.

John nodded as if there could be no other conclusion. "She *is* a clipper, modified for my personal use." His voice rang with the delight of a proud parent. "They're not great for cargo, being so slim and so high above water, and not used much anymore since steam took over with the opening of the Suez Canal just after the war, but they're great as private yachts if freedom and adventure are what you're after." He looked up at the masts rising forever and criss-crossed with intricate rigging. "I spent my youth apprenticing to build these. Now I have one of my own." Emily smiled up at him first, and then the ship. She loved her friend's appreciation for value one produced through one's own skill, rather than simply the wealth to purchase it. She understood the joy of commitment to creating what you want, even if what you want is a musical language instead of a work of art to look at or hold—or to sail on, for that matter.

"I wish I could carry you over to the island on the *Silver Queen*, Emily." John made no effort to hide the concern in his voice. "You won't enjoy the ride on the steamer. I don't understand why you insist on going that way, and to be honest, can't fathom why you want to perform for the inmates of the Women's Lunatic Asylum in the first place. I wonder if you've gone a little crazy yourself." His smile, not unkind, showed he was not to be taken seriously.

Leaning toward him to set her point, Emily gripped her gloved hands tighter on the violin case. "I told you when I asked you to come with me, John. I met a woman from Germany in a shirtwaist factory Connie and I visited with a seamstress friend. The worker told us her sister ended up in the asylum because she didn't speak English. The owner was suspicious she was complaining of conditions in the factory and he committed her to get her out of his way."

Mackay nodded, taking off his hat and tapping it on his other hand. "Women and their children are often consigned for being on the wrong side of society. . . ." His voice trailed off, as if he'd been much affected by thoughts of the lives of women and orphans. Emily shook her head at him, a frown darkening her usually bright eyes.

"I'm impressed by your thoughtfulness, John, knowing you to be one of the most powerful men in America. To take away a woman's freedom and home on a selfish whim of dominance is surely criminal, even if our society and culture support the injustice. Don't you think so?"

John Mackay lowered his eyes to study the hat in his hands. Then raising them again to hers, he shifted the hat brim a few times in his fingers but never wavered from meeting her gaze. "Even though my gender should place me contrary to the argument, I happen to agree with you," he said. "But many men *are* mindful of their humanity, Emily, taking the responsibility concurrent with their supremacy very seriously. There are undoubtedly many poor wretches who belong in the asylum for their own safety, and to get the medical attention they need—"

"And many who don't," she interrupted. "The former, one might call patients, but the latter, prisoners." She could feel a feverish glow spreading up to her forehead. She kept a steady gaze leveled out at the slips with their tangle of masts stenciling the skyline, afraid that if she looked at John she'd lose her nerve.

Somehow, chance and her youngest son had conspired to bring her inner turmoil to help the beleaguered, powerless, homeless immigrants arriving in New York. Emily couldn't imagine how a young woman would survive with none of the advantages she'd had as a thirteen-year-old visitor from England. She knew little of these women in the asylum except that no one wanted anything to do with them. The knowledge that they could be pulled off the street, either literally or by outright lies, set her mind and heart on a tumultuous journey away from her worries about her own future. She didn't need investigative help. She didn't need Johnny Dunne or the *New York Times*. She needed someone with personal knowledge of life in the tenements and immigrant populations. She needed John Mackay.

"I'm going, John, and that's that. But I'm very glad you're with me," she added, softly, the clouds of her discontent clearly visible over her expressive face.

He didn't hear her in the sudden uproar swelling from the cobble-stones, followed by pounding pebbles and snarling catcalls behind them. He pulled Emily closer to the dock to avoid a caravan of unruly onlookers following a covered wagon. Some men and women ran alongside pounding on the wagon's sides, while others ran behind trying to hang on to the bars over the window in back. They seemed a surprising mix of well-dressed city folk, merchants, scruffy sailors, and dockworkers, and swarms of cats and dogs stirred to a frenzy by the bad behavior of their human counterparts. Street hooligans also ran alongside the wagon throwing stones at it with surprisingly accurate aim and percussive results. Emily could imagine the sound their projectiles made inside the wagon, flinching when one ricocheted to land at her feet.

"Well, here come your lunatics, Emily." John stepped forward, holding her with one arm so she was totally shielded from the parade of hecklers following the asylum wagon. She took a frightened breath, and then slipped under his arm to the front again.

"It's all right, John. I need to see what's happening. And besides, I have you to protect me," she said, with a genuine smile of gratitude, flashing her still-charming dimples and immediately defusing the objection that died in his throat. "Why do the crowds jeer and leer at them so? I don't understand. Are they afraid the women's misfortune might rub off on them? Can't the attendants keep them away and protect the womenfolk from such harsh treatment?"

"Oh Emily, my dear, this is nothing compared to what they're going to face inside the asylum, I fear. I've never worked up close with the indigent or insane, but there must be a good reason for hiding them away as society does."

"Don't be so sure!" Emily snapped, deepening patches of scarlet rising from her chest to her cheeks, eyes riveted on the approaching wagon. "Charles Dickens has been writing for a long time about taking people we don't want to deal with off the streets. Most of *us* have no idea what happens to *them*, and would just as soon we never do. But you, John, you've always had a very different view of your duty to help those in need. That's why I wanted you to come with me . . . as well as for your athletic build!" she added, with a rueful smile, which did nothing to even her complexion or brighten her expression.

"So, you're becoming an advocate for the beleaguered female immigrants of New York, is that it, Emily?"

"I've always had concern for them, John. I've discussed their fate with my boys almost since they were born on this soil in a privileged home, unlike the majority here in this city, for that matter."

"There are many ways to be without a home, Emily, and it's not always about privilege."

"Obviously, but you know the saying, 'fat sorrow is better than lean sorrow.'" She rested her violin case down on the ground at last with a sigh. She was beginning to feel very tired before she'd even reached her destination. *If I'm tired now, how must those poor souls in the wagon feel?*

"You've helped people with the basics of physical survival for a long time, John, and always anonymously without need for recognition. I hope my music can help these women toward a spiritual endurance they might not have any other way." Suddenly overwhelmed and trying to shut out the very sights and sounds she'd told John she needed to see, Emily closed her eyes for a moment.

"Are you well?" he asked again. Her face seemed pale, reflecting the unbecoming gray of her outfit. He reached for her violin case. "May I . . . ?"

Vaguely, she shook her head. "You don't have to . . ." Her voice trailed off, but she let her violin slip from her hand into his.

"We help each other, Emily," the silver king reassured her, holding her prized Guarneri firmly with the care he knew it required. He could see her shoulders relax. "I applaud your desire to feed the souls of unfortunate immigrants. I can't do that. I feed their bodies, instead. Come on, then. We'll be boarding in a minute." He nodded in the direction of the slips.

"What a sight. Is that battered old thing what we've been waiting for?" Emily stared at a side-wheeler now docked between two sleek sailboats. A charred smokestack rose above the other masts near the pier, reminding her of a less graceful but increasingly necessary advancement in water travel many still chose to ignore. "I didn't know there were any of these around here. What is it?"

"Have you forgotten the very first steamboat was built right on our East River?" John chuckled. "And almost one hundred years ago, at that. Well, maybe more like sixty, but a long time ago, at any rate. This one is more of a packet," he added.

"A what?" Emily was still staring at the flat, steel-hulled ferry with two masts at either end, one flying the American flag and the other a white flag with black letters: **B.I.**; a low railing around the entire deck was the only structure other than what appeared to be a makeshift cabin, just a wooden box with some windows cut away as an afterthought. The ship reminded her of a top-heavy bathing tub with paddle wheels.

"Packets are meant to carry a little cargo short distances and some people, too. But this one's obviously been converted just to ferry inmates to the island. *B.I.—Blackwell's Island*. It's no showboat, that's for sure." John shook his head slightly, then looked away as he grew silent for fear of upsetting Emily.

"Is it quite safe, John?"

"Not as safe as a sailboat, certainly. The worries many have about boiler explosions have been borne out. There's something unnatural about stoking a huge fire on a boat. But this thing's clearly been around a long time . . . and fully in use," he added, somewhat contritely, looking at the peeling paint and signs of rust visible from where they stood. "I'm sure it will make the trip safely at least one more time," he added, clearly sorry for his sarcasm as he saw terror in Emily's eyes.

"Look how fearful the patients being brought up are," Emily whispered. "The sight of that packet doesn't exactly reassure them. Or me, either," she added, unnecessarily.

They both watched as two women were carried out of the wagon on stretchers toward the decrepit steamer waiting in the slip just ahead of them.

"Why are they first?" Emily asked.

"They're either so physically or mentally ill it's believed they'll contaminate the others," John explained. They watched in grim silence as more women were then led out of the wagon one or two at a time and marched up the boarding plank to disappear onto the steamer.

"How unnerving to think one could catch mental illness from another," Emily said, still staring at the steamer.

"I know," John answered. "I recognize that's the fear. There really isn't much understood about it, and there's always a chance it's caused by something that could render it catching." Emily frowned as she watched, unable to grasp what he was saying.

Finally, one last inmate was led to the boat and the wagon backed away from the dock. There was no room to turn around down near the slips, so the driver jumped out to help the horse back up from his head, tapping once or twice with his whip on the creature's left shoulder or right to adjust the direction, threading the wagon through the milling crowds until the street widened enough for it to turn in a circle. Emily watched as the quiet old horse hung his head, a victim of the heaviness she felt herself. His despairing, dull eyes reminded her of the pain shared by all living creatures. How many of these horrid trips had the dependable animal made in his lifetime?

"Are you sure about this?" John asked. "We can still hire our own skiff."

Emily paused for a moment, and then shook her head, starting toward the loading plank and forcing her friend to quicken his pace to catch up. A grimy man reeking of whiskey stood beside the loading ramp to help Emily up. The breeze blew the liquor fumes on his breath her way, causing her to reel from the stench. John reached out to steady her. "Enough fuel right there to start a fire," John grumbled in her ear.

Emily was too stunned by the assault of the vapors exuding from the man's mouth and pores to comment at first. "My God! Was he in the wagon with the women?" she finally breathed. "If so, I'm surprised they're all still conscious." John chuckled, but Emily did not.

The liquor-soaked guard scanned Emily from head to toe with his rheumy eyes. Matted hair of no discernible color protruded from his oily cap, which he whipped off in the mock-chivalry of a gentleman. Spitting out a huge wad of tobacco juice beside her feet, he smeared his mouth on the back of his filthy sleeve, grinning at her all the while. Suddenly the imposing figure of John Mackay stepped up next to her, his presence moving the sailor away until he disappeared completely. Only the stench of his greedy appetite for rye hung in the air around them like a fog.

"I suppose we should follow him," Emily said, with a disgust she took no effort to hide.

John shook his head. "Not necessary. There's no room inside these old steamers and there are quite a lot of prisoners . . . patients. Between them and the attendants, and possibly doctors, there won't be an extra inch. If you think that man's breath reeked up here in the open air, just imagine what that closed-in space will smell like."

"It's all part of taking away the women's humanity when there's nothing left to steal. I want to understand what they're up against. Please, escort me down there," Emily said, quietly, all the while hanging back slightly as if to slow the completion of the task.

"Shall we leave your violin up here for safekeeping then?" John asked.

"No!" she cried, trying to grab it from his right hand.

"It's all right, Emily. I'll hold on to it for you, then. Let's get this over with." He moved to the cabin they'd seen the attendant disappear into, grasping the violin case in his left hand and stepping over the high threshold as he held open the door for her with his right. She followed slowly.

Gasping, both from the shock of the sight inside and lack of oxygen, Emily stopped so abruptly she could feel her violin forced against her back as John stumbled to recover his balance behind her. She turned and clutched the case, holding it tightly to her chest before moving forward to face the atmosphere in the dirty steamer cabin. It took a few seconds for her eyes to refocus in the thick, dank air, with only slim bars of light straggling through a few high, closed portholes. She knew she'd disappear in the gloom, dressed as she was: gray and plain. She'd blend with everyone else in a place where standing out was the last thing one wanted; and disappearing was a goal so alien she couldn't believe the plan had occurred to her, though she was glad of it now.

Seated on narrow benches under the slim, filthy glass openings, inhabitants of the asylum wagon were packed shoulder to shoulder, arranged like butcher shop produce against the cabin walls. At the far end of the room, a small, foul-smelling bunk ran between two pillars. One of the first prisoners off the wagon, a young girl, was being lowered from the wooden slab as Emily and John entered. Had she not been ill already, the filthy cot would most assuredly have made her so. Emily didn't spot the older woman who'd also come off before the others, and hoped she'd been smart enough to fade into the background to avoid the soiled bed of disease and pestilence. But John saw the elderly patient tied to one of the pillars so as not to slip away. She had neither a place to lie nor the ability to sit.

Noticing two female guards move close on either side of the portal they'd just entered, Emily wondered how she'd have viewed those fearful sentries had John Mackay not been with her. Colossal creatures in makeshift, pieced-together dresses, the women were competing, spitting on the floor with tobacco juice in a bizarre form of target practice. Every time one of the patients shifted on the bench or rose to look out a high window, one of the matrons would glower like a thunder cloud and growl, "Si'down!" Emily jumped the first time she heard the barked command but steeled herself to hold still from then on—not difficult, as she was concentrating on holding her breath to avoid the stench in the cabin. She never looked at John, nor he at her, but she felt the roomful of eyes on them both.

Unaware of anything other than the vile atmosphere, Emily paid no attention to the movement of the boat covering the short distance across the river until it stopped, and the older inmate Emily had originally lost sight of was untied by one of the gargantuan sentinels. She felt a pang of remorse, having imagined the older woman better off than the others if she'd escaped. The young girl on the cot was also taken off roughly by two male attendants. At least fresh air would be her welcome. John moved as if to leave next, but Emily put out her hand to stop him.

"Let's go last," she said in a low voice. "I want to watch them off, one at a time." She felt him stop beside her but couldn't look at his face for fear of losing her hard-won composure. Finally, the last prisoner, a young woman of about twenty, seemingly sane but frightened, was escorted by two attendants, a man and a woman, to the plank. Moving up directly behind her, Emily could see the man's fingers sink in the flesh of the girl's arm as he pulled her to the bridge.

"Where are we?" the girl asked, pale eyes darting.

"Blackwell's Island," her tormentor answered.

"What are those?" She raised her free arm and pointed up the shore with a shaking hand.

"They be coffins and corpses," he said darkly, "gettin' ready to go back to Manhattan on the ship you come over on. Don't bother lookin' around. Plenty of time for that at the asylum, as you're not leavin' till you go like them." He nodded toward the line of coffins waiting to be carried to the steamship. Putting his large fist in the middle of her back, he shoved her along the plank to the waiting ambulance wagon, already filled with the other steamship inhabitants. The springboard was put up and a policeman and mail carrier leaped behind as it moved off fast.

"What's their hurry if no one's ever going to leave?" Emily muttered. She hugged her violin closer, and John slipped his arm around her shoulder, an intimacy she'd never have welcomed had the shock of what they'd just experienced not called for it.

"What now?" Emily asked, in a daze.

"What indeed," John muttered.

CHAPTER FIFTEEN

THE UNCOMFORTABLE BOAT TRIP to Blackwell's Island, to say nothing of the corpses lined up for transport, would discourage anyone from making the trip by choice, as Emily just had. Why, John wondered, was it so much harder to bear the sight of privation through the eyes of the innocent? Growing up in the streets himself as the son of a poverty-stricken immigrant, teased and tormented by gangs for the stutter he couldn't control as a child, there was little he hadn't already seen and lived through. But how these hardships must grieve someone with the disciplined, cultivated mind and gentle, caring heart of Emily de Koningh! Her artistic sensibilities must truly be writhing from the dearth of civility she'd just witnessed, now cruelly assuring her the violin could give these poor creatures nothing they really needed. The thought made it hard for him to breathe, knowing so well the depth of Emily's passion for her instrument.

"Let's walk to the asylum," he suggested. "I think we could both use the air and the exercise, and judging from the sight of those green lawns ahead I'd say we're in for a more pleasurable excursion than the one we've just endured." Together they started off in the same direction they'd seen the ambulance go, Emily setting each foot down quickly and deliberately, as if she'd never considered what a joy it was to have the freedom of choice until now.

"Slow down," John said, "your breathing, I mean. It's just a performance like any other."

"No, indeed it is *not*," Emily muttered. "Every audience is different and an integral part of the performance. I can't imagine what this one will be like." But whether she referred to the audience or her concert, he was never to know. She clutched the violin case at her side as if it contained her salvation, which in truth it did. Was it possible these women would remind her of why she played it in the first place? She took a slow, resolute breath in, counted to three, and let it out to the count of five. The ride by steamship just before and visions of gruesome caskets at their arrival faded with every calming lungful she controlled in and out.

"I hardly think that sign is necessary!" John's voice broke into her walking meditation. Her head jerked up as a putrid smell stopped her measured breaths.

"What in the name of heaven is that?" she gasped, thrusting the back of her gloved hand over her nose and mouth.

"Well, if we're to believe the placard, it's meant to be the kitchen," John groaned. "That's why this sign warning pedestrians to advance no further is unnecessary. Who would ever want to get closer?" Emily shook her head, trying to answer without uncovering her nose, and also to get rid of the image of food to be eaten by the female inmates coming from such a place.

They hurried past the warning sign to a walkway leading around the building she'd taken no notice of before while lost in her thoughts. Stopping suddenly, she was shocked by the incongruity of its fairy-tale architecture. The octagonal Italianate mansion of blue-gray stone with white trim was a five-story castle rising from the ground like a wedding cake. Its layers of decreasing diameter reached for the sky and ended in a decorative wrought-iron widows' walk on the roof. Surely that offered an incomparable view of the East River.

"Where did this come from?" she whispered to John, unable to take her eyes from the mirage shimmering at the edge of the island.

"Oh, it's always been here; or at least for the past fifty years," he answered.

"Who put it here, and why?" She finally focused on the sign over the front door announcing the NEW YORK CITY LUNATIC ASYLUM — 1841. Misinterpreting her question, John looked pensive for a moment before he offered the information he thought she wanted.

"Alexander Jackson Davis," he intoned, obviously proud he'd come up with the name he'd been looking for. "America's number-one architect and designer of her most beautiful buildings."

"Good Lord! Why would they employ an artist of his renown for a building to house lunatics . . . or prisoners . . . or any of society's misfits they want to hide away? What is it in our culture that boasts such grand schemes for such mean purposes? I've seen the Tombs downtown, and you'd never know it was a prison from its Egyptian Revival grandeur. What was it Mr. Dickens called it: *'An enchanter's palace in a melodrama'*?"

"Guilt!" John Mackay looked up at the blue slate rotunda of the lunatic asylum. "Guilt makes us try to convince God and ourselves we're treating those in need as Christ wants us to."

"A prison built with guilt. A gilded cage . . . ," she muttered. "I don't think God is fooled," Emily groaned, staring up again at the beautiful façade. "What happened to Davis?" she asked, unable to take her eyes off the architect's handiwork. "You never hear of him anymore."

"Disappeared after the War Between the States. Don't think he was able to adjust to the changing tastes of the new wealth."

"Ah, well maybe that's to his credit," Emily said, a little softer. "Though I wonder at his taking this job in the first place." John noticed a surer sound in her voice.

"It's just a building, Emily, not an offense to the morals of humanity."

"I wonder, John. I think perhaps that's just exactly what it is."

"Guilt by association?" He felt able to relax a bit as Emily gained assurance.

"Absolutely," she shuddered, just as a man in a starched white coat came out of the entrance to the asylum and moved toward them.

Suddenly, an emaciated young woman raced out of the building behind the man in the coat. Her long, dull dark hair was matted, and in fact the only things about her that shone were her eyes, glittering with a fevered intensity. "Please!" she called on the top step. Her gray cotton flannel slip seemed to be taking the place of a dress and looked as if years of use had pounded it flat into a brittle piece of straw. She had a tattered blanket clutched to her chest.

The man in the crisp white coat turned to stop her. On the back of his collar was printed PHYSICIAN 16~ B.I. Taking the woman by the shoulders, he spun her around just in time for a female attendant, even taller than himself, to grab the woman and pull her back through the door. Emily could see a stamp also on the back of the woman's cotton flannel slip. "Lunatic asylum, B.I.H. six," she read out loud.

"Who is . . . ?" she began.

"Blackwell's Island, Hall 6," John broke in, below his breath.

"My Lord, John. Everything is the language of a prison. Why not just say so? Is there any way out of this place . . . alive?" She stared at the physician's starched white coat disappearing through the limestone portal, soon swallowed up by the dark, unfathomable interior.

"Look at the inscription over the portal: *'While I live, I hope,'*" she read, in a strangled whisper. "It should be: *'Whoever enters here leaves all hope behind.'*" Grasping John Mackay's arm, Emily turned, almost pushing him back down the stairs to the walkway and lawn they'd just come from before she stopped, out of breath. "Let's get them out of there for the performance, John, out in the sunshine and fresh air. Can you help me with that?" She still grasped his arm with one hand while the other clutched the violin. John met her gaze as long as possible, but then looked away to the river just visible through a stand of oak trees along the island's banks.

"All right, Emily. I'll do my best. But you must remember we have no real influence here. This is not our realm." His clear blue eyes had clouded over, anticipating trouble.

"Isn't it a public institution? Aren't we the public? We have every right to involve ourselves in the joyless lives of these people," she hissed, obviously too close to tears for John's comfort. He was beginning to regret his involvement in her plan in many ways. How had she convinced him to accompany her on this naïve and useless mission?

"Emily, I know they won't allow a performance on the lawn down by the river, they have to worry about escapes. But perhaps in the locked exercise courtyard . . ." His voice trailed off as he saw the dark storm clouds collecting on her face again.

"No!" She exploded with a vehemence he wasn't used to from her. "It has to be someplace on the island they've not been before. I don't want it associated with their everyday horrors."

"But I thought the point was to bring your music to them, not bring them to you." His tone was stronger, calmer, as he knew he was making an important point she couldn't reject.

"Yes, within reason. But how could I have known how terrible this place is? I want them outside, somewhere nature can remind them of what they need to hold on to . . . to believe in."

John Mackay, used to success created by the power of his own energy, looked lost and exasperated. Finally, he brushed his blond mustache with a slow, pensive stroke. "I wonder . . ." He narrowed his gaze and looked up. "Would the roof be acceptable? I see an iron railing that's high enough to keep the guards happy but open enough to give us the air and light you want for the inmates. I'll bet the view is amazing. A little disorienting perhaps, but . . ."

"What could be better than being disoriented when reality is so horrible? Yes! Please try, John. Disorientation is exactly what I'm after. The roof would be perfect."

"How do you do . . . hello . . . everyone," Emily said, a little too softly to be heard past the first row of inmates. She wasn't used to announcing her performance on stage. That would never be accepted by either a sophisticated audience or an acclaimed venue. Distance was considered a necessity for proper appreciation and respect. In truth, the silence before she began to play had always helped her leave the present stage behind for a place of quiet focus. But this setting clearly had different requirements and distancing herself from her audience was the last thing she wanted to do. She could feel a gentle breeze being pulled across the East River lifting the edge of her skirt and the white collar on her blouse. The water was just visible through a row of trees in the distance below the roof of the rotunda.

"Hello," she said again, loud enough this time to be heard by the back row of inmates pressed against the wrought-iron fencing on the far side of the asylum roof. She wished the officials had agreed to more than the thirty women they'd allowed on the roof at one time. She couldn't help noticing the looks of vacancy from the inmates, a contrast to the closed faces of the male doctors and matrons scattered among them.

"My name is Emily de Koningh, and I'm a violinist." She lifted her instrument up from its safe place slipped between her elbow and waist with a little smile, as if to introduce it to her audience, as well as to reassure herself. Tucking it comfortably back under her left arm against her rib cage, and with her bow hanging down at her right side, she asked, "How many of you have heard a violin played before?"

Three hands went up, all those belonging to inmates. Either the doctors and attendants had never heard one, or preferred not to respond.

"Where did you hear it?" Emily pointed her bow at one of the women with her hand up.

"At home. In England," the woman answered quietly.

Emily nodded and smiled. "I did too. And you?" she asked, gesturing toward a tiny young woman looking no more than a child.

"Germany," the woman said, barely above a whisper. Emily had to lean forward to hear her. "My father made bows," she added, a little louder. Emily nodded, looked at her bow, and smiled broadly back at the woman. *We're almost family*, her smile seemed to say. She pointed at the third woman, even though her hand had long since gone down.

"Italy," she answered, with a thick accent. "But *it* was a *fee*-dle."

"Same thing!" Emily said, brightly. "We're all fiddlers, and proud of it. Have you ever seen a fiddlehead fern in the forest?" She held the violin by its body and lifted it up high for their viewing when she saw the curiosity on their faces. "Does this remind you of those ferns?" She turned the violin so they could see the neck. The Guarneri's scroll ornamentation could not be missed. "We fiddlers love feeling so close to those ferns when we play, but we love the sound under our left ear even more. I hope you love the sound, too. You'll find it can set you free if you'll let it. Where you go in your own head when you listen is up to you. Yes, music can set you free. I know. I've escaped many difficult things and know I'll be using my violin to escape for the rest of my life."

"You're already free! What do you know about being trapped like an animal?" someone cried out. She didn't look to see who. It could have been any woman's voice.

"We women all know something about that," Emily said, slowly. "A cage can be many things, but music can get past them all. Just listen."

She walked to the other side of her makeshift stage so that those on the east side of the roof could see her better, and she them. She easily spotted John Mackay against the fence, hat in hand, and another strangely familiar face beside him at his shoulder. She almost gasped, recognizing the red hair and beard of Robert Haussmann. How and why had John brought him to the island without her knowing? *Focus. Don't lose your place.*

"The man who wrote this first piece I want to play for you was imprisoned by his deafness. He'd had a hard childhood, losing his mother early and caring for his alcoholic father. His music helped him with his sadness and bitterness, but when he went deaf at a young age, possibly because of the explosions of cannons all around him, and couldn't even hear his own music, he felt completely lost. It was only the memories of music he'd heard once in his head that kept him sane. And I don't think you'll find this piece the work of an angry, disillusioned man. Just listen, please." She'd tried to share her feelings on her face but knew now she had to switch to another tongue she was more fluent in. It took more effort than she was used to.

She moved back to the center of the roof, rested her violin on her left shoulder and tucked it under her chin. Taking one of her deep, calming breaths, she lifted the bow in her right hand and involuntarily closed her eyes as she started the achingly sweet strains of Beethoven's Violin Romance No. 2. But without the full orchestra accompanying her, she jumped over the parts where they would have joined, and started playing too fast. Realizing it would take away the sweet quality she wanted to share, she stopped for the first time in her life on stage. Her eyes flew open in surprise as the audience of inmates came into full view.

"That's fine, dearie," one of the inmates called out. "You just take your time. We're with you. You can start again whenever you like." Emily nodded slightly. A big lump seemed to be stuck in her throat, so she took another deep breath and let it out slowly while she swallowed.

But why did I close my eyes? Because she always did, to separate

herself from the audience and stage and world. This time she kept
them open, determined to hold the inmates whenever she could
connect with them. There were John Mackay and Robert Haussmann again in her peripheral vision. And good Lord! Was Corey
next to Robert? It must be her imagination. The cascade of possibilities made her feel slightly mad and nauseated. Had John thought that
having those who were part of her musical life in the audience would
help? If so, he was so wrong. *Focus, focus*! Surely Robert was saying it
now as he had when she was a child.

One more deep breath and she started Beethoven's Romance
again, but this time with the slow, thin sweetness of a crystalline
thread of honey. Her eyes met those of a smiling old woman partway
back. Had she been the one to call out assurance? No matter. They
were all in it together, and Emily's violin would carry them off
together as well. For all its ancient artistic beauty, the Guarneri could
support the weight of the world if it had to. She'd always loved that
so many stories had passed through the wood of its body; first from
the composers, then translated by the musicians like her, and on to
the world around them. And that's all she was doing now. Sharing
the stories of life with people who needed to make sense of them,
easing a troubled mind or mending a broken heart. It wasn't about
the notes and tempo being perfect. It was about telling Beethoven's
story of how to transcend pain to these women at the lunatic asylum.
Plain and simple. That's what it was.

"Did you catch their cries of joy, sense how free they felt listening,
see the smiles, feel the peace?" Emily's words tumbled out
unchecked in the doctor's office after the concert. Surrounded by the
powerful men she called friends, she looked from one face to
another.

"Did you hear the one who started singing? And all the others joining in with her at the end?" Emily's dark eyes glistened, as did her black hair against the glow of her flushed cheeks and damp forehead. She looked out over the men as if they'd become her audience. "Surely, it's obvious if we want them to have a chance to return to a sane, productive life we must give them the keys to do it. They need music in the asylum, as we all do anywhere we live."

She had that post-concert luminosity Robert Haussmann knew well after all the years he'd taught her and their many performances together. She leaned so far forward in her chair in the physician's office he was afraid she might fall off. Looking at her now, with that familiar radiance illuminating her face, he could hardly believe she'd just spent the last half hour playing in this women's jail. Where were the lovely satin gowns he was so used to seeing her in, the feathers or ribbons in her hair, the throngs of well-dressed audience members streaming down the hall to meet her afterward? The press, the managers, and, yes, even the royalty?

The grim reality of this place was reflected in Emily's strange, dull gray skirt, and the distinctly institutional echoes ricocheting around the plaster walls and hard floors. They reinforced his wonder that she could ever have agreed to bring her singular, beautiful tone here. He didn't know what she was becoming . . . what she was thinking . . . what she wanted. Her eccentricities were finally getting the better of her and perhaps of all who were connected to her. He sighed, smoothing the glossy beaver brim of his hat resting on his lap, and glanced wistfully at the river out the window. He imagined that he, too, might be locked up here by some awful, nightmare twist of fate and shivered at the thought. John Mackay's raised voice brought Robert back to the room. That unusual event, the increased volume from a man who almost never showed excess emotion, was just what Robert needed to remind him to stay present.

"You don't understand, Emily," John was saying with an exasperation Robert had seldom noted in this self-assured kingpin of incomparable wealth. "You're being naïve. You can't just throw money at this place and expect it to accomplish anything!" Emily was sitting up in her chair now, her back so straight and eyes so steely he felt sorry for John, who seemed to be the target of her anger. "It's not that I don't want to help," John continued, leaning forward in his chair to her right and clearly hoping to soften the sting of Emily's expression. "It's just that the problem isn't really here. It's out there " He waved his gray kid-gloved hand to indicate a world of trouble outside the institution's walls.

"Something has to be done to change public opinion and the way our government handles these . . . problems; these people," John continued. "That's where the money might make a difference, but it will take time. You want help for them right now, and that I can't do." John glared at Emily, his complexion showing the heightened color of his Irish ancestry. Robert stared at his former pupil to see how she would resolve this unusual disagreement with her comrade.

Before she could respond, the door opened quietly and one of the doctors came in, closing it silently behind him again as he stood watching, clearly feeling the weight of the formerly explosive discourse imposing silence on them all now. Robert wondered what this man might imagine was going on. He doubted such a group of the city's elite citizens had ever been gathered together behind the asylum's walls before.

"And you, Robert."

Emily's voice made him jump and he grasped his hat a bit tighter than he'd intended. She was still glowering at John Mackay, but surprised Robert with her change of direction. She must have felt Robert's eyes on her instinctively and knew when to move. Why hadn't he looked elsewhere? He smoothed his hat again to repair the mark he'd just made in the brim.

"What would you have me do, Emily?" he asked, hesitantly. "How can I possibly be of help?" The air in the room seemed heavy and still, making it difficult to think or breathe.

"Teach them, Robert. Didn't you see that piano in the parlor room on our way downstairs after the concert?" She moved her eyes to his, slowly and deliberately. Robert nodded, distinctly recalling the criminally destroyed ancient upright and bench. He'd seen a few like that before in his life, and he could feel the sound they made setting his teeth on edge without needing to hear it.

"Awful, Emily, just ghastly," he said, grimacing. "I could no more teach on an instrument like that than fly to the moon. But to be perfectly honest, I have no time or desire to teach in an insane asylum. I have a full schedule and earn my living schooling those who can pay. No, Emily, this is not a place I ever want to come again. I am only here . . . for you."

She was silent, no doubt feeling the increasing mass of the room's atmosphere of resistance. Robert could guess her thoughts: *Where were the men she used to call friends? How could they turn on her so fast the first time she asked them for help? Didn't they care about these poor women? About her?*

Robert glanced around at the others for support, but noticed they were all looking elsewhere, lest they be called on to speak again; all but Corey. Robert watched, fascinated, as Emily's husband unwound his long frame from the hard wooden chair and stretched his legs. Slivers of sun darted between scudding clouds outside to highlight Corey's once bright yellow hair. It looked cooler than it had in his childhood; the still-blond strands suggested a towheaded boy instead of a middle-aged man. Robert knew that boy at his piano then, better than the man across the room now. He'd taught Corey in his father's library long before either one of them had met Emily Alden.

"I see your point, Em," Corey said, a quiet smile spreading from his mouth to his high Dutch cheekbones and finally his eyes. That was the way his father's smile moved as well. Was it just Robert's advancing years clarifying patterns around him he'd not noted in the past? "Give the women the way to make their own music," Corey was saying. "Get them a new piano, make sure some of them can play, and then, I'd suggest they form a chorus they could continue themselves. There's nothing like singing together to give one courage." He moved behind Emily's chair, placing his hands on her shoulders. She turned her head to look up at him.

"I could get the piano replaced," he said, gently squeezing her shoulder. "Mr. Steinway would be generous, I think. But I couldn't come every week to give lessons. They just need a few inmates who can play accompaniment and the rest could be a chorus." A look of quiet desperation started to spread across Emily's face.

"Perhaps someone ... else ... could come to take them on," Corey continued. "We just have to find someone with the time and inclination." Emily raised her right hand from her lap, in a gesture reminding Robert of a royal benediction, but she dropped it again seeing the lack of commitment coming from the pianists in the room.

"Yes," she said. "I'd like to make a difference, but I can't do it alone." She'd apparently forgotten her other friends in the room as she held Corey where he stood with her big, dark eyes.

"We do want to thank you for coming to play for the patients today, Mrs. de Koningh," the doctor intoned, an inscrutable smile lifting the corners of his mouth but extending no further. His pale eyes reminded Robert of an albino with too little melanin to color the irises. They gave him a ghostly appearance that he imagined added to the apprehension of inmates facing him for the first time. Emily had fixed her gaze on him. Apparently she'd gained a heightened appreciation for eye contact that day.

"The music was ... nice," the doctor continued, "and we're especially grateful for including your illustrious ... friends," he added, smiling in an attempt to connect with the men seated around Emily. His eyes lingered on the robust figure of John Mackay in his elegant light wool suit and holding his gold-headed walking stick and hat on his lap. Everyone recognized the silver king these days, New York being particularly blessed to have him living full-time on its shores. The city advertised its delight with newspaper articles headed by portraits of the king as often as twice a week.

Then the doctor looked up at Emily's husband standing behind her chair, towering above everyone in what might be considered an unnerving display of superiority unless you knew him well enough to know better. Between Mr. Mackay's physique and the exquisite perfection of Robert's own prolific red hair and beard, his elegant beaver hat resting on his knee, the supremacy of Mrs. de Koningh's husband seemed to add to the doctor's sense of inferiority. Most likely the good doctor wasn't used to having many men around in the women's asylum, offering a challenge he'd not faced for a long time. It was obvious from his attitude that he was usually the most senior person in the room.

"Can I answer any questions for you?" the doctor asked, putting his hand on the doorknob as if their response was a foregone conclusion. It seemed he wanted to make them disappear to smooth out the rest of his afternoon. He started to pull the door open to encourage their compliance.

"Just a moment, Dr. . . . Physician 16—B.I. . . . Are you called anything else?" Emily's voice had a quiet, not unpleasant timbre, but its tone warned that disappearing through the door again would not be wise.

"Dr. Dent, Mrs. de Koningh," he said, closing the door but making no move to come into the room or shake her hand. He wasn't used to women like her at the asylum, either.

"You are the doctor who met us at the portal to the asylum?" she asked.

"Indeed, he is," John Mackay spoke up, perhaps feeling that this simple solidarity was called for and could be spared. "However, one of his patients proved in need of his attention at that moment we entered, which is perhaps why we never met, officially," he added. Robert found himself wondering at whom John Mackay's camaraderie was aimed.

"Ah yes, Gertrude . . ." Dr. Dent's voice drifted off as if the memory was of little significance. "Any other questions, Mrs. de Koningh?" The inscrutable smile had all but disappeared. In its place a frozen stare suggested there had better be no more inquiries. But he hadn't counted on the tenacity of the pretty violinist surrounded by her courtiers. Seeing her eyes meet those of the silver king in a kind of communion, the doctor braced himself.

"Yes, Gertrude. Exactly!" she said, with a satisfaction Robert couldn't miss. "'Gertrude' means 'the warrior,' I believe. How ironic. I've long taken pleasure in the significance of names," she added, smiling into a past only she and Corey could see. The doctor reached for the doorknob again. "I also saw Gertrude at the concert," Emily continued, firmly, her change in tone insisting that she wouldn't permit being ignored. "And I noticed the same blanket wrapped around her. Has she no other garments to keep her warm? I don't see the other patients so attired in this unusually mild spring weather." Her deep, dark eyes bored into the doctor's pale, colorless ones.

"There are sixteen hundred insane women on Blackwell's Island, madame, and they're all properly cared for. Gertrude chooses to wrap her baby in that blanket. It's more for protection from the other inmates than the elements."

"What? She has a baby here in the asylum?" Emily sprang to her feet as if propelled by a force of incalculable power. The other men also rose from their seats, all lifted by the female performer's irresistible pull. "That's horrible!" she cried. "She cannot bring up a baby in this place. I want her out of here!" Emily was clearly close to tears.

Corey stepped up, placing his hand back on her shoulder and squeezing it a little. "You've got to calm down," he muttered to Emily, and turning to the doctor, he said, "We'd like to meet Gertrude and her . . ."

". . . daughter." Dr. Dent finished the sentence for him. "Quite impossible," he said, the enigmatic smile brushing his lips, as if his return to his own domain and control pleased him. A sharp intake of breath from Emily told him his statement had upset her, as intended. Even Robert was offended by his smug confidence.

"My dear friend, I think you're wrong." John Mackay stepped forward, lifting his head a little to look at the doctor through narrowed eyes. Dr. Dent said nothing in the direct line of the silver king's fire. He glanced around, as if becoming aware of a game of chess where the moves of others had not been anticipated.

"We understand why you can't accommodate us by bringing Mrs. . . . Gertrude, to see Mrs. de Koningh here. But perhaps we could show our concern with a contribution of some kind, to the asylum for your discretionary use." John Mackay's gaze leveled off to a normal position, but his voice dropped to a quiet breath. Robert was aware that the silver king had made a major peace offering and hoped Emily understood that, too. He knew how difficult it was to get her to let go of an idea once she'd fixed on it. Dr. Dent looked from Robert to Corey, and finally at Emily. Dr. Dent shook his head, and with an odd shrug of his shoulders, opened the door and left the room.

The team seemed to let out a collective sigh of relief, but Robert noticed Emily was grim and silent, sitting bolt upright and stiff on the edge of her chair. None of them had worked in partnership with her in the way she'd wanted them to, and even John Mackay's financial offering was unlikely to earn her praise. Robert knew that expression he'd seen many times on his young pupil's face before she'd outgrown her stubborn childhood frustrations. It asked why no one would help her get the things she wanted in life, and why she was always on her own.

CHAPTER SIXTEEN

"HELLO, MATTHEW!"

Welcomed across the threshold of the Steinway Hall on Fourteenth Street by the company's best salesman and floor manager, Corey tried to leave his unhappiness at the entrance, smile with sincerity, and put a spring in his step. Sometimes even that small effort seemed too much lately.

He'd never thought about or expected work with a salary, and so he'd taken Mr. Steinway's original offer to hire him in sales and marketing for Steinway & Sons in the East almost as a joke. He was to be the company's Young Artist in Residence, with a commission paid on each customer he brought in. At first he'd just enjoyed having a title. But when his contracts to perform dwindled while Emily's increased, he soon came to realize the job offered a chance for autonomy he couldn't refuse. Working in the rarified world of beautiful new instruments gave him a feeling of legitimacy, of having a meaningful place in the world of music. He'd enjoyed being Steinway's representative, but soon came to believe it was little more than another promotional lure Mr. Steinway had created to keep pianos in the public eye whenever possible. It had been his first job, and now he was about to leave it, hopefully with a modicum of humility and gratitude where it was owed to the son of the piano company's founder.

"Mr. Steinway's waiting for you," Matthew said, as Corey walked into the combination concert hall and sales floor. "How was the trip down south? Is your father well?"

"Yes. Everything went well," Corey said, removing his hat and gloves. "I missed New York though, and have to admit I'm salivating over the chance to touch one of these gorgeous instruments again." He waved his hat as if saluting the pianos distributed around the showroom floor. "There's nothing like these beauties where I've just come from," he added, looking down at the Art Case piano from 1857 guarding the entrance.

"I've heard sales are up again, Matthew. Is that so?"

"Indeed, they are! You know, it's amazing when you think of it. A year after we opened in '54 we were making about two pianos a week and selling seventy-four a year. We thought that was wonderful. Now, not even twenty years later, we're making a piano every hour of the day and selling almost three thousand a year! How did you do down south? Any takers now that they don't have to rely on Confederate money anymore?"

"Can't be sure yet," Corey said, untruthfully. "Maybe one or two when the dust settles. I just got back so I'm not sure who will follow through."

"One or two what?" boomed out from behind him, amplified by the open space and marble floor of the two-thousand-seat auditorium behind the showroom. William Steinway appeared through the door, as large as his voice and looking familiarly disheveled.

"Just uprights, Mr. Steinway," Corey answered. "The order of the day in the South right now seems to be, *something to fit in the parlor, please.*" He'd hoped to hide his dismal sales debacle indefinitely but had been caught by the one man he'd wanted to avoid, and he felt embarrassed.

"Well, we need to sell uprights, too, Adriaan. But if you don't stop calling me *Mr.* I'll have you barred from the door in the future. I'm not that much older than you are!" Fifteen years Corey's senior, the

German immigrant looked much more mature, mostly because of his size and shagginess.

"I'll find a way to drop the *mister*, sir, when you stop calling me *Adriaan*. I've told you, only my parents and a few of my mother's relatives have ever called me that." Corey grinned at the big bear of a man he'd first met with Robert Haussmann when he was a boy. Even before he became the leader of the company, Steinway had been an impressive presence with his heft, the dark beard devouring his face and neck, and his almost blond hair cut tall at the top and flat on the sides. Corey imagined him as permanently crowned with a Prussian helmet.

He and Robert had subsequently spent many afternoons in Corey's early adolescence trying out pianos at the showroom, and later at the factory in Astoria. Over the years, he'd secured a kind of friendship with Mr. Steinway, more because of the longevity of their acquaintance rather than any commonality, he thought. Steinway & Sons' great success was largely due to its engineering and marketing, thanks to this son, but Corey had very little interest in technology. Their triumph made other German immigrants proud, but to Corey the company's accomplishments now made him feel unnecessary. He was, after all, an artist, not a businessman, and certainly not a salesman. He believed that music should never be an enterprise. He'd tell Mr. Steinway he was leaving before he was asked to go.

"I don't see why you have any interest in the uprights if your other sales are up so much," Corey said, suddenly hundreds of miles away in his head, playing the warped old upright with Marcy Bond in the gazebo at the Negroes' concert in West Virginia. It made him long for that other life.

Mr. Steinway watched him quietly, in no rush for Corey to say whatever he wanted to. "After my father died a few years ago and I took over," he finally said, "I vowed I'd get a broader distribution between the models so we could carry the business through all kinds of economic challenges. But still, ninety percent of our business is in square pianos, with only five percent in uprights. That's why I'd love to expand those sales down south."

"You mean the grand sales are only around five percent, too?" Corey looked in horror from a beautiful, graceful grand piano on the floor near him to a smaller, chunkier, square piano placed closer to the center of the room.

"Yes. The square piano is already going out of favor in Europe, but it's still preferred here." William Steinway moved across the floor past different displays of instruments and cases, letting his hand linger lightly over each one he passed as if connecting with the body of a beloved family member without making any demands of them. "It's ironic that the tariffs our government put on pianos which have permitted our industry to expand have also slowed the sharing of the technology and demand for the larger instruments, so now we want to sell in Europe as much as we do here."

"More than ironic," Corey said, following Mr. Steinway's lead with a light touch on one of the uprights he was nearest. He couldn't resist playing a little syncopation with his right hand. Pianos were to make music with after all, not just to look at.

"Come into my office, please," his employer said, leading the way. Adjusting his rimless spectacles as he sat down behind his desk, he looked to Corey like a big owl in a faded black waistcoat. There was nothing menacing about him, but somehow just the fact of his family's spectacular achievements after coming to America penniless only two decades earlier was enough to give him command of any room or situation. Corey couldn't avoid feeling an admiration unrequired by his friend and boss. He may have been no more than fifteen years Corey's senior, but the wisdom of this owl was evident in everything he touched. His beautiful mansion on Long Island Sound, his lovely wife and children, and his hugely successful business coalesced into the most perfect life any man could want, but few could expect. The unavoidable admiration Corey felt had probably been responsible for his mistakenly accepting a job he didn't want and knew he probably couldn't do.

"Let's talk," Steinway said. "I want to hear your assessment of the possibilities for reparations to the economy of the South and what you find there, culturally speaking. Has reconstruction delivered on its promises?"

"It has not," Corey said. "And in some ways, I'm afraid it never will."

"Oh my," William Steinway muttered, adjusting his spectacles carefully so as not to get fingerprints on the round lenses. "This is not the optimistic report I'd hoped for. Can you elaborate a little? What do you attribute the slowness of the recovery to?"

"I'm undoubtedly not the right person to ask," Corey said. "I'm uniquely uninterested in business and commerce in general or the politics that seem to control both most of the time, so, many of the high points pass me by." His boss moved in his large leather chair, making Corey feel he must have sounded spoiled, and perhaps even rude, to a man who lived for commerce of all kinds.

"But ask me about the music," Corey went on, "and there I can keep you engaged most of the day and night." He smiled at his employer and tried to ease the tension he'd felt responsible for. "We all have our proclivities," Corey continued, "and music is mine. That's what I came to talk with you about." He stopped there, hoping he'd get a sign that he was released from the purgatory where his thoughtless comment about the business of selling pianos had put him. But no signal came to ease his discomfort.

Finally, William Steinway said, "Talk away, Corey. I'm listening." He reached over to open his box of cigars, offering Corey one with a questioning nod. Corey shook his head and waited while the German entrepreneur cut off the tip and lit it from his silver box of matches on the desk. The wise owl settled back comfortably in his chair and said, not unkindly, "You seem to be having some trouble talking about it, whatever 'it' is. Please, feel free to say whatever you like. I'm a good listener." He put the cigar down in the ashtray on his desk and sat back in his chair as if he had all the time in the world. Corey couldn't have asked for a better opportunity to explain his decision to leave Steinway & Sons. He knew it was his turn to speak.

"I appreciate this," he began. "I know how busy you are," and then with his inner ear for rhythm as acute as ever, he recognized it was best to keep rolling quickly along. "I've been rather lost lately . . ." He began again: ". . . unable to find my balance in anything I'm doing. I need to make some changes in my life, and one of the first must be my resignation from Steinway & Sons, as I'm not contributing anything of value. I hope you'll understand that I see it as my own failure to fit in where I can offer something, and not your wonderful company's inability to suit itself to me."

William Steinway continued to watch and listen without moving, and Corey felt as if he was testing his thoughts on himself, in a room where no one could overhear to judge or rebuke him. This seemed an opportunity not to be missed. The floodgates keeping his unsettling passions at bay were opening, and every emotional insecurity and doubt started to rush out. He heard himself, as if in a dream, describing his discomfort with the hallowed institutions of marriage, family, home, and work, ending with the greatest force on Emily. His dissatisfaction with the tether trapping him from such a young age to the present, before he'd had a chance to figure the world out for himself, seemed unfair at best and cruel at worst with only one life to live. He finally stopped to come up for air and found his boss had put out his cigar and was leaning forward at his desk as if to catch every word. Corey had almost forgotten he was there, and so apologized for what must have seemed like an incoherent tirade.

"I fear I've taken advantage of your willing support," he said, a little sheepishly. "I didn't mean to. It's been so long since I've spoken to a sympathetic ear I'm afraid I overdid it." He knew his apology would be more effective if he looked contrite, but the relief of unburdening himself to a man who surely understood his sense of entrapment made him feel so good he looked more pleased than sorry. He was just settling into the aura of goodwill he imagined when Steinway's president started to speak, and his tone brought Corey up so suddenly he almost rose from his chair.

"Even though we're not much more than a decade apart in age, we're in entirely oppositional universes when it comes to our outlooks on the world," William Steinway said, his voice never rising nor gaining volume even as his gaze took on a hard, unwavering quality. "I hear you make your argument for your freedom, as you've put it, which is already a natural right of all males of human origin. But I may have a different view from most men of today as I've lived a rather different life, with a wife who believes in her own freedom. Perhaps this is a little of your problem, too; a wife who insists on the liberty to live in ways others in society don't acknowledge as her right. Have I misinterpreted your point of view so far?" Corey writhed uncomfortably in his chair but shook his head.

"Good. I thought not." He nodded, picking up his cigar and relighting it slowly. Corey had to wait while the once-lit Figurado gave its smoker trouble because of its unusual torpedo shape. Beads of perspiration broke out under Corey's collar, and he tried to readjust it to a more comfortable position, but there didn't seem to be one. As soon as the cigar had been successfully relit, he leaned back from the desk a little, inhaling the smoke and exhaling slowly. Corey felt as if an hour had passed and had no idea what to expect or how he'd survive the waiting. He and this enormously successful, self-made commercial giant could have little in common but their masculinity, but he couldn't imagine where this discussion would lead.

"There's a lot more we share in common than our positions as men in this society," William Steinway said, as if he'd read Corey's mind. "We're actually close enough in age to be of the same generation, and we both got married incredibly young, too young in my belief, but many don't acknowledge it. My wife and I were married close to the time you and your wife married as well. For us, it was just before the war, and for you, just after. Regina was only seventeen, and I twenty-six. We made our own choices then, believing ourselves to know better than anyone how ready we were. But my father was as resistant as yours, I'm sure, yet of course we thought we knew better."

Corey shook his head. "My father was injured and held behind enemy lines when Emily and I decided to marry, so we conveniently imagined he'd be delighted since he'd known her from childhood. But her father was set against it until long after we wed, though I think that was his disapproval of me rather than our ages."

William Steinway nodded. "And so you see the parallels already. I would also deny I enjoyed more worldly freedoms than you did, as I'd trained in various piano factories at my father's insistence since I was eleven, with no time off for good behavior." This time Corey nodded and smiled, feeling the shared understanding of patriarchal expectations. For years, his own father had pressured him to pay more attention to the importation of cloth than the acquisition of a piano repertoire.

"But even though we all have different proclivities, as you point out," his employer continued, running his index finger along the top of his nameplate on the desk announcing his role as president of Steinway & Sons, "there are some laws of nature that cannot be changed no matter how the circumstances surrounding them may alter. Among those, the need for fidelity to a spouse and family ranks supreme."

"I don't think all men would agree with you," Corey said, watching the unusual German immigrant as he spoke.

"I don't care about all men, or all women, for that matter," he said. "I only care about what I know to be true, and I urge you to listen to me. You're in an extremely dangerous position now, and your life could go either way, depending on what you decide to do next." Again he tamped the virtually untouched cigar out in his ashtray and folded his hands on the desk, leaning toward Corey as if to deliver something delicate of grave importance.

"You feel you should have your autonomy, although I sense you worry a little about the effect that will have on your family and your wife and well you might. I have the reverse dilemma, but it is no less devastating for being the inconsistency of a woman as opposed to a man." Corey adjusted himself again in his seat, remembering the very public humiliation meted out by New York society for Mrs. Steinway's multiple affairs.

"I tell you nothing you haven't heard or read before," William Steinway went on, obviously aware of Corey's discomfort. "Yet it still kills me just to acknowledge the betrayal and is no less painful because Regina is a woman rather than a man. My point being, it's wrong for any human being to treat another who trusts them that way. Ever. I don't believe that is the kind of culture human society can flourish in. I urge you to take the time to figure your life out before you upend the family that loves you." He looked so distraught Corey could have almost believed he knew Emily and his boys personally, which he didn't.

"Give it time," Mr. Steinway urged again, bushy dark brows pulled together over his almost invisible glasses. "I know it's not what you want to hear, but it's the truth. Get the perspective you need before you have no way back. I'm not some elderly curmudgeon telling you this," he added, "although the advice may sound like the kind you're used to getting from acquaintances of another generation."

Corey let out a little breath, realizing when he did that he'd been holding it too long. He was embarrassed to find his hands shaking and gripped them together in his lap to steady the tremors. Things seemed so impossibly clear and simple for this man, probably because he lacked the sensitivity of an artist. Corey was unaware that he'd started to guard himself from others' advice with a cloak of individuality. He missed something when Steinway started to speak again but was instantly jerked back to the present.

"My wife's affairs will undoubtedly end in divorce," William Steinway was saying, quietly, "because she's not taken the time to step back from them to let another viewpoint in. If that's where Regina is going, the children, or at least one of my sons, will go with her as he's young. Your children are immature, too, are they not?" Corey nodded, realizing his employer was literally reaching halfway across his desk toward him now. He could think of nothing to say, the shock of William Steinway's revelation was so stinging.

A knock on the office door made Corey start, but Steinway just looked up and called out for the person to come in. The curly dark head of his secretary appeared through the opening, apologizing for the intrusion, and announcing that Mr. Daimler's servant had delivered something to the showroom. He held up a long tube package, and Steinway nodded, reaching out as he asked him to hand it over. The young man bustled into the room, looking much as Steinway did himself, slightly disheveled but extremely purposeful, and laid it on his desk. "I need to remind you that the woman applying for the teaching job at your school will be here in an hour," the young man said. "I'll be at lunch, no doubt, so Matthew will announce her." He smiled at Corey and turned to disappear as quickly as he'd come.

"Gottlieb Daimler?" Corey said, eyeing the package. "The engineer?"

William pushed back in his chair, almost as if needing some way to rest and calm himself. Clearly he was feeling pressure as Corey did. "Yes," he nodded, distractedly. "Daimler has just been made technical manager of Gasmotorenfabrik Deutz." He rolled the tube package back and forth a bit on his desk looking up at Corey in a refusal to be distracted.

"Don't run the risk of losing everything you have inside just because you're enticed by the view outside," he went on. "If you need to adjust your work and find something more artistically rewarding, of course you should leave us. You talk of proclivities. I agree we must all do what calls us, but that can be accomplished in so many ways. Nothing is handed to us." He lifted the tube up and pried off the seal on the end, slowly slipping a roll of drawings out and leaving it on his desk.

"I, for example, don't care about music," he said, unrolling the drawings the rest of the way and holding down the corners with his hand, a paperweight, and letter opener. "I only care about it in its culturally supportive role I accept as a European. But I *am* passionate about engineering," he said, looking back at the drawings on his desk. "I like to make things I can hold in my hand. That's why I've made an alliance with Mr. Daimler. I want to learn all I can from him about the manufacture of engines. I'd like to help him make them right here in my own factory in Astoria someday!" His eyes lit up with the pleasure of a small child.

"Good heavens!" Corey exclaimed. "I had no idea . . . that you cared so much for machinery that you've found a way to work on it here. What a surprise!"

"Not to me," Steinway chuckled. "But perhaps you start to see my point. I don't have to give up what I love because I'm committed to carrying out my father's dream. I just have to adapt it to my . . . proclivities!" Corey nodded slowly, still not sure exactly what he was hearing or why. "And there are so many other things that fascinate me that might seem to have nothing directly to do with pianos, but everything is relational." He leaned back in his chair, finally looking relaxed and happy. At that moment there came another tap on the door and a secretary reappeared, this time without waiting to be told to enter. "She's here, the teacher, but I have Matthew keeping her busy with a cup of coffee and a sandwich. They'll be occupied for at least twenty minutes, so I'm going for my own lunch now. Goodbye," he announced, shutting the door again. William laughed outright. He seemed to enjoy his employee's lack of reverence.

"Why are you interviewing teachers?" Corey asked. "Is she a music teacher?"

William Steinway shook his head. "I'm building a company town on my land on Long Island right now. It will house all the workers for Steinway & Sons and provide a school, church, hospital, and transportation. You might think a social project a vastly different kind of business endeavor, but it isn't. It makes my company more stable because the lives of its workers are enhanced, so it satisfies both my role as head of Steinway & Sons, and my penchant for social equity." His eyes seemed to glow now behind his rimless lenses, and Corey couldn't tell if it came from within or reflected somehow from the glass.

"And your desire to make things, machines, advance technology . . . that's gone into more than the frames and strings of pianos, I guess," Corey said, looking at this man with a new kind of admiration.

"Oh indeed, it never stops!" William Steinway laughed. "I've bought the rights to cut a tunnel from my development in Astoria under the East River to Manhattan. I want to run transportation and goods underground instead of dealing with the problems and costs of surface transit. And I want to make New York City less congested and traffic less daunting. We need public transportation, Corey, and I want to work on making it happen!"

"I'm . . . astounded," Corey breathed. "I'm also happy to see you so completely engaged in things that are of benefit to . . . everyone. It's an amazing and unusual accomplishment." He knew he was staring as if he'd never seen his employer before, which was almost true.

"But do you see my point, Corey?" His employer looked worried again, and Corey suddenly felt as if he needed to escape the intensity of the office. He uncrossed his legs and leaned forward, making what he hoped was an obvious preparation to stand. "You can talk all you like of your 'proclivities,'" William Steinway went on, emphasizing the last word with something like distaste, "but no one with your advantages and connections is trapped unless they want to be." He looked at Corey as the wise black owl he'd seemed when they'd first entered the office to sit down. Corey returned his gaze, unable to assimilate all he'd heard yet, and started to focus on finding escape while avoiding the rudeness he felt he'd begun their talk with. But Steinway looked so solid, so sure, so fulfilled in his seat across the desk, Corey not only had trouble relating to him but couldn't figure out how to end their conversation. He'd done what he'd intended, informing his employer of his resignation, and he couldn't order all he'd heard after that and needed time alone to try.

As if he understood Corey's dilemma, William Steinway smiled and started to adjust in his seat, also as if preparing to stand himself. "You might consider doing something new in an entirely new place," he said, lightly, "yet taking your family with you to assure them they won't be losing you." Corey finally felt a return to the specific gave him the opportunity he needed to respond.

"Emily was born in England, but I don't think she'd ever want to move back to Europe and I'm not sure I'd want to go with her if she did. I was looking for some kind of . . . independence, not the entanglements of a family . . ."

"Go!" his boss exploded. "It will be the perfect opportunity to see them in an entirely new light. And they you, I might add." Corey pulled back in his chair, aware that this benign bit of advice he'd sought from his boss had somehow turned into an ultimatum for living.

"Sometimes . . . ," William Steinway said, after a pause filled with too many possibilities, "sometimes the very things we think we most want to escape become the wonders of our world we couldn't live without. It would be a shame to throw anything away you might find you wanted later." At that, he rose to his feet, pulling Corey up involuntarily by an invisible thread neither would have known was there. They'd come so far together in such a short time, they moved to the door almost as one.

"I have another thought for you," William Steinway said, suddenly coming to a complete stop with Corey almost running into him from behind. As massive as the Steinway son seemed, Corey was at least a head taller, and his height gave him a confidence his personality might have lacked without it. William Steinway looked at him as if they were the oldest, and dearest, of friends, which they had never been. Old acquaintances would be more accurate, Corey thought. Yet why then did he feel so completely at ease?

"What's your thought?" Corey asked, rotating the brim of his bowler loosely in his hands as if they'd been sharing the easiest, most pleasurable talk imaginable. Corey waited. Something he recognized, ironically, he'd never been particularly good at.

"I'm opening the first European Steinway Hall in London next year if all goes well. Why don't you help me out there, Corey, in any way you like? We'll need a lot of help with everything, including booking the musicians to perform as we're up and running. You could even perform yourself if you felt it appropriate to the audiences you find." Corey had stopped fiddling with his hat and was standing still in place, staring at his boss in what he knew was obvious abject disbelief. He'd come into the room a half-hour earlier to quit his job, and now found himself offered another.

"It would position you right in the middle of the music business and the artists who work in Europe. It'll set you up with friends of the kind that will make you feel appreciated and worthwhile from the start, with none of that social pressure you probably abhor." Corey grinned and nodded at just the same time as his boss. "Your wife probably has a ready-made circle of connections from her childhood in England and her performances abroad, so it would be good for you to have some of your own, separate from hers right from the start." Corey stared down at William Steinway, who was now flushed with excitement, his pale skin above his profuse, dark beard turning such a rosy glow he half-expected the man's glasses to fog up.

"Think on it, please," his boss implored, grasping Corey's thin right hand between two of his own paw-like ones. "You can't think straight when everything seems stacked against you. I know. So take my offer and plan an immediate future that will support and nurture you." Corey stayed frozen to his spot, still unable to figure out how they'd gotten to this new vision of his future. "Why don't you stay awhile and play a little?" Steinway suggested, opening the door to his office. "There's a beautiful grand piano on the floor you could try."

"Thank you, thank you for your time and your goodwill. No one could ask for more," Corey said, with a slight inclination of his head. "You've helped me more than you could know. I owe you a huge debt. And yes, I will play a little before I go. I see you have some potential buyers on the floor now, so I'll try to lead them to a purchase." He turned to go and then stopped suddenly. "One more thing . . . with your proclivity for social equity, I wonder if Steinway & Sons would be willing to donate an upright to the Women's Lunatic Asylum on Blackwell's Island. My wife has been doing some work there and I'd like to help her get a music program going for the patients." A huge grin spread across William Steinway's face as he nodded and pumped Corey's hand.

"What a great idea," he exclaimed enthusiastically. "Now you're getting the point. Find projects you can work on together and heaven knows what personal good can come of it." Having smiled at each other and shaken hands, Corey took off across the showroom as his employer stood watching on the threshold of his office doorway. He raised an eyebrow as Corey passed the grand piano to stand at a small upright against the wall. Running his hands over the keys in bright, flowing arpeggios to get a feel for the instrument's action and tone, he then launched into a syncopated song his boss had never heard before. But it had the buyers who'd come in all smiling and swaying in place.

William Steinway turned back into his office and closed the door on the music with a sigh, eyeing the plans for his collaboration with Gottlieb Daimler on his desk. He found the music bothersome when he was trying to work, but then, as his young employee had noted, everyone possessed different proclivities.

CHAPTER SEVENTEEN

EMILY WASN'T SURE WHAT SOUND WOKE HER, or if there had been any noise at all. She listened carefully, quieting her breathing so she could pick up the slightest disturbance in the air. She'd never been comfortable going to sleep with the gaslight still burning, a precaution even truer for candles, no matter how generous the drip pan or sconce. The midnight darkness in Corey's dressing room seemed to blanket even the walls, except where a fluorescent shaft of moonlight laid down a diagonal swath across the desk below the window. She wondered if the eerie intensity of light could have been what disturbed her. Or perhaps it was something within herself.

She'd realized she'd fallen asleep, as she often did, reading the score for her next violin lesson or performance. She saw it lying on the floor by the love seat where it had slipped from her hand and lap when her fatigue finally betrayed her. Camille Saint-Saëns's new *First Piano Trio* was introducing her to chamber music in a new way. Her choice had pleased Jacques Offenbach's friend who was, after all, paying for the performance. And for this exquisite, delicate, and typically French offering, she was delighted to give up her solo position on stage to join a cellist and pianist.

The sheet music lay at her feet displaying the opening marked "Allegro Vivace" and living up to its cheerful label with a lot of dancing dots for the piano's keys, though not much for the violin and cello. But the page with the slow movement lay sideways underneath the opening, showing the violin's gorgeous refrain and the cello's response, their turn to communicate while the piano took a rest. Now, when the French only seemed interested in opera, Camille Saint-Saëns was almost single-handedly working with chamber music, which so many of his countrymen continued to think of as something German and therefore both undesirable and unworthy of attention. Emily knew of his fame for larger orchestral works and instrumental concertos, but now Saint-Saëns was spending a great deal of time and effort writing these intimate pieces. She still hadn't found her pianist or cellist for the performance yet but was building so many new friendships thanks to her foray into chamber music that she didn't worry. And of course, Robert could always help her with that if necessary.

After her performance at the women's asylum, Emily was finding this new way of connecting with other musicians and her audience fascinating, and she wanted to explore it more thoroughly in performance. So far, she'd only spent a few late afternoons sight-reading with others at the violin maker's shop and with friends of Robert's at his house. But she thought perhaps she'd found herself in this collaboration, something she'd had no idea she was looking for. Emily was learning that she didn't have to fly alone to soar. She glanced out the window when she heard the bell of the small French desk clock ringing twice through the silence of the night; two o'clock and Corey still wasn't home.

Resting her dark head on one of the love seat's cushions, she looked slowly around the still dressing room. As her vision adjusted to the dim light, she could make out the armoires and bureaus placed around the perimeter of the room. It was a big space for a dressing closet because it had begun as Corey's small bedroom when he was a boy. It was almost adjacent to the large bedroom she'd been given when she arrived at the age of thirteen, and once they were married and Corey moved in with her, the transformation from small child's room to large dressing space was a natural one. He'd developed a mature taste for the kind of beautiful, stylish clothes he'd worn often as a little boy without thought. But small velvet jackets with silk collars had become large waistcoats with rows of silk ascots to broaden their usefulness, so space to house his wardrobe was now a necessity. In addition, the dressing room made a private retreat for him, something she'd recognized his need for when the children were born soon after their marriage. Her privacy had not been so easily ensured, but that was motherhood.

She was careful not to change her position for fear of making too much noise. She wanted her presence to come as a surprise, so he'd be unable to prepare a retreat in advance. She'd chosen this room for their watershed moment tonight, so he'd feel safe once they began to talk. She'd also picked her cream-colored silk dressing gown to wear knowing he was partial to it and would recognize instinctively she was making a peace offering even before they began. He always said the color and sheen of it enhanced the warm glow of her skin and brown eyes. She wasn't sure she found it terribly becoming, but it was about his partialities tonight, not hers. Before she could move to stand, she heard the sound that had most likely woken her, a soft swishing noise on the stairs and now the hall carpet outside Corey's dressing room door. She held her breath as the door slowly pushed open.

"It's you," she said, ignoring the sheet music on the floor beside her and rising slowly. "I've been waiting. We have to talk." Corey said nothing but stared at her with his hand still on the door handle. "I've been waiting for you so I wouldn't fall asleep, but that happened anyway," she added with a soft, rueful smile only she could see in the dark. For some reason she didn't quite understand, a deep calm had enveloped her, quieting her pulse and the usual flashes of anger she had to subdue when confronting Corey's late-night forays. She had no idea where the unfamiliar sense of assurance had come from, but she thought perhaps it had much to do with her decision to have the discussion with him she should have had years ago, to say nothing of over the most recent months. There were no more options for her, and thus no fear of lies and deception. It seemed a great relief to plan a talk of simple truths without embellishment for avoidance; finally.

"Come," she said, raising her hand to him where he still stood in the doorway. He moved in and took her hand slowly. She'd never run through this scene in her mind's eye, never wondered how he would react. Until her circumstances changed so radically due to Klaas's marriage plans she realized her life would never be the same no matter what she did; she hadn't considered facing Corey's demons with him. But now, here he was, looking no more physically besieged than anyone would at two in the morning, not smelling of alcohol or any the worse for whatever environment he'd been in all night while she waited for him. It was something deeper, something in his eyes that made him seem utterly overwhelmed.

"Yes, we do need to talk," he said, as if he'd rehearsed the same lines she had.

"Sit here on the love seat with me," she said. "There are few choices in your dressing room, but this will do." She let go of his hand gently and sat at the end of the down cushion in the impression her body had made when she'd fallen asleep, leaving Corey more than half of the unused portion of the seat. He hesitated, worrying her that he might refuse. But slowly he sat down next to her, still watching her in the same stoic silence he'd entered the room with.

"So let's begin, then," she said, respectful of the stillness around them and his air of emotional delicacy, something she felt she'd developed an expertise for since recovering from her own crisis of losing her child and nearly losing her life in the fire, as well. "Do you want to tell me about what's going on, Corey? I fear you're going to collapse if you don't get it off your chest." Suddenly he looked up at her and she could see tears wetting his cheeks. Still, she sat quietly as one would with an injured animal, resisting the urge to move too fast to offer something he might not want and thus scaring him away.

"I do," he whispered. "But you're the last person I can talk to about it. All of my troubles revolve around you—you and the children." She heard him sobbing quietly, which only made her resolve stronger.

"I'm your best friend, Corey," she stated, calmly. "I always have been right from the beginning. There's nothing you can't tell me." She paused so the incontrovertible truth would sink in and settle in his depths. Then, she started again.

"Sometimes I feel as if our marriage has gotten in the way of our friendship, and that's not something I want any more than you do. So, let's start with you telling me everything that's bothering you, and we'll see if your trust in me is justified." She raised her hand to brush his hair gently out of his eyes, as she'd always done, but put it down again quickly, still mindful of his unexplained self-imposed injuries and not wanting to make them any worse. "Tell me," she said. And then she sat and waited.

She had no idea how long they sat that way in silence together. The desk clock chimed and continued to tick off the minutes, the angle of the swath of moonlight increased, and her breath came in and out as if she were preparing to go onstage. But she was already there, so all she could do was watch and wait for him to speak, and then for her turn to answer. She thought of the intimacy of the language of the Saint-Saëns piano trio and how much it mirrored the dance they were doing. Finally, he turned to look up at the window. The light coming in showed suffering on his face that made her reach for his hand again, but she put it down instead to let it rest on her lap.

His voice was thin and reedy, as if he lacked the strength to get it out into the air. "All these late nights and early mornings . . . they start and end in piano bars but don't seem to lead to anything more in my future. I'm looking for something . . . something I caught a glimpse of when I was down south . . . a kind of connection with the music and the audience I found one night playing with a minstrel band on Mrs. Stovall's plantation . . ." He stopped, as if he'd lost sight of what he'd been watching in his mind's eye. "I've been gone in some kind of darkness I can't explain." Emily took one long breath. She still wanted to listen more and speak less, but she knew he needed to understand she was paying attention, and that there were going to be no recriminations.

"Do you know when the darkness started?" she asked. "Are you sure it was when you went down south with your father this last time?" But she knew that it was. From the minute she heard about the socializing that delayed their return home, she knew. Now it was important that Corey tell her himself instead of her telling him. If they were ever going to share the kind of relationship and trust they started with, this night would have to end right. She realized he was crying silently again next to her while her mind raced. All he needed to know was that she was waiting. The balance was so delicate—not too much care and not too little. She found herself fascinated with the level of control she needed to stay quiet while he talked.

"Yes," he whispered finally, "it was on that trip. The music . . . and the musicians' relationship to it was different, and something I want to find again somehow. It made me feel as if I was needed . . . as if I had an important part to play. But that's not all . . ." He stopped as his voice lost momentum, and Emily was afraid she'd have to encourage him again. Still, she waited, and finally he took another breath and started over.

"The Widow Stovall has a beautiful niece who introduced me to those musicians and the music." So, there it was, the beautiful niece. This wasn't about developing Corey's art; it was about dealing with his boredom in his work. Once he'd shared her passion and belief that the music was everything, but apparently no more. The beautiful niece had come upon a lost child.

"Somehow, she attacked every resistance I've ever had and pulled me into a world unlike anything I've experienced before," Corey was saying. "I don't know why. It just seemed what I've always wanted but never known." Suddenly he seemed to be moving along more easily, relieved to have someone to share his inner conflict with. "Have you noticed I've been living with a kind of bleakness for a while now? How could you not! My music seems to be going nowhere while yours expands, and the home and children most people find fulfilling, or say they do, make me feel trapped and bereft. *Is this all there is?* rings in my head." Emily shifted her position, unable to sit still after that declaration. How could there be anything as important as love, children, and family? She wasn't even sure music meant more. But Corey accepted her silence as encouragement to go on rather than the shock and agony following it, and so he did.

"When I got in that free place away from here, I couldn't help comparing everything in my life with it. I felt so lost, realizing none of the things I was supposed to be grateful for made me happy."

"Even the children?" Emily asked, almost under her breath. "I thought the children were your greatest joy." She looked at him with an expression of disbelief she was glad he couldn't see in the shadows as he stared at the carpet in front of the love seat. He wasn't playing the part she'd expected and prepared for. He seemed to be improvising his answers from a score she'd never learned. *Breathe and swallow,* she told herself. Don't let the hurt distract you. Your part isn't over yet.

"... even the children," he said. "All I could think of down there was finding time to be alone with Marcy Bond, and thoughts of the boys made me angry and impatient to get free of weights that tied me down to everything up here. Don't you see, I really am lost. I don't know what or who I am anymore, or where I'm going." He slipped his head down on the sofa back, eyes wide open and staring at the ceiling from a face wet with tears.

"Go on," Emily said, quietly. "Don't stop now."

"I wrote the widow's niece, Marcy, as soon as I got back here, but she made it clear she didn't want to hear from me again. She said we could always be friends, but of course that won't be possible because we never really were. So now I don't have her, and I know I've betrayed you and my family, but I don't feel any remorse for it." He shut his eyes slowly with a grimace, as if they stung too much to keep open. "I don't feel anything at all except the referred pain of what I once was. There's nothing left of me. I keep looking for help everywhere I go and with anyone I meet, but none comes." He lifted his head from the sofa back and turned it to look at Emily through his swollen lids. "I'm telling you this, but you're my wife and the one person I should keep it all from. Still, I must talk to someone, and for some reason, I want to tell you because you're the only one who wants to hear." He clutched one of the pillows and hid his face in it.

The numbness and shock Emily had thought she'd prepared for began to fill her with a kind of dread she'd never known before. This was her very own family falling apart before her in a wash of tears for a tragedy that had already happened. In an instant she knew there was nothing she could have done to prevent it, and in an odd way, nothing Corey could have done, either. Neither one of them had realized all the growing up they'd had to do and were prevented from by their early marriage. Blame served no purpose. All she could do now was show him she understood and help him back on his feet again for the sake of her home and children. She wished there were someone else to turn to for help, just this once, but there wasn't. If he believed in himself, he'd believe in her and the family, too, eventually. That was her only hope.

"Take your time," she said, folding her capable little hands in her lap, one over the other. "You need to get your balance back, and I'll be here to help with that." She smiled at him but refrained from touching him again. "The children will, too," she added. "You'll find them more help than you realize now."

"Why are you doing this?" Corey whispered, staring at her as if he'd only just seen her in the room sitting beside him there. "Why aren't you angry with me?" he finished, shaking his head as if he couldn't translate what she'd been saying.

"I understand what you've been through, and how that feeling of being trapped has robbed you of your own will," she said, sitting up very straight and still. "I'll help if I can. You can count on me. I'm not saying I know what to do because I don't, but I'll do what I can to help." She looked straight ahead, realizing Corey hadn't been listening to the substance of what she'd been saying, only the general sense of it, which would have to be enough.

"What can we do, Emi?" he murmured, eyes shut. "We can't go on as we are, can we?"

"Yes, I think we can," she said, rising slowly from the love seat. "But not as we are or were." She turned to look at him, and afraid she might be losing him to his despair again, she said, "You'll have your time to figure things out without fear of anything happening or guilt about what you're doing. I'll have time to see if I can't help you find your place within our family again, maybe a different place than we thought at first, leaving room for your career separate from mine, and time to figure out all of this away from here."

"What do you mean?" he asked, opening his eyes and pushing his hair off his forehead. He straightened up a little inside his loose shirt. "Are you saying we should run away?"

"In a way . . . let's leave here together," Emily said, sounding as if she'd just had the idea she'd been working on ever since Klaas had told them of his impending marriage to the Widow Stovall. "Let's go to Europe for a while. We can rent a place in Paris perhaps, and expand our careers much more easily than we can here." Corey frowned, and she hesitated, realizing there was still some work to do to get him to full acceptance. "The new music community there is vibrant, and you should have plenty of creative musicians to work with, if you want to." She leaned over farther so she could see his face better, trying to make eye contact in the dark, which was virtually impossible.

"My father says there's wonderful choral music going on in England now, too, and there are many more venues for popular music than there are here." She couldn't tell if she was making an impression because he didn't move. So, worried that there was too much attention focused on him, she decided to try to normalize what she was saying by including herself. "I've been working on some of the new French chamber music lately, and I'd love to get closer to the source." She looked down at the Saint-Saëns's sheet music, hoping Corey would see that the reality of what she said was already starting. By way of some divine assistance it was illuminated now in the stream of moonlight from the window.

"I still have European connections to musicians, also," she continued, before she realized that might be one of the major problems of their marriage she shouldn't mention, so she moved on quickly. "And the children would benefit greatly from living abroad. What better education could they have or a more exciting place to be than Paris or some other capitals of Europe during this time of worldwide peace and prosperity? Let's just pack up our little household and go, Corey." She grabbed both his hands and finally looked directly in his eyes. "It will be a fresh start."

Understandably, Corey seemed stunned, but he pulled her to him and threw his arms around her. "Why are you so good to me?" he whispered next to her hair. "How will I ever be able to thank you?" He rocked her from side to side as he held on to her.

"We're old friends, remember?" she whispered back to him. "Just don't you forget it. Now you'll want to get cleaned up before bed. We might have an hour or two of rest before we must get up again." She let him go as if it had been his idea, but she had in fact been moving him away from her and toward the bathroom without his awareness. He smiled and kissed the top of her head, unbuttoning his waistcoat and pulling off his silk ascot as he turned toward the bathroom door, disappearing behind it. She could hear him turning on the water.

Sinking down in the middle of the carpet next to the Saint-Saëns piano trio in a slither of her silk dressing gown, she buried her face in her arms and let out a soft wail of agony unlike any sound she'd ever heard or felt before. "My children, my family, my home," she moaned. "How could they do this to me?" She rocked back and forth, the pain finally seeping out and running away from her, taking the only course open to it. "I'll never forgive them," she sobbed. "But I'll save my family despite them all."

Hearing the running water stopping in the bathroom, she grabbed her sheet music and pulled herself up, slipping quickly out the dressing room door. She knew what she had to do now, and for many years to come, and the first step was to escape this house and everything it represented, taking the people and things that meant the most with her when she went.

CHAPTER EIGHTEEN

"JESUS, MARY, AND JOSEPH!" the elderly kitchen maid swore under her breath. Scrubbing the top of the little Sterling stove in the pantry so hard she vibrated, a small cross at her neck bobbing back and forth in time to her movements in support of her task. Apron hiked up under her bust as far as she could get it to cover as much of her torso as possible, Mary made a bizarre sight, tendrils of white and black hair departing her bun in every direction. Her arms were encased in Emily's cast-off, elbow-length kid evening gloves, in hopes of protecting her skin from the water and sodium bicarbonate she used to clean the stove.

"Mary! You look a fine sight; as if you're going out to a ball with your apron on." Emily had entered the pantry from across the kitchen so quietly she couldn't have been heard, even if Mary's attention hadn't been focused on her cleaning job.

"Aye!" Mary squealed. "You scared me half to death. I'll warrant . . . yes, I'm right!" She glanced over her shoulder. "Ya've no shoes on, so no wonder I couldn't hear ya. When will ya ever learn, Miss Emily? Ya *must wear shoes* in this kitchen." Mary shook her heavy, brown bristled scrubbing brush at Emily in mock threat. But seeing her mistress grinning amiably back at her, Mary, too, broke into a huge smile, putting the brush down on top of the stove to take a break.

"Never been one for shoes, have ya, Miss Emily? Not as a child and neither as a woman. Some things don't change around here."

Emily glanced guiltily down at her bare toes peeking out from her skirt and wiggled them. Bare feet had been her ritual in the kitchen since she was thirteen. "You won't tell on me, will you, Mary? It wouldn't do for the boys to know how good their mother is at breaking rules."

"And always has been," Mary added, shaking the bristling scrubbing brush at Emily again. "They all know. Ever since ya was my favorite little girl, ya've been doin' things your own way." Suddenly, Mary's cheerful expression dissolved before Emily's eyes. She was the queen of instant drama, Emily knew; a fact that had always endeared her to the young, rebellious girl who'd arrived at the de Koningh mansion alone so long ago. "Yes, they do," Mary sputtered as if she were about to cry.

"Do what? Know you love me or that I break rules?" Emily put her hand on the aging woman's shoulder.

"Do change. Things do change around here. Entirely too many things of late. I'm going to miss ya . . . and Master Corey . . . and the boys . . . and the music and the friends, and . . . everythin'." She finished with a choke.

"Oh Mary, I'm pleased to hear you say that, because we're all going to miss you and everyone here so much, too." Emily squeezed the little maid's shoulder but didn't want to throw her arms around the aproned *kitchen royal* in wet kid gloves for fear she, too, would start to cry.

Suddenly, the bell rang marking an arrival at the mansion's front door, a welcome diversion, and Emily grabbed the opportunity to escape Mary's moaning. The goodbyes had increased to a daily outpouring, forcing Emily into an emotional retreat every time she anticipated another. Settling her family in Europe would be a major challenge; she'd expected that. But leaving New York City was becoming a personal upheaval she'd somehow ignored until now.

The trouble lay in the mansion itself, not so much the city it stood in. She hadn't appreciated quite how much of her emotional skin lay here.

"It must be Klaas," she announced. Pausing for a moment, then rising slowly, she said, "I'll get it, Mary. You're too busy, and I don't see Tom or anyone else around." Giving the maid a reassuring pat on the shoulder again, she started for the back stairs, almost forgetting to slip into her shoes waiting at the bottom landing.

"Shoes!" Mary sniffed after her, using the upper sleeve of her uniform to wipe her right eye where it had suddenly started to water again. "How'll she get on without me?" she muttered. "How'll we get on without her?" She whispered the afterthought before turning back to attack the stove's many surface blemishes.

Emily stopped at the pantry door for a minute, turning to look over the long kitchen table, big double oven, and familiar cabinets filled with the china and implements of comfort and creativity she'd come to think of as hers during her life at the de Koningh home. She'd fixed every one of them in her mind's eye so she could recall them whenever she got homesick in the future. One last look at Mary's back bent over the pantry stove, and she turned to climb the steep, wooden risers to greet her father-in-law, just home from his daily carriage ride in the park.

Every step up the narrow staircase seemed to take on a significance it never had before, and even the loose boards of the groaning saddle at the top had to be acknowledged today instead of skipped over, as they usually were. She'd found herself paying attention to everything in the house, lately; minute details of art, architecture, and atmosphere could not escape her need to grasp them. They were all being clutched to her heart. She had to hold tight to everything, somehow. Well, maybe not everything. She was leaving the grandmother clock behind, even though it was hers, given to her by Robert Haussmann on one of her birthdays. How jealous William had been on that day, wishing the gift had been given to him instead of her.

How mesmerized the new baby, Connie, had been by the shiny brass pendulum swinging with metronomic precision.

Emily stopped in front of her "clock of the grand*mother*," as Robert's friend who'd procured it had called it. It stood demurely in the shell alcove across from the grand marble staircase. She admired the little clock's feminine size and charm. True, it had never been in scale with the large foyer or height of the ceiling, but the clock's feminine attributes ran to more than a pretty face and diminutive body. It was dependable, steadfast, lovely to listen to as its chimes sang out through the house on the hour, and it had kept an eye on her and her children when there were no other women in the mansion. Now, of course, with Klaas's marriage to the Widow Stovall and the arrival of her niece, there would be two new women in the de Koningh home, and so the little clock wouldn't be missed if Emily felt the need to take it to France with her. But oddly enough, she did not. She needed a fresh start, and some of the things she'd collected around her for protection weren't going to be a part of it.

Her eyes swept up the curved marble staircase to the first-floor landing, where she and twelve-year-old Corey had once dropped spitballs over the banister into the silver tray on the table below. The sight of the smooth newel post at the end of the handrail brought an involuntary smile, as she pictured two generations of de Koningh children sliding down and catapulting many feet onto the polished marble floor of the entry. The hard landing had been worth the joy of the flight. Memories of Emily's life in this house cascaded relentlessly once they got started, making it hard to focus on events of today with so many yesterdays crowding in.

"Didn't anyone hear me? I fear you're going deaf faster than I am," Klaas exclaimed peevishly from behind, making Emily jump. She'd forgotten why she'd come to the foyer in the first place.

"Forgive me," she said, turning to kiss her father-in-law, hesitantly. She wasn't sure how he was feeling about her, or she about him for that matter, since his seemingly crass announcement of his intentions to marry. She'd purposely not crossed his path since then. "I hear so many voices from the past in my head these days, Klaas, I'm indeed somewhat deaf to the present," she said, noticing how much frailer he'd gotten in the years after the war. But pulling away again, she saw the spark of his soft blue eyes verifying his still-vibrant spirit

"Lost in the nostalgia of departure, were you?" Klaas asked, pulling off his gloves and laying them on the hall table. "Powerful thing, nostalgia."

"I know. I have to get rid of it and move on, and I will," Emily assured him. "But this has been my home almost forever, and maybe you can't appreciate how hard it is to leave." He narrowed his gaze as if to see her better.

"There's much in the lessons of this house and your past to stand you in good stead in the future. Better to live with them and learn from them than get rid of the nostalgia completely," he said. "But you mustn't let it rule your life."

"Oh, I won't forget any of this, or you," Emily said. "I couldn't. Every move I make, sight I see, sound I hear, or note I play will remind me of you and this house." She knew she looked too fierce, like the often-surly little girl she had once been, now grown; not at all how she'd intended to part from him.

"Come here, Lady Liberty," Klaas said, pulling her close and rocking her imperceptibly as he'd done when she was a child. "Remember when I used to call you that?"

"Of course." She nodded, even as her head rested on his shoulder. "I loved that you and I had private names for each other. It made me feel I was remarkably close, but still special. Do you remember yours?" She pulled back again to give him a mischievous grin that deepened her dimples. He paused. "You don't, do you?" she teased.

"Santa," he whispered. "Santa Klaas; you got away with it when no one else could have."

"It was apt. Every day in this household was a Christmas gift to a little girl with no home of her own," Emily said, suddenly serious again. "Somehow, you were my mother, father, and friend all at once." She looked away again, keenly aware of how lucky she'd been. "Are you tired?" she asked. "You've been out all afternoon. Why don't we have some tea together in the library."

"Wonderful idea!" He smiled back at her. "But I'm thinking maybe something a little stronger . . ." His voice faded as he tucked her arm through his and they turned toward the hall. They walked slowly, linked together down to the library, both wrapped in the protection of shared memories no one else could know or take away. Emily felt he was making a special effort to be particularly close and loving with her now, and it made her wonder about his knowledge of Corey's infidelity. He probably didn't know that she and Corey had talked, and so would never bring up the subject unless she did. She stopped just before they came to the massive oak door to the music room, as she'd always called it because of the piano and the bookshelves filled with musical scores as well as books. She suddenly felt an urgency to step into her new role as a fully fledged woman of another world.

"Klaas, I've talked with Corey about his time down south and his difficulty getting settled with the family again now that he's home. He told me he'd discussed it with you. I want to thank you for not siding with or against him. He needs space, I think, as do we all right now."

"Ah, Emily, my dear," Klaas sighed. "I applaud you for not removing him forcibly from your heart and your marriage. I know how hard it must be to live with his betrayal, for that's just what it was. But if you can do that and rise to a different level, I believe he'll come back to you and all of us." Emily looked away for a moment but said nothing before looking back at Klaas. He seemed to misunderstand her silence for hesitancy, which made him try to explain.

"Remember that Cory's exceeding charm as a child was always aimed at making life better for everyone around him," Klaas said. "His choice was always the joy over the sorrow. We all benefited: his mother, me, and you as well. You would not have made the adjustment you did to your own harsh beginnings without his help. He deserves ours now. Please say you'll give him time." Klaas seized and held on to Emily's hand as he spoke, making her feel more uncomfortable than she could understand. Forming an alliance with her husband's father to nurture and indulge his son made her feel she'd suddenly become the caretaker instead of the one in need, and as if she were being recruited to work against herself.

Ever since her visit to the asylum, she'd wondered if mental disorders could be treated as a physical illness, exposed to the care of a trained physician so help for the patient was taken more seriously. Maybe Corey needed that kind of help. But why was it always the men who got the consideration? She nodded slightly, anger and hurt rising in her throat. It was important to stop what felt like an invasion of her family's privacy. And Corey had perhaps been a lightning rod for her problems with all the other men in her life, so he actually needed less attention while she needed more.

"Look at that," she said, lifting her head and taking a deep breath. A change of subject was paramount if she and Klaas were to remain on good terms in the future. "The wallpaper has never lost its lighter rectangular spot where the Philip de Koninck landscape painting was removed. I rather like that reminder of times past, too. Where did the painting end up? Schuylerville or Schenectady, with Mrs. de Koningh's Dutch relatives?"

"Wrong!" Klaas said, disoriented by her quick shift of focus, but taking obvious pleasure in correcting her and seemingly oblivious to his part in her sadness. "It's right here where it came from."

"Where?" She eyed the blank wall again. "You brought it back? But why?"

"It left to keep my wife happy when she went to her family during the war. But as she's gone now, I saw no reason to leave it with them."

"Ah yes, it must be quite valuable. Best to return it to the mansion." She noted Klaas's eyes were sparkling more than usual, and he looked almost as if he was holding his breath.

"I brought it back for you!" he exclaimed.

"For me?" Emily gasped. "But I never had a particular attachment to it," she said, almost apologetically. It seemed to her there were many things he'd misunderstood.

"No, but Robert Haussmann did!" Klaas burst out, gleefully. "I remember well you told me his analysis of it and how he missed it when it left. I thought you might like to give him something to remember you by." Emily stared back at her father-in-law, her amazement showing clearly in the lift of her dark eyebrows and swell of her huge brown eyes.

"Klaas, you are . . . such a surprise," Emily whispered. "It will mean the world to Robert. And I love the idea of leaving things behind to enhance memories, instead of the other way around."

Klaas nodded. "It should make you feel lighter and freer," he said, smiling into her eyes so she thought she could see his kind, warm heart she'd come to appreciate as a child.

He pushed the oak door to the library open for Emily to pass through, and she was overwhelmed by the knowledge that of all the things and people she'd miss from New York, Klaas de Koningh would indeed be principal among them even with the hurt he'd done to her and her family. This gentle man had guided and supported her as a child. He'd set an example for her as a parent, both protective and liberating, exacting, yet open-minded. She was so lucky Corey hadn't resented her time with his father. She remembered how she'd thought often of Klaas when he'd disappeared during the war, and how she'd noted Corey's likeness to his father, both physically and temperamentally. Maybe Klaas hadn't been so cruel after all in thinking she and Corey needed a push out and a fresh start. She'd known him to be right most often.

She must remember her early impressions of Klaas. Look at the father now, and you could possibly see the son in the future, and how much of her own sons were there? She'd best be prepared. Suddenly realizing she'd stopped just inside the room with her musings, while

Klaas had already moved past her to the piano, she saw Robert Haussmann sitting on the piano bench. He rose as they came in to meet them.

"Robert," Klaas was saying. "Emily and I . . . were just talking about you." She saw the two men with hands clasped silhouetted against the big glass doors to the garden. The sight seemed framed for her, but Robert's reaction brought it back to life. He bowed his head very slightly, but his old Prussian stance was gone. When she'd first met her future professor, he'd pulled himself up a few inches and clicked his heels together, a holdover, Corey had assured the young Emily, of the professor's European background. Emily didn't know when it had disappeared, but it was gone now.

"Emily, I'm going to go get your present for Robert. Will you keep him busy while I do that?" Klaas winked at her, enjoying the look of confusion on Robert Haussmann's face.

"I shall," Emily assured him. "Robert, are you here for the children's lessons? Did you send someone to get them?"

"William went to find Connie," Robert said, still watching Klaas depart with a frown.

"I'm so sorry they've kept you waiting," Emily muttered, moving in from the door as Klaas left through it. "They should be here, eagerly awaiting your arrival. I've warned them of how precious your time is. Really, this makes me quite angry." She moved over to the piano, running her hand slowly along the curve of its top in a gesture both loving and respectful at the same time.

"We can't expect the boys to share the enthusiasm you and Corey displayed at their age," Robert said, watching her hand, now resting on the piano. "You two were uniquely motivated."

"I know," Emily laughed. "You're good to remind me we'll have no more musicians in this family, without making me feel guilty or upset about it." She pulled her hand back and slipped it into the folds of her skirt. "But I still feel they can benefit from a musical education, Robert. It's important to learn another language."

"I agree," he nodded. "But William has recently stated he feels he's wasting his time with music. He'd rather learn French."

"Ha! William would," Emily scoffed with a mock scowl. She let out a sigh and turned to look out at the garden, already springing to life with the tulip magnolias boasting huge, deeply veined buds. "It will soon be warm," she whispered, "and I shall soon be gone, and he'll be learning French," she added with a sigh.

"Are you sure you want to go?" Robert asked, quietly.

"I don't know . . . ," her voice trailed off. Without looking at Robert, she said, "I wish you were coming." She must have sensed his surprise, as she added quickly, "It won't be home without you, Robert."

"It's not supposed to be," he said. "It's meant to be your fresh start, yours and Corey's. It's a wonderful opportunity for a new life. Are you still wary of your father's motives for encouraging you? Does Corey also doubt him? But you know Europe well, Emily. You'll be welcomed there, and your music will flourish."

"This . . . America . . . is my home, Robert. I told you that a long time ago."

"Oh, come now. Home is where your passions are . . . your family, friends, music—"

"It's more complicated than that," Emily interrupted. She looked at Robert for a moment, and then away again. "It may also be where your demons are not, where you feel safe."

"What do you mean, 'demons'?" Robert peered at Emily more closely. He heard something odd in her voice.

"Why did you never return to Europe yourself?" she asked him, still looking away. "You have roots there and family, history, and friends, and they appreciate music at a higher level."

"Ah, yes, I see what you mean. I suppose we set up our homes when we stop running away. Why do you always have the last word, Emily? Even as a child, that stubborn will of yours couldn't be overcome."

"I fear I may be lonely," she said, to the garden, "with only myself for company, the very person I wish to leave behind."

"You'll have the children, and Corey; your *own* father . . . and your music . . . and many old friends will visit you on their way through France and England." Robert struggled to soothe a troubled side of her he felt he'd not seen before. Maybe it had been there all along and he'd just missed it.

Emily turned to look at him without really seeing him. She moved around to the piano's keyboard and lifted the cover. "I'm not going away, all the way to Europe, to have everyone follow me," she said. "And none of my friends have any reason to go to Europe anyway, now that the war is over." She slipped between the keyboard and piano bench, sitting down with her hands in her lap, as if now that she was there she had no idea what to do with them.

"But Jacques Offenbach lives in Paris; John Mackay visits twice a year to see his wife and daughters; your children's British grandfather will finally be able to see his grandsons grow; and Johnny Dunne is moving there, too."

Emily's head jerked up. "What," she whispered. "What do you mean?"

"You didn't know? He's been made bureau chief for Paris. I'm surprised you hadn't heard." Robert looked at Emily, studying her emotive change to see if it showed on her face. In fact, something dark was there but he couldn't tell what it was.

"I've been distracted, busy with the move . . . ," she murmured.

"Well, it's good news, isn't it? I'm sure you'll be seeing a lot of him." He continued to watch her carefully.

"I sincerely hope not," Emily said, so low Robert wasn't quite sure he'd heard her. But it didn't matter, because William and Connie came tumbling into the room, followed by their father, whose legs were at least three times as long as theirs. They came to an abrupt halt at Robert's feet, and Connie looked up at him through his curly blond mop of hair.

"Father says we must 'pologize for being late, Professor, and so we do," he exclaimed, eyes shining and clothes oddly disarranged in direct contrast to his brother's military neatness. William rolled his eyes.

"He gets worse all the time," William said. "He's such a *child*." His feigned superiority and boredom made the adults in the room smile.

Corey placed the tray he'd been carrying with ice water on it down on the bar. "It's not a crime to be a child, William," Corey said. "We've all been there." The water ritual had started twenty years before, when Corey and Emily began their music lessons together in the library. At one time both had been ill, and the water helped to soothe their throats and tame their lingering coughs. A glass for their professor was always included. And now, the tradition continued. Connie danced and skipped in place, reminding Emily of a drop of cold water on a hot griddle.

"Will Mary and Tom and Bessie come with us?" Connie crowed, moving over to Emily on the piano bench to straddle it on the end, his pudgy legs sticking out on both sides.

"No. Grandpa Klaas needs them here with him to run this big house, and Bessie can't give up all her wonderful customers. We don't need an army of servants to help us, Connie. We're all perfectly capable, and the house we're renting in France will be small in comparison with this one."

"But who will take care of us?"

"Your father and I will."

"I mean, when you're working."

"Good question," Corey said, looking at Emily pointedly. "Your mother's new friend from Blackwell's Island, Gertrude, will be coming to take care of you and William when we're working. We're delighted she can join us—"

"And her baby girl," Emily interrupted, trying to push Connie's hair out of his eyes. "She needs help and so do we, so it's a mutually beneficial arrangement."

"What? You're bringing one of those prisoners with us to France?" William stood frozen to his spot on the carpet next to Robert Haussmann. The horror on his face and in his voice was genuine.

"A patient, William. Gertrude was not a prisoner. It's an important distinction. She's done nothing wrong," Emily explained to her oldest son, as firmly as she could without letting the anger she felt seep into her voice. "She speaks three languages, but not English very well. That was the cause of the *misunderstanding* in her . . . situation," she finished, trying to be less defensive and more matter of fact. But she looked up at Robert Haussmann, and saw that he, too, had stiffened, a fact that had not escaped William, either.

"Oh, no," William moaned. "My parents have gone mad, Professor Haussmann. Surely you can reason with them." Emily was struck by the level of adolescence she could hear in her childish son's voice. It would doubtless mean many unwelcome challenges for her and Corey in the future.

"A baby girl," Connie squealed with delight. "Gertrude has a baby girl. At last, I'll have my little sister. I've wanted her for so, so long. Thank you, thank you," he squealed again, at the same level, while he looked first from Corey to Emily, and then back to Corey again.

"What's all this excitement?" Klaas asked as he came into the library. "Can I be a part of it, too?"

"Of course, Father." Corey went to Klaas as he entered. "Can I help you with that?" He reached out his hand toward a large brown package Klaas was carrying, but Klaas turned slightly away from him, and looked at Emily. "No, your wife has to help me." He winked at her. "Come on over, Emily," he ordered.

She rose and slipping Connie off the bench before her so they could both stand, she put him on his little feet and straightened up to go to Klaas. Connie moved to join her, but she stopped him with one hand, and bending down, said to him, "No, my darling. You'll have to wait to see the surprise, too. It's not for you, this time. It's for the professor." All eyes turned to Robert Haussmann, as he looked at Emily first, and then turned to Klaas in disbelief.

Emily went to Klaas, and he handed her the rectangular, brown paper package he'd brought into the room. It had twine tied around numerous times, and a rope handle attached at the center of the longer side to make it easier to carry. Knowing Klaas wasn't strong enough to lift a package of serious weight, Emily figured it must be more cumbersome than heavy. She took it from him easily, smiling into his eyes as she did so, and turned to hand it over to Robert.

"For you," she said. "With the love and gratitude this family owes its best friend." He looked completely at a loss to know what to do, and so she picked up the shears on the desk beside him and carefully severed the cords that bound the package.

"Now Robert, the rest is up to you," she said, stepping back. William and Connie drew in closer, and Corey shifted his position as well, to see better.

"Open it, Professor. We can't stand to wait any longer," William cried, apparently happily regressing to the childish excitement of opening gifts.

Slowly, the paper was pulled off, and a landscape painting of incomparable beauty appeared. "The Philip de Koninck!" Corey exclaimed. "How wonderful. What a fabulous idea, Father."

"It's not mine," Klaas said, smiling. "I gave it to Emily, and she is giving it to Robert."

"The professor always loved it," Corey told the boys, both of whom were standing in a kind of wonder that said they didn't know what was happening.

"Let's lift it into the light so we can see it better," Corey suggested, but no one moved. He finally reached down carefully to raise the painting, holding it so the sun from the garden would bring the picture to life in the most natural way. Robert Haussmann still stood dumbfounded, neither moving nor talking. "Oh my," Corey breathed, "it is so special. I had forgotten."

They all watched as Corey gently rested the painting on top of the piano, with the brown paper underneath. Light from the garden windows poured over the landscape, boldly painted by some member of the family hundreds of years before any of them were born. The billows of tinted atmosphere filling much of the canvas seemed to transform into clouds of moving shades of blue and gray. The natural midday light lit the canvas as it could never have been illuminated hanging on an interior wall. The flat lowland countryside seemed to shimmer in differing green shades due to the movement of the clouds scudding over it. There were no people or animals in sight, and only a tiny red-roofed house peeking through some foliage.

"Moving, moving, always moving," Corey murmured, as he tipped the picture to see it better. "That river curving through the middle of it adds so much life."

"Lovely." Klaas nodded in agreement.

"Can I see, can I see?" Connie cried, pushing up on his tiptoes behind the backs of all the adults grouped around the piano to stare at the painting.

"It's always made me feel so entirely free," Corey said, seemingly unaware of his young son. "It's the elevation, painted from the view of a bird. It brings the past, present, and future all together. You see everything from 'up here,' instead of just what's around you 'down there.'"

"Like a deity," Emily added.

"Yes," Corey nodded. "That made me feel unconstrained, not bound by the things of this earth."

Suddenly a vision of Johnny Dunne swept through Emily's mind like the scudding clouds. She could see him as she'd first met him in St. Stephen's Square, but soberer, with worldly responsibilities on his shoulders; the Paris Johnny to come, not the Vienna Johnny that was. She glanced at Corey, then back at the landscape.

"Free?" she said. "No, it doesn't make me feel that way. We're never free. Just because there's movement," she glanced down at the clouds and river in the scene on the piano, "that doesn't mean we don't take our past with us wherever we go."

"I want to *see*!" Connie howled, unaccustomed to being ignored by anyone but his brother. He tugged on Emily's skirt, and she picked him up with a groan, indicating that he, too, had changed from a baby to something much bigger and heavier.

"Oh!" he breathed, smiling broadly when the dramatic landscape came into view. He leaned forward over it, forcing Emily to lean back a little to counter his weight. "But it has crackers all over it," he exclaimed, snapping upright so fast Emily had to compensate with the top of her own body, banging heads with Connie.

"Lord, Con. Be careful around the picture! And what do you mean?" Her tone moved from irritated to alarmed in one inflection. "Has someone spilled on it or something?" They all bent closer to the canvas, trying to see Connie's crackers. All except William, whose chin just cleared the piano top, and so was at the perfect level to focus.

"He means cracks," William snorted, rolling his eyes. "There are lots of little cracks on the painting, that's all. And it's kind of dirty, too."

"Really?" Corey bent down close to it himself. "Well, from this viewpoint, I can see he's right."

"I was the one who said . . . ," William began.

"Both of you are right." Corey interrupted William's claim to fame. "It's not in great shape, Father. Do you think the relatives treated it badly?"

"No, indeed," Robert Haussmann said, speaking for the first time since the surprise of his fine gift had been revealed. "It's incredibly old, and antiques are meant to show their age. It's part of their . . . allure. And I do remember the cracked varnish when I first saw it in the hall some twenty years ago, although the light wasn't good enough to see as much as we do here."

"Let me have a look, please," Klaas said, moving in closer and adjusting his small wire-framed spectacles up on the bridge of his nose for greater magnification. He stepped in front of Corey who ceded his position. "The boys are right," Klaas said, finally. "It needs a good cleaning and restoration. We can't have it reminding Professor Haussmann of the de Koninghs in that condition!"

"Oh no, it's fine," Robert objected.

"It isn't, Professor Haussmann; anything but fine. And that said, the frame is somewhat the worse for wear. It needs gilding, but I'm not sure its baroque heft is appropriate to the picture now, anyway," Klaas added.

"It's a period piece," Robert said. "I'm sure it's fine with a little peeling gilt."

"But the whole point of the picture is to escape the boundaries of man's daily life, Professor. I think this frame is too . . . confining. It's too closed, the painting needs to be . . . liberated. Shall we find it a new frame and get rid of that gilt?" Klaas suggested, cheerfully. He looked around from Corey to Emily, and then Robert, remembering to meet the eyes of the children as well, since they were truly the future. They all nodded at the same time, except Robert, who still seemed overwhelmed by everything to do with the gift he'd just received.

He spoke up, finally. "This was painted by a family member of yours, Mr. de Koningh, was it not? In 1660?" He glanced down at the dated signature.

"It was," Klaas affirmed with a nod. "He was said to be a pupil of Rembrandt van Rijn, and lived his entire life in Amsterdam, born and died there. You can see Rembrandt's influence in it, can't you?"

"Most certainly," Robert said, "but . . ."

"And I think he also became a rather prosperous businessman, unlike his wayward maestro. Yet in the end, the maestro is remembered as the most important Dutch painter in history, and Philip de Koninck . . ."

"It's much too personal!" Robert burst out. "Too valuable. I can't accept such a gift!"

Emily let Connie slip down, out of her arms, and turning to Robert, put her hand in his. "Robert," she said looking into his eyes, "do you remember when you gave me your violin?" Robert flinched from the shock of her hand in his or the memory, she couldn't quite tell.

"I presume they're of equal monetary value," she went on, quietly. "But their true value surely lies in their beauty and the joy they give as works of art. There's no way to measure that." They stood holding each other's hands, looking into each other's eyes, and barely breathing. "Every time I picked up the Guarneri," she continued, "I thought of you. I hope you'll feel the same way about me . . . about all of us . . . when you look at your painting. If you prefer the gilt frame, we'll leave it on, although I think some restorative work on the painting is in order. You'd want the Guarneri worked on if it needed care, so you can't object to getting a little cosmetic uplift for the painting." She squeezed Robert's hand, but wouldn't let it go.

He looked from her around the room, swaying a little as if the library had started swimming in front of his eyes. Finally, he looked back at Emily. "All right, Emily," he said. "The painting will come to live with me and always have a place of honor in my home. Thank you. Thank you all," he added, unable to look anywhere but at his own feet in a vain attempt to steady himself. Corey turned and put one hand on Robert's shoulder, and the other on Emily's, but she slipped out from under it.

"And I have something else for you," Emily said, turning to the piano and taking the Guarneri's case off it. "The time has come for me to return this most wonderful gift once loaned to me by you," she said, holding the case up to him with a small smile.

"What?" Robert looked so stunned even his shoulders fell. "Why?"

"Because it's time for me to find my musical voice. I need my own violin now, Robert, and there are going to be many chances to find a new one in Europe. Maybe even a more modern one built in the 1800s—with a sweeter tone, more suitable for the smaller performance spaces I'll be playing in." She could see he looked so stricken that she kept her explanation rolling on to allow him to adjust. "I was thinking perhaps of a French instrument, maybe one of Monsieur Boulenger's. His business was in Frith Street, Soho, for many years. Did you ever go there? I remember the shop. He made excellent instruments . . ." her voice trailed off. Corey moved closer between the two of them. He looked worried as he glanced from one to the other. Robert was frozen in place, seeming as if he'd forgotten how to breathe. Finally, he gave a small sigh, looking directly at Emily as if he finally saw her.

"But the Guarneri suits your personality, Emily, especially now, and it always has," he said softly. "It's such a collaborative instrument, perfect for the chamber music you're becoming so enamored of. A Stradivarius, or even a Boulenger, would be touchier, less likely to do your bidding. You have to be very gentle with them, terribly diplomatic . . ." He looked almost desperate as his voice died out, clearly not finishing the thought out loud. Then he took a breath and started again.

"And besides, you'll need an instrument for practice and for your early commitments when you first arrive in Europe. Why don't you take the Guarneri with you to tide you over until you've finally found exactly what you want?" He smiled a little, seemingly confident that he'd found a compromise she couldn't refuse. "I well remember the first time you played the Guarneri in my house . . . Bach, I think. It was so beautiful, and you were so well matched with the instrument . . ."

She smiled back, giving his hand a squeeze, and then letting it go. "You know how much this instrument meant to me when you loaned it to me, and for all the years that followed." She looked at him directly with the concern she knew would show. "I'll never forget your generosity or caring in support of my musical life, but no,

Robert," she said, firmly. "It's best that I'm forced to move swiftly and decisively when I get there. Finding a new instrument should not be put off because I conveniently have my old one under my chin. Besides, I can rent one for the first month or so. I hadn't thought of the violin as a wily pet likely to bite or obey me depending on how I handled it, but I'll keep your description in mind when I make my rounds. Don't worry about me," she urged cheerfully. "Anyway, you know that bringing up two boys has changed me a good deal," she went on, her dimples appearing briefly as she winked at the others. "I've learned all manner of subtlety in getting what I want and even learned to listen more than I talk, which is undoubtedly the greatest skill of all. I relish the search for a new instrument."

"In art, as in life, it's not about things . . . ," Corey said, looking down first at the red-bearded man, and then at his own dark-haired wife, ". . . but the meanings of things, isn't it?" Emily couldn't quite tell why, but she felt at that moment they were all moving on to something different, and she was glad of it. She put the Guarneri's case in Robert's hand.

"Thank you," she said, although who she was talking to was anybody's guess. "And now, let's leave Robert and the boys here for their last music lesson together in this house. We all have much to do ourselves and little time to do it in, so off we go." She slipped her arm through Corey's and swept Klaas up with her other arm as she started to move them all toward the door.

"You are an amazing young woman," Klaas murmured, leaning over to put a light kiss on her cheek as she closed the door behind them. He started to move toward the stairs, looking a bit sadder than she'd seen him since he'd returned home. She knew he'd wanted to welcome change but wondered if this wasn't more than he'd considered. She and Corey stood side by side, watching the senior de Koningh slowly climb the shallow risers.

"It's hard to be the one left behind," Corey said quietly, shaking his head a little. "Even though he has many new things to look forward to, I wonder if he might not be thinking his entire life as he's known it will end when we go."

"Yes, well, that's all to the good, I think," Emily said, narrowing her gaze as if adjusting to Klaas's changing perspective. "I hope someday he'll forget my less than charitable acceptance of his plans for his new life," she added, thoughtfully. "I wonder if we should stay for his wedding. Do you think he needs us for support? I'd like to meet these women myself," she added. "I don't know if he should get my blessing until I've been introduced to them both."

"No, indeed we should not," Corey answered, looking away, and pulling his collar up as if to protect himself from a harsh wind. "We humans all struggle to arm ourselves against our worst fears," he said. "It's only natural," he added, watching his father disappear from the top landing. Emily was staring straight ahead as Klaas vanished from sight. "I wonder if his marriage is meant to insulate him from his age in the only way he can imagine. I suppose we must let that happen in whatever way he wants it to. I don't think we should hover around trying to control the outcome."

Emily nodded. "I shudder to think of the control I brought to bear on everything in my life for such a long time. Even you, Corey," she said with surprise in her voice. "Maybe since the first time I met you here in the house as a child, I've been trying to form you into a vision for my future. Why would the one who wanted most to be free of constraint try to govern everyone else?" She shook her head slowly.

"And you," Corey said, without changing either his focus on his father's retreat or his tone of voice. "Will you ever be able to forgive me?"

"I didn't mention forgiveness," she replied slowly, without taking her eyes off the empty place where Klaas had been at the top of the stairs. "I don't think it has anything to do with forgiveness," she said, turning to look up at Corey. "All I can offer is acceptance. A religious person would probably call it grace, the grace of God."

"What's the difference?" Corey asked, quietly, shifting his eyes from his father's space back to his wife's face.

"Oh, I think of it as something that takes a lot of hard work." She narrowed her gaze into the now empty entrance hall. "Commitment and discipline are part of it; both things I know something about. And acceptance takes time." She moved a little as if to prepare to depart from the hall. "But you know," she started again, finally turning to look up at Corey and directly into his eyes again, "you offered me my first chance to play music. You heard what I needed and gave it to me, just as partners would in a chamber music pairing. I wouldn't be who I am today without my violin, and you championing my cause so long ago. I owe you my life for it, most assuredly. I haven't forgotten that, and never will."

"Then why don't we see how good we can both get at acceptance again," Corey said. "The better we get, the freer we'll be. Isn't personal freedom what we're both after?"

Emily smiled slightly, turning to start up the stairs herself, but she feared Corey would see that she hadn't nodded. Unnoticed, she slipped the de Koningh sapphire engagement ring off her finger and dropped it in her pocket. She couldn't wear it when she played the violin, anyway. It could be saved for William's future bride. Looking down at her small, strong fingers she realized she already felt freer. She belonged more to herself now.

"We've all got parts to play in making this family a success," he called after her, seeing her move lightly, yet surely and relentlessly up the stairs. She could feel him watching and thought about what he'd just said. *Yes, we all have our parts but there's always a first violin to lead the others.* She didn't stop until she'd reached the top.

She turned to him from way above on the landing, wondering what lay ahead now for each one of them. It was the first time since she'd come to the house as a child that she'd looked forward to finding out what was waiting outside its walls. But it wasn't a fear for herself that caused her to pause this time. Her concern was for them all, and that changed everything.

BOOK GROUP QUESTIONS

Designed to start a discussion, not finish one.

1. Why are the children upset visiting the Central Park Zoo in Chapter One? Do they both have the same worries? What themes are exposed in this chapter?

2. What issues around immigration are raised by the discussion of John Mackay's rise to fame?

3. How does the boy on the train to West Virginia inspire Corey's thoughts of his own family at home in New York?

4. Why is the location of the Greenbriar Hotel a good symbol of reconstruction?

5. Why is Corey unimpressed by the idea of public education in the South?

6. Why does Corey appear unfriendly to Marcy Bond when they first meet?

7. How does Robert feel Emily and her family when she requests that he accompany her on her trip to Chicago? What is most important to him?

8. Why does Emily object to the speed of the new trains?

9. How does she react to the gossip about her on the train?

10. Is Robert interested in the newer technologies of the times?

11. Why are the officials keeping Emily hidden from the public on her trip back to New York after the fire?

12. Does Johnny understand Emily's dilemma after the fire?

13. Is Emily feeling relieved of the burden of another child?

14. Does Johnny understand Emily's feelings about her family and ambivalence over her restrictions due to social mores? Does Emily?

15. Is the trip downtown in the snowstorm a crossroad for Corey? If so, why? And if not, why not?

16. What has the house come to represent for Emily?

BOOK GROUP QUESTIONS

17. Is the de Koningh mansion the Gilded Cage referred to in the book's title?

18. Does Emily feel antagonistic or simply ambivalent about the men in her life?

19. How does she feel about her father's ideas for her future without Klaas and the mansion?

20. Does Emily's decline into shame surprise you? Where the Widow Stovall is concerned, is her reaction understandable? How do you feel about Emily after hearing about her plan involving Johnny?

21. Did Emily know about how the women's insane asylum was used before learning more from Bessie?

22. Is her plan to go to the asylum rational? Will she get the help she needs from the men in her life?

23. Does she feel differently about the plight of women in the world after playing for the inmates?

24. What does Corey learn from William Steinway?

25. Does Emily see a move to Europe as an escape and the fresh start she needs?

26. Why do Emily and Klaas want to give Robert a gift?

27. Why does Emily return Robert's violin to him? Is that a wise move?

28. Has Emily accepted Corey's infidelity? Does she forgive him?

29. How is she going to deal with living with him in the future? Has he freed her?

30. Does Emily end up understanding more about what family is?

31. Does Corey (the prodigal son) understand the difference between grace and acceptance?

32. What roles do forgiveness and acceptance play in their future?

ACKNOWLEDGMENTS

A sequel is such a different animal from its predecessor. There are expectations to be met, and that changes everything. I heard from friends, and readers of the prequel, *Certain Liberties*, with ideas, questions, suggestions, and wonderful historical references. Fascinating books and pictures were sent and loaned as part of the collaboration between *Certain Liberties* readers and the author of *The Gilded Cage*—me!

I can't thank every one of those vicarious teammates by name, but I must acknowledge that I'd never have put the finished book between covers and out in the world without my wonderful editors Walter Bode and the divine Dan Janeck. To say that its earthly form would have never happened without designer Katie Holeman is an understatement. I thank everyone on the team personally, because you made it the absolute best book it could possibly be. And that's all I could ask for. Thank you!

—*Sidney S. Stark*

ABOUT THE AUTHOR

Sidney S. Stark is the author of the Emily Alden Trilogy and a book of personal essays, *Twilight Perspectives*, all published by Momentum Ink Press. She has founded and led writing workshops and retreats sponsored by Momentum Ink Press in New York and Vermont. Born in Manhattan, Sidney owns homes in both New York and Stowe, Vermont. She is a passionate supporter of the performing arts and young musicians wherever she lives. You can find more of Sidney's writing on her blog TheUnblockedWriter.com.

Momentum Ink Press is a cooperative advancing the work of writers unavailable through traditional commercial publishers. Each book is carefully reviewed by a collection of authors, editors, and designers ensuring an authentic artistic version of the writer's best work. By selecting and reading a Momentum Ink Press book you are joining and supporting a community of readers and writers committed to quality in literature. We hope you appreciate our books as much as we enjoy bringing them to you.

www.ingramcontent.com/pod-product-compliance
Lightning Source LLC
Chambersburg PA
CBHW050535260626
47157CB00002B/308